# BEAKER'S DOZEN

# BEAKER'S
# DOZEN

# NANCY KRESS

A Tom Doherty Associates Book
New York

BEAKER'S DOZEN

Edited by David G. Hartwell

A Tor Book
Published by Tom Doherty Associates, Inc.
175 Fifth Avenue
New York, NY 10010

Tor Books on the World Wide Web:
http://www.tor.com

Tor® is a registered trademark of Tom Doherty Associates, Inc.

Design by Maura Fadden Rosenthal

Library of Congress Cataloging-in-Publication Data

Kress, Nancy.
Beaker's dozen / Nancy Kress.—1st ed.
       p.      cm.
"A Tom Doherty Associates book."
ISBN 0-312-86537-6 (acid-free paper)
I. Title.
PS3561.R46B36      1998
813'.54—dc21    98-11579
                        CIP

First Edition: August 1998

Printed in the United States of America

0 9 8 7 6 5 4 3 2 1

"Always True to Thee, In My Fashion" first appeared in *Isaac Asimov's Science Fiction Magazine*, January 1997

"Ars Longa" first appeared in *By Any Other Fame*, ed. Mike Resnick and Martin H. Greenberg, DAW, 1994

"Beggars in Spain" first appeared in *Isaac Asimov's Science Fiction Magazine*, April 1991. Simultaneous appearance: Axolotl Press

"Dancing on Air" first appeared in *Isaac Asimov's Science Fiction Magazine*, July 1993

"Evolution" first appeared in *Isaac Asimov's Science Fiction Magazine*, October 1995

"Fault Lines" first appeared in *Isaac Asimov's Science Fiction Magazine*, August 1995

"Feigenbaum Number" first appeared in *Omni*, December 1995

"Flowers of Aulit Prison" *Isaac Asimov's Science Fiction Magazine*, October/November 1996

"Grant Us This Day" *Isaac Asimov's Science Fiction Magazine*, September 1993

"Margin of Error" first appeared in *Omni*, October 1994

"Sex Education" first appeared in *Intersections: The Sycamore Hill Anthology*, eds. John Kessel, Mark L. van Name, and Richard Butner, Tor, 1996

"Summer Wind" first appeared in *Ruby Slippers, Golden Tears*, eds. Ellen Datlow and Terri Windling, Avon, 1995

"Unto the Daughters" first appeared in *Sisters in Fantasy*, eds. Susan Shwartz and Martin H. Greenberg, Roc, 1995

# CONTENTS

# INTRODUCTION

THERE'S ALWAYS SOMETHING SLIGHTLY EMBARRASSING ABOUT WRITING AN introduction to one's own short stories: What does one write? Received wisdom says—correctly—that the stories should speak for themselves. Modesty says—also correctly—that one cannot write "This author is terrific!" Prudence says that one should not announce that now, in the time that has passed since their writing, all the stories' flaws have become glaringly obvious to the author, who sits wondering why she didn't strong-arm a friend into writing the introduction in her place.

But, in this case, I actually do have something I want to say. Not directly about the stories, which should speak for themselves (see above), but about the context in which they were written. That context is the last decade of the twentieth century, when strange and wondrous things are happening in science labs around the world.

Scientists in Scotland clone a sheep from an adult cell.

Researchers decipher the entire DNA sequence, every last gene, used by the bacterium *Escherichia coli*.

Pharming—the practice of genetically engineering animals to produce pharmaceuticals for human use—becomes a burgeoning industry.

A research group in Japan discovers that large fragments of human chromosomes, with up to one thousand genes, can be incorporated into the mouse genome.

Human genes are identified for many inheritable tendencies, including breast cancer.

The twenty-first century, it's often remarked, will transform our knowledge of biology in the same way that the twentieth century transformed physics. With knowledge, of course, comes application. And with the application of all we are learning about genetic engineering come social and ethical questions, some of them knotty.

This is where science fiction enters, stage left. Scientific laboratories are where the new technologies are rehearsed. Science fiction rehearses the implications of those technologies. What might we eventually do with our newfound power? Should we do it? Who should do it? Who will be affected? How? Is that a good thing or not? For whom?

Of the thirteen stories in this book, eight are concerned with what might come out of the beakers and test tubes and gene sequencers of microbiology. Not everything in these stories will come to pass. Possibly nothing in them will; fiction is not prediction. But I hope the stories at least will raise questions about the world rushing in on us at the speed—not of light—but of thought.

And, oh yeah . . . I hope you enjoy reading the stories as well. Without that, there's really no point, is there? But you'll be the sole, best judge of that.

—Nancy Kress
March 29, 1998

# BEGGARS IN SPAIN

This story represents several milestones in my career as a writer. It was the first story I wrote after I left my job as a corporate copy-writer in order to write fiction full-time. It won my first (and only) Hugo. More substantially, it represents the first of many stories concerned with the possibilities of genetic engineering.

Of the thirteen stories in this book, six are primarily about genetic engineering: five as applied to people and one as applied to bacteria. In addition, another three stories deal with the effects on the human mind of designer drugs, pharmaceuticals created from the DNA level up. Clearly what we have here is an obsession.

Why? I don't know. The introduction to this collection states that it's because the coming century is going to be the Century of Microbiology, in which the scientific breakthroughs in that field will equal those of physics in the twentieth century. That is true, but I didn't write "Beggars in Spain" because of that truth. Although I'm fascinated by microbiology, this story was written not from intellectual fascination but from a much simpler and older emotion: envy. I need at least eight hours of sleep a night, prefer-ably nine, and I resent it quite a bit. The Sleepless need none. I wish I could have had the genetic engineering that went into cre-ating Leisha, and so have claimed it the only way writers can: on paper.

# ONE

THEY SAT STIFFLY ON HIS ANTIQUE EAMES CHAIRS, TWO PEOPLE WHO didn't want to be here, or one person who didn't want to and one who resented the other's reluctance. Dr. Ong had seen this before. Within two minutes he was sure: the woman was the silently furious resister. She would lose. The man would pay for it later, in little ways, for a long time.

"I presume you've performed the necessary credit checks already," Roger Camden said pleasantly, "so let's get right on to details, shall we, Doctor?"

"Certainly," Ong said. "Why don't we start by your telling me all the genetic modifications you're interested in for the baby."

The woman shifted suddenly on her chair. She was in her late twenties—clearly a second wife—but already had a faded look, as if keeping up with Roger Camden was wearing her out. Ong could easily believe that. Mrs. Camden's hair was brown, her eyes were brown, her skin had a brown tinge that might have been pretty if her cheeks had had any color. She wore a brown coat, neither fashionable nor cheap, and shoes that looked vaguely orthopedic. Ong glanced at his records for her name: Elizabeth. He would bet people forgot it often.

Next to her, Roger Camden radiated nervous vitality, a man in late middle age whose bullet-shaped head did not match his careful haircut and Italian-silk business suit. Ong did not need to consult his file to recall anything about Camden. A caricature of the bullet-shaped head had been the leading graphic for yesterday's online edition of the *Wall Street Journal:* Camden had led a major coup in cross-border data-atoll investment. Ong was not sure what cross-border data-atoll investment was.

"A girl," Elizabeth Camden said. Ong hadn't expected her to speak first. Her voice was another surprise: upper-class British. "Blonde. Green eyes. Tall. Slender."

Ong smiled. "Appearance factors are the easiest to achieve, as I'm sure you already know. But all we can do about slenderness is give her a genetic disposition in that direction. How you feed the child will naturally—"

"Yes, yes," Roger Camden said, "that's obvious. Now: intelligence. *High* intelligence. And a sense of daring."

"I'm sorry, Mr. Camden, personality factors are not yet understood well enough to allow genet—"

"Just testing," Camden said, with a smile that Ong thought was probably supposed to be lighthearted.

Elizabeth Camden said, "Musical ability."

"Again, Mrs. Camden, a disposition to be musical is all we can guarantee."

"Good enough," Camden said. "The full array of corrections for any potential gene-linked health problem, of course."

"Of course," Dr. Ong said. Neither client spoke. So far theirs was a fairly modest list, given Camden's money; most clients had to be argued out of contradictory genetic tendencies, alteration overload, or unrealistic expectations. Ong waited. Tension prickled in the room like heat.

"And," Camden said, "no need to sleep."

Elizabeth Camden jerked her head sideways to look out the window.

Ong picked up a paper magnet from his desk. He made his voice pleasant. "May I ask how you learned whether that genetic-modification program exists?"

Camden grinned. "You're not denying it exists. I give you full credit for that, Doctor."

Ong held his temper. "May I ask how you learned whether the program exists?"

Camden reached into an inner pocket of his suit. The silk crinkled and pulled; body and suit came from different classes. Camden was, Ong remembered, a Yagaiist, a personal friend of Kenzo Yagai himself. Camden handed Ong hard copy: program specifications.

"Don't bother hunting down the security leak in your data banks, Doctor. You won't find it. But if it's any consolation, neither will anybody else. Now." He leaned forward suddenly. His tone changed. "I know that you've created twenty children who don't need to sleep at all, that so far nineteen are healthy, intelligent, and psychologically normal. In fact, they're better than normal; they're all unusually precocious. The oldest is already four years old and can read in two languages. I know you're thinking of offering this genetic modification on the open market in a few years. All I want is a chance to buy it for my daughter *now*. At whatever price you name."

Ong stood. "I can't possibly discuss this with you unilaterally, Mr. Camden. Neither the theft of our data—"

"Which wasn't a theft—your system developed a spontaneous bubble regurgitation into a public gate. You'd have a hell of a time proving otherwise—"

"—*nor* the offer to purchase this particular genetic modification lie in my sole area of authority. Both have to be discussed with the Institute's board of directors."

"By all means, by all means. When can I talk to them, too?"

"You?"

Camden, still seated, looked up at him. It occurred to Ong that there were few men who could look so confident eighteen inches below eye level. "Certainly. I'd like the chance to present my offer to whoever has the actual authority to accept it. That's only good business."

"This isn't solely a business transaction, Mr. Camden."

"It isn't solely pure scientific research, either," Camden retorted. "You're a for-profit corporation here. *With* certain tax breaks available only to firms meeting certain fair-practice laws."

For a minute Ong couldn't think what Camden meant. "Fair-practice laws . . ."

". . . are designed to protect minorities who are suppliers. I know it hasn't ever been tested in the case of customers, except for redlining in Y-energy installations. But it could be tested, Dr. Ong. Minorities are entitled to the same product offerings as nonminorities. I know the Institute would not welcome a court case, Doctor. None of your twenty genetic beta-test families is either Black or Jewish."

"A court . . . but you're not Black *or* Jewish!"

"I'm a different minority. Polish-American. The name was Kaminsky." Camden finally stood. And smiled warmly. "Look, it is preposterous. You know that, and I know that, and we both know what a grand time journalists would have with it anyway. And you know that I don't want to sue you with a preposterous case just to use the threat of premature and adverse publicity to get what I want. I don't want to make threats at all, believe me I don't. I just want this marvelous advancement you've come up with for my daughter." His face changed, to an expression Ong wouldn't have believed possible on those particular features: wistfulness. "Doctor, do you know how much more I could have accomplished if I hadn't had to *sleep* all my life?"

Elizabeth Camden said harshly, "You hardly sleep now."

Camden looked down at her as if he had forgotten she was there. "Well, no, my dear, not now. But when I was young . . . college, I might have been able to finish college and still support . . . Well. None of that matters now. What matters, Doctor, is that you and I and your board come to an agreement."

"Mr. Camden, please leave my office now."

"You mean before you lose your temper at my presumptuousness? You wouldn't be the first. I'll expect to have a meeting set up by the end of next week, whenever and wherever you say, of course. Just let my personal secretary, Diane Clavers, know the details. Anytime that's best for you."

Ong did not accompany them to the door. Pressure throbbed behind his temples. In the doorway Elizabeth Camden turned. "What happened to the twentieth one?"

"What?"

"The twentieth baby. My husband said nineteen of them are healthy and normal. What happened to the twentieth?"

The pressure grew stronger, hotter. Ong knew that he should not answer; that Camden probably already knew the answer even if his wife didn't; that he, Ong, was going to answer anyway; that he would regret the lack of self-control, bitterly, later.

"The twentieth baby is dead. His parents turned out to be unstable. They separated during the pregnancy, and his mother could not bear the twenty-four-hour crying of a baby who never sleeps."

Elizabeth Camden's eyes widened. "She killed it?"

"By mistake," Camden said shortly. "Shook the little thing too hard." He frowned at Ong. "Nurses, Doctor. In shifts. You should have picked only parents wealthy enough to afford nurses in shifts."

"That's horrible!" Mrs. Camden burst out, and Ong could not tell if she meant the child's death, the lack of nurses, or the Institute's carelessness. Ong closed his eyes.

When they had gone, he took ten milligrams of cyclobenzaprine-III. For his back—it was solely for his back. The old injury was hurting again. Afterward he stood for a long time at the window, still holding the paper magnet, feeling the pressure recede from his temples, feeling himself calm down. Below him Lake Michigan lapped peacefully at the shore; the police had driven away the homeless in another raid just last night, and they hadn't yet had time to return. Only their debris remained, thrown into the bushes of the lakeshore park: tattered blankets, newspapers, plastic bags like pathetic trampled standards. It was illegal to sleep in the park, illegal to enter it without a resident's permit, illegal to be homeless and without a residence. As Ong watched, uniformed park attendants began methodically spearing newspapers and shoving them into clean self-propelled receptacles.

Ong picked up the phone to call the chairman of Biotech Institute's board of directors.


Four men and three women sat around the polished mahogany table of the conference room. *Doctor, lawyer, Indian chief,* thought Susan Melling, looking from Ong to Sullivan to Camden. She smiled. Ong caught the smile and looked frosty. Pompous ass. Judy Sullivan, the Institute lawyer, turned to speak in a low voice to Camden's lawyer, a thin nervous man with the look of being owned. The owner, Roger Camden, the Indian chief himself, was the happiest-looking person in the room. The lethal little man—what did it take to become that rich, starting from nothing? She, Susan, would certainly never know—radiated excitement. He beamed, he glowed, so unlike the usual parents-to-be that Susan was intrigued. Usually the prospective daddies and mommies—especially the daddies—sat there looking as if they were at a corporate merger. Camden looked as if he were at a birthday party.

Which, of course, he was. Susan grinned at him, and was pleased when he grinned back. Wolfish, but with a sort of delight that could only be called innocent—what would he be like in bed? Ong frowned majestically and rose to speak.

"Ladies and gentlemen, I think we're ready to start. Perhaps introductions are in order. Mr. Roger Camden, Mrs. Camden, are of course our clients. Mr. John Jaworski, Mr. Camden's lawyer. Mr. Camden, this is Judith Sullivan, the Institute's head of Legal; Samuel Krenshaw, representing Institute Director Dr. Brad Marsteiner, who unfortunately couldn't be here today; and Dr. Susan Melling, who developed the genetic modification affecting sleep. A few legal points of interest to both parties—"

"Forget the contracts for a minute," Camden interrupted. "Let's talk about the sleep thing. I'd like to ask a few questions."

Susan said, "What would you like to know?" Camden's eyes were very blue in his blunt-featured face; he wasn't what she had expected. Mrs. Camden, who apparently lacked both a first name and a lawyer, since Jaworski had been introduced as her husband's but not hers, looked either sullen or scared, it was difficult to tell which.

Ong said sourly, "Then perhaps we should start with a short presentation by Dr. Melling."

Susan would have preferred a Q&A, to see what Camden would ask. But she had annoyed Ong enough for one session. Obediently she rose.

"Let me start with a brief description of sleep. Researchers have known for a long time that there are actually three kinds of sleep. One is 'slow-wave sleep,' characterized on an EEG by delta waves. One is 'rapid-eye-movement sleep,' or REM sleep, which is much lighter sleep and contains most dreaming. Together these two make up 'core sleep.' The third type of sleep is 'optional sleep,' so-called because people seem to get along without it with no ill effects, and some short sleepers don't do it at all, sleeping naturally only three or four hours a night."

"That's me," Camden said. "I trained myself into it. Couldn't everybody do that?"

Apparently they were going to have a Q&A after all. "No. The actual sleep mechanism has some flexibility, but not the same amount for every person. The raphe nuclei on the brain stem—"

Ong said, "I don't think we need that level of detail, Susan. Let's stick to basics."

Camden said, "The raphe nuclei regulate the balance among neurotransmitters and peptides that leads to a pressure to sleep, don't they?"

Susan couldn't help it; she grinned. Camden, the laser-sharp ruthless financier, sat trying to look solemn, a third-grader waiting to have his homework praised. Ong looked sour. Mrs. Camden looked away, out the window.

"Yes, that's correct, Mr. Camden. You've done your research."

Camden said, "This is my *daughter*," and Susan caught her breath. When was the last time she had heard that note of reverence in anyone's voice? But no one in the room seemed to notice.

"Well, then," Susan said, "you already know that the reason people sleep is because a pressure to sleep builds up in the brain. Over the past twenty years, research has determined that's the *only* reason. Neither slow-wave sleep nor REM sleep serve functions that can't be carried on while the body and brain are awake. A lot goes on during sleep, but it can go on during wakefulness just as well, if other hormonal adjustments are made.

"Sleep served an important evolutionary function. Once Clem Pre-Mammal was done filling his stomach and squirting his sperm around, sleep kept him immobile and away from predators. Sleep was an aid to survival. But now it's a left-over mechanism, a vestige like the appendix. It switches on every night, but the need is gone. So we turn off the switch at its source, in the genes."

Ong winced. He hated it when she oversimplified like that. Or maybe it was the lightheartedness he hated. If Marsteiner were making this presentation, there'd be no Clem Pre-Mammal.

Camden said, "What about the need to dream?"

"Not necessary. A left-over bombardment of the cortex to keep it on semialert in case a predator attacked during sleep. Wakefulness does that better."

"Why not have wakefulness instead then? From the start of the evolution?"

He was testing her. Susan gave him a full, lavish smile, enjoying his brass. "I told you. Safety from predators. But when a modern predator attacks—say, a cross-border data-atoll investor—it's safer to be awake."

Camden shot at her, "What about the high percentage of REM sleep in fetuses and babies?"

"Still an evolutionary hangover. Cerebrum develops perfectly well without it."

"What about neural repair during slow-wave sleep?"

"That does go on. But it can go on during wakefulness, if the DNA is programmed to do so. No loss of neural efficiency, as far as we know."

"What about the release of human growth enzyme in such large concentrations during slow-wave sleep?"

Susan looked at him admiringly. "Goes on without the sleep. Genetic adjustments tie it to other changes in the pineal gland."

"What about the—"

"The *side effects*?" Mrs. Camden said. Her mouth turned down. "What about the bloody side effects?"

Susan turned to Elizabeth Camden. She had forgotten she was there. The younger woman stared at Susan, mouth turned down at the corners.

"I'm glad you asked that, Mrs. Camden. Because there are side effects." Susan paused; she was enjoying herself. "Compared to their age mates, the nonsleep children—who have *not* had IQ genetic manipulation—are more intelligent, better at problem-solving, and more joyous."

Camden took out a cigarette. The archaic, filthy habit surprised Susan. Then she saw that it was deliberate: Roger Camden was drawing attention to an ostentatious display to draw attention away from what he was feeling. His cigarette lighter was gold, monogrammed, innocently gaudy.

"Let me explain," Susan said. "REM sleep bombards the cerebral cortex with random neural firings from the brain stem; dreaming occurs because the poor besieged cortex tries so hard to make sense of the activated images and memories. It spends a lot of energy doing that. Without that energy expenditure, nonsleep cerebrums save the wear-and-tear and do better at coordinating real-life input. Thus, greater intelligence and problem-solving.

"Also, doctors have known for sixty years that antidepressants, which lift the mood of depressed patients, also suppress REM sleep entirely. What they have proved in the past ten years is that the reverse is equally true: suppress REM sleep and people don't *get* depressed. The nonsleep kids are cheerful, outgoing . . . *joyous*. There's no other word for it."

"At what cost?" Mrs. Camden said. She held her neck rigid, but the corners of her jaw worked.

"No cost. No negative side effects at all."

"So far," Mrs. Camden shot back.

Susan shrugged. "So far."

"They're only four years old! At the most!"

Ong and Krenshaw were studying her closely. Susan saw the moment the Camden woman realized it; she sank back into her chair, drawing her fur coat around her, her face blank.

Camden did not look at his wife. He blew a cloud of cigarette smoke. "Everything has costs, Dr. Melling."

She liked the way he said her name. "Ordinarily, yes. Especially in genetic modification. But we honestly have not been able to find any here, despite looking." She smiled directly into Camden's eyes. "Is it too much to believe that just once the universe has given us something wholly good, wholly a step forward, wholly beneficial? Without hidden penalties?"

"Not the universe. The intelligence of people like you," Camden said, surprising Susan more than anything else that had gone before. His eyes held hers. She felt her chest tighten.

"I think," Dr. Ong said dryly, "that the philosophy of the universe may be beyond our concerns here. Mr. Camden, if you have no further medical questions, perhaps we can return to the legal points Ms. Sullivan and Mr. Jaworski have raised. Thank you, Dr. Melling."

Susan nodded. She didn't look again at Camden. But she knew what he said, how he looked, that he was there.

The house was about what she had expected, a huge mock-Tudor on Lake Michigan north of Chicago. The land was heavily wooded between the gate and the house, open between the house and the surging water. Patches of snow dotted the dormant grass. Biotech had been working with the Camdens for four months, but this was the first time Susan had driven to their home.

As she walked toward the house another car drove up behind her. No, a truck, continuing around the curved driveway to a service entry at the side of the house. One man rang the service bell; a second began to unload a plastic-wrapped playpen from the back of the truck. White, with pink and yellow bunnies. Susan briefly closed her eyes.

Camden opened the door himself. She could see his effort not to look worried. "You didn't have to drive out, Susan; I'd have come into the city!"

"No, I didn't want you to do that, Roger. Mrs. Camden is here?"

"In the living room." Camden led her into a large room with a stone fireplace, English country-house furniture, and prints of dogs or boats, all hung eighteen inches too high; Elizabeth Camden must have done the decorating. She did not rise from her wing chair as Susan entered.

"Let me be concise and fast," Susan said, "I don't want to make this any more drawn-out for you than I have to. We have all the amniocentesis, ultrasound, and Langston test results. The fetus is fine, developing normally for two weeks, no problems with the implant on the uterine wall. But a complication has developed."

"What?" Camden said. He took out a cigarette, looked at his wife, and put it back unlit.

Susan said quietly, "Mrs. Camden, by sheer chance both your ovaries released eggs last month. We removed one for the gene surgery. By more sheer chance the second was fertilized and implanted. You're carrying two fetuses."

Elizabeth Camden grew still. "Twins?"

"No," Susan said. Then she realized what she had said. "I mean, yes.

They're twins, but nonidentical. Only one has been genetically altered. The other will be no more similar to her than any two siblings. It's a so-called normal baby. And I know you didn't want a so-called normal baby."

Camden said, "No. I didn't."

Elizabeth Camden said, "I did."

Camden shot her a fierce look that Susan couldn't read. He took out the cigarette again, and lit it. His face was in profile to Susan, and he was thinking intently; she doubted he knew the cigarette was there, or that he was lighting it. "Is the baby being affected by the other one's being there?"

"No," Susan said. "No, of course not. They're just . . . coexisting."

"Can you abort it?"

"Not without aborting both of them. Removing the unaltered fetus would cause changes in the uterine lining that would probably lead to a spontaneous miscarriage of the other." She drew a deep breath. "There's that option, of course. We can start the whole process over again. But as I told you at the time, you were very lucky to have the *in vitro* fertilization take on only the second try. Some couples take eight or ten tries. If we started all over, the process could be a lengthy one."

Camden said, "Is the presence of this second fetus harming my daughter? Taking away nutrients or anything? Or will it change anything for her later on in the pregnancy?"

"No. Except that there is a chance of premature birth. Two fetuses take up a lot more room in the womb, and if it gets too crowded, birth can be premature. But the—"

"How premature? Enough to threaten survival?"

"Most probably not."

Camden went on smoking. A man appeared at the door. "Sir, London calling. James Kendall for Mr. Yagai."

"I'll take it." Camden rose. Susan watched him study his wife's face. When he spoke, it was to her. "All right, Elizabeth. All right." He left the room.

For a long moment the two women sat in silence. Susan was aware of the disappointment; this was not the Camden she had expected to see. She became aware of Elizabeth Camden watching her with amusement.

"Oh, yes, Doctor. He's like that."

Susan said nothing.

"Completely overbearing. But not this time." She laughed softly, with excitement. "Two. Do you . . . do you know what sex the other one is?"

"Both fetuses are female."

"I wanted a girl, you know. And now I'll have one."

"Then you'll go ahead with the pregnancy."

"Oh, yes. Thank you for coming, Doctor."

She was dismissed. No one saw her out. But as she was getting into her car, Camden rushed out of the house, coatless. "Susan! I wanted to thank you. For coming all the way out here to tell us yourself."

"You already thanked me."

"Yes. Well. You're sure the second fetus is no threat to my daughter?"

Susan said deliberately, "Nor is the genetically altered fetus a threat to the naturally conceived one."

He smiled. His voice was low and wistful. "And you think that should matter to me just as much. But it doesn't. And why should I fake what I feel? Especially to you?"

Susan opened her car door. She wasn't ready for this, or she had changed her mind, or something. But then Camden leaned over to close the door, and his manner held no trace of flirtatiousness, no smarmy ingratiation. "I better order a second playpen."

"Yes."

"And a second car seat."

"Yes."

"But not a second night-shift nurse."

"That's up to you."

"And you." Abruptly he leaned over and kissed her, a kiss so polite and respectful that Susan was shocked. Neither lust nor conquest would have shocked her; this did. Camden didn't give her a chance to react; he closed the car door and turned back toward the house. Susan drove toward the gate, her hands shaky on the wheel until amusement replaced shock: It *had* been a deliberate, blatant, respectful kiss, an engineered enigma. And nothing else could have guaranteed so well that there would have to be another.

She wondered what the Camdens would name their daughters.


Dr. Ong strode the hospital corridor, which had been dimmed to half-light. From the nurse's station in Maternity a nurse stepped forward as if to stop him—it was the middle of the night, long past visiting hours—got a good look at his face, and faded back into her station. Around a corner was the viewing glass to the nursery. To Ong's annoyance, Susan Melling stood pressed against the glass. To his further annoyance, she was crying.

Ong realized that he had never liked the woman. Maybe not any women. Even those with superior minds could not seem to refrain from being made damn fools by their emotions.

"Look," Susan said, laughing a little, swiping at her face. "Doctor—*look.*"

Behind the glass Roger Camden, gowned and masked, was holding up a baby in a white undershirt and pink blanket. Camden's blue eyes—theatrically blue—a man really should not have such garish eyes—glowed. The baby's head was covered with blond fuzz; it had wide eyes and pink skin. Camden's eyes above the mask said that no other child had ever had these attributes.

Ong said, "An uncomplicated birth?"

"Yes," Susan Melling sobbed. "Perfectly straightforward. Elizabeth is fine. She's asleep. Isn't she beautiful? He has the most adventurous spirit I've ever known." She wiped her nose on her sleeve; Ong realized that she was drunk. "Did I ever tell you that I was engaged once? Fifteen years ago, in med school? I broke it off because he grew to seem so ordinary, so boring. Oh, God, I shouldn't be telling you all this. I'm sorry. I'm sorry."

Ong moved away from her. Behind the glass Roger Camden laid the baby in a small wheeled crib. The nameplate said BABY GIRL CAMDEN #1 5.9 POUNDS. A night nurse watched indulgently.

Ong did not wait to see Camden emerge from the nursery or to hear Susan Melling say to him whatever she was going to say. Ong went to have the OB paged. Melling's report was not, under the circumstances, to be trusted. A perfect, unprecedented chance to record every detail of gene alteration with a nonaltered control, and Melling was more interested in her own sloppy emotions. Ong would obviously have to do the report himself, after talking to the OB. He was hungry for every detail. And not just about the pink-cheeked baby in Camden's arms. He wanted to know everything about the birth of the child in the other glass-sided crib: BABY GIRL CAMDEN #2. 5.1 POUNDS. The dark-haired baby with the mottled red features, lying scrunched down in her pink blanket, asleep.

# TWO

LEISHA'S EARLIEST MEMORY WAS FLOWING LINES THAT WERE NOT there. She knew they were not there because when she reached out her fist to touch them, her fist was empty. Later she realized that the flowing lines were light: sunshine slanting in bars between curtains in her room, between the wooden blinds in the dining room, between the crisscross lattices in the conservatory. The day she realized the golden flow was light she laughed out loud with the sheer joy of discovery, and Daddy turned from putting flowers in pots and smiled at her.

The whole house was full of light. Light bounded off the lake, streamed across the high white ceilings, puddled on the shining wooden floors. She and Alice moved continually through light, and sometimes Leisha would stop and tip back her head and let it flow over her face. She could feel it, like water.

The best light, of course, was in the conservatory. That's where Daddy liked to be when he was home from making money. Daddy potted plants and watered trees, humming, and Leisha and Alice ran between the wooden tables of flowers with their wonderful earthy smells, running from the dark side of the conservatory where the big purple flowers grew to the sunshine side with sprays of yellow flowers, running back and forth, in and out of the light. "Growth," Daddy said to her, "flowers all fulfilling their promise. Alice, be careful! You almost knocked over that orchid!" Alice, obedient, would stop running for a while. Daddy never told Leisha to stop running.

After a while the light would go away. Alice and Leisha would have their baths, and then Alice would get quiet, or cranky. She wouldn't play nice with Leisha, even when Leisha let her choose the game or even have all the best dolls. Then Nanny would take Alice to bed, and Leisha would talk with Daddy some more until Daddy said he had to work in his study with the papers that made money. Leisha always felt a moment of regret that he had to go do that, but the moment never lasted very long because Mamselle would arrive and start Leisha's lessons, which she liked. Learning things was so interesting! She could already sing twenty songs and write all the letters in the alphabet and count to fifty. And by the time lessons were done, the light had come back, and it was time for breakfast.

Breakfast was the only time Leisha didn't like. Daddy had gone to the office, and Leisha and Alice had breakfast with Mommy in the big dining room. Mommy sat in a red robe, which Leisha liked, and she didn't smell funny or talk funny the way she would later in the day, but still breakfast wasn't fun. Mommy always started with The Question.

"Alice, sweetheart, how did you sleep?"

"Fine, Mommy."

"Did you have any nice dreams?"

For a long time Alice said no. Then one day she said, "I dreamed about a horse. I was riding him." Mommy clapped her hands and kissed Alice and gave her an extra sticky bun. After that Alice always had a dream to tell Mommy.

Once Leisha said, "I had a dream, too. I dreamed light was coming in the window and it wrapped all around me like a blanket and then it kissed me on my eyes."

Mommy put down her coffee cup so hard that coffee sloshed out of it. "Don't lie to me, Leisha. You did not have a dream."

"Yes, I did," Leisha said.

"Only children who sleep can have dreams. Don't lie to me. You did not have a dream."

"Yes I did! I did!" Leisha shouted. She could see it, almost: the light streaming in the window and wrapping around her like a golden blanket.

"I will not tolerate a child who is a liar! Do you hear me, Leisha— I won't tolerate it!"

"You're a liar!" Leisha shouted, knowing the words weren't true, hating herself because they weren't true but hating Mommy more and that was wrong, too, and there sat Alice stiff and frozen with her eyes wide, Alice was scared and it was Leisha's fault.

Mommy called sharply, "Nanny! Nanny! Take Leisha to her room at once. She can't sit with civilized people if she can't refrain from telling lies!"

Leisha started to cry. Nanny carried her out of the room. Leisha hadn't even had her breakfast. But she didn't care about that; all she could see while she cried was Alice's eyes, scared like that, reflecting broken bits of light.

But Leisha didn't cry long. Nanny read her a story, and then played Data Jump with her, and then Alice came up and Nanny drove them both into Chicago to the zoo where there were wonderful animals to see, animals Leisha could not have dreamed—nor Alice *either*. And by the time they came back Mommy had gone to her room and Leisha knew that she would stay there with the glasses of funny-smelling stuff the rest of the day and Leisha would not have to see her.

But that night, she went to her mother's room.

"I have to go to the bathroom," she told Mamselle. Mamselle said, "Do you need any help?" maybe because Alice still needed help in the bathroom. But Leisha didn't, and she thanked Mamselle. Then she sat on the toilet for a minute even though nothing came, so that what she had told Mamselle wouldn't be a lie.

Leisha tiptoed down the hall. She went first into Alice's room. A little light in a wall socket burned near the crib. There was no crib in Leisha's room. Leisha looked at her sister through the bars. Alice lay on her side with her eyes closed. The lids of the eyes fluttered quickly, like curtains blowing in the wind. Alice's chin and neck looked loose.

Leisha closed the door very carefully and went to her parents' room.

They didn't sleep in a crib but in a huge enormous bed, with enough room between them for more people. Mommy's eyelids weren't fluttering; she lay on her back making a hrrr-hrrr sound through her nose. The funny smell was strong on her. Leisha backed away and tiptoed over to Daddy. He looked like Alice, except that his neck and chin looked even looser, folds of skin collapsed like the tent that had fallen down in the back yard. It scared Leisha to see him like that. Then Daddy's eyes flew open so suddenly that Leisha screamed.

Daddy rolled out of bed and picked her up, looking quickly at Mommy. But she didn't move. Daddy was wearing only his underpants. He carried Leisha out into the hall, where Mamselle came rushing up saying, "Oh, Sir, I'm sorry, she just said she was going to the bathroom—"

"It's all right," Daddy said. "I'll take her with me."

"No!" Leisha screamed, because Daddy was only in his underpants and his neck had looked all funny and the room smelled bad because of Mommy. But Daddy carried her into the conservatory, set her down on a bench, wrapped himself in a piece of green plastic that was supposed to cover up plants, and sat down next to her.

"Now, what happened, Leisha? What were you doing?"

Leisha didn't answer.

"You were looking at people sleeping, weren't you?" Daddy said, and because his voice was softer Leisha mumbled, "Yes." She immediately felt better; it felt good not to lie.

"You were looking at people sleeping because you don't sleep and you were curious, weren't you? Like Curious George in your book?"

"Yes," Leisha said. "I thought you said you made money in your study all night!"

Daddy smiled. "Not all night. Some of it. But then I sleep, although not very much." He took Leisha on his lap. "I don't need much sleep, so I get a lot more done at night than most people. Different people need different amounts of sleep. And a few, a very few, are like you. You don't need any."

"Why not?"

"Because you're special. Better than other people. Before you were born, I had some doctors help make you that way."

"Why?"

"So you could do anything you want to and make manifest your own individuality."

Leisha twisted in his arms to stare at him; the words meant nothing. Daddy reached over and touched a single flower growing on a tall potted tree. The flower had thick white petals like the cream he put in coffee, and the center was a light pink.

"See, Leisha—this tree made this flower. Because it *can*. Only this tree can make this kind of wonderful flower. That plant hanging up there can't, and those can't either. Only this tree. Therefore the most important thing in the world for this tree to do is grow this flower. The flower is the tree's individuality—that means just *it*, and nothing else—made manifest. Nothing else matters."

"I don't understand, Daddy."

"You will. Someday."

"But I want to understand *now*," Leisha said, and Daddy laughed with pure delight and hugged her. The hug felt good, but Leisha still wanted to understand.

"When you make money, is that your indiv . . . that thing?"

"Yes," Daddy said happily.

"Then nobody else can make money? Like only that tree can make that flower?"

"Nobody else can make it just the way I do."

"What do you do with the money?"

"I buy things for you. This house, your dresses, Mamselle to teach you, the car to ride in."

"What does the tree do with the flower?"

"Glories in it," Daddy said, which made no sense. "Excellence is what counts, Leisha. Excellence supported by individual effort. And that's *all* that counts."

"I'm cold, Daddy."

"Then I better bring you back to Mamselle."

Leisha didn't move. She touched the flower with one finger. "I want to sleep, Daddy."

"No, you don't, sweetheart. Sleep is just lost time, wasted life. It's a little death."

"Alice sleeps."

"Alice isn't like you."

"Alice isn't special?"

"No. You are."

"Why didn't you make Alice special, too?"

"Alice made herself. I didn't have a chance to make her special."

The whole thing was too hard. Leisha stopped stroking the flower and slipped off Daddy's lap. He smiled at her. "My little questioner. When you grow up, you'll find your own excellence, and it will be a new order, a specialness the world hasn't ever seen before. You might even be like Kenzo Yagai. He made the Yagai generator that powers the world."

"Daddy, you look funny wrapped in the flower plastic." Leisha laughed. Daddy did, too. But then she said, "When I grow up, I'll make my specialness find a way to make Alice special, too," and Daddy stopped laughing.

He took her back to Mamselle, who taught her to write her name, which was so exciting she forgot about the puzzling talk with Daddy. There were six letters, all different, and together they were *her name*. Leisha wrote it over and over, laughing, and Mamselle laughed too. But later, in the morning, Leisha thought again about the talk with Daddy. She thought of it often, turning the unfamiliar words over and over in her mind like small hard stones, but the part she thought about most wasn't a word. It was the frown on Daddy's face when she told him she would use her specialness to make Alice special, too.


Every week Dr. Melling came to see Leisha and Alice, sometimes alone, sometimes with other people. Leisha and Alice both liked Dr. Melling, who laughed a lot and whose eyes were bright and warm. Often Daddy was there, too. Dr. Melling played games with them, first with Alice and Leisha separately and then together. She took their pictures and weighed them. She made them lie down on a table and stuck little metal things to their temples, which sounded scary but wasn't because there were so many machines to watch, all making interesting noises, while they were lying there. Dr. Melling was as good at answering questions as Daddy. Once Leisha said, "Is Dr. Melling a special person? Like Kenzo Yagai?" And Daddy laughed and glanced at Dr. Melling and said, "Oh, yes, indeed."

When Leisha was five she and Alice started school. Daddy's driver took them every day into Chicago. They were in different rooms, which disappointed Leisha. The kids in Leisha's room were all older. But from the first day she adored school, with its fascinating science equipment and electronic drawers full of math puzzlers and other children to find countries on the map with. In half a year she had been moved to yet a different room, where the kids were still older, but they were nonetheless nice to her. Leisha started to learn Japanese. She loved drawing the beautiful characters on thick white paper. "The Sauley School was a good choice," Daddy said.

But Alice didn't like the Sauley School. She wanted to go to school on the same yellow bus as Cook's daughter. She cried and threw her paints on the floor at the Sauley School. Then Mommy came out of her room—Leisha hadn't seen her for a few weeks, although she knew Alice had—and threw some candlesticks from the mantelpiece on the floor. The candlesticks, which were china, broke. Leisha ran to pick up the pieces while Mommy and Daddy screamed at each other in the hall by the big staircase.

"She's my daughter, too! And I say she can go!"

"You don't have the right to say anything about it! A weepy drunk, the most rotten role model possible for both of them . . . and I thought I was getting a fine English aristocrat!"

"You got what you paid for! Nothing! Not that you ever needed anything from me or anybody else!"

"Stop it!" Leisha cried. "Stop it!" There was silence in the hall.

Leisha cut her fingers on the china; blood streamed onto the rug. Daddy rushed in and picked her up. "Stop it," Leisha sobbed, and didn't understand when Daddy said quietly, "*You* stop it, Leisha. Nothing *they* do should touch you at all. You have to be at least that strong."

Leisha buried her head in Daddy's shoulder. Alice transferred to Carl Sandburg Elementary School, riding there on the yellow school bus with Cook's daughter.

A few weeks later Daddy told them that Mommy was going away to a hospital, to stop drinking so much. When Mommy came out, he said, she was going to live somewhere else for a while. She and Daddy were not happy. Leisha and Alice would stay with Daddy and they would visit Mommy sometimes. He told them this very carefully, finding the right words for truth. Truth was very important, Leisha already knew. Truth was being true to yourself, your specialness. Your individuality. An individual respected facts, and so always told the truth.

Mommy—Daddy did not say but Leisha knew—did not respect facts.

"I don't want Mommy to go away," Alice said. She started to cry. Leisha thought Daddy would pick Alice up, but he didn't. He just stood there looking at them both.

Leisha put her arms around Alice. "It's all right, Alice. It's all right! We'll make it all right! I'll play with you all the time we're not in school so you don't miss Mommy!"

Alice clung to Leisha. Leisha turned her head so she didn't have to see Daddy's face.

# THREE

KENZO YAGAI WAS COMING TO THE UNITED STATES TO LECTURE. THE title of his talk, which he would give in New York, Los Angeles, and Chicago, with a repeat in Washington as a special address to Congress, was "The Further Political Implications of Inexpensive Power." Leisha Camden, eleven years old, was going to have a private introduction after the Chicago talk, arranged by her father.

She had studied the theory of cold fusion at school, and her global studies teacher had traced the changes in the world resulting from Yagai's patented, low-cost applications of what had, until him, been unworkable theory: the rising prosperity of the Third World; the death throes of the old communistic systems; the decline of the oil states; the renewed economic power of the United States. Her study group had written a news script, filmed with the school's professional-quality equipment, about how a 1985 American family lived with expensive energy costs and a belief in tax-supported help, while a 2019 family lived with cheap energy and a belief in the contract as the basis of civilization. Parts of her own research puzzled Leisha.

"Japan thinks Kenzo Yagai was a traitor to his own country," she said to Daddy at supper.

"No," Camden said, "*some* Japanese think that. Watch out for generalizations, Leisha. Yagai patented and licensed Y-energy in the United States because here there were at least the dying embers of individual enterprise. Because of his invention, our entire country has slowly swung back toward an individual meritocracy, and Japan has slowly been forced to follow."

"Your father held that belief all along," Susan said. "Eat your peas, Leisha." Leisha ate her peas. Susan and Daddy had only been married less than a year; it still felt a little strange to have her there. But nice. Daddy said Susan was a valuable addition to their household: intelligent, motivated, and cheerful. Like Leisha herself.

"Remember, Leisha," Camden said, "a man's worth to society and to himself doesn't rest on what he thinks other people should do or be or feel, but on himself. On what he can actually do, and do well. People trade what they do well, and everyone benefits. The basic tool of civilization is the contract. Contracts are voluntary and mutually beneficial. As opposed to coercion, which is wrong."

"The strong have no right to take anything from the weak by force," Susan said. "Alice, eat your peas, too, honey."

"Nor the weak to take anything by force from the strong," Camden said. "That's the basis of what you'll hear Kenzo Yagai discuss tonight, Leisha."

Alice said, "I don't like peas."

Camden said, "Your body does. They're good for you."

Alice smiled. Leisha felt her heart lift; Alice didn't smile much at dinner any more. "My body doesn't have a contract with the peas."

Camden said, a little impatiently, "Yes, it does. Your body benefits from them. Now eat."

Alice's smile vanished. Leisha looked down at her plate. Suddenly she saw a way out. "No, Daddy, look—Alice's body benefits, but the peas don't! It's not a mutually beneficial consideration, so there's no contract! Alice is right!"

Camden let out a shout of laughter. To Susan he said, "Eleven years old . . . *eleven*." Even Alice smiled, and Leisha waved her spoon triumphantly, light glinting off the bowl and dancing silver on the opposite wall.

But even so, Alice did not want to go hear Kenzo Yagai. She was going to sleep over at her friend Julie's house; they were going to curl their hair together. More surprisingly, Susan wasn't coming either. She and Daddy looked at each other a little funny at the front door, Leisha thought, but Leisha was too excited to think about this. She was going to hear *Kenzo Yagai*.

Yagai was a small man, dark and slim. Leisha liked his accent. She liked, too, something about him that took her a while to name. "Daddy," she whispered in the half-darkness of the auditorium, "he's a joyful man."

Daddy hugged her in the darkness.

Yagai spoke about spirituality and economics. "A man's spirituality, which is only his dignity as a man, rests on his own efforts. Dignity and worth are not automatically conferred by aristocratic birth; we have only to look at history to see that. Dignity and worth are not automatically conferred by inherited wealth. A great heir may be a thief, a wastrel, cruel, an exploiter, a person who leaves the world much poorer than he found it. Nor are dignity and worth automatically conferred by existence itself. A mass murderer exists, but is of negative worth to his society and possesses no dignity in his lust to kill.

"No, the only dignity, the only spirituality, rests on what a man can achieve with his own efforts. To rob a man of the chance to achieve, and to trade what he achieves with others, is to rob him of his spiritual dignity as a man. This is why communism has failed in our time. *All* co-ercion—all force to take from a man his own efforts to achieve—causes spiritual damage and weakens a society. Conscription, theft, fraud, violence, welfare, lack of legislative representation—*all* rob a man of his chance to choose, to achieve on his own, to trade the results of his achievement with others. Coercion is a cheat. It produces nothing new. Only freedom—the freedom to achieve, the freedom to trade freely the results of achievement—creates the environment proper to the dignity and spirituality of man."

Leisha applauded so hard her hands hurt. Going backstage with Daddy, she thought she could hardly breathe. Kenzo Yagai!

But backstage was more crowded than she had expected. There were cameras everywhere. Daddy said, "Mr. Yagai, may I present my daughter Leisha," and the cameras moved in close and fast—on *her.* A Japanese man whispered something in Kenzo Yagai's ear, and he looked more closely at Leisha. "Ah, yes."

"Look over here, Leisha," someone called, and she did. A robot camera zoomed so close to her face that Leisha stepped back, startled. Daddy spoke very sharply to someone, then to someone else. The cameras didn't move. A woman suddenly knelt in front of Leisha and thrust a microphone at her. "What does it feel like to never sleep, Leisha?"

"What?"

Someone laughed. The laugh was not kind. "Breeding geniuses . . ."

Leisha felt a hand on her shoulder. Kenzo Yagai gripped her very firmly, and pulled her away from the cameras. Immediately, as if by magic, a line of Japanese men formed behind Yagai, parting only to let Daddy through. Behind the line, the three of them moved into a dressing room, and Kenzo Yagai shut the door.

"You must not let them bother you, Leisha," he said in his wonderful accent. "Not ever. There is an old Asian proverb: 'The dogs bark but the caravan moves on.' You must never let your individual caravan be slowed by the barking of rude or envious dogs."

"I won't," Leisha breathed, not sure yet what the words really meant, knowing there was time later to sort them out, to talk about them with Daddy. For now she was dazzled by Kenzo Yagai, the actual man himself who was changing the world without force, without guns, by trading his special individual efforts. "We study your philosophy at my school, Mr. Yagai."

Kenzo Yagai looked at Daddy. Daddy said, "A private school. But Leisha's sister also studies it, although cursorily, in the public system. Slowly, Kenzo, but it comes. It comes." Leisha noticed that he did not say why Alice was not here tonight with them.

Back home, Leisha sat in her room for hours, thinking over everything that had happened. When Alice came home from Julie's the next morning, Leisha rushed toward her. But Alice seemed angry about something.

"Alice—what is it?"

"Don't you think I have enough to put up with at school already?" Alice shouted. "Everybody knows, but at least when you stayed quiet it didn't matter too much! They'd stopped teasing me! Why did you have to do it?"

"Do what?" Leisha said, bewildered.

Alice threw something at her: a hard-copy morning paper, on newsprint flimsier than the Camden systems used. The paper dropped open at Leisha's feet. She stared at her own picture, three columns wide, with Kenzo Yagai. The headline said, "Yagai and the Future: Room For the Rest of Us? Y-Energy Inventor Confers With 'Sleep-Free' Daughter of Mega-Financier Roger Camden."

Alice kicked the paper. "It was on TV last night too—on *TV*. I work hard not to look stuck-up or creepy, and you go and do this! Now Julie probably won't even invite me to her slumber party next week!" She rushed up the broad curving stairs to her room.

Leisha looked down at the paper. She heard Kenzo Yagai's voice in her head: *The dogs bark but the caravan moves on.* She looked at the empty stairs. Aloud she said, "Alice—your hair looks really pretty curled like that."

# FOUR

I WANT TO MEET THE REST OF THEM," LEISHA SAID. "WHY HAVE YOU KEPT them from me this long?"

"I haven't kept them from you at all," Camden said. "Not offering is not the same as denial. Why shouldn't you be the one to do the asking? You're the one who now wants it."

Leisha looked at him. She was fifteen, in her last year at the Sauley School. "Why didn't you offer?"

"Why should I?"

"I don't know," Leisha said. "But you gave me everything else."

"Including the freedom to ask for what you want."

Leisha looked for the contradiction, and found it. "Most things that you provided for my education I didn't ask for, because I didn't know enough to ask and you as the adult did. But you've never offered the opportunity for me to meet any of the other sleepless mutants—"

"Don't use that word," Camden said sharply.

"—so you must either think it was not essential to my education or else you had another motive for not wanting me to meet them."

"Wrong," Camden said. "There's a third possibility. That I think meeting them is essential to your education, that I do want you to, but this issue provided a chance to further the education of your self-initiative by waiting for *you* to ask."

"All right," Leisha said, a little defiantly; there seemed to be a lot of defiance between them lately, for no good reason. She squared her shoulders. Her new breasts thrust forward. "I'm asking. How many of the Sleepless are there, who are they, and where are they?"

Camden said, "If you're using that term—'the Sleepless'—you've already done some reading on your own. So you probably know that there are 1,082 of you so far in the United States, more in foreign countries, most of them in major metropolitan areas. Seventy-nine are in Chicago, most of them still small children. Only nineteen anywhere are older than you."

Leisha didn't deny reading any of this. Camden leaned forward in his study chair to peer at her. Leisha wondered if he needed glasses. His hair was completely gray now, sparse and stiff, like lonely broom straws. The *Wall Street Journal* listed him among the hundred richest men in America; *Women's Wear Daily* pointed out that he was the only billionaire in the country who did not move in the society of international parties, charity balls, and social secretaries. Camden's jet ferried him to business meetings around the world, to the chairmanship of the Yagai Economics Institute, and to very little else. Over the years he had grown richer, more reclusive, and more cerebral. Leisha felt a rush of her old affection.

She threw herself sideways into a leather chair, her long slim legs dangling over the arm. Absently she scratched a mosquito bite on her thigh. "Well, then, I'd like to meet Richard Keller." He lived in Chicago and was the beta-test Sleepless closest to her own age. He was seventeen.

"Why ask me? Why not just go?"

Leisha thought there was a note of impatience in his voice. He liked her to explore things first, then report on them to him later. Both parts were important.

Leisha laughed. "You know what, Daddy? You're predictable."

Camden laughed, too. In the middle of the laugh Susan came in. "He certainly is not. Roger, what about that meeting in Buenos Aires on Thursday? Is it on or off?" When he didn't answer, her voice grew shriller. "Roger? I'm talking to you!"

Leisha averted her eyes. Two years ago Susan had finally left genetic research to run Camden's house and schedule; before that she had tried hard to do both. Since she had left Biotech, it seemed to Leisha, Susan had changed. Her voice was tighter. She was more insistent that Cook and the gardener follow her directions exactly, without deviation. Her blond braids had become stiff sculptured waves of platinum.

"It's on," Roger said.

"Well, thanks for at least answering. Am I going?"

"If you like."

"I like."

Susan left the room. Leisha rose and stretched. Her long legs rose on tiptoe. It felt good to reach, to stretch, to feel sunlight from the wide windows wash over her face. She smiled at her father, and found him watching her with an unexpected expression.

"Leisha—"

"What?"

"See Keller. But be careful."

"Of what?"

But Camden wouldn't answer.


The voice on the phone had been noncommittal. "Leisha Camden? Yes, I know who you are. Three o'clock on Thursday?" The house was modest, a thirty-year-old colonial on a quiet suburban street where small children on bicycles could be watched from the front window. Few roofs had more than one Y-energy cell. The trees, huge old sugar maples, were beautiful.

"Come in," Richard Keller said.

He was no taller than she, stocky, with a bad case of acne. Probably no genetic alterations except sleep, Leisha guessed. He had thick dark hair, a low forehead, and bushy black brows. Before he closed the door Leisha saw him stare at her car and driver, parked in the driveway next to a rusty ten-speed bike.

"I can't drive yet," she said. "I'm still fifteen."

"It's easy to learn," Richard said. "So, you want to tell me why you're here?"

Leisha liked his directness. "To meet some other Sleepless."

"You mean you never have? Not any of us?"

"You mean the rest of you know each other?" She hadn't expected that.

"Come to my room, Leisha."

She followed him to the back of the house. No one else seemed to be home. His room was large and airy, filled with computers and filing cabinets. A rowing machine sat in one corner. It looked like a shabbier version of the room of any bright classmate at the Sauley School, except there was more space without a bed. She walked over to the computer screen.

"Hey—you working on Boesc equations?"

"On an application of them."

"To what?"

"Fish migration patterns."

Leisha smiled. "Yeah, that would work. I never thought of that."

Richard seemed not to know what to do with her smile. He looked at the wall, then at her chin. "You interested in Gaea patterns? In the environment?"

"Well, no," Leisha confessed. "Not particularly. I'm going to study politics at Harvard. Pre-law. But of course we had Gaea patterns at school."

Richard's gaze finally came unstuck from her face. He ran a hand through his dark hair. "Sit down, if you want."

Leisha sat, looking appreciatively at the wall posters, shifting green on blue, like ocean currents. "I like those. Did you program them yourself?"

"You're not at all what I pictured," Richard said.

"How did you picture me?"

He didn't hesitate. "Stuck up. Superior. Shallow, despite your IQ."

She was more hurt than she had expected to be.

Richard blurted. "You're one of only two Sleepless who're really rich. You and Jennifer Sharifi. But you already know that."

"No, I don't. I've never checked."

He took the chair beside her, stretching his stocky legs straight in front of him, in a slouch that had nothing to do with relaxation. "It makes sense, really. Rich people don't have their children genetically modified to be superior—they think any offspring of theirs is already superior. By their values. And poor people can't afford it. We Sleepless are upper-middle class, no more. Children of professors, scientists, people who value brains and time."

"My father values brains and time," Leisha said. "He's the biggest supporter of Kenzo Yagai."

"Oh, Leisha, do you think I don't already know that? Are you flashing me or what?"

Leisha said with great deliberateness, "I'm *talking* to you." But the next minute she could feel the hurt break through on her face.

"I'm sorry," Richard muttered. He shot off his chair and paced to the computer and back. "I *am* sorry. But I don't . . . I don't understand what you're doing here."

"I'm lonely," Leisha said, astonished at herself. She looked up at him. "It's true. I'm lonely. I am. I have friends and Daddy and Alice. But no one really knows, really understands—what? I don't know what I'm saying."

Richard smiled. The smile changed his whole face, opened up its dark planes to the light. "I do. Oh, do I. What do you do when they say, 'I had such a dream last night?' "

"Yes!" Leisha said. "But that's even really minor. It's when *I* say, 'I'll look that up for you tonight' and they get that funny look on their face that means, 'She'll do it while I'm asleep.' "

"But that's even really minor," Richard said. "It's when you're playing basketball in the gym after supper and then you go to the diner for food and then you say, 'Let's have a walk by the lake,' and they say, 'I'm really tired. I'm going home to bed now.' "

"But that's really minor," Leisha said, jumping up. "It's when you really are absorbed by the movie and then you get the point and it's so goddamn beautiful you leap up and say, 'Yes! Yes!' and Susan says, 'Leisha, really, you'd think nobody but you ever enjoyed anything before.' "

"Who's Susan?" Richard said.

The mood was broken. But not really; Leisha could say, "My stepmother," without much discomfort over what Susan had promised to be and what she had become. Richard stood inches from her, smiling that joyous smile, understanding, and suddenly relief washed over Leisha so strong that she walked straight over to him and put her arms around his neck, only tightening them when she felt his startled jerk. She started to sob—she, Leisha, who never cried.

"Hey," Richard said. "Hey."

"Brilliant," Leisha said, laughing. "Brilliant remark."

She could feel his embarrassed smile. "Wanta see my fish migration curves instead?"

"No," Leisha sobbed, and he went on holding her, patting her back awkwardly, telling her without words that she was home.

Camden waited up for her, although it was past midnight. He had been smoking heavily. Through the blue air he said quietly, "Did you have a good time, Leisha?"

"Yes."

"I'm glad," he said, and put out his last cigarette, and climbed the stairs—slowly, stiffly, he was nearly seventy now—to bed.

They went everywhere together for nearly a year: swimming, dancing, the museums, the theater, the library. Richard introduced her to the others, a group of twelve kids between fourteen and nineteen, all of them intelligent and eager. All Sleepless.

Leisha learned.

Tony Indivino's parents, like her own, had divorced. But Tony, fourteen, lived with his mother, who had not particularly wanted a Sleepless child, while his father, who had, acquired a red sports car and a young girlfriend who designed ergonomic chairs in Paris. Tony was not allowed to tell anyone—relatives, schoolmates—that he was Sleepless. "They'll think you're a freak," his mother said, eyes averted from her son's face. The one time Tony disobeyed her and told a friend that he never slept, his mother beat him. Then she moved the family to a new neighborhood. He was nine years old.

Jeanine Carter, almost as long-legged and slim as Leisha, was training for the Olympics in ice skating. She practiced twelve hours a day, hours no Sleeper still in high school could ever have. So far the newspapers had not picked up the story. Jeanine was afraid that if they did, they would somehow not let her compete.

Jack Bellingham, like Leisha, would start college in September. Unlike Leisha, he had already started his career. The practice of law had to wait for law school; the practice of investing required only money. Jack didn't have much, but his precise financial analyses parlayed six hundred dollars saved from summer jobs to three thousand dollars through stock-market investing, then to ten thousand dollars, and then he had enough to qualify for information-fund speculation. Jack was fifteen, not old enough to make legal investments; the transactions were all in the name of Kevin Baker, the oldest of the Sleepless, who lived in Austin. Jack told Leisha, "When I hit eighty-four percent profit over two consecutive quarters, the data analysts logged onto me. Just sniffing. Well, that's their job, even when the overall amounts are actually small. It's the patterns they care about. If they take the trouble to cross-reference data banks and come up with the fact that Kevin is a Sleepless, will they try to stop us from investing somehow?"

"That's paranoid," Leisha said.

"No, it's not," Jeanine said. "Leisha, you don't *know.*"

"You mean because I've been protected by my father's money and caring," Leisha said. No one grimaced; all of them confronted ideas openly, without shadowy allusions. Without dreams.

"Yes," Jeanine said. "Your father sounds terrific. And he raised you to think that achievement should not be fettered—Jesus Christ, he's a Yagaiist. Well, good. We're glad for you." She said it without sarcasm. Leisha nodded. "But the world isn't always like that. They hate us."

"That's too strong," Carol said. "Not hate."

"Well, maybe," Jeanine said. "But they're different from us. We're better, and they naturally resent that."

"I don't see what's natural about it," Tony said. "Why shouldn't it be just as natural to admire what's better? We do. Does any one of us resent Kenzo Yagai for his genius? Or Nelson Wade, the physicist? Or Catherine Raduski?"

"We don't resent them because we *are* better," Richard said. "Q.E.D."

"What we should do is have our own society," Tony said. "Why should we allow their regulations to restrict our natural, honest achievements? Why should Jeanine be barred from skating against them and Jack from investing on their same terms just because we're Sleepless? Some of them are brighter than others of them. Some have greater persistence. Well, we have greater concentration, more biochemical stability, and more time. All men are not created equal."

"Be fair, Jack—no one has been barred from anything yet," Jeanine said.

"But we will be."

"*Wait,*" Leisha said. She was deeply troubled by the conversation. "I mean, yes, in many ways we're better. But you quoted out of context, Tony. The Declaration of Independence doesn't say all men are created equal in ability. It's talking about rights and power; it means that all are created equal *under the law.* We have no more right to a separate society or to being free of society's restrictions than anyone else does. There's no other way to freely trade one's efforts, unless the same contractual rules apply to all."

"Spoken like a true Yagaiist," Richard said, squeezing her hand.

"That's enough intellectual discussion for me," Carol said, laughing. "We've been at this for hours. We're at the beach, for Chrissake. Who wants to swim with me?"

"I do," Jeanine said. "Come on, Jack."

All of them rose, brushing sand off their suits, discarding sunglasses. Richard pulled Leisha to her feet. But just before they ran into the water, Tony put his skinny hand on her arm. "One more question, Leisha. Just to think about. If we achieve better than most other people, and if we trade with the Sleepers when it's mutually beneficial, making no distinction there between the strong and the weak—what obligation do we have to those so weak they don't have anything to trade with us? We're already going to give more than we get; do we have to do it when we get nothing at all? Do we have to take care of their deformed and handicapped and sick and lazy and shiftless with the products of our work?"

"Do the Sleepers have to?" Leisha countered.

"Kenzo Yagai would say no. He's a Sleeper."

"He would say they would receive the benefits of contractual trade even if they aren't direct parties to the contract. The whole world is better-fed and healthier because of Y-energy."

"Come on!" Jeanine yelled. "Leisha, they're ducking me! Jack, you stop that! Leisha, help me!"

Leisha laughed. Just before she grabbed for Jeanine, she caught the look on Richard's face, and on Tony's: Richard frankly lustful, Tony angry. At her. But why? What had she done, except argue in favor of dignity and trade?

Then Jack threw water on her, and Carol pushed Jack into the warm spray, and Richard was there with his arms around her, laughing.

When she got the water out of her eyes, Tony was gone.


Midnight. "Okay," Carol said. "Who's first?"

The six teen-agers in the brambly clearing looked at each other. A Y-lamp, kept on low for atmosphere, cast weird shadows across their faces and over their bare legs. Around the clearing Roger Camden's trees stood thick and dark, a wall between them and the closest of the estate's outbuildings. It was very hot. August air hung heavy, sullen. They had voted against bringing an air-conditioned Y-field because this was a return to the primitive, the dangerous; let it be primitive.

Six pairs of eyes stared at the glass in Carol's hand.

"Come *on*," she said. "Who wants to drink up?" Her voice was jaunty, theatrically hard. "It was difficult enough to get this."

"How *did* you get it?" said Richard, the group member—except for Tony—with the least influential family contacts, the least money. "In a drinkable form like that?"

"Jennifer got it," Carol said, and five sets of eyes shifted to Jennifer Sharifi, who two weeks into her visit with Carol's family was confusing them all. She was the American-born daughter of a Hollywood movie star and an Arab prince who had wanted to found a Sleepless dynasty. The movie star was an aging drug addict; the prince, who had taken his fortune out of oil and put it into Y-energy when Kenzo Yagai was still licensing his first patents, was dead. Jennifer Sharifi was richer than Leisha would someday be, and infinitely more sophisticated about procuring things. The glass held interleukin-1, an immune-system booster, one of many substances which as a side effect induced the brain to swift and deep sleep.

Leisha stared at the glass. A warm feeling crept through her lower belly, not unlike the feeling when she and Richard made love. She caught Jennifer watching her, and flushed.

Jennifer disturbed her. Not for the obvious reasons she disturbed Tony and Richard and Jack: the long black hair, the tall, slim body in shorts and halter. Jennifer didn't laugh. Leisha had never met a Sleepless who didn't laugh, nor one who said so little, with such deliberate casualness. Leisha found herself speculating on what Jennifer Sharifi wasn't saying. It was an odd sensation to feel toward another Sleepless.

Tony said to Carol, "Give it to me!"

Carol handed him the glass. "Remember, you only need a little sip."

Tony raised the glass to his mouth, stopped, and looked at them over the rim from his fierce eyes. He drank.

Carol took back the glass. They all watched Tony. Within a minute he lay on the rough ground; within two, his eyes closed in sleep.

It wasn't like seeing parents sleep, siblings, friends. It was Tony. They looked away, avoided each other's eyes. Leisha felt the warmth between her legs tug and tingle, faintly obscene. She didn't look at Jennifer.

When it was Leisha's turn, she drank slowly, then passed the glass to Richard. Her head turned heavy, as if it were being stuffed with damp rags. The trees at the edge of the clearing blurred. The portable lamp blurred, too. It wasn't bright and clean anymore but squishy, blobby; if she touched it, it would smear. Then darkness swooped over her brain, taking it away: *taking away her mind.* "Daddy!" She tried to call, to clutch for him, but then the darkness obliterated her.

Afterward, they all had headaches. Dragging themselves back through the woods in the thin morning light was torture, compounded by an odd shame. They didn't touch each other. Leisha walked as far away from Richard as she could.

Jennifer was the only one who spoke. "So now we know," she said, and her voice held a strange satisfaction.

It was a whole day before the throbbing left the base of Leisha's skull, or the nausea her stomach. She sat alone in her room, waiting for the misery to pass, and despite the heat, her whole body shivered.

There had not even been any dreams.

_____

"I want you to come with me tonight," Leisha said, for the tenth or twelfth time. "We both leave for college in just two days; this is the last chance. I really want you to meet Richard."

Alice lay on her stomach across her bed. Her hair, brown and lusterless, fell around her face. She wore an expensive yellow jumpsuit, silk by Ann Patterson, which rucked up around her knees.

"Why? What do you care if I meet Richard or not?"

"Because you're my sister," Leisha said. She knew better than to say "my twin." Nothing got Alice angry faster.

"I don't want to." The next moment Alice's face changed. "Oh, I'm sorry, Leisha—I didn't mean to sound so snotty. But . . . but I don't want to."

"It won't be all of them. Just Richard. And just for an hour or so. Then you can come back here and pack for Northwestern."

"I'm not going to Northwestern."

Leisha stared at her.

Alice said, "I'm pregnant."

Leisha sat on the bed. Alice rolled onto her back, brushed the hair out of her eyes, and laughed. Leisha's ears closed against the sound. "Look at you," Alice said. "You'd think it was _you_ who was pregnant. But you never would be, would you, Leisha? Not until it was the proper time. Not you."

"How?" Leisha said. "We both had our caps put in. . . ."

"I had the cap removed," Alice said.

"You wanted to get pregnant?"

"Damn flash I did. And there's not a thing Daddy can do about it. Except, of course, cut off all credit completely, but I don't think he'll do that, do you?" She laughed again. "Even to me?"

"But Alice . . . why? Not just to anger Daddy!"

"No," Alice said. "Although you would think of that, wouldn't you? Because I want something to love. Something of my _own_. Something that has nothing to do with this house."

Leisha thought of herself and Alice running through the conservatory, years ago, her and Alice, darting in and out of the sunlight. "It hasn't been so bad growing up in this house."

"Leisha, you're stupid. I don't know how anyone so smart can be so stupid. Get out of my room! Get out!"

"But Alice—a _baby_—"

"Get out!" Alice shrieked. "Go to Harvard! Go be successful! Just get out!"

Leisha jerked off the bed. "Gladly! You're irrational, Alice. You don't think ahead, you don't plan, a *baby*—" But she could never sustain anger. It dribbled away, leaving her mind empty. She looked at Alice, who suddenly put out her arms. Leisha went into them.

"You're the baby," Alice said wonderingly. "You *are*. You're so . . . I don't know what. You're a baby."

Leisha said nothing. Alice's arms felt warm, felt whole, felt like two children running in and out of sunlight. "I'll help you, Alice. If Daddy won't."

Alice abruptly pushed her away. "I don't need your help."

Alice stood. Leisha rubbed her empty arms, fingertips scraping across opposite elbows. Alice kicked the empty, open trunk in which she was supposed to pack for Northwestern, and then abruptly smiled a smile that made Leisha look away. She braced herself for more abuse. But what Alice said, very softly, was, "Have a good time at Harvard."

# FIVE

S HE LOVED IT.

From the first sight of Massachusetts Hall, older than the United States by a half century, Leisha felt something that had been missing in Chicago: Age. Roots. Tradition. She touched the bricks of Widener Library, the glass cases in the Peabody Museum, as if they were the grail. She had never been particularly sensitive to myth or drama; the anguish of Juliet seemed to her artificial, that of Willy Loman merely wasteful. Only King Arthur, struggling to create a better social order, had interested her. But now, walking under the huge autumn trees, she suddenly caught a glimpse of a force that could span generations, fortunes left to endow learning and achievement the benefactors would never see, individual effort spanning and shaping centuries to come. She stopped, and looked at the sky through the leaves, at the buildings solid with purpose. At such moments she thought of Camden, bending the will of an entire genetic research institute to create her in the image he wanted.

Within a month, she had forgotten all such mega-musings.

The work load was incredible, even for her. The Sauley School had encouraged individual exploration at her own pace; Harvard knew what it wanted from her, at its pace. In the past twenty years, under the academic leadership of a man who in his youth had watched Japanese economic domination with dismay, Harvard had become the controversial leader of a return to hard-edged learning of facts, theories, applications, problem-solving, and intellectual efficiency. The school accepted one of every two hundred applicants from around the world. The daughter of England's prime minister had flunked out her first year and been sent home.

Leisha had a single room in a new dormitory, the dorm because she had spent so many years isolated in Chicago and was hungry for people, the single so she would not disturb anyone else when she worked all night. Her second day a boy from down the hall sauntered in and perched on the edge of her desk.

"So you're Leisha Camden."

"Yes."

"Sixteen years old."

"Almost seventeen."

"Going to outperform us all, I understand, without even trying."

Leisha's smile faded. The boy stared at her from under lowered downy brows. He was smiling, his eyes sharp. From Richard and Tony and the others Leisha had learned to recognize the anger that presents itself as contempt.

"Yes," Leisha said coolly, "I am."

"Are you sure? With your pretty little-girl hair and your mutant little-girl brain?"

"Oh, leave her alone, Hannaway," said another voice. A tall blond boy, so thin his ribs looked like ripples in brown sand, stood in jeans and bare feet, drying his wet hair. "Don't you ever get tired of walking around being an asshole?"

"Do you?" Hannaway said. He heaved himself off the desk and started toward the door. The blond moved out of his way. Leisha moved into it.

"The reason I'm going to do better than you," she said evenly, "is because I have certain advantages you don't. Including sleeplessness. And then after I outperform you, I'll be glad to help you study for your tests so that you can pass, too."

The blond, drying his ears, laughed. But Hannaway stood still, and into his eyes came an expression that made Leisha back away. He pushed past her and stormed out.

"Nice going, Camden," the blond said. "He deserved that."

"But I meant it," Leisha said. "I will help him study."

The blond lowered his towel and stared. "You did, didn't you? You meant it."

"Yes! Why does everybody keep questioning that?"

"Well," the boy said, "*I* don't. You can help me if I get into trouble." Suddenly he smiled. "But I won't."

"Why not?"

"Because I'm just as good at anything as you are, Leisha Camden."

She studied him. "You're not one of us. Not Sleepless."

"Don't have to be. I know what I can do. Do, be, create, trade."

She said, delighted, "You're a Yagaiist!"

"Of course." He held out his hand. "Stewart Sutter. How about a fishburger in the Yard?"

"Great," Leisha said. They walked out together, talking excitedly. When people stared at her, she tried not to notice. She was here. At Harvard. With space ahead of her, time, to learn, and with people like Stewart Sutter who accepted and challenged her.

All the hours he was awake.


She became totally absorbed in her class work. Roger Camden drove up once, walking the campus with her, listening, smiling. He was more at home than Leisha would have expected: he knew Stewart Sutter's father and Kate Addams's grandfather. They talked about Harvard, business, Harvard, the Yagai Economics Institute, Harvard. "How's Alice?" Leisha asked once, but Camden said he didn't know; she had moved out and did not want to see him. He made her an allowance through his attorney. While he said this, his face remained serene.

Leisha went to the Homecoming Ball with Stewart, who was also majoring in pre-law but was two years ahead of Leisha. She took a weekend trip to Paris with Kate Addams and two other girlfriends, taking the Concorde III. She had a fight with Stewart over whether the metaphor of superconductivity could apply to Yagaiism, a stupid fight they both knew was stupid but had anyway, and afterward they became lovers. After the fumbling sexual explorations with Richard, Stewart was deft, experienced, smiling faintly as he taught her how to have an orgasm both by herself and with him. Leisha was dazzled. "It's so *joyful*," she said, and Stewart looked at her with a tenderness she knew was part disturbance but didn't know why.

At midsemester she had the highest grades in the freshman class. She got every answer right on every single question on her midterms. She and Stewart went out for a beer to celebrate, and when they came back Leisha's room had been destroyed. The computer was smashed, the data banks wiped, hard copies and books smoldered in a metal wastebasket. Her clothes were ripped to pieces, her desk and bureau hacked apart. The only thing untouched, pristine, was the bed.

Stewart said, "There's no way this could have been done in silence.

Everyone on the floor—hell, on the floor *below*—had to know. Someone will talk to the police." No one did. Leisha sat on the edge of the bed, dazed, and looked at the remnants of her Homecoming gown. The next day Dave Hannaway gave her a long, wide smile.

Camden flew east, taut with rage. He rented her an apartment in Cambridge with E-lock security and a bodyguard named Toshio. After he left, Leisha fired the bodyguard but kept the apartment. It gave her and Stewart more privacy, which they used to endlessly discuss the situation. It was Leisha who argued that it was an aberration, an immaturity.

"There have always been haters, Stewart. Hate Jews, hate Blacks, hate immigrants, hate Yagaiists who have more initiative and dignity than you do. I'm just the latest object of hatred. It's not new, it's not remarkable. It doesn't mean any basic kind of schism between the Sleepless and Sleepers."

Stewart sat up in bed and reached for the sandwiches on the night stand. "Doesn't it? Leisha, you're a different kind of person entirely. More evolutionarily fit, not only to survive but to prevail. Those other objects of hatred you cite—they were all powerless in their societies. They occupied *inferior* positions. You, on the other hand—all three Sleepless in Harvard Law are on the *Law Review.* All of them. Kevin Baker, your oldest, has already founded a successful bio-interface software firm and is making money, a lot of it. Every Sleepless is making superb grades, none has psychological problems, all are healthy, and most of you aren't even adults yet. How much hatred do you think you're going to encounter once you hit the high-stakes world of finance and business and scarce endowed chairs and national politics?"

"Give me a sandwich," Leisha said. "Here's my evidence you're wrong: you yourself. Kenzo Yagai. Kate Addams. Professor Lane. My father. Every Sleeper who inhabits the world of fair trade and mutually beneficial contracts. And that's most of you, or at least most of you who are worth considering. You believe that competition among the most capable leads to the most beneficial trades for everyone, strong and weak. Sleepless are making real and concrete contributions to society, in a lot of fields. That has to outweigh the discomfort we cause. We're *valuable* to you. You know that."

Stewart brushed crumbs off the sheets. "Yes. I do. Yagaiists do."

"Yagaiists run the business and financial and academic worlds. Or they will. In a meritocracy, they *should.* You underestimate the majority of people, Stew. Ethics aren't confined to the ones out front."

"I hope you're right," Stewart said. "Because, you know, I'm in love with you."

Leisha put down her sandwich.

"Joy," Stewart mumbled into her breasts, "you are joy."

When Leisha went home for Thanksgiving, she told Richard about Stewart. He listened tight-lipped.

"A Sleeper."

"A *person*," Leisha said. "A good, intelligent, achieving person!"

"Do you know what your good intelligent achieving Sleepers have done, Leisha? Jeanine has been barred from Olympic skating. 'Genetic alteration, analogous to steroid abuse to create an unsportsmanlike advantage.' Chris Devereaux has left Stanford. They trashed his laboratory, destroyed two years' work in memory-formation proteins. Kevin Baker's software company is fighting a nasty advertising campaign, all underground of course, about kids using software designed by nonhuman minds. Corruption, mental slavery, satanic influences: the whole bag of witch-hunt tricks. Wake up, Leisha!"

They both heard his words. Minutes dragged by. Richard stood like a boxer, forward on the balls of his feet, teeth clenched. Finally he said, very quietly, "Do you love him?"

"Yes," Leisha said. "I'm sorry."

"Your choice," Richard said coldly. "What do you do while he's asleep? Watch?"

"You make it sound like a perversion!"

Richard said nothing. Leisha drew a deep breath. She spoke rapidly but calmly, a controlled rush: "While Stewart is asleep I work. The same as you do. Richard—don't do this. I didn't mean to hurt you. And I don't want to lose the group. I believe the Sleepers are the same species as we are. Are you going to punish me for that? Are you going to *add* to the hatred? Are you going to tell me that I can't belong to a wider world that includes all honest, worthwhile people whether they sleep or not? Are you going to tell me that the most important division is by genetics and not by economic spirituality? Are you going to force me into an artificial choice, us or them?"

Richard picked up a bracelet. Leisha recognized it; she had given it to him in the summer. His voice was quiet. "No. It's not a choice." He played with the gold links a minute, then looked at her. "Not yet."

By spring break, Camden walked more slowly. He took medicine for his blood pressure, his heart. He and Susan, he told Leisha, were getting a divorce. "She changed, Leisha, after I married her. You saw that. She was independent and productive and happy, and then after a few years she stopped all that and became a shrew. A whining shrew." He shook his head in genuine bewilderment. "You saw the change."

Leisha had. A memory came to her: Susan leading her and Alice in "games" that were actually controlled cerebral-performance tests, Susan's braids dancing around her sparkling eyes. Alice had loved Susan then, as much as Leisha had.

"Dad, I want Alice's address."

"I told you up at Harvard, I don't have it," Camden said. He shifted in his chair, the impatient gesture of a body that never expected to wear out. In January Kenzo Yagai had died of pancreatic cancer; Camden had taken the news hard. "I make her allowance through an attorney. By her choice."

"Then I want the address of the attorney."

The attorney, a quenched-looking man named John Jaworski, refused to tell Leisha where Alice was. "She doesn't want to be found, Ms. Camden. She wanted a complete break."

"Not from me," Leisha said.

"Yes," Jaworski said, and something flickered in his eyes, something she had last seen in Dave Hannaway's face.

She flew to Austin before returning to Boston, making her a day late for classes. Kevin Baker saw her instantly, canceling a meeting with IBM. She told him what she needed, and he set his best datanet people on it, without telling them why. Within two hours she had Alice's address from Jaworski's electronic files. It was the first time, she realized, that she had ever turned to one of the Sleepless for help, and it had been given instantly. Without trade.

Alice was in Pennsylvania. The next weekend Leisha rented a hovercar and driver—she had learned to drive, but only groundcars as yet—and went to High Ridge, in the Appalachian Mountains.

It was an isolated hamlet, twenty-five miles from the nearest hospital. Alice lived with a man named Ed, a silent carpenter twenty years older than she, in a cabin in the woods. The cabin had water and electricity but no newsnet. In the early spring light the earth was raw and bare, slashed with icy gullies. Alice and Ed apparently worked at nothing. Alice was eight months pregnant.

"I didn't want you here," she said to Leisha. "So why are you?"

"Because you're my sister."

"God, look at you. Is that what they're wearing at Harvard? Boots like that? When did you become fashionable, Leisha? You were always too busy being intellectual to care."

"What's this all about, Alice? Why here? What are you doing?"

"Living," Alice said. "Away from dear Daddy, away from Chicago, away from drunken, broken Susan—did you know she drinks? Just like Mom. He does that to people. But not to me. I got out. I wonder if you ever will."

"Got out? To *this?*"

"I'm happy," Alice said angrily. "Isn't that what it's supposed to be about? Isn't that the aim of your great Kenzo Yagai—happiness through individual effort?"

Leisha thought of saying that Alice was making no efforts that she could see. She didn't say it. A chicken ran through the yard of the cabin. Behind, the mountains rose in layer upon layer of blue haze. Leisha thought what this place must have been like in winter, cut off from the world where people strived toward goals, learned, changed.

"I'm glad you're happy, Alice."

"Are you?"

"Yes."

"Then I'm glad, too," Alice said, almost defiantly. The next moment she abruptly hugged Leisha, fiercely, the huge, hard mound of her belly crushed between them. Alice's hair smelled sweet, like fresh grass in sunlight.

"I'll come see you again, Alice."

"Don't," Alice said.

# SIX

"Sleepless Mutie Begs for Reversal of Gene Tampering," screamed the headline in the Food Mart. " 'Please Let Me Sleep Like Real People!' Child Pleads."

Leisha typed in her credit number and pressed the news kiosk for a printout, although ordinarily she ignored the electronic tabloids. The headline went on circling the kiosk. A Food Mart employee stopped stacking boxes on shelves and watched her. Bruce, Leisha's bodyguard, watched the employee.

She was twenty-two, in her final year at Harvard Law, editor of the *Law Review,* clearly first in her graduating class. The closest three contenders were Jonathan Cocchiara, Len Carter, and Martha Wentz. All Sleepless.

In her apartment she skimmed the printout. Then she accessed the Groupnet run from Austin. The files had more news stories about the child, with comments from other Sleepless, but before she could call them up Kevin Baker came online himself, on voice.

"Leisha. I'm glad you called. I was going to call you."

"What's the situation with this Stella Bevington, Kev? Has anybody checked it out?"

"Randy Davies. He's from Chicago but I don't think you've met him; he's still in high school. He's in Park Ridge, Stella's in Skokie. Her parents wouldn't talk to him—they were pretty abusive, in fact—but he got to see Stella face-to-face anyway. It doesn't look like an abuse case, just the usual stupidity: parents wanted a genius child, scrimped and saved, and now they can't handle that she *is* one. They scream at her to sleep, get emotionally abusive when she contradicts them, but so far no violence."

"Is the emotional abuse actionable?"

"I don't think we want to move on it yet. Two of us will keep in close touch with Stella—she does have a modem, and she hasn't told her parents about the net—and Randy will drive out weekly."

Leisha bit her lip. "A tabloid shitpiece said she's seven years old."

"Yes."

"Maybe she shouldn't be left there. I'm an Illinois resident, I can file an abuse grievance from here if Candy's got too much in her briefcase. . . ." *Seven years old.*

"No. Let it sit a while. Stella will probably be all right. You know that."

She did. Nearly all of the Sleepless stayed all right, no matter how much opposition came from the stupid segment of society. And it was only the stupid segment, Leisha argued, a small if vocal minority. Most people could, and would, adjust to the growing presence of the Sleepless, when it became clear that that presence included not only growing power but growing benefits to the country as a whole.

Kevin Baker, now twenty-six, had made a fortune in microchips so revolutionary that Artificial Intelligence, once a debated dream, was yearly closer to reality. Carolyn Rizzolo had won the Pulitzer Prize in drama for her play *Morning Light*. She was twenty-four. Jeremy Robinson had done significant work in superconductivity applications while still a graduate student at Stanford. William Thaine, *Law Review* editor when Leisha first came to Harvard, was now in private practice. He had never lost a case. He was twenty-six, and the cases were becoming important. His clients valued his ability more than his age.

But not everyone reacted that way.

Kevin Baker and Richard Keller had started the datanet that bound the Sleepless into a tight group, constantly aware of each other's personal fights. Leisha Camden financed the legal battles, the educational costs of Sleepless whose parents were unable to meet them, the support of children in emotionally bad situations. Rhonda Lavelier got herself licensed as a foster mother in California, and whenever possible the Group maneuvered to have young Sleepless who were removed from their homes assigned to Rhonda. The Group now had three licensed lawyers; within the next year it would gain four more, licensed to practice in five different states.

The one time they had not been able to remove an abused Sleepless child legally, they kidnapped him.

Timmy DeMarzo, four years old. Leisha had been opposed to the action. She had argued the case morally and pragmatically—to her they were the same thing—thus: If they believed in their society, in its fundamental laws and in their ability to belong to it as free-trading productive individuals, they must remain bound by the society's contractual laws. The Sleepless were, for the most part, Yagaiists. They should already know this. And if the FBI caught them, the courts and press would crucify them.

They were not caught.

Timmy DeMarzo—not even old enough to call for help on the datanet, they had learned of the situation through the automatic police-record scan Kevin maintained through his company—was stolen from his own back yard in Wichita. He had lived the last year in an isolated trailer in North Dakota; no place was too isolated for a modem. He was cared for by a legally irreproachable foster mother who had lived there all her life. The foster mother was second cousin to a Sleepless, a broad cheerful woman with a much better brain than her appearance indicated. She was a Yagaiist. No record of the child's existence appeared in any data bank: not the IRS's, not any school's, not even the local grocery store's computerized checkout slips. Food specifically for the child was shipped in monthly on a truck owned by a Sleepless in State College, Pennsylvania. Ten of the Group knew about the kidnapping, out of the total 3,428 sleepless born in the United States. Of those, 2,691 were part of the Group via the net. An additional 701 were as yet too young to use a modem. Only thirty-six Sleepless, for whatever reason, were not part of the Group.

The kidnapping had been arranged by Tony Indivino.

"It's Tony I wanted to talk to you about," Kevin said to Leisha. "He's started again. This time he means it. He's buying land."

She folded the tabloid very small and laid it carefully on the table. "Where?"

"Allegheny Mountains. In southern New York State. A lot of land. He's putting in the roads now. In the spring, the first buildings."

"Jennifer Sharifi still financing it?" It had been six years since the interleukin-drinking in the woods, but the evening remained vivid to Leisha. So did Jennifer Sharifi.

"Yes. She's got the money to do it. Tony's starting to get a following, Leisha."

"I know."

"Call him."

"I will. Keep me informed about Stella."

She worked until midnight at the *Law Review,* then until 4:00 A.M. preparing her classes. From four to five she handled legal matters for the Group. At 5:00 A.M. she called Tony, still in Chicago. He had finished high school, done one semester at Northwestern, and at Christmas vacation had finally exploded at his mother for forcing him to live as a Sleeper. The explosion, it seemed to Leisha, had never ended.

"Tony? Leisha."

"The answers are yes, yes, no, and go to hell."

Leisha gritted her teeth. "Fine. Now tell me the questions."

"Are you really serious about the Sleepless withdrawing into their own self-sufficient society? Is Jennifer Sharifi willing to finance a project the size of building a small city? Don't you think that's a cheat of all that can be accomplished by patient integration of the Group into the mainstream? And what about the contradictions of living in an armed restricted city and still trading with the Outside?"

"I would never tell *you* to go to hell."

"Hooray for you," Tony said. After a moment he added, "I'm sorry. That sounds like one of *them.*"

"It's wrong for us, Tony."

"Thanks for not saying I couldn't pull it off."

She wondered if he could. "We're not a separate species, Tony."

"Tell that to the Sleepers."

"You exaggerate. There are haters out there, there are *always* haters, but to give up . . ."

"We're not giving up. Whatever we create can be freely traded: software, hardware, novels, information, theories, legal counsel. We can travel in and out. But we'll have a safe place to return *to.* Without the leeches who think we owe them blood because we're better than they are."

"It isn't a matter of owing."

"Really?" Tony said. "Let's have this out, Leisha. All the way. You're a Yagaiist—what do you believe in?"

"Tony . . ."

"*Do it,*" Tony said, and in his voice she heard the fourteen-year-old she had been introduced to by Richard. Simultaneously, she saw her father's face: not as he was now, since the bypass, but as he had been when she was a little girl, holding her on his lap to explain that she was special.

"I believe in voluntary trade that is mutually beneficial. That spiritual dignity comes from supporting one's life through one's own efforts, and from trading the results of those efforts in mutual cooperation throughout the society. That the symbol of this is the contract. And that we need each other for the fullest, most beneficial trade."

"Fine," Tony bit off. "Now what about the beggars in Spain?"

"The what?"

"You walk down a street in a poor country like Spain and you see a beggar. Do you give him a dollar?"

"Probably."

"Why? He's trading nothing with you. He has nothing to trade."

"I know. Out of kindness. Compassion."

"You see six beggars. Do you give them all a dollar?"

"Probably," Leisha said.

"You would. You see a hundred beggars and you haven't got Leisha Camden's money. Do you give them each a dollar?"

"No."

"Why not?"

Leisha reached for patience. Few people could make her want to cut off a comlink; Tony was one of them. "Too draining on my own resources. My life has first claim on the resources I earn."

"All right. Now consider this. At Biotech Institute—where you and I began, dear pseudo-sister—Dr. Melling has just yesterday—"

"*Who?*"

"Dr. Susan Melling. Oh, God, I completely forgot—she used to be married to your father!"

"I lost track of her," Leisha said. "I didn't realize she'd gone back to research. Alice once said . . . never mind. What's going on at Biotech?"

"Two crucial items, just released. Carla Dutcher has had first-month fetal genetic analysis. Sleeplessness is a dominant gene. The next generation of the Group won't sleep either."

"We all knew that," Leisha said. Carla Dutcher was the world's first pregnant Sleepless. Her husband was a Sleeper. "The whole world expected that."

"But the press will have a field day with it anyway. Just watch. Muties Breed! New Race Set to Dominate Next Generation Of Children!"

Leisha didn't deny it. "And the second item?"

"It's sad, Leisha. We've just had our first death."

Her stomach tightened. "Who?"

"Bernie Kuhn. Seattle." She didn't know him. "A car accident. It looks pretty straightforward; he lost control on a steep curve when his brakes failed. He had only been driving a few months. He was seventeen. But the significance here is that his parents have donated his brain and body to Biotech, in conjunction with the pathology department at the Chicago Medical School. They're going to take him apart to get the first good look at what prolonged sleeplessness does to the body and brain."

"They should," Leisha said. "That poor kid. But what are you so afraid they'll find?"

"I don't know. I'm not a doctor. But whatever it is, if the haters can use it against us, they will."

"You're paranoid, Tony."

"Impossible. The Sleepless have personalities calmer and more reality-oriented than the norm. Don't you read the literature?"

"Tony—"

"What if you walk down that street in Spain and a hundred beggars each want a dollar and you say no and they have nothing to trade you but they're so rotten with anger about what you have that they knock you down and grab it and then beat you out of sheer envy and despair?"

Leisha didn't answer.

"Are you going to say that's not a human scenario, Leisha? That it never happens?"

"It happens," Leisha said evenly. "But not all that often."

"Bullshit. Read more history. Read more *newspapers*. But the point is: What do you owe the beggars then? What does a good Yagaiist who believes in mutually beneficial contracts do with people who have nothing to trade and can only take?"

"You're not—"

"*What,* Leisha? In the most objective terms you can manage, what do we owe the grasping and nonproductive needy?"

"What I said originally. Kindness. Compassion."

"Even if they don't trade it back? Why?"

"Because . . ." She stopped.

"Why? Why do law-abiding and productive human beings owe anything to those who neither produce very much nor abide by just laws? What philosophical or economic or spiritual justification is there for owing them anything? Be as honest as I know you are."

Leisha put her head between her knees. The question gaped beneath her, but she didn't try to evade it. "I don't know. I just know we do."

"*Why?*"

She didn't answer. After a moment, Tony did. The intellectual challenge was gone from his voice. He said, almost tenderly, "Come down in the spring and see the site for Sanctuary. The buildings will be going up then."

"No," Leisha said.

"I'd like you to."

"No. Armed retreat is not the way."

Tony said, "The beggars are getting nastier, Leisha. As the Sleepless grow richer. And I don't mean in money."

"Tony—" she said, and stopped. She couldn't think what to say.

"Don't walk down too many streets armed with just the memory of Kenzo Yagai."

In March, a bitterly cold March with wind whipping down the Charles River, Richard Keller came to Cambridge. Leisha had not seen him for three years. He didn't send her word on the Groupnet that he was coming. She hurried up the walk to her townhouse, muffled to the eyes in a red wool scarf against the snowy cold, and he stood there blocking the doorway. Behind Leisha, her bodyguard tensed.

"Richard! Bruce, it's all right, this is an old friend."

"Hello, Leisha."

He was heavier, sturdier-looking, with a breadth of shoulder she didn't recognize. But the face was Richard's, older but unchanged: dark low brows, unruly dark hair. He had grown a beard.

"You look beautiful," he said.

Inside, she handed him a cup of coffee. "Are you here on business?" From the Groupnet she knew that he had finished his master's and had done outstanding work in marine biology in the Caribbean but had left that a year ago and disappeared from the net.

"No. Pleasure." He smiled suddenly, the old smile that opened up his dark face. "I almost forgot about that for a long time. Contentment, yes. We're all good at the contentment that comes from sustained work. But pleasure? Whim? Caprice? When was the last time you did something silly, Leisha?"

She smiled. "I ate cotton candy in the shower."

"Really? Why?"

"To see if it would dissolve in gooey pink patterns."

"Did it?"

"Yes. Lovely ones."

"And that was your last silly thing? When was it?"

"Last summer," Leisha said, and laughed.

"Well, mine is sooner than that. It's now. I'm in Boston for no other reason than the spontaneous pleasure of seeing you."

Leisha stopped laughing. "That's an intense tone for a spontaneous pleasure, Richard."

"Yup," he said, intensely. She laughed again. He didn't.

"I've been in India, Leisha. And China and Africa. Thinking, mostly. Watching. First I traveled like a Sleeper, attracting no attention. Then I set out to meet the Sleepless in India and China. There are a few, you know, whose parents were willing to come here for the operation. They pretty much are accepted and left alone. I tried to figure out why desperately poor countries—by our standards anyway; over there Y-energy is mostly available only in big cities—don't have any trouble accepting the superiority of Sleepless, whereas Americans, with more prosperity than any time in history, build in resentment more and more."

Leisha said, "Did you figure it out?"

"No. But I figured out something else, watching all those communes and villages and *kampongs*. We are too individualistic."

Disappointment swept Leisha. She saw her father's face: *Excellence is what counts, Leisha. Excellence supported by individual effort. . . .* She reached for Richard's cup. "More coffee?"

He caught her wrist and looked up into her face. "Don't misunderstand me, Leisha. I'm not talking about work. We are too much individuals in the rest of our lives. Too emotionally rational. Too much alone. Isolation kills more than the free flow of ideas. It kills joy."

He didn't let go of her wrist. She looked down into his eyes, into depths she hadn't seen before. It was the feeling of looking into a mine shaft, both giddy and frightening, knowing that at the bottom might be gold or darkness. Or both.

Richard said softly, "Stewart?"

"Over long ago. An undergraduate thing." Her voice didn't sound like her own.

"Kevin?"

"No, never—we're just friends."

"I wasn't sure. Anyone?"

"No."

He let go of her wrist. Leisha peered at him timidly. He suddenly laughed. "Joy, Leisha." An echo sounded in her mind, but she couldn't place it, and then it was gone and she laughed too, a laugh airy and frothy and pink cotton candy in summer.

---

"Come home, Leisha. He's had another heart attack."

Susan Melling's voice on the phone was tired. Leisha said, "How bad?"

"The doctors aren't sure. Or say they're not sure. He wants to see you. Can you leave your studies?"

It was May, the last push toward her finals. The *Law Review* proofs were behind schedule. Richard had started a new business, marine consulting to Boston fishermen plagued with sudden inexplicable shifts in ocean currents, and was working twenty hours a day. "I'll come," Leisha said.

Chicago was colder than Boston. The trees were half-budded. On Lake Michigan, filling the huge east windows of her father's house, whitecaps tossed up cold spray. Leisha saw that Susan was living in the house; her brushes were on Camden's dresser, her journals on the credenza in the foyer.

"Leisha," Camden said. He looked old. Grey skin, sunken cheeks, the fretful and bewildered look of men who accepted potency like air, indivisible from their lives. In the corner of the room, on a small eighteenth-century slipper chair, sat a short, stocky woman with brown braids.

"*Alice.*"

"Hello, Leisha."

"*Alice.* I've looked for you . . ." The wrong thing to say. Leisha had looked, but not very hard, deterred by the knowledge that Alice had not wanted to be found. "How are you?"

"I'm fine," Alice said. She seemed remote, gentle, unlike the angry Alice of six years ago in the raw Pennsylvania hills. Camden moved painfully on the bed. He looked at Leisha with eyes which, she saw, were undimmed in their blue brightness.

"I asked Alice to come. And Susan. Susan came a while ago. I'm dying, Leisha."

No one contradicted him. Leisha, knowing his respect for facts, remained silent. Love hurt her chest.

"John Jaworski has my will. None of you can break it. But I wanted to tell you myself what's in it. The past few years I've been selling, liquidating. Most of my holdings are accessible now. I've left a tenth to Alice, a tenth to Susan, a tenth to Elizabeth, and the rest to you, Leisha, because you're the only one with the individual ability to use the money to its full potential for achievement."

Leisha looked wildly at Alice, who gazed back with her strange remote calm. "Elizabeth? My . . . mother? Is alive?"

"Yes," Camden said.

"You told me she was dead! Years and years ago!"

"Yes. I thought it was better for you that way. She didn't like what
you were, was jealous of what you could become. And she had nothing to give you. She would only have caused you emotional harm."

*Beggars in Spain . . .*

"That was wrong, Daddy. You were *wrong*. She's my mother. . . ."
She couldn't finish the sentence.

Camden didn't flinch. "I don't think I was. But you're an adult now.
You can see her if you wish."

He went on looking at her with his bright, sunken eyes, while
around Leisha the air heaved and snapped. Her father had lied to her.
Susan watched her closely, a small smile on her lips. Was she glad to see
Camden fall in his daughter's estimation? Had she all along been that
jealous of their relationship, of Leisha . . . ?

She was thinking like Tony.

The thought steadied her a little. But she went on staring at Camden,
who went on staring back implacably, unbudged, a man positive even
on his deathbed that he was right.

Alice's hand was on her elbow, Alice's voice so soft that no one but
Leisha could hear. "He's done talking now, Leisha. And after a while
you'll be all right."


Alice had left her son in California with her husband of two years,
Beck Watrous, a building contractor she had met while waiting on ta-
bles in a resort on the Artificial Islands. Beck had adopted Jordan,
Alice's son.

"Before Beck there was a real bad time," Alice said in her remote
voice. "You know, when I was carrying Jordan I actually used to dream
that he would be Sleepless? Like you. Every night I'd dream that, and
every morning I'd wake up and have morning sickness with a baby that
was only going to be a stupid nothing like me. I stayed with Ed—in the
Appalachian Mountains, remember? You came to see me there once—
for two more years. When he beat me, I was glad. I wished Daddy
could see. At least Ed was touching me."

Leisha made a sound in her throat.

"I finally left because I was afraid for Jordan. I went to California, did nothing but eat for a year. I got up to 190 pounds." Alice was, Leisha estimated, five-foot-four. "Then I came home to see Mother."

"You didn't tell me," Leisha said. "You knew she was alive and you didn't tell me."

"She's in a drying-out tank half the time," Alice said, with brutal simplicity. "She wouldn't see you if you wanted to. But she saw me, and she fell slobbering all over me as her 'real' daughter, and she threw up on my dress. And I backed away from her and looked at the dress and knew it *should* be thrown up on, it was so ugly. Deliberately ugly. She started screaming how Dad had ruined her life, ruined mine, all for you. And do you know what I did?"

"What?" Leisha said. Her voice was shaky.

"I flew home, burned all my clothes, got a job, started college, lost fifty pounds, and put Jordan in play therapy."

The sisters sat silent. Beyond the window the lake was dark, unlit by moon or stars. It was Leisha who suddenly shook, and Alice who patted her shoulder.

"Tell me . . ." Leisha couldn't think what she wanted to be told, except that she wanted to hear Alice's voice in the gloom, Alice's voice as it was now, gentle and remote, without damage any more from the damaging fact of Leisha's existence. Her very existence as damage. "Tell me about Jordan. He's five now? What's he like?"

Alice turned her head to look levelly into Leisha's eyes. "He's a happy, ordinary little boy. Completely ordinary."


Camden died a week later. After the funeral, Leisha tried to see her mother at the Brookfield Drug and Alcohol Abuse Center. Elizabeth Camden, she was told, saw no one except her only child, Alice Camden Watrous.

Susan Melling, dressed in black, drove Leisha to the airport. Susan talked deftly, determinedly, about Leisha's studies, about Harvard, about the *Law Review*. Leisha answered in monosyllables, but Susan persisted, asking questions, quietly insisting on answers: When would Leisha take her bar exams? Where was she interviewing for jobs? Gradually Leisha began to lose the numbness she had felt since her father's casket was lowered into the ground. She realized that Susan's persistent questioning was a kindness.

"He sacrificed a lot of people," Leisha said suddenly.

"Not me," Susan said. "Only for a while there, when I gave up my work to do his. Roger didn't respect sacrifice much."

"Was he wrong?" Leisha said. The question came out with a kind of desperateness she hadn't intended.

Susan smiled sadly. "No. He wasn't wrong. I should never have left my research. It took me a long time to come back to myself after that."

*He does that to people,* Leisha heard inside her head. Susan? Or Alice? She couldn't, for once, remember clearly. She saw her father in the old conservatory, now empty, potting and repotting the exotic flowers he had loved.

She was tired. It was muscle fatigue from stress, she knew; twenty minutes of rest would restore her. Her eyes burned from unaccustomed tears. She leaned her head back against the car seat and closed her eyes.

Susan pulled the car into the airport parking lot and turned off the ignition. "There's something I want to tell you, Leisha."

Leisha opened her eyes. "About the will?"

Susan smiled tightly. "No. You really don't have any problems with how he divided the estate, do you? It seems reasonable to you. But that's not it. The research team from Biotech and Chicago Medical has finished its analysis of Bernie Kuhn's brain."

Leisha turned to face Susan. She was startled by the complexity of Susan's expression. It held determination, and satisfaction, and anger, and something else Leisha could not name.

Susan said, "We're going to publish next week, in the *New England Journal of Medicine.* Security has been unbelievably restricted—no leaks to the popular press. But I want to tell you now, myself, what we found. So you'll be prepared."

"Go on," Leisha said. Her chest felt tight.

"Do you remember when you and the other Sleepless kids took interleukin-1 to see what sleep was like? When you were sixteen?"

"How did you know about that?"

"You kids were watched a lot more closely than you think. Remember the headache you got?"

"Yes." She and Richard and Tony and Carol and Brad and Jeanine . . . no, not Jeanine. Jennifer. It had been Jennifer in the woods with them.

"Interleukin-1 is what I want to talk about. At least partly. It's one of a whole group of substances that boost the immune system. They stimulate the production of antibodies, the activity of white blood cells, and a host of other immunoenhancements. Normal people have surges of IL-1 released during the slow-wave phases of sleep. That means that they—we—are getting boosts to the immune system during sleep. One of the questions we researchers asked ourselves twenty-eight years ago was: will Sleepless kids who don't get those surges of IL-1 get sick more often?"

"I've never been sick," Leisha said.

"Yes, you have. Chicken pox and three minor colds by the end of your fourth year," Susan said precisely. "But in general you were all a very healthy lot. So we researchers were left with the alternate theory of sleep-driven immunoenhancement: that the burst of immune activity existed as a counterpart to a greater vulnerability of the body in sleep to disease, probably in some way connected to the fluctuations in body temperature during REM sleep. In other words, sleep *caused* the immune vulnerability that endogenous pyrogens like IL-1 counteracted. Sleep was the problem, immune-system enhancements were the solution. Without sleep, there would be no problem. Are you following this?"

"Yes."

"Of course you are. Stupid question." Susan brushed her hair off her face. It was going gray at the temples. There was a tiny brown age spot beneath her right ear.

"Over the years we collected thousands, maybe hundreds of thousands, of Single Photon Emission Tomography scans of you kids' brains, plus endless EEGs, samples of cerebrospinal fluid, and all the rest of it. But we couldn't really see inside your brains, really know what's going on in there. Until Bernie Kuhn hit that embankment."

"Susan," Leisha said, "give it to me straight. Without more buildup."

"You're not going to age."

"What?"

"Oh, cosmetically, a little—sagging due to gravity, maybe. But the absence of sleep peptides and all the rest of it affects the immune and tissue-restoration systems in ways we don't understand. Bernie Kuhn had a perfect liver. Perfect lungs, perfect heart, perfect lymph nodes, perfect pancreas, perfect medulla oblongata. Not just healthy, or young—*perfect*. There's a tissue regeneration enhancement that clearly derives from the operation of the immune system but is radically different from anything we ever suspected. Organs show no wear and tear, not even the minimal amount expected in a seventeen-year-old. They just repair themselves, perfectly, on and on . . . and on."

"For how long?" Leisha whispered.

"Who the hell knows? Bernie Kuhn was young. Maybe there's some compensatory mechanism that cuts in at some point and you'll all just collapse, like an entire fucking gallery of Dorian Grays. But I don't think so. Neither do I think it can go on forever; no tissue regeneration can do that. But a long, long time."

Leisha stared at the blurred reflections in the car windshield. She saw her father's face against the blue satin of his casket, banked with white roses. His heart, unregenerated, had given out.

Susan said, "The future is all speculative at this point. We know that the peptide structures that build up the pressure to sleep in normal people resemble the components of bacterial cell walls. Maybe there's a connection between sleep and pathogen receptivity. We don't know. But ignorance never stopped the tabloids. I wanted to prepare you because you're going to get called supermen, *homo perfectus,* who-all-knows what. Immortal."

The two women sat in silence. Finally Leisha said, "I'm going to tell the others. On our datanet. Don't worry about the security. Kevin Baker designed Groupnet; nobody knows anything we don't want them to."

"You're that well organized already?"

"Yes."

Susan's mouth worked. She looked away from Leisha. "We better go in. You'll miss your flight."

"Susan . . ."

"What?"

"Thank you."

"You're welcome," Susan said, and in her voice Leisha heard the thing she had seen before in Susan's expression and had not been able to name: it was longing.

*Tissue regeneration. A long, long time,* sang the blood in Leisha's ears on the flight to Boston. *Tissue regeneration.* And, eventually: *immortal.* No, not that, she told herself severely. Not that. The blood didn't listen.

"You sure smile a lot," said the man next to her in first class, a business traveler who had not recognized Leisha. "You coming from a big party in Chicago?"

"No. From a funeral."

The man looked shocked, then disgusted. Leisha looked out the window at the ground far below. Rivers like microcircuits, fields like neat index cards. And on the horizon, fluffy white clouds like masses of exotic flowers, blooms in a conservatory filled with light.

---

The letter was no thicker than any hard-copy mail, but hard-copy mail addressed by hand to either of them was so rare that Richard was nervous. "It might be explosive." Leisha looked at the letter on their hall credenza. MS. LIESHA CAMDEN. Block letters, misspelled.

"It looks like a child's writing," she said.

Richard stood with head lowered, legs braced apart. But his expression was only weary. "Perhaps deliberately like a child's. You'd be more open to a child's writing, they might have figured."

" 'They'? Richard, are we getting that paranoid?"

He didn't flinch from the question. "Yes. For the time being."

A week earlier the *New England Journal of Medicine* had published Susan's careful, sober article. An hour later the broadcast and datanet news had exploded in speculation, drama, outrage, and fear. Leisha and Richard, along with all the Sleepless on the Groupnet, had tracked and charted each of four components, looking for a dominant reaction: speculation ("The Sleepless may live for centuries, and this might lead to the following events. . . ."); drama ("If a Sleepless marries only Sleepers, he may have lifetime enough for a dozen brides, and several dozen children, a bewildering blended family. . . ."); outrage ("Tampering with the law of nature has only brought among us unnatural so-called people who will live with the unfair advantage of time: time to accumulate more kin, more power, more property than the rest of us could ever know. . . ."); and fear ("How soon before the Super-race takes over?")

"They're all fear, of one kind or another," Carolyn Rizzolo finally said, and the Groupnet stopped its differentiated tracking.

Leisha was taking the final exams of her last year of law school. Each day comments followed her to the campus, along the corridors and in the classroom; each day she forgot them in the grueling exam sessions, in which all students were reduced to the same status of petitioner to the great university. Afterward, temporarily drained, she walked silently back home to Richard and the Groupnet, aware of the looks of people on the street, aware of her bodyguard Bruce striding between her and them.

"It will calm down," Leisha said. Richard didn't answer.

The town of Salt Springs, Texas, passed a local ordinance that no Sleepless could obtain a liquor license, on the grounds that civil rights statutes were built on the "all men were created equal" clause of the Declaration of Independence, and Sleepless clearly were not covered.

There were no Sleepless within a hundred miles of Salt Springs and no one had applied for a new liquor license there for the past ten years, but the story was picked up by United Press and by Datanet News, and within twenty-four hours heated editorials appeared, on both sides of the issue, across the nation.

More local ordinances were passed. In Pollux, Pennsylvania, the Sleepless could be denied an apartment rental on the grounds that their prolonged wakefulness would increase both wear-and-tear on the landlord's property and utility bills. In Cranston Estates, California, Sleepless were barred from operating twenty-four hour businesses: "unfair competition." Iroquois County, New York, barred them from serving on county juries, arguing that a jury containing Sleepless, with their skewed idea of time, did not constitute "a jury of one's peers."

"All those statutes will be thrown out in superior courts," Leisha said. "But God! The waste of money and docket time to do it!" A part of her mind noticed that her tone as she said this was Roger Camden's.

The state of Georgia, in which some sex acts between consenting adults were still a crime, made sex between a Sleepless and a Sleeper a third-degree felony, classing it with bestiality.

Kevin Baker had designed software that scanned the newsnets at high speed, flagged all stories involving discrimination or attacks on Sleepless, and categorized them by type. The files were available on Groupnet. Leisha read through them, then called Kevin. "Can't you create a parallel program to flag defenses of us? We're getting a skewed picture."

"You're right," Kevin said, a little startled. "I didn't think of it."

"Think of it," Leisha said, grimly. Richard, watching her, said nothing.

She was most upset by the stories about Sleepless children. Shunning at school, verbal abuse by siblings, attacks by neighborhood bullies, confused resentment from parents who had wanted an exceptional child but had not bargained for one who might live centuries. The school board of Cold River, Iowa, voted to bar Sleepless children from conventional classrooms because their rapid learning "created feelings of inadequacy in others, interfering with their education." The board made funds available for Sleepless to have tutors at home. There were no volunteers among the teaching staff. Leisha started spending as much time on Groupnet with the kids, talking to them all night long, as she did studying for her bar exams, scheduled for July.

Stella Bevington stopped using her modem.

Kevin's second program cataloged editorials urging fairness toward

Sleepless. The school board of Denver set aside funds for a program in which gifted children, including the Sleepless, could use their talents and build teamwork through tutoring even younger children. Rive Beau, Louisiana, elected Sleepless Danielle du Cherney to the City Council, although Danielle was twenty-two and technically too young to qualify. The prestigious medical research firm of Halley-Hall gave much publicity to their hiring of Christopher Amren, a Sleepless with a Ph.D. in cellular physics.

Dora Clarq, a Sleepless in Dallas, opened a letter addressed to her and a plastic explosive blew off her arm.

Leisha and Richard stared at the envelope on the hall credenza. The paper was thick, cream-colored, but not expensive, the kind of paper made of bulky newsprint dyed the shades of vellum. There was no return address. Richard called Liz Bishop, a Sleepless who was majoring in criminal justice in Michigan. He had never spoken with her before—neither had Leisha—but she came on the Groupnet immediately and told them how to open it. Or, she could fly up and do it if they preferred. Richard and Leisha followed her directions for remote detonation in the basement of the townhouse. Nothing blew up. When the letter was open, they took it out and read it:

> Dear Ms. Camden,
>
> You been pretty good to me and I'm sorry to do this but I quit. They are making it pretty hot for me at the union not officially but you know how it is. If I was you I wouldn't go to the union for another bodyguard I'd try to find one privately. But be careful. Again I'm sorry but I have to live too.
>
> Bruce

"I don't know whether to laugh or cry," Leisha said. "The two of us getting all this equipment, spending hours on this setup so an explosive won't detonate. . . ."

"It's not as if I at least had a whole lot else to do," Richard said. Since the wave of anti-Sleepless sentiment, all but two of his marine consulting clients, vulnerable to the marketplace and thus to public opinion, had canceled their accounts.

Groupnet, still up on Leisha's terminal, shrilled in emergency override. Leisha got there first. It was Tony Indivino.

"Leisha. I need your legal help, if you'll give it. They're trying to fight me on Sanctuary. Please fly down here."

Sanctuary was raw brown gashes in the late-spring earth. It was situated in the Allegheny Mountains of southern New York State, old hills rounded by age and covered with pine and hickory. A superb road led from the closest town, Conewango, to Sanctuary. Low, maintenance-free buildings, whose design was plain but graceful, stood in various stages of completion. Jennifer Sharifi, unsmiling, met Leisha and Richard. She hadn't changed much in six years but her long black hair was uncombed and her dark eyes enormous with strain. "Tony wants to talk to you, but first he asked me to show you both around."

"What's wrong?" Leisha asked quietly.

Jennifer didn't try to evade the question. "Later. First look at Sanctuary. Tony respects your opinion enormously, Leisha; he wants you to see everything."

The dormitories each held fifty, with communal rooms for cooking, dining, relaxing, and bathing, and a warren of separate offices and studios and labs for work. "We're calling them 'dorms' anyway, despite the etymology," Jennifer said, and even in this remark, which from anybody else would have been playful, Leisha heard the peculiar combination of Jennifer's habitual deliberate calm with her present strain.

She was impressed, despite herself, with the completeness of Tony's plans for lives that would be both communal and intensely private. There was a gym, a small hospital—"By the end of next year, we'll have eighteen board/certified doctors, you know, and four of them are thinking of coming here"—a daycare facility, a school, and an intensive-crop farm. "Most of the food will come in from the outside, of course. So will most people's jobs, although they'll do as much of them as possible from here, over datanets. We're not cutting ourselves off from the world, only creating a safe place from which to trade with it." Leisha didn't answer.

Apart from the power facilities, self-supported Y-energy, she was most impressed with the human planning. Tony had interested Sleepless from virtually every field they would need both to care for themselves and to deal with the outside world. "Lawyers and accountants come first," Jennifer said. "That's our first line of defense in safeguarding ourselves. Tony recognizes that most modern battles for power are fought in the courtroom and boardroom."

But not all. Last, Jennifer showed them the plans for physical defense. For the first time, her taut body seemed to relax slightly.

Every effort had been made to stop attackers without hurting them.

Electronic surveillance completely circled the 150 square miles Jennifer had purchased. Some *counties* were smaller than that, Leisha thought, dazed. When breached, a force field a half-mile within the E-gate activated, delivering electric shocks to anyone on foot—"but only on the *outside* of the field. We don't want any of our kids hurt," Jennifer said. Unmanned penetration by vehicles or robots was identified by a system that located all moving metal above a certain mass within Sanctuary. Any moving metal that did not carry a special signaling device designed by Donald Pospula, a Sleepless who had patented important electronic components, was suspect.

"Of course, we're not set up for an air attack or an outright army assault," Jennifer said. "But we don't expect that. Only the haters in self-motivated hate."

Leisha touched the hard-copy of the security plans with one finger. They troubled her. "If we can't integrate ourselves into the world . . . Free trade should imply free movement."

Jennifer said swiftly, "Only if free movement implies free minds," and at her tone Leisha looked up. "I have something to tell you, Leisha."

"What?"

"Tony isn't here."

"Where is he?"

"In Cattaraugus County Jail in Conewango. It's true we're having zoning battles about Sanctuary—zoning! In this isolated spot! But this is something else, something that just happened this morning. Tony's been arrested for the kidnapping of Timmy DeMarzo."

The room wavered. "FBI?"

"Yes."

"How . . . how did they find out?"

"Some agent eventually cracked the case. They didn't tell us how. Tony needs a lawyer, Leisha. Bill Thaine has already agreed, but Tony wants you."

"Jennifer—I don't even take the bar exams until July!"

"He says he'll wait. Bill will act as his lawyer in the meantime. Will you pass the bar?"

"Of course. But I already have a job lined up with Morehouse, Kennedy & Anderson in New York. . . ." She stopped. Richard was looking at her hard, Jennifer inscrutably. Leisha said quietly, "What will he plead?"

"Guilty," Jennifer said, "with—what is it called legally? Extenuating circumstances."

Leisha nodded. She had been afraid Tony would want to plead not guilty: more lies, subterfuge, ugly politics. Her mind ran swiftly over extenuating circumstances, precedents, tests to precedents. . . . They could use *Clements* v. *Voy*. . . .

"Bill is at the jail now," Jennifer said. "Will you drive in with me?" She made the question a challenge.

"Yes," Leisha said.

In Conewango, the county seat, they were not allowed to see Tony. William Thaine, as his attorney, could go in and out freely. Leisha, not officially an attorney at all, could go nowhere. This was told to them by a man in the D.A.'s office whose face stayed immobile while he spoke to them, and who spat on the ground behind their shoes when they turned to leave, even though this left him with a smear of spittle on his courthouse floor.

Richard and Leisha drove their rental car to the airport for the flight back to Boston. On the way Richard told Leisha he was leaving. He was moving to Sanctuary, now, even before it was functional, to help with the planning and building.


She stayed most of the time in her townhouse, studying ferociously for the bar exams or checking on the Sleepless children through Groupnet. She had not hired another bodyguard to replace Bruce, which made her reluctant to go outside very much; the reluctance in turn made her angry with herself. Once or twice a day she scanned Kevin's electronic news clippings.

There were signs of hope. The *New York Times* ran an editorial, widely reprinted on the electronic news services:

PROSPERITY AND HATRED:
A LOGIC CURVE WE'D RATHER NOT
SEE

The United States has never been a country that much values calm, logic, and rationality. We have, as a people, tended to label these things "cold." We have, as a people, tended to admire feeling and action: We exalt in our stories and our memorials—not the creation of the Constitution but its defense at Iwo Jima; not the intellectual achievements of a Linus Pauling but the heroic passion of a Charles Lindbergh; not the inventors of the monorails and computers that unite us but the composers of the angry songs of rebellion that divide us.

A peculiar aspect of this phenomenon is that it grows stronger in times of prosperity. The better off our citizenry, the greater their contempt for the calm reasoning that got them there, and the more passionate their indulgence in emotion. Consider, in the past century, the gaudy excesses of the roaring twenties and the antiestablishment contempt of the sixties. Consider, in our own century, the unprecedented prosperity brought about by Y-energy—and then consider that Kenzo Yagai, except to his followers, was seen as a greedy and bloodless logician, while our national adulation goes to neo-nihilist writer Stephen Castelli, to "feelie" actress Brenda Foss, and to daredevil gravity-well diver Jim Morse Luter.

But most of all, as you ponder this phenomenon in your Y-energy houses, consider the current outpouring of irrational feeling directed at the "Sleepless" since the publication of the joint findings of the Biotech Institute and the Chicago Medical School concerning Sleepless tissue regeneration.

Most of the Sleepless are intelligent. Most of them are calm, if you define that much-maligned word to mean directing one's energies into solving problems rather than to emoting about them. (Even Pulitzer Prize winner Carolyn Rizzolo gave us a stunning play of ideas, not of passions run amuck.) All of them show a natural bent toward achievement, a bent given a decided boost by the one-third more time in their days to achieve. Their achievements lie, for the most part, in logical fields rather than emotional ones: Computers. Law. Finance. Physics. Medical research. They are rational, orderly, calm, intelligent, cheerful, young, and possibly very long-lived.

And, in our United States of unprecedented prosperity, they are increasingly hated.

Does the hatred that we have seen flower so fully over the past few months really grow, as many claim, from the "unfair advantage" the Sleepless have over the rest of us in securing jobs, promotions, money, and success? Is it really envy over the Sleepless' good fortune? Or does it come from something more pernicious, rooted in our tradition of shoot-from-the-hip American action: hatred of the logical, the calm, the considered? Hatred in fact of the superior mind?

If so, perhaps we should think deeply about the founders of this country: Jefferson, Washington, Paine, Adams—inhabitants of the Age of Reason, all. These men created our orderly and balanced system of laws precisely to protect the property and achievements created by the individual efforts of balanced and rational minds. The Sleepless may be our severest internal test yet of our own sober belief in law and order. No, the Sleepless were *not,* "created equal," but our attitudes toward them should be examined with a care equal to our soberest jurisprudence. We may not like what we learn about our own motives, but our credibility as a people may depend on the rationality and intelligence of the examination.

Both have been in short supply in the public reaction to last month's research findings.

Law is not theater. Before we write laws reflecting gaudy and dramatic feelings, we must be very sure we understand the difference.

Leisha hugged herself, gazing in delight at the screen, smiling. She called the *New York Times* and asked who had written the editorial. The receptionist, cordial when she answered the phone, grew brusque. The *Times* was not releasing that information, "prior to internal investigation."

It could not dampen her mood. She whirled around the apartment, after days of sitting at her desk or screen. Delight demanded physical action. She washed dishes, picked up books. There were gaps in the furniture patterns where Richard had taken pieces that belonged to him; a little quieter now, she moved the furniture to close the gaps.

Susan Melling called to tell her about the *Times* editorial; they talked warmly for a few minutes. When Susan hung up, the phone rang again.

"Leisha? Your voice still sounds the same. This is Stewart Sutter."

"Stewart." She had not seen him for four years. Their romance had lasted two years and then dissolved, not from any painful issue so much as from the press of both their studies. Standing by the comm terminal, hearing his voice, Leisha suddenly felt again his hands on her breasts in the cramped dormitory bed: All those years before she had found a good use for a bed. The phantom hands became Richard's hands, and a sudden pain pierced her.

"Listen," Stewart said, "I'm calling because there's some information I think you should know. You take your bar exams next week, right? And then you have a tentative job with Morehouse, Kennedy & Anderson."

"How do you know all that, Stewart?"

"Men's room gossip. Well, not as bad as that. But the New York legal community—that part of it, anyway—is smaller than you think. And you're a pretty visible figure."

"Yes," Leisha said neutrally.

"Nobody has the slightest doubt you'll be called to the bar. But there is some doubt about the job with Morehouse, Kennedy. You've got two senior partners, Alan Morehouse and Seth Brown, who have changed their minds since this . . . flap. 'Adverse publicity for the firm,' 'turning law into a circus,' blah blah blah. You know the drill. But you've also got two powerful champions, Ann Carlyle and Michael Kennedy, the old man himself. He's quite a mind. Anyway, I wanted you to know all this so you can recognize exactly what the situation is and know whom to count on in the infighting."

"Thank you," Leisha said. "Stew . . . why do you care if I get it or not? Why should it matter to you?"

There was a silence on the other end of the phone. Then Stewart said, very low, "We're not all noodleheads out here, Leisha. Justice does still matter to some of us. So does achievement."

Light rose in her, a bubble of buoyant light.

Stewart said, "You have a lot of support here for that stupid zoning fight over Sanctuary, too. You might not realize that, but you do. What the Parks Commission crowd is trying to pull is . . . but they're just being used as fronts. You know that. Anyway, when it gets as far as the courts, you'll have all the help you need."

"Sanctuary isn't my doing. At all."

"No? Well, I meant the plural you."

"Thank you. I mean that. How are you doing?"

"Fine. I'm a daddy now."

"Really! Boy or girl?"

"Girl. A beautiful little bitch named Justine, drives me crazy. I'd like you to meet my wife sometime, Leisha."

"I'd like that," Leisha said.

She spent the rest of the night studying for her bar exams. The bubble stayed with her. She recognized exactly what it was: joy.

It was going to be all right. The contract, unwritten, between her and her society—Kenzo Yagai's society, Roger Camden's society—would hold. With dissent and strife and yes, some hatred. She suddenly thought of Tony's beggars in Spain, furious at the strong because the beggars were not. Yes. But it would hold.

She believed that.

She did.

# SEVEN

LEISHA TOOK HER BAR EXAMS IN JULY. THEY DID NOT SEEM HARD TO her. Afterward three classmates, two men and a woman, made a fakely casual point of talking to Leisha until she had climbed safely into a taxi whose driver obviously did not recognize her, or stop signs. The three were all Sleepers. A pair of undergraduates, cleanshaven blond men with the long faces and pointless arrogance of rich stupidity, eyed Leisha and sneered. Leisha's female classmate sneered back.

Leisha had a flight to Chicago the next morning. Alice was going to join her there. They had to clean out the big house on the lake, dispose of Roger's personal property, put the house on the market. Leisha had had no time to do it earlier.

She remembered her father in the conservatory, wearing an ancient flat-topped hat he had picked up somewhere, potting orchids and jasmine and passion flowers.

When the doorbell rang she was startled; she almost never had visitors. Eagerly, she turned on the outside camera—maybe it was Jonathan or Martha, back in Boston to surprise her, to celebrate—why hadn't she thought before about some sort of celebration?

Richard stood gazing up at the camera. He had been crying.

She tore open the door. Richard made no move to come in. Leisha saw that what the camera had registered as grief was actually something else: tears of rage.

"Tony's dead."

Leisha put out her hand, blindly. Richard didn't take it.

"They killed him in prison. Not the authorities—the other prisoners. In the recreation yard. Murderers, rapists, looters, scum of the earth—and they thought they had the right to kill *him* because he was different."

Now Richard did grab her arm, so hard that something, some bone, shifted beneath the flesh and pressed on a nerve. "Not just different—*better*. Because he was better, because we all are, we goddamn just don't stand up and shout it out of some misplaced feeling for *their* feelings . . . God!"

Leisha pulled her arm free and rubbed it, numb, staring at Richard's contorted face.

"They beat him to death with a lead pipe. No one even knows how they got a lead pipe. They beat him on the back of the head and then they rolled him over and—"

"Don't!" Leisha said. It came out a whimper.

Richard looked at her. Despite his shouting, his violent grip on her arm, Leisha had the confused impression that this was the first time he had actually seen her. She went on rubbing her arm, staring at him in terror.

He said quietly, "I've come to take you to Sanctuary, Leisha. Dan Jenkins and Vernon Bulriss are in the car outside. The three of us will carry you out, if necessary. But you're coming. You see that, don't you? You're not safe here, with your high profile and your spectacular looks. You're a natural target if anyone is. Do we have to force you? Or do you finally see for yourself that we have no choice—the bastards have left us no choice—except Sanctuary?"

Leisha closed her eyes. Tony, at fourteen, at the beach. Tony, his eyes ferocious and shining, the first to reach out his hand for the glass of interleukin-1. Beggars in Spain.

"I'll come."


She had never known such anger. It scared her, coming in bouts throughout the long night, receding but always returning again. Richard held her in his arms, sitting with their backs against the wall of her library, and his holding made no difference at all. In the living room Dan and Vernon talked in low voices.

Sometimes the anger erupted in shouting, and Leisha heard herself and thought, *I don't know you*. Sometimes it became crying, sometimes talking about Tony, about all of them. Neither the shouting nor the crying nor the talking eased her at all.

Planning did, a little. In a cold, dry voice she didn't recognize, Leisha told Richard about the trip to close the house in Chicago. She had to go; Alice was already there. If Richard and Dan and Vernon put Leisha on the plane, and Alice met her at the other end with union bodyguards, she should be safe enough. Then she would change her return ticket from Boston to Conewongo and drive with Richard to Sanctuary.

"People are already arriving," Richard said. "Jennifer Sharifi is organizing it, greasing the Sleeper suppliers with so much money they can't resist. What about this townhouse here, Leisha? Your furniture and terminal and clothes?"

Leisha looked around her familiar office. Law books, red and green and brown, lined the walls although most of the same information was online. A coffee cup rested on a printout on the desk. Beside it was the receipt she had requested from the taxi driver this afternoon, a giddy souvenir of the day she had passed her bar exams; she had thought of having it framed. Above the desk was a holographic portrait of Kenzo Yagai.

"Let it rot," Leisha said.

Richard's arm tightened around her.


"I've never seen you like this," Alice said, subdued. "It's more than just clearing out the house, isn't it?"

"Let's get on with it," Leisha said. She yanked a suit from her father's closet. "Do you want any of this stuff for your husband?"

"It wouldn't fit."

"The hats?"

"No," Alice said. "Leisha—what is it?"

"Let's just *do* it!" She yanked all the clothes from Camden's closet, piled them on the floor, scrawled FOR VOLUNTEER AGENCY on a piece of paper, and dropped it on top of the pile. Silently, Alice started adding clothes from the dresser, which already bore a taped paper bearing the words, ESTATE AUCTION.

The curtains were already down throughout the house; Alice had done that yesterday. She had also rolled up the rugs. Sunset glared red on the bare wooden floors.

"What about your old room?" Leisha said. "What do you want there?"

"I've already tagged it," Alice said. "A mover will come Thursday."

"Fine. What else?"

"The conservatory. Sanderson has been watering everything, but he didn't really know what needed how much, so some of the plants are—"

"Fire Sanderson," Leisha said curtly. "The exotics can die. Or have them sent to a hospital, if you'd rather. Just watch out for the ones that are poisonous. Come on, let's do the library."

Alice sat slowly on a rolled-up rug in the middle of Camden's bedroom. She had cut her hair; Leisha thought it looked ugly, like jagged brown spikes around her broad face. She had also gained more weight. She was starting to look like their mother.

Alice said, "Do you remember the night I told you I was pregnant? Just before you left for Harvard?"

"Let's do the library!"

"Do you?" Alice said. "For God's sake, can't you just once listen to someone else, Leisha? Do you have to be so much like Daddy every single minute?"

"I'm not Daddy!"

"The hell you're not. You're exactly what he made you. But that's not the point. Do you remember that night?"

Leisha walked over the rug and out the door. Alice simply sat. After a minute Leisha walked back in. "I remember."

"You were near tears," Alice said implacably. Her voice was quiet. "I don't even remember exactly why. Maybe because I wasn't going to college after all. But I put my arms around you, and for the first time in years—years, Leisha—I felt you really were my sister. Despite all of it—the roaming the halls all night and the showoff arguments with Daddy and the special school and the artificially long legs and golden hair—all that crap. You seemed to need me to hold you. You seemed to need me. You seemed to *need*."

"What are you saying?" Leisha demanded. "That you can only be close to someone if they're in trouble and need you? That you can only be a sister if I was in some kind of pain, open sores running? Is that the bond between you Sleepers? 'Protect me while I'm unconscious, I'm just as crippled as you are'?"

"No," Alice said. "I'm saying that *you* could be a sister only if you were in some kind of pain."

Leisha stared at her. "You're stupid, Alice."

Alice said calmly, "I know that. Compared to you, I am. I know that."

Leisha jerked her head angrily. She felt ashamed of what she had just said, and yet it was true, and they both knew it was true, and anger still lay in her like a dark void, formless and hot. It was the formless part that was the worst. Without shape, there could be no action; without action, the anger went on burning her, choking her.

Alice said, "When I was twelve Susan gave me a dress for our birthday. You were away somewhere, on one of those overnight field trips your fancy progressive school did all the time. The dress was silk, pale blue, with antique lace—very beautiful. I was thrilled, not only because it was beautiful but because Susan had gotten it for me and gotten software for you. The dress was mine. Was, I thought, *me.*" In the gathering gloom Leisha could barely make out her broad, plain features. "The first time I wore it a boy said, 'Stole your sister's dress, Alice? Snitched it while she was *sleeping?*' Then he laughed like crazy, the way they always did.

"I threw the dress away. I didn't even explain to Susan, although I think she would have understood. Whatever was yours was yours, and whatever wasn't yours was yours, too. That's the way Daddy set it up. The way he hard-wired it into our genes."

"You, too?" Leisha said. "You're no different from the other envious beggars?"

Alice stood up from the rug. She did it slowly, leisurely, brushing dust off the back of her wrinkled skirt, smoothing the print fabric. Then she walked over and hit Leisha in the mouth.

"Now do you see me as real?" Alice asked quietly.

Leisha put her hand to her mouth. She felt blood. The phone rang, Camden's unlisted personal line. Alice walked over, picked it up, listened, and held it calmly out to Leisha. "It's for you."

Numb, Leisha took it.

"Leisha? This is Kevin. Listen, something's happened. Stella Bevington called me, on the phone, not Groupnet; I think her parents took away her modem. I picked up the phone and she screamed, 'This is Stella! They're hitting me, he's drunk—' and then the line went dead. Randy's gone to Sanctuary—hell, they've *all* gone. You're closest to her, she's still in Skokie. You better get there fast. Have you got bodyguards you trust?"

"Yes," Leisha said, although she hadn't. The anger, finally, took form. "I can handle it."

"I don't know how you'll get her out of there," Kevin said. "They'll recognize you, they know she called somebody, they might even have knocked her out. . . ."

"I'll handle it," Leisha said.

"Handle what?" Alice said.

Leisha faced her. Even though she knew she shouldn't, she said, "What your people do. To one of ours. A seven-year-old kid who's getting beaten by her parents because she's Sleepless—because she's *better* than you are—" She ran down the stairs and out to the rental car she had driven from the airport.

Alice ran right down with her. "Not your car, Leisha. They can trace a rental car just like that. My car."

Leisha screamed, "If you think you're—"

Alice yanked open the door of her battered Toyota, a model so old the Y-energy cones weren't even concealed but hung like drooping jowls on either side. She shoved Leisha into the passenger seat, slammed the door, and rammed herself behind the wheel. Her hands were steady. "Where?"

Blackness swooped over Leisha. She put her head down, as far between her knees as the cramped Toyota would allow. It had been two—no, three—days since she had eaten. Not since the night before the bar exams. The faintness receded, swept over her again as soon as she raised her head.

She told Alice the address in Skokie.


"Stay way in the back," Alice said. "And there's a scarf in the glove compartment—put it on. Low, to hide as much of your face as possible."

Alice had stopped the car along Highway 42. Leisha said, "This isn't—"

"It's a quick-guard place. We have to look like we have some protection, Leisha. We don't need to tell him anything. I'll hurry."

She was out in three minutes with a huge man in a cheap dark suit. He squeezed into the front seat beside Alice and said nothing at all. Alice did not introduce him.

The house was small, a little shabby, with lights on downstairs, none upstairs. The first stars shone in the north, away from Chicago. Alice said to the guard, "Get out of the car and stand here by the car door—no, more in the light—and don't do anything unless I'm attacked in some way." The man nodded. Alice started up the walk. Leisha scrambled out of the back seat and caught her sister two-thirds of the way to the plastic front door.

"Alice, what the hell are you doing? *I* have to—"

"Keep your voice down," Alice said, glancing at the guard. "Leisha, *think*. You'll be recognized. Here, near Chicago, with a Sleepless daughter—these people have looked at your picture in magazines for years. They've watched long-range holovids of you. They know you. They know you're going to be a lawyer. Me they've never seen. I'm nobody."

"Alice—"

"For Chrissake, get back in the car!" Alice hissed, and pounded on the front door.

Leisha drew off the walk, into the shadow of a willow tree. A man opened the door. His face was completely blank.

Alice said, "Child Protection Agency. We got a call from a little girl, this number. Let me in."

"There's no little girl here."

"This is an emergency, priority one," Alice said. "Child Protection Act 186. Let me in!"

The man, still blank-faced, glanced at the huge figure by the car. "You got a search warrant?"

"I don't need one in a priority-one child emergency. If you don't let me in, you're going to have legal snarls like you never bargained for."

Leisha clamped her lips together. No one would believe that, it was legal gobbledygook, . . . Her lip throbbed where Alice had hit it.

The man stood aside to let Alice enter.

The guard started forward. Leisha hesitated, then let him. He entered with Alice.

Leisha waited, alone, in the dark.

In three minutes they were out, the guard carrying a child. Alice's broad face gleamed pale in the porch light. Leisha sprang forward, opened the car door, and helped the guard ease the child inside. The guard was frowning, a slow puzzled frown shot with wariness.

Alice said, "Here. This is an extra hundred dollars. To get back to the city by yourself."

"Hey . . ." the guard said, but he took the money. He stood looking after them as Alice pulled away.

"He'll go straight to the police," Leisha said despairingly. "He has to, or risk his union membership."

"I know," Alice said. "But by that time we'll be out of the car."

"*Where?*"

"At the hospital," Alice said.

"Alice, we can't—" Leisha didn't finish. She turned to the back seat. "Stella? Are you conscious?"

"Yes," said the small voice.

Leisha groped until her fingers found the rear-seat illuminator. Stella lay stretched out on the seat, her face distorted with pain. She cradled her left arm in her right. A single bruise colored her face, above the left eye. Her red hair was tangled and dirty.

"You're Leisha Camden," the child said, and started to cry.

"Her arm's broken," Alice said.

"Honey, can you . . ." Leisha's throat felt thick, she had trouble getting the words out ". . . can you hold on till we get you to a doctor?"

"Yes," Stella said. "Just don't take me back there!"

"We won't," Leisha said. "Ever." She glanced at Alice and saw Tony's face.

Alice said, "There's a community hospital about ten miles south of here."

"How do you know that?"

"I was there once. Drug overdose," Alice said briefly. She drove hunched over the wheel, with the face of someone thinking furiously. Leisha thought, too, trying to see a way around the legal charge of kidnapping. They probably couldn't say the child came willingly. Stella would undoubtedly cooperate but at her age and in her condition she was probably *non sui juris,* her word would have no legal weight. . . .

"Alice, we can't even get her into the hospital without insurance information. Verifiable online."

"Listen," Alice said, not to Leisha but over her shoulder, toward the back seat, "here's what we're going to do, Stella. I'm going to tell them you're my daughter and you fell off a big rock you were climbing while we stopped for a snack at a roadside picnic area. We're driving from California to Philadelphia to see your grandmother. Your name is Jordan Watrous and you're five years old. Got that, honey?"

"I'm seven," Stella said. "Almost eight."

"You're a very large five. Your birthday is March 23. Can you do this, Stella?"

"Yes," the little girl said. Her voice was stronger.

Leisha stared at Alice. "Can *you* do this?"

"Of course I can," Alice said. "I'm Roger Camden's daughter."

Alice half-carried, half-supported Stella into the Emergency Room of the small community hospital. Leisha watched from the car: the short stocky woman, the child's thin body with the twisted arm. Then she drove Alice's car to the farthest corner of the parking lot, under the dubious cover of a skimpy maple, and locked it. She tied the scarf more securely around her face.

Alice's license plate number, and her name, would be in every police and rental-car databank by now. The medical banks were slower; often they uploaded from local precincts only once a day, resenting the governmental interference in what was still, despite a half-century of battle, a private-sector enterprise. Alice and Stella would probably be all right in the hospital. Probably. But Alice could not rent another car.

Leisha could.

But the data file that would flash to rental agencies on Alice Camden Watrous might or might not include that she was Leisha Camden's twin.

Leisha looked at the rows of cars in the lot. A flashy luxury Chrysler, an Ikeda van, a row of middle-class Toyotas and Mercedes, a vintage '99 Cadillac—she could imagine the owner's face if that were missing—ten or twelve cheap runabouts, a hovercar with the uniformed driver asleep at the wheel. And a battered farm truck.

Leisha walked over to the truck. A man sat at the wheel, smoking. She thought of her father.

"Hello," Leisha said.

The man rolled down his window but didn't answer. He had greasy brown hair.

"See that hovercar over there?" Leisha said. She made her voice sound young, high. The man glanced at it indifferently; from this angle you couldn't see that the driver was asleep. "That's my bodyguard. He thinks I'm inside, the way my father told me to, getting this lip looked at." She could feel her mouth swollen from Alice's blow.

"So?"

Leisha stamped her foot. "So I don't want to be inside. He's a shit and so's Daddy. I want *out*. I'll give you four thousand bank credits for your truck. Cash."

The man's eyes widened. He tossed away his cigarette and looked again at the hovercar. The driver's shoulders were broad, and the car was within easy screaming distance.

"All nice and legal," Leisha said, trying to smirk. Her knees felt watery.

"Let me see the cash."

Leisha backed away from the truck, to where he could not reach her. She took the money from her arm clip. She was used to carrying a lot of cash; there had always been Bruce, or someone like Bruce. There had always been safety.

"Get out of the truck on the other side," Leisha said, "and lock the door behind you. Leave the keys on the seat, where I can see them from here. Then I'll put the money on the roof where you can see it."

The man laughed, a sound like gravel pouring. "Regular little Dabney Engh, aren't you? Is that what they teach you society debs at your fancy schools?"

Leisha had no idea who Dabney Engh was. She waited, watching the man try to think of a way to cheat her, and tried to hide her contempt. She thought of Tony.

"All right," he said, and slid out of the truck.

"Lock the door!"

He grinned, opened the door again, and locked it. Leisha put the money on the roof, yanked open the driver's door, clambered in, locked the door, and powered up the window. The man laughed. She put the key into the ignition, started the truck, and drove toward the street. Her hands trembled.

She drove slowly around the block twice. When she came back, the man was gone, and the driver of the hovercar was still asleep. She had wondered if the man would wake him, out of sheer malice, but he had not. She parked the truck and waited.

An hour and a half later Alice and a nurse wheeled Stella out of the Emergency entrance. Leisha leaped out of the truck and yelled, "Coming, Alice!" waving both her arms. It was too dark to see Alice's expression; Leisha could only hope that Alice showed no dismay at the battered truck, that she had not told the nurse to expect a red car.

Alice said, "This is Julie Bergadon, a friend that I called while you were setting Jordan's arm." The nurse nodded, uninterested. The two women helped Stella into the high truck cab; there was no back seat. Stella had a cast on her arm and looked drugged.

"How?" Alice said as they drove off.

Leisha didn't answer. She was watching a police hovercar land at the other end of the parking lot. Two officers got out and strode purposefully toward Alice's locked car under the skimpy maple.

"My God," Alice said. For the first time, she sounded frightened.

"They won't trace us," Leisha said. "Not to this truck. Count on it."

"Leisha." Alice's voice spiked with fear. "Stella's *asleep.*"

Leisha glanced at the child, slumped against Alice's shoulder. "No, she's not. She's unconscious from painkillers."

"Is that all right? Normal? For . . . her?"

"We can black out. We can even experience substance-induced

sleep." Tony and she and Richard and Jennifer in the midnight woods. . . . "Didn't you know that, Alice?"

"No."

"We don't know very much about each other, do we?"

They drove south in silence. Finally Alice said, "Where are we going to take her, Leisha?"

"I don't know. Any one of the Sleepless would be the first place the police would check—"

"You can't risk it. Not the way things are," Alice said. She sounded weary. "But all my friends are in California. I don't think we could drive this rust bucket that far before getting stopped."

"It wouldn't make it anyway."

"What should we do?"

"Let me think."

At an expressway exit was a pay phone. It wouldn't be data-shielded, as Groupnet was. Would Kevin's open line be tapped? Probably.

There was no doubt the Sanctuary line would be.

Sanctuary. All of them were going there or already there, Kevin had said. Holed up, trying to pull the worn Allegheny Mountains around them like a safe little den. Except for the children like Stella, who could not.

Where? With whom?

Leisha closed her eyes. The Sleepless were out; the police would find Stella within hours. Susan Melling? But she had been Alice's all-too-visible stepmother, and was a cobeneficiary of Camden's will; they would question her almost immediately. It couldn't be anyone traceable to Alice. It could only be a Sleeper that Leisha knew, and trusted, and why should anyone at all fit that description? Why should she risk so much on anyone who did?

She stood a long time in the dark phone kiosk. Then she walked to the truck. Alice was asleep, her head thrown back against the seat. A tiny line of drool ran down her chin. Her face was white and drained in the bad light from the kiosk. Leisha walked back to the phone.

"Stewart? Stewart Sutter?"

"Yes?"

"This is Leisha Camden. Something has happened." She told the story tersely, in bald sentences. Stewart did not interrupt.

"Leisha—" Stewart said, and stopped.

"I need help, Stewart." *'I'll help you, Alice.' 'I don't need your help.'*

A wind whistled over the dark field beside the kiosk and Leisha shivered. She heard in the wind the thin keen of a beggar. In the wind, in her own voice.

"All right," Stewart said, "this is what we'll do. I have a cousin in Ripley, New York, just over the state line from Pennsylvania, the route you'll be driving east. It has to be in New York; I'm licensed in New York. Take the little girl there. I'll call my cousin and tell her you're coming. She's an elderly woman, was quite an activist in her youth. Her name is Janet Patterson. The town is—"

"What makes you so sure she'll get involved? She could go to jail. And so could you."

"She's been in jail so many times you wouldn't believe it. Political protests going all the way back to Vietnam. But no one's going to jail. I'm now your attorney of record, I'm privileged. I'm going to get Stella declared a ward of the state. That shouldn't be too hard with the hospital records you established in Skokie. Then she can be transferred to a foster home in New York. I know just the place, people who are fair and kind. Then Alice—"

"Stella's resident in Illinois. You can't—"

"Yes, I can. Since those research findings about the Sleepless lifespan have come out, legislators have been railroaded by stupid constituents scared or jealous or just plain angry. The result is a body of so-called law riddled with contradictions, absurdities, and loopholes. None of it will stand in the long run—or at least I hope not—but in the meantime it can all be exploited. I can use it to create the most goddamn convoluted case for Stella that anybody ever saw, and in the meantime she won't be returned home. But that won't work for Alice. She'll need an attorney licensed in Illinois."

"We have one," Leisha said. "Candace Holt."

"No, not a Sleepless. Trust me on this, Leisha. I'll find somebody good. There's a guy in—are you crying?"

"No," Leisha said, crying.

"Ah, God," Stewart said. "Bastards. I'm sorry all this happened, Leisha."

"Don't be," Leisha said.

When she had directions to Stewart's cousin, she walked back to the truck. Alice was still asleep, Stella still unconscious. Leisha closed the truck door as quietly as possible. The engine balked and roared, but Alice didn't wake.

There was a crowd of people with them in the narrow and darkened cab: Stewart Sutter, Tony Indivino, Susan Melling, Kenzo Yagi, Roger Camden.

To Stewart Sutter she said, You called to inform me about the situation at Morehouse, Kennedy. You are risking your career and your cousin for Stella. And you stand to gain nothing. Like Susan telling me in advance about Bernie Kuhn's brain. Susan, who lost her life to Daddy's dream and regained it by her own strength. A contract without consideration for each side is not a contract: Every first-year student knows that.

To Kenzo Yagai she said, Trade isn't always linear. You missed that. If Stewart gives me something, and I give Stella something, and ten years from now Stella is a different person because of that and gives something to someone else as yet unknown—it's an ecology. An ecology of trade, yes, each niche needed, even if they're not contractually bound. Does a horse need a fish? Yes.

To Tony she said, Yes, there are beggars in Spain who trade nothing, give nothing, do nothing. But there are *more* than beggars in Spain. Withdraw from the beggars, you withdraw from the whole damn country. And you withdraw from the possibility of the ecology of help. That's what Alice wanted, all those years ago in her bedroom. Pregnant, scared, angry, jealous, she wanted to help *me*, and I wouldn't let her because I didn't need it. But I do now. And she did then. Beggars need to help as well as be helped.

And finally, there was only Daddy left. She could *see* him, bright-eyed, holding thick-leaved exotic flowers in his strong hands. To Camden she said, You were wrong. Alice *is* special. Oh, Daddy—the specialness of Alice! You were wrong.

As soon as she thought this, lightness filled her. Not the buoyant bubble of joy, not the hard clarity of examination, but something else: sunshine, soft through the conservatory glass, where two children ran in and out. She suddenly felt light herself, not buoyant but translucent, a medium for the sunshine to pass clear through, on its way to somewhere else.

She drove the sleeping woman and the wounded child through the night, east, toward the state line.

# FEIGENBAUM NUMBER

*"Feigenbaum Number" is that well-known SF phenomenon: the portmanteau story. A writer reads something by someone else: a story, or a scientific article, or maybe merely a reference to some event or phenomenon. Something happens in whatever deep part of the mind these things happen, and the new concept mates with another older, known concept to produce a hybrid offspring.*

*One of the stimuli for "Feigenbaum Number" was a* New Destinies *essay by Charles Sheffield, "The Unlicked Bear Whelp." This article dealt with chaos theory, but the part of it that sparked my imagination concerned iterated function theory. Being math-impaired, I had never heard of iterated function theory. Nor had I heard of its shimmering, suggestive components: strange attractors; convergence; the Feigenbaum number, at which predictable behavior changes to chaotic behavior. Metaphorically heady stuff for a lapsed English major.*

*The other concept packed into this portmanteau, the Platonic idea that there exists an ideal state of which reality is merely a poor reflection, I had known about for a long time. I used it in an early story, "Shadows on the Cave Wall" (in* Universe 11, *1981). Now it cross-fertilized with iterated function theory to produce the question: What if the Platonic state were subject to the law of convergence? And someone was fated to experience that?*

*Fifteen years later, I saw Tom Stoppard's marvelous play Arcadia, which mates iterated function theory with the collapse of artistic romanticism. Stoppard's Thomasina Coverly is a far more enchanting creature than my Jack. She also lives in a far more enchanting world—which makes you wonder which way the convergence is actually going.*

*"Behold! Human beings living in an underground den. . . .
Like ourselves, they see only their own shadows, or the
shadows of one another, which the fire throws on the opposite walls of the cave."*
—Plato, *The Republic*


I ROSE FROM THE BED, LEAVING DIANE SPRAWLED ACROSS THE RUM-
pled sheets, smiling, lipstick smeared and large belly sweaty. She
said, "Wow."

"Wow yourself," I said and turned to the mirror. Behind me, the
other woman rose ghostly from the bed and crossed, smiling, to the
window.

Diane said, "Come back to bed, Jack."

"Can't. I have to go. Student appointment."

"So what's new?" In the mirror I saw her eyes narrow, her mouth
tighten. The other woman turned from the window, laughing, one slim
graceful arm pushing back a tendril of chestnut hair.

Diane skinned her brown hair back from her face. "Is it too much
to ask, Jack, *honey,* that just once after we make love you don't go
rushing off like there's a three-alarm fire? Just *once?"*

I didn't answer.

"I mean, how do you think that makes me feel? Slam-bam-thank-
you-ma'am. We have an actual relationship here, we've been going out
for three months, it doesn't seem a lot to ask that after we make love
you don't just—"

I didn't interrupt. I couldn't. The dizziness was strong this time;
soon the nausea would follow. Sex did that. The intensity. Diane
ranted, jerking herself to a kneeling position on the bed, framed by

lumpy maroon window curtains opened a crack to a neighbor's peeling frame house and weedy garden. Across the room the other Diane stood framed by crimson silk draperies opened a crack to a mellowed-wood cottage riotous with climbing roses. She blew me a light-hearted kiss. Her eyes glowed with understanding.

The nausea came.

"—*can't* seem to understand how it makes me *feel* to be treated like—"

I clutched the edge of the dresser, which was both a scratched pressed-board "reproduction" and a polished cherrywood lowboy. Two perfume bottles floated in front of me: yellow plastic spraybottle and clean-lined blown glass. I squeezed my eyes shut. The ghostly Diane disappeared in the act of sauntering, slim and assured, toward the bathroom.

"—don't even really look at me, not when we make love or—"

Eyes shut, I groped for the bedroom door.

"Jack!"

I slammed the doors, both of them, and left the apartment before Diane could follow. With her sloppy anger, her overweight nakedness, her completely justified weeping.

Outside was better. I drove my Escort to campus. The other car, the perfectly engineered driving machine with the sleek and balanced lines, shimmered in and out around me, but the vertigo didn't return. I'd never gotten very intense about cars, and over the years I'd learned to handle the double state of anything that wasn't too intense. The rest I avoided. Mostly.

The Aaron Fielding Faculty Office Building jutted boxlike three stories from the asphalt parking lot, and it blended its three floors harmoniously with a low hillside whose wooded lines were repeated in horizontal stretches of brick and wood. The poster-cluttered lobby was full of hurried students trying to see harried advisors, and it was a marble atrium where scholars talked eagerly about the mind of man. I walked down the corridor toward my cubicle, one of a row allotted to teaching assistants and post-docs.

But Dr. Frances Schraeder's door was open, and I couldn't resist.

She sat at her terminal, working, and when I knocked on the door-jamb (scarred metal, ghostly graceful molding), she looked up and smiled. "Jack! Come look at this!"

I came in, with so much relief my eyes prickled. The material Fran's long, age-spotted fingers were held poised over her keyboard, and the ideal Fran's long, age-spotted fingers echoed them. The ideal Fran's white hair was fuller, but no whiter, and both were cut in simple short caps. The material Fran wore glasses, but both Frans' bright blue eyes, a little sunken, shone with the same alert tranquillity.

She was the only person I'd ever seen who came close to matching what she should have been.

"This is the latest batch of phase-space diagrams," Fran said. "The computer just finished them—I haven't even printed them yet."

I crouched beside her to peer at the terminal.

"Don't look any more disorganized to me than the last bunch."

"Nor to me, either, unfortunately. Same old, same old." She laughed: in chaos theory, there is no same old, same old. The phase-space diagrams were infinitely complex, never repeating, without control.

But not completely. The control was there, not readily visible, a key we just didn't recognize with the mathematics we had. Yet.

An ideal no one had seen.

"I keep thinking that your young mind will pick up something I've missed," Fran said. "I'll make you a copy of these. Plus, Pyotr Solenski has published some new work in Berlin that I think you should take a look at. I downloaded it from the net and emailed you."

I nodded, but didn't answer. For the first time today, calm flowed through me, soothing me.

Calm.

Rightness.

*Numbers.*

Fran had done good, if undistinguished, work in pure mathematics all her life. For the last few years she—and I as her graduate student— had worked in the precise and austere world of iterated function theory, where the result of a given equation is recycled as the starting value of the next repetition of the same equation. If you do that, the results are predictable: the sequences will converge on a given set of numbers. No matter what initial value you plug into the equation, with enough iterations you end up at the same figures, called attractors. Every equation can generate a set of attractors, which iterations converge on like homing pigeons flying back to their nests.

Until you raise the value plugged into the equation past a point called the Feigenbaum number. Then the sequences produced lose all regularity. You can no longer find any pattern. Attractors disappear. The behavior of even fairly simple equations becomes chaotic. The pigeons fly randomly, blind and lost.

Or do they?

Fran—like dozens of other pure mathematicians around the world—looked at all that chaos, and sorted through it, and thought she glimpsed an order to the pigeons' flight. A chaotic order, a controlled randomness. We'd been looking at nonlinear differential equations, and at their attractors, which cause iterated values not to converge but to *diverge*. States which start out only infinitesimally separated go on to diverge more and more and more . . . and more, moving toward some hidden values called, aptly enough, *strange attractors*. Pigeons from the same nest are drawn, through seeming chaos, to points we can identify but not prove the existence of.

Fran and I had a tentative set of equations for those idealized points.

Only tentative. Something wasn't right. We'd overlooked something, something neither of us could see. It was there—I *knew* it—but we couldn't see it. When we did, we'd have proof that any physical system showing an ultradependence on initial conditions must have a strange attractor buried somewhere in its structure. The implications would be profound—for chaos mathematics, for fluid mechanics, for weather control.

For me.

I loved looking for that equation. Sometimes I thought I could glimpse it, behind the work we were doing, almost visible to me. But not often. And the truth I hadn't told Fran, couldn't tell her, was that I didn't need to *find* it, not in the way she did. She was driven by the finest kind of intellectual hunger, a true scientist. I just wanted the peace and calm of looking. The same calm I'd found over the years in simple addition, in algebra, in calculus, in Boolean logic. In numbers, which were not double state but just themselves, no other set of integers or constants or fractals lying behind these ones, better and fuller and more fulfilled. Mathematics had its own arbitrary assumptions—but no shadows on the cave wall.

So I spent as long with Fran in front of the terminal as I could, and printed out the last batch of phase space diagrams and spent time with those, and went over our work yet again, and read Pyotr Solenski's work, and then I could no longer put off returning to the material world.


As soon as I walked into Introduction to Set Theory, my nausea returned.

Mid-October. Two more months of teaching this class, twice a week, ninety minutes a session, to keep my fellowship. I didn't know if I could do it. But without the fellowship, I couldn't work with Fran.

Thirty-two faces bobbed in front of me, with thirty-two shimmering ghostly behind them. Different. So different. Jim Mulcahy: a sullen slouching eighteen-year-old with acned face and resentful eyes, flunking out—and behind him, the quiet assured Jim, unhamstrung by whatever had caused that terrible resentfulness, whatever kept him from listening to me or studying the text. Jessica Harris: straight A's, thin face pinched by anxiety, thrown into panic whenever she didn't instantly comprehend some point—and behind her, the confident Jessica who could wait a minute, study the logic, take pleasure in her eventual mastery of it. Sixty-four faces, and sixty-four pieces of furniture in two rooms, and sometimes when I turned away to the two blackboards (my writing firm on the pristine surface, and quavery over dust-filled scratches), even turning away wasn't enough to clear my head.

"The students complain you don't look at them when you talk," my Department Chair had said. "And you don't make yourself available after class to deal with their problems."

He'd shimmered behind himself, a wise leader and an overworked bureaucrat.

Nobody had any questions. Nobody stayed after class. Nobody in the first thirty-four students had any comments on infinite sets, and the second thirty-four I couldn't hear, couldn't reach.

I left the classroom with a raging headache, and almost tripped over a student in the hall.

Chairs lined the corridor walls (water-stained plaster; lively-textured stucco) for students to wait for faculty, or each other, or enlightenment. One chair blocked fully a third of my doorway, apparently shifted there by the girl who sat, head down, drawing in a notebook. My headache was the awful kind that clouds vision. I banged my knee into a corner of the chair (graffiti on varnish on cheap pine; clean hand-stained hardwood). My vision cleared but my knee throbbed painfully.

"Do you *mind* not blocking the doorway, miss?"

"Sorry." She didn't look up, or stop drawing.

*"Please move the damned chair."*

She hitched it sideways, never raising her eyes from the paper. The chair banged along the hall floor, clanging onto my throbbing brain. Beside her, the other girl shrugged humorously, in charming self-deprecation.

I forced myself. "Are you waiting for me? To see about the class?"

"No." Still she didn't look up, rude even for a student. I pushed past her, and my eyes fell on her drawing paper.

It was full of numbers: a table for binomial distribution of coin-tossing probabilities, with $x$ as the probability of throwing $n$ heads, divided by the probability of throwing an equal number of heads and tails. The columns were neatly labeled. She was filling in the numbers as rapidly as her pen could write, to seven decimal places. From memory, or mental calculation?

I blurted, "Most people don't do that."

"Is that an observation, an insult, or a compliment?"

All I could see of both girls were the bent tops of their heads: lank dirty blonde, feathery golden waves.

She said, "Because if it's an observation, then consider that I said, 'I already know that.' "

The vertigo started to take me.

"If it's an insult, then I said, 'I'm not most people.' "

I put out one hand to steady myself against the wall.

"And if it's a compliment, I said, 'Thanks.' I guess."

The hallway pulsed. Students surged toward me, sixty-four of them, except that I was only supposed to teach thirty-two and they weren't the ones who really wanted to learn, they were warped and deformed versions of what they should have been and I couldn't teach them because I hated them too much. For not being what they could have. For throwing off my inner balance, the delicate metaphysical ear that co-ordinates reality with ideal with acceptance. For careening past the Feigenbaum number, into versions of themselves where attraction was replaced by turbulent chaos. . . . I fell heavily against the wall, gulping air.

"Hey!" The girl looked up. She had a scrawny, bony face with a too-wide mouth, and a delicate, fine-boned face with rosy generous lips. But mostly I saw her eyes. They looked at me with conventional concern, and then at the wall behind me, and then back at me, and shock ran over me like gasoline fire. The girl reached out an arm to steady me, but her gaze had already gone again past me, as mine did everywhere but in the mirror, inexorably drawn to what I had never seen: the other Jack shimmering behind me, the ideal self I was not.

"It affects you differently than me," Mia said over coffee in the student cafeteria. I'd agreed to go there only because it was nearly empty. "I don't get nauseated or light-headed. I just get mad. It's such a fucking *waste.*"

She sat across from me, and the other Mia sat behind her, green eyes hopeful in her lovely face. Hopeful that we could share this, that she was no longer alone, that I might be able to end her loneliness. The physical Mia didn't look hopeful. She looked just as furious as she said she was.

"Nine times out of ten, Jack, people could *become* their ideal selves, or at least a whole lot fucking closer, if they just tried. They're just too lazy or screwed up to put some backbone into it."

I looked away from her. "For me," I said hesitantly, "I guess it's mostly the unfairness of it that's such a burden. Seeing the ideal has interfered with every single thing I've ever wanted to do with my life." Except mathematics.

She squinted at me. " 'Unfairness'? So what? Just don't give into it."

"I think it's a little more complicated than—"

"It's not. In fact, it's real simple. Just do what you want, anyway. And don't whine."

"I'm not—"

"You are. Just don't let the double vision stop you from trying anything you want to. *I* don't." She glared belligerently. Behind her, the other Mia radiated determination tempered by acceptance.

"Mia, I do try to do the things I want. Math. My dissertation. Teaching." Not that I wanted to be doing that.

"Good," she snapped, and looked over my shoulder. "Double vision doesn't have to defeat us if we don't let it."

I said, "Have you ever found any others like us?" What did my ideal self look like? What strengths could she see on his face?

"No, you're the only one. I thought I was alone."

"Me, too. But if there's two of us, there could be more. Maybe we should—"

"Damn it, Jack, at least *look* at me when you're talking to me!"

Slowly my gaze moved back to her face. Her physical face. Her mouth gaped in anger; her eyes had narrowed to ugly slits. My gaze moved back.

"Stop it, you asshole! Stop it!"

"Don't call me names, Mia."

"Don't tell me what to do! You have no right to tell me what to do! You're no different from—"

I said, "Why would I look at *you* if I could look at her?"

She stood up so abruptly that her chair fell over. Then she was gone. I put my hands over my eyes, blotting out all sight. Of everything.


"What was this system before it started to diverge?" Fran said.

She held in her hands a phase space diagram I hadn't seen before. Her eyes sparkled. Even so, there was something heavy around her mouth, something that wasn't in the Fran behind her, and for a minute I was so startled I couldn't concentrate on the print-outs. The ideal Fran, too, looked different from the day before. Her skin glowed from within, almost too strongly, as if a flashlight burned behind its pale fine-grained surface.

"That was rhetorical, Jack. I know what the system was before it diverged—the equations are there on the desk. But this one looks different. See . . . here. . . ."

She pointed and explained. Nonlinear systems with points that start out very close together tend to diverge from each other, into chaos. But there was something odd about these particular diagrams: they were chaotic, as always around a strange attractor, but in non-patterns I hadn't seen before. I couldn't quite grasp the difference. Almost, but not quite.

I said, "Where are those original equations?"

"There. On that paper—no, that one."

"You're using *Arnfelser's Constant?* Why?"

"Look at the equations again."

I did, and this time I recognized them, even though subatomic particle physics is not my field. James Arnfelser had won the Nobel two years ago for his work on the behavior of electron/positron pairs during the first thirty seconds of the universe's life. Fran was mucking around with the chaos of creation.

I looked at the phase space diagrams again.

She said, "You can almost see it, can't you? Almost . . . see . . ."

"Fran!"

She had her hand to her midriff. "It's nothing, Jack. Just indigestion on top of muscle tension on top of sleeplessness. I was up all night on those equations."

"Sit down."

"No, I'm fine. Really I am." She smiled at me, and the skin around her eyes, a mass of fine wrinkles, stretched tauter. And behind her, the other Fran didn't smile. At all. She looked at me, and I had the insane idea that somehow, for the first time, she *saw* me.

It was the first time I'd ever seen them diverge.

"Fran, I want you to see a doctor."

"You're good to be so concerned. But I'm fine. Look, Jack, here on the diagram . . ."

Both Frans lit up with the precise pleasure of numbers. And I—out of cowardice, out of relief—let them.


". . . can't understand a thing in this fucking course."

The voice was low, male, the words distinct but the speaker not identifiable. I turned from writing equations on the board. Thirty-two/-sixty-four faces swam in front of me. "Did one of you say something?"

Silence. A few girls looked down at their notebooks. The rest of the students stared back at me, stony. I turned back to the board and wrote another half equation.

". . . fucking moron who couldn't teach a dog to piss." A different voice.

My hand, holding the chalk, shook. I went on writing.

". . . shouldn't be allowed in front of a classroom." This time, a girl.

I turned around again. My stomach churned. The students stared back at me. They were all in on this, or at least tacitly complicit.

I heard my voice shake. "If you have any complaints about how this course is being taught, you are advised to take them up with the Department Chair, or to express them on the course evaluation form distributed at the end of the semester. Meanwhile, we have additional work to cover." I turned back to the board.

". . . fucking prick who can't make anything clear."

My chalk stopped, in the middle of writing an integer. I couldn't make it move again. No matter how hard I concentrated, the chalk wouldn't complete the number.

". . . trying to make us flunk so *he* looks bigger."

Slowly I turned to face the class.

They sat in front of me, slumping or smirking or grinning inanely. Empty faces. Stupid faces. A few embarrassed faces. Fourth-rate minds, interested only in getting by, ugly gaping maws into which we were supposed to stuff the brilliance of Maxwell and Boltzmann and von Neumann and Russell and Arnfelser. So they could masticate it and spit it on the floor.

And behind them . . . behind them . . .

"Get out," I said.

One hundred twenty-eight eyes opened wide.

"You heard me!" I heard myself screaming. "Get out of my class-room! Get out of this university! You don't belong here, it's criminal that you're here, you none of you are worth the flame to set you on fire! Get out! You've diverged too far from what you . . . what you . . ."

A few boys in the front row sauntered out. A girl in the back started to cry. Then some of them were yelling at me, shrieking. Only the shrieking wasn't in my classroom, it was in the hall, down the hall, it was sirens and bells and outside the window, an Emergency Medical van, and they were carrying Fran out on a stretcher, her long-fingered hand dangling limply over the side, and nobody would listen to me ex-plain that the terrible thing was not that she wasn't moving but that lying on the stretcher so quietly were not two Frans, as there should have been, but only one. Only one.


I didn't go to the funeral.

I took Fran's last set of diagrams, and copied her files off her hard drive, and packed a bag. Before I checked into the Morningside Motel on Route 64, I left messages on Diane's answering machine, and the Department Chair's, and my landlady's.

"—*don't want to see you again. It's not your fault, but I mean it. I'm sorry.*"

"*I resign my teaching fellowship, and my status as a postdoc at this university.*"

"*My rent is paid through the end of the month. I will not be re-turning. Please pack my things and send them to my sister, COD, at this address. Thank you.*"

I bolted the motel door, unwrapped two bottles of Jack Daniels, and raised my glass to the mirror.

But no toast came. To *him*? Who would not have been doing this stupid melodramatic thing? Who would have seen Fran's death as the random event it was, and grieved it with courage and grace? Who would have figured out the best way to cope with his problems from a healthy sense of balance undestroyed by knowing exactly what he could never, ever, ever measure up to? I'd be damned if I'd drink to him.

"To Fran," I said, and downed it straight, and went on downing it straight until I couldn't see the other, better room lurking behind this one.

---

Even drunk, you dream.

I didn't know that. I'd expected the hangovers, and the throwing up, and the terrible, blessed blackouts. I'd expected the crying jag. And the emotional pain, like a dull drill. But I'd never been drunk for four days before. I'd thought that when I slept the pain would go away, into oblivion. I didn't know I'd dream.

I dreamed about numbers.

They swam in front of me, pounded the inside of my eyelids, chased me through dark and indistinct landscapes. They hunted me with knives and guns and fire. They hurt. I didn't wake screaming, or disoriented, but I did wake sweating, and in the middle of the night I hung over the toilet, puking, while numbers swam around me on the wavering, double floor. The numbers wouldn't go away. And neither would the thing I was trying to drink myself out of. No matter how drunk I got, the double vision stayed. Except for the equations, and they hurt just as much as the polished floor I couldn't touch, the cool sheets I couldn't feel, the competent Jack I couldn't be. Maybe the equations hurt more. They were Fran's.

*Take Arnfelser's constant. Plug it into a set of equations describing a nonlinear system. . . .*

*Phase space diagrams. Diverging, diverging, gone. A small difference in initial states and you get widely differing states, you get chaos. . . .*

*Take Arnfelser's constant. Use it as* r. *Let* x *equal . . .*

*A small difference in initial states. A Fran who diverged only a small amount, a Jack who . . .*

*Take Arnfelser's equation . . .*

I almost saw it. But not quite.

I wasn't good enough to see it. Only *he* was.

I poured another whiskey.

The knock on the door woke me. It sounded like a battering ram.

"Get out. I paid at the desk this morning. I don't want maid service!"

The shouting transferred the battering ram to my head, but the knocking ceased.

Someone started picking the lock.

I lay on the bed and watched, my anger mounting. The chain was on the door. But when the lock was picked, the door opened the length of the chain, and a hand inserted a pair of wirecutters. Two pairs of wire-cutters, physical and ideal. Four hands. I didn't even move. If the motel owner wanted me, he could have me. Or the cops. I had reached some sort of final decimal place—I simply didn't care.

The chain, cheap lightweight links, gave way, and the door opened. Mia walked in.

"Christ, Jack. Look at you."

I lay sprawled across the bed, and both Mias wrinkled their noses at the smell.

I said, even though it wasn't what I meant, "How the fuck did you get in here?"

"Well, didn't you *see* how I got in here? Weren't you even conscious?" She walked closer and went on staring at me, in soiled underwear, the empty bottle on the floor. Something moved behind their eyes.

"How did you find me?" It hurt to speak.

"Hacked your Visa account. You put this dump on it."

"Go away, Mia."

"When I'm good and ready. Jesus, look at you."

"So don't."

I tried to roll over, but couldn't, so I closed my eyes.

Mia said, "I didn't think you had it in you. No, I really didn't." Her tone was so stupid—such a mix of ignorance and some sort of stupid feminine idealization of macho asshole behavior—that I opened my eyes again. She was smiling.

"Get. Out. Now."

"Not till you tell me what this is all about. Is it Dr. Schraeder? They told me you two were pals."

Fran. The pain started again. And the numbers.

"That's it, isn't it, Jack? She was your friend, not just your advisor. I'm sorry."

I said, "She was the only person I ever met who was what she was supposed to be."

"Yeah? Well, then, I'm really sorry. I'm not what I'm supposed to be, I know. And you sure the hell aren't. Although, you know . . . you look closer to him this morning than you ever did on campus. More . . . real."

I couldn't shove her out the door, and I couldn't stop her talking, and I couldn't roll over without vomiting. So I brought my arm up and placed it across my eyes.

"Don't cry, Jack. Please don't cry."

"I'm not—"

"On second thought, do cry. Why the fuck *not?* Your friend is dead. Go ahead and cry, if you want to!" And she knelt beside me, despite what I must smell like and look like, and put her arms around me while, hating every second of it, I cried.

When I was done, I pushed her away. Drawing every fiber of my body into it, I hauled myself off the bed and toward the bathroom. My stomach churned and the rooms wavered. It took two hands to grope along the wall to the shower.

The water hit me, hard and cold and stinging. I stood under it until I was shivering, and it took that long to realize I still had my briefs on. Bending over to strip them off was torture. My toothbrush scraped raw the inside of my mouth, and the nerves in my brain. I didn't even care that when I staggered naked into the bedroom, Mia was still there.

She said, "Your body is closer to his than your face."

"Get out, Mia."

"I told you, when I'm ready. Jack, there aren't any more of us. At least not that I know of. Or that you do. We can't fight like this."

I groped in my overnight bag, untouched for four days, for fresh underwear. Mia seemed different than she had in the cafeteria: gentler, less abrasive, although she looked the same. I didn't care which—or who— she was.

"We need each other," Mia said, and now there was a touch of desperation in her voice. I didn't turn around.

"Jack—listen to me, at least. See me!"

"I see you," I said. "And I don't want to. Not you, not anybody. Get out, Mia."

"No."

"Have it your way."

I pulled on my clothes, gritted my teeth to get on my shoes, left them untied. I braced myself to push past her.

She stood in the exact center of the room, her hands dangling helplessly at her sides. Behind her the other Mia stood gracefully, her dropping body full of sorrow. But the physical Mia, face twisted in an ugly grimace, was the only one looking at me.

I stopped dead.

They always both looked at me. At the same time. Everybody's both: Mia, Diane, Fran, the department chair, my students. Where one looked, the other looked. Always.

Mia said, more subdued than I had ever heard her. "Please don't leave me alone with this, Jack. I . . . need you."

The other Mia looked across the room, not over my shoulder. Not at *him*. At . . . what?

From a small difference in initial states you get widely differing states with repeated iterations. Diverging, diverging, chaos . . . and somewhere in there, the strange attractor. The means to make sense of it.

And just like that, I saw the pattern in the phase space diagrams. I saw the equations.

"Jack? Jack!"

"Just let me . . . write them down. . . ."

But there wasn't any chance I'd forget them. They were there, so clear and obvious and perfect, exactly what Fran and I had been searching for.

Mia cried, "You can't just *leave!* We're the only two people like this!"

I finished scribbling the equations and straightened. My head ached, my stomach wanted to puke, my intestines prickled and squirmed. My eyes were so puffy I could barely see out of them. But I saw her, looking at me with her scared bravado, and I saw the other one, not looking at me at all. Diverging. She was right—we were the only two people like this, linked in our own chaotic system. And the states I could see were diverging.

"No," I got out, just before I had to go back into the bathroom. "There aren't two. Soon . . . only one of you."

She stared at me like I was crazy, all the time I was puking. And the other Jack was doing God knows what.

I didn't really care.

I haven't published the equations yet.

I will, of course. They're too important not to publish: proof that any physical system showing an ultradependence on initial conditions must have a strange attractor buried somewhere in its structure. The implications for understanding chaos are profound. But it's not easy to publish this kind of innovation when you no longer have even a post-doc position at a decent university. Even though Fran's name will go first on the article.

I may just put it out on the Internet. Without prior peer review, without copyright protection, without comment. Out onto the un-structured, shifting realities of the net. After all, I don't really need for-mal attention. I don't really want it.

I have what I wanted: relief. The other faces—other rooms, other buildings, other gardens—are receding from me now. I catch only glimpses of them out of the corner of my eye, diminished in size by the distance between us, and getting smaller all the time. Diverging toward their own strange attractors.

It's not the same for Mia. When she said at the Morningside Motel that I looked more like the ideal Jack than ever before, it wasn't a compliment to my unshaven frowziness. For her, the phase space diagrams are *converging*. She can barely discern the ideal separate from the physical now; the states are that close. She smiles at everyone. People are drawn to her as to a magnet; she treats them as if their real selves are their ideal ones.

For now.

The crucial characteristic about chaotic systems is that they change unpredictably. Not as unpredictably as before the Schraeder Equations, but still unpredictably. Once you fall into the area past the Feigenbaum number, states converge or diverge chaotically. Tomorrow Mia could see something else. Or I could.

I have no idea what the ideal Mia was looking at when she gazed across the motel room, away from both me and him. When you are not the shadow on the cave wall but the genuine ideal, what is the next state?

I don't want to know. But it doesn't matter whether or not I want it. If that state of life comes into being, then it does, and all we can do is chase it through the chaos of dens and labyrinths and underground caves, trying to pin it momentarily with numbers, as our states diverge from what we know toward something I cannot even imagine, and don't want to.

Although, of course, that, too, may change.

# MARGIN OF ERROR

*Some writers write long. Some writers write short. Each can learn
to do the opposite, usually, but often they find it no fun.*

*I naturally write medium. My favorite length is the novella.
Left to myself, I would write nothing but novellas, which give me
room to build an alternate reality but not so much room that I become lost and foundering in the terrain. However, I'm not always
left to myself. Economic imperatives dictate that, to survive, authors must write novels. Editors occasionally dictate that, to publish in a given forum, authors must write short-shorts.*

*Ellen Datlow, fiction editor of* Omni *magazine in its print in-
carnation, asked me for a story under two thousand words. I
grumbled, but Ellen stood firm. The result, "Margin of Error," is
2,200 words, which was the best I could squeeze it down to, even
though the entire story includes only one scene and three speaking
characters. Plus a frog. Had this been a regular story, I'm sure the
frog would have gotten at least one "Ribbit."*

PAULA CAME BACK IN A BLAZE OF GLORY, HER INSTITUTE UNIFORM WITH its pseudo-military medals crisp and bright, her spine straight as an engineered diamond-fiber rod. I heard her heels clicking on the sidewalk and I looked up from the bottom porch step, a child on my lap. Paula's face was genemod now, the blemishes gone, the skin fine-pored, the cheekbones chiseled under green eyes. But I would have known that face anywhere. No matter what she did to it.

"Karen?" Her voice held disbelief.

"Paula," I said.

"*Karen?*" This time I didn't answer. The child, my oldest, twisted in my arms to eye the visitor. The slight movement made the porch step creak.

It was the kind of neighborhood where women sat all morning on porches or stoops, watching children play on the sidewalk. Steps sagged; paint peeled; small front lawns were scraped bare by feet and tricycles and plastic wading pools. Women lived a few doors down from their mothers, both of them growing heavier every year. There were few men. The ones there were, didn't seem to stay long.

I said, "How did you find me?"

"It wasn't hard," Paula said, and I knew she didn't understand my smile. Of course it wasn't hard. I had never intended it should be. This was undoubtedly the first time in nearly five years that Paula had looked.

She lowered her perfect body gingerly onto the porch steps. My little girl, Lollie, gazed at her from my lap. Then Lollie opened her cupped hands and smiled. "See my frog, lady?"

"Very nice," Paula said. She was trying hard to hide her contempt, but I could see it. For the sad imprisoned frog, for Lollie's dirty face, for the worn yard, for the way I looked.

"Karen," Paula said, "I'm here because there's a problem. With the project. More specifically, with the initial formulas, we think. With portion of the nanoassembler code from five years ago, when you were . . . still with us."

"A problem," I repeated. Inside the house, a baby wailed. "Just a minute."

I set Lollie down and went inside. Lori cried in her crib. Her diaper reeked. I put a pacifier in her mouth and cradled her in my left arm. With the right arm I scooped Timmy from his crib. When he didn't wake, I jostled him a little. I carried both babies back to the porch, deposited Timmy in the portacrib, and sat down next to Paula.

"Lollie, go get me a diaper, honey. And wipes. You can carry your frog inside to get them."

Lollie went; she's a sweet-natured kid. Paula stared incredulously at the twins. I unwrapped Lori's diaper and Paula grimaced and slid farther away.

"Karen—are you listening to me? This is *important!*"

"I'm listening."

"The nanocomputer instructions are off, somehow. The major results check out, obviously—" *Obviously.* The media had spent five years exclaiming over the major results.

"—but there are some odd foldings in the proteins of the twelfth-generation nanoassemblers."

Twelfth generation. The nanocomputer attached to each assembler replicates itself every six months. That was one of the project's checks and balances on the margin of error. It had been five and a half years. Twelfth generation was about right.

"Also," Paula continued, and I heard the strain in her voice, "there are some unforeseen macro-level developments. We're not sure yet that they're tied to the nanocomputer protein folds. There might not be any connection. What we're trying to do now is cover all the variables."

"You must be working on fairly remote variables if you're reduced to asking me."

"Well, yes, we are. Karen, do you have to do that *now?*"

"Yes." I scraped the shit off Lori with one edge of the soiled diaper. Lollie danced out of the house with a clean one. She sat beside me, whispering to her frog.

Paula said, "What I need . . . what the project needs—"

I said, "Do you remember the summer we collected frogs? We were maybe eight and ten. You'd become fascinated reading about that experiment where they threw a frog in boiling water but it jumped out, and then they put a frog in cool water and gradually increased the temperature to boiling until the stupid frog just sat there and died. Remember?"

"Karen—"

"I collected sixteen frogs for you, and when I found out what you were going to do with them, I cried and tried to let them go. But you boiled eight of them anyway. The other eight were controls. I'll give you that—proper scientific method. To reduce the margin of error, you said."

"Karen—we were just kids . . ."

I put the clean diaper on Lori. "Not all kids behave like that. Lollie doesn't. But you wouldn't know that, would you? Nobody in your set has children. You should have had a baby, Paula."

She barely hid her shudder. But then, most of the people we knew felt the same way.

She said, "What the project needs is for you to come back and work on the same small area you did originally. Looking for something—anything—you might have missed in the protein-coded instructions to successive generations of nanoassemblers."

"No," I said.

"It's not really a matter of choice. The macro-level problems—I'll be frank, Karen. It looks like a new form of cancer, one nobody's ever seen. Unregulated replication of some very weird cells."

"So take the cellular nanomachinery out." I crumpled the stinking diaper and set it out of the baby's reach. Closer to Paula.

"You know we can't do that! The project's irreversible!"

"Many things are irreversible," I said. Lori started to fuss. I picked her up, opened my blouse, and gave her the breast. She sucked greedily. Paula glanced away. She has had nanomachinery in her perfect body, making it perfect, for five years now. Her breasts will never look swollen, blue-veined, sagging.

"Karen, listen—"

"No—you listen," I said quietly. "Eight years ago you convinced Zweigler I was only a minor member of the research team, included only because I was your sister. I've always wondered, by the way, how you did that—were you sleeping with him, too? Seven years ago you got me shunted off into the minor area of the project's effect on female gametes—which nobody cared about because it was already clear there was no way around sterility as a side effect. Nobody thought it was too high a price for a perfect, self-repairing body, did they? Except me."

Paula didn't answer. Lollie carried her frog to the wading pool and set it carefully in the water.

I said, "I didn't mind working on female gametes, even if it was a backwater, even if you got star billing. I was used to it, after all. As kids, you were always the cowboy; I got to be the horse. You were the astronaut, I was the alien you conquered. Remember? One Christmas you used up all the chemicals in your first chemistry set and then stole mine."

"I don't think trivial childhood incidents matter in—"

"Of course you don't. And I never minded. But I did mind when five years ago you made copies of all my notes and presented them as yours, while I was so sick during my pregnancy with Lollie. You claimed *my* work. Stole it. Just like the chemistry set. And then you eased me off the project."

"What you did was so minor—"

"If it was so minor, why are you here asking for my help now? And why would you imagine for half a second I'd give it to you?"

She stared at me, calculating. I stared back coolly. Paula wasn't used to me cool, I could see that. I'd always been the excitable one. Excitable, flighty, unstable—that's what she'd told Zweigler. A security risk.

Timmy fussed in his portacrib. I stood up, still nursing Lori, and scooped him up with my free arm. Back on the steps, I juggled Timmy to lie across Lori on my lap, pulled back my blouse, and gave him the other breast. This time Paula didn't permit herself a grimace.

She said, "Karen, what I did was wrong. I know that now. But for the sake of the project, not for me, you have to—"

"You *are* the project. You have been from the first moment you grabbed the headlines away from Zweigler and the others who gave their life to that work. 'Lovely Young Scientist Injects Self With Perfect-Cell Drug!' 'No Sacrifice Too Great To Circumvent FDA Shortsightedness, Heroic Researcher Declares.' "

Paula said flatly, "You're jealous. You're obscure and I'm famous. You're a mess and I'm beautiful. You're—"

"A milch cow? While you're a brilliant researcher? Then solve your own research problems."

"This was your area—"

"Oh, Paula, they were *all* my areas. I did more of the basic research than you did, and you know it. But you knew how to position yourself with Zweigler, to present key findings at key moments, to cultivate the right connections . . . all that stuff you do so well. And, of course, I was still under the delusion we were partners. I just didn't realize it was a barracuda partnering a goldfish."

From the wading pool Lollie watched us with big eyes. "Mommy . . ."

"It's okay, honey. Mommy's not mad at you. Look, better catch your frog—he's hopping away."

She shrieked happily and dove for the frog. Paula said softly, "I had no idea you were so angry after all this time. You've changed, Karen."

"But I'm not angry. Not any more. And you never knew what I was like before. You never bothered to know."

"I knew you never wanted a scientific life. Not the way I did. You always wanted kids. Wanted . . . *this.*" She waved her arm around the shabby yard. David left eighteen months ago. He sends money. It's never enough.

"I wanted a scientific establishment that would let me have both. And I wanted credit for my work. I wanted what was mine. How did you do it, Paula—end up with what was yours and what was mine, too?"

"Because you were distracted by babyshit and frogs!" Paula yelled, and for the first time I saw how scared she really was. Paula didn't make admissions like that. A tactical error. I watched her stab desperately for a way to regain the advantage. A way to seize the offensive.

I seized it first. "You should have left David alone. You already had Zweigler; you should have left me David. Our marriage was never the same after that."

She said, "I'm dying, Karen."

I turned my head from the nursing babies to look at her.

"It's true. My cellular machinery is running wild. Just in the last few months. The nanoassemblers are creating weird structures, destructive enzymes. For five years they replicated perfectly and now . . . for five years it all performed *exactly* as it was programmed to—"

I said, "It still is."

Paula sat very still. Lori had fallen asleep. I juggled her into the portacrib and nestled Timmy more comfortably on my lap. Lollie chased her frog around the wading pool. I squinted to see if Lollie's lips were blue; the weather was really too cool for her to be in the water very long.

Paula choked out, "You programmed the assembler machinery in the ovaries to—"

"Nobody much cares about women's ovaries. Only fourteen percent of college-educated women want to muck up their lives with kids. Recent survey result. Less than one percent margin of error."

"—you actually sabotaged . . . hundreds of women have been injected by now, maybe *thousands*—"

"Oh, there's a reverser enzyme," I said. "Completely effective if you take it before the twelfth-generation replication. You're the only person that's been injected that long. I just discovered the reverser a few months ago, tinkering with my old notes for something to do in what your friends probably call my idle domestic prison. That's provable, incidentally. All my notes are computer-dated."

Paula whispered, "Scientists don't *do* this—"

"Too bad you wouldn't let me be one."

"Karen—"

"Don't you want to know what the reverser is, Paula? It's engineered from human chorionic gonadotropin. The pregnancy hormone. Too bad you never wanted a baby."

She went on staring at me. Lollie shrieked and splashed with her frog. Her lips *were* turning blue. I stood up, laid Timmy next to Lori in the portacrib, and buttoned my blouse.

"You made an experimental error twenty-five years ago," I said to Paula. "Too small a sample population. Sometimes a frog jumps out."

I went to lift my daughter from the wading pool.

# FAULT LINES

*In the fall of 1994 I sublet an apartment in New York. That was
the season I became fascinated by New York City cops.*

*There was no reason for this. Writers take such fits, and the
best thing to do is go along and see if the fit leads anywhere. So for
a month I eavesdropped on cops, visited precinct stations, went to
lectures by police officers, searched out newspaper stories on the
NYPD. I discovered how cops referred to a precinct ("the Four-
six"), what percentage of New York cops are female (fourteen),
the amount of paperwork required to document one arrest (incredible), and what a "public service homicide" is (the Mob murder of a criminal that, in the opinion of police, the city would be
better off without anyway). In the newspapers I followed the
struggle between Mayor Giuliani and the police commissioner, between Internal Affairs and the Thirtieth Precinct, between drug
pushers and drug busters, who sometimes turned out to be the
same people. I don't read many detective novels; for me, this was
new territory. I was completely absorbed.*

*When the fit passed, as eventually such fits do, I was left with
a black leather NYPD jacket without the insignia, and this story.*

*If the truth shall kill them, let them die.*

—Immanuel Kant

THE FIRST DAY OF SCHOOL, WE HAD ASSAULT-WITH-INTENT IN MS. Kelly's room.

I was in my room next door, 136, laying down the law to 7C math. The usual first-day bullshit: turn in homework every day, take your assigned seat as soon as you walk in, don't bring a weapon or an abusive attitude into my classroom or you'll wish you'd never been born. The kids would ignore the first, do the others—for me anyway. Apparently not for Jenny Kelly.

"Mr. Shaunessy! Mr. Shaunessy! Come quick, they throwing chairs next door! The new teacher crying!" A pretty, tiny girl I recognized from last year: Lateesha Jefferson. Her round face glowed with excitement and satisfaction. A riot! Already! On the very first day!

I looked over my class slowly, penetratingly, letting my gaze linger on each upturned face. I took my time about it. Most kids dropped their eyes. Next door, something heavy hit the wall. I lowered my voice, so everybody had to strain to hear me.

"Nobody move while I'm gone. You all got that?"

Some heads nodded. Some kids stared back, uncertain but cool. A few boys smirked and I brought my unsmiling gaze to their faces until they stopped. Shouts filtered through the wall.

"Okay, Lateesha, tell Ms. Kelly I'm coming." She took off like a shot, grinning, Paul Revere in purple leggings and silver shoes.

I limped to the door and turned for a last look. My students all sat quietly, watching me. I saw Pedro Valesquez and Steven Cheung surreptiously scanning my jacket for the bulge of a service revolver that of course wasn't there. My reputation had become so inflated it rivaled the NYC budget. In the hall Lateesha screamed in a voice that could have deafened rock stars, "Mr. Shaunessy coming! You hos better stop!"

In 134, two eighth-grade girls grappled in the middle of the floor. For a wonder, neither seemed to be armed, not even with keys. One girl's nose streamed blood. The other's blouse was torn. Both screamed incoherently, nonstop, like stuck sirens. Kids raced around the room. A chair had apparently been hurled at the chalkboard, or at somebody once standing in front of the chalkboard; chair and board had both cracked. Jenny Kelly yelled and waved her arms. Lateesha was wrong; Ms. Kelly wasn't crying. But neither was she helping things a hell of a lot. A few kids on the perimeter of the chaos saw me and fell silent, curious to see what came next.

And then I saw Jeff Connors, leaning against the window wall, arms folded across his chest, and his expression as he watched the fighting girls told me everything I needed to know.

I took a huge breath, letting it fill my lungs. I bellowed at top volume, and with no facial expression whatsoever, "Freeze! Now!"

And everybody did.

The kids who didn't know me looked instantly for the gun and the backup. The kids who did know me grinned, stifled it, and nodded slightly. The two girls stopped pounding each other to twist toward the noise—my bellow had shivered the hanging fluorescents—which was time enough for me to limp across the floor, grab the girl on top, and haul her to her feet. She twisted to swing on me, thought better of it, and stood there, panting.

The girl on the floor whooped, leaped up, and tensed to slug the girl I held. But then she stopped. She didn't know me, but the scene had alerted her: nobody yelling anymore, the other wildcat quiet in my grip, nobody racing around the room. She glanced around, puzzled.

Jeff still leaned against the wall.

They expected me to say something. I said nothing, just stood there, impassive. Seconds dragged by. Fifteen, thirty, forty-five. To adults, that's a long time. To kids, it's forever. The adrenaline ebbs away.

A girl in the back row sat down at her desk.

Another followed.

Pretty soon they were all sitting down, quiet, not exactly intimidated but interested. This was different, and different was cool. Only the two girls were left, and Jeff Connors leaning on the window, and a small Chinese kid whose chair was probably the one hurled at the chalkboard. I saw that the crack ran right through words printed neatly in green marker:

Ms. Kelly
English 8E

After a minute, the Chinese kid without a chair sat on his desk.

Still I said nothing. Another minute dragged past. The kids were uneasy now. Lateesha said helpfully, "Them girls supposed to go to the nurse, Mr. Shaunessy. Each one by they own self."

I kept my grip on the girl with the torn blouse. The other girl, her nose gushing blood, suddenly started to cry. She jammed her fist against her mouth and ran out of the room.

I looked at each face, one at a time.

Eventually I released my grip on the second girl and nodded at Lateesha. "You go with her to the nurse."

Lateesha jumped up eagerly, a girl with a mission, the only one I'd spoken to. "You come on, honey," she said, and led away the second girl, clucking at her under her breath.

Now they were all eager for the limelight. Rosaria said quickly, "They fighting over Jeff, Mr. Shaunessy."

"No they ain't," said a big, muscled boy in the second row. He was scowling. "They fighting cause Jonelle, she dissed Lisa."

"No, they—"

Everybody had a version. They all jumped in, intellectuals with theories, arguing with each other until they saw I wasn't saying anything, wasn't trying to sort through it, wasn't going to participate. One by one, they fell silent again, curious.

Finally Jeff himself spoke. He looked at me with his absolutely open, earnest, guileless expression and said, "It was them suicides, Mr. Shaunessy."

The rest of the class looked slightly confused, but willing to go along with this. They knew Jeff. But now Ms. Kelly, excluded for five full minutes from her own classroom, jumped in. She was angry. *"What suicides?* What are you talking about, uh . . . ?"

Jeff didn't deign to supply his name. She was supposed to know it. He spoke directly to me. "Them old people. The ones who killed theirselves in that hospital this morning. And last week. In the newspaper."

I didn't react. Just waited.

"You know, Mr. Shaunessy," Jeff went on, in that same open, confiding tone. "Them old people shooting and hanging and pushing theirselves out of windows. At their age. In their sixties and seventies and eighties." He shook his head regretfully.

The other kids were nodding now, although I'd bet my pension none of them ever read anything in any newspaper.

"It just ain't no example to us," Jeff said regretfully. "If even the people who are getting three good meals a day and got people waiting on them and don't have to work or struggle no more with the man—if *they* give up, how we supposed to think there's anything in this here life for us?"

He leaned back against the window and grinned at me: triumphant, regretful, pleading, an inheritor of a world he hadn't made. His classmates glanced at each other sideways, glanced at me, and stopped grinning.

"A tragedy, that's what it is," Jeff said, shaking his head. "A tragedy. All them old people, deciding a whole life just don't make it worth it to stick to the rules. How *we* supposed to learn to behave?"

"You have to get control of Jeff Connors," I told Jenny Kelly at lunch in the faculty room. This was an exposed-pipes, flaking-plaster oasis in the basement of Benjamin Franklin Junior High. Teachers sat jammed together on folding metal chairs around brown Formica tables, drinking coffee and eating out of paper bags. Ms. Kelly had plopped down next to me and practically demanded advice. "That's actually not as hard as it might look. Jeff's a hustler, an operator, and the others follow him. But he's not uncontrollable."

"Easy for you to say," she retorted, surprising me. "They look at you and see the macho ex-cop who weighs what? Two-thirty? Who took out three criminals before you got shot, and has strong juice at Juvenile Hall. They look at me and see a five-foot-three, one-hundred-twenty-pound nobody they can all push around. Including Jeff."

"So don't let him," I said, wondering how she'd heard all the stories about me so fast. She'd only moved into the district four days ago.

She took a healthy bite of her cheese sandwich. Although she'd spent the first half of the lunch period in the ladies' room, I didn't see any tear marks. Maybe she fixed her makeup to cover tear stains. Margie used to do that. Up close Jenny Kelly looked older than I'd thought at first: twenty-eight, maybe thirty. Her looks weren't going to make it any easier to control a roomful of thirteen-year-old boys. She pushed her short blonde hair off her face and looked directly at me.

"Do you really carry a gun?"

"Of course not. Board of Education regs forbid any weapons by anybody on school property. You know that."

"The kids think you carry."

I shrugged.

"And you don't tell them otherwise."

I shrugged again.

"Okay, I can't do that either," she said. "But I'm not going to fail at this, Gene. I'm just not. You're a big success here, everybody says so. So tell me what I *can* do to keep enough control of my classes that I have a remote chance of actually teaching anybody anything."

I studied her, and revised my first opinion, which was that she'd be gone by the end of September. No tear stains, not fresh out of college, able to keep eating under stress. The verbal determination I discounted; I'd heard a lot of verbal determination from rookies when I was on the Force, and most of it melted away three months out of Police Academy. Even sooner in the City School District.

"You need to do two things," I said. "First, recognize that these kids can't do without connection to other human beings. Not for five minutes, not for one minute. They're starved for it. And to most of them, 'connection' means arguing, fighting, struggling, even abuse. It's what they're used to, and it's what they'll naturally create, because it feels better to them than existing alone in a social vacuum for even a minute. To compete with that, to get them to disengage from each other long enough to listen to you, you have to give them an equally strong connection to *you*. It doesn't have to be intimidation, or some bullshit fantasy about going up against the law. You can find your own way. But unless you're a strong presence—very strong, very distinctive—of one kind or another, they're going to ignore you and go back to connecting with each other."

"Connection," she said, thinking about it. "What about connecting to the material? English literature has some pretty exciting stuff in it, you know."

"I'll take your word for it. But no books are exciting to most of these kids. Not initially. They can only connect to the material through a person. They're that starved."

She took another bite of sandwich. "And the second thing?"

"I already told you. Get control of Jeff Connors. Immediately."

"Who is he? And what was all that bullshit about old people killing themselves?"

I said, "Didn't you see it on the news?"

"Of course I did. The police are investigating, aren't they? But what did it have to do with my classroom?"

"Nothing. It was a diversionary tactic. A cover-up."

"Of what?"

"Could be a lot of things. Jeff will use whatever he hears to confuse and mislead, and he hears everything. He's bright, unmotivated, a natural leader, and—unbelievably—not a gang member. You saw him— no big gold, no beeper. His police record is clean. So far, anyway."

Jenny said, "You worked with him a little last year."

"No, I didn't work with him. I controlled him in class, was all." She'd been asking about me.

"So if *you* didn't really connect with him, how do I?"

"I can't tell you that," I said, and we ate in silence for a few minutes. It didn't feel strained. She looked thoughtful, turning over what I'd told her. I wondered suddenly whether she'd have made a good cop. Her ears were small, I noticed, and pink, with tiny gold earrings in the shape of little shells.

She caught me looking, and smiled, and glanced at my left hand.

So whoever she'd asked about me hadn't told her everything. I gulped my last bite of sandwich, nodded, and went back to my room before 7H came thundering up the stairs, their day almost over, one more crazy period where Mr. Shaunessy actually expected them to pay attention to some weird math instead of their natural, intense, contentious absorption in each other.


Two more elderly people committed suicide, at the Angels of Mercy Nursing Home on Amsterdam Avenue.

I caught it on the news, while correcting 7H's first-day quiz to find out how much math they remembered from last year. They didn't remember squat. My shattered knee was propped up on the hassock beside the bones and burial tray of a Hungry Man Extra-Crispy Fried Chicken.

". . . identified as Giacomo della Francesca, 78, and Lydia Smith, 80. The two occupied rooms on the same floor, according to nursing home staff, and both had been in fairly good spirits. Mrs. Smith, a widow, threw herself from the roof of the eight-story building. Mr. della Francesca, who was found dead in his room, had apparently stabbed himself. The suicides follow very closely on similar deaths this morning at the Beth Israel Retirement Home on West End Avenue. However, Captain Michael Doyle, NYPD, warned against premature speculation about—"

I shifted my knee. This Captain Doyle must be getting nervous; this was the third pair of self-inflicted fatalities in nursing homes within ten days. Old people weren't usually susceptible to copycat suicides. Pretty soon the *Daily News* or the *Post* would decide that there was actually some nut running around Manhattan knocking off the elderly. Or that there was a medical conspiracy backed by Middle East terrorists and extraterrestrials. Whatever the tabloids chose, the NYPD would end up taking the blame.

Suddenly I knew, out of nowhere, that Margie was worse.

I got these flashes like that, out of nowhere, and I hated it. I never used to. I used to know things the way normal people know things, by seeing them or reading them or hearing them or reasoning them through. Ways that made sense. Now, for the last year, I get these flashes of knowing things some other way, thoughts just turning up in my mind, and the intuitions are mostly right. Mostly right, and nearly always bad.

This wasn't one of my nights to go to the hospital. But I flicked off the TV, limped to the trash to throw away my dinner tray, and picked up the cane I use when my leg has been under too much physical stress. The phone rang. I paused to listen to the answering machine, just in case it was Libby calling from Cornell to tell me about her first week of classes.

"Gene, this is Vince Romano." Pause. "Bucky." Pause. "I know it's been a long time."

I sat down slowly on the hassock.

"Listen, I was sorry to hear about Margie. I was going to . . . you were . . . it wasn't . . ." Despite myself, I had to grin. People didn't change. Bucky Romano never could locate a complete verb.

He finished floundering. ". . . to say how sorry I am. But that's not why I'm calling." Long pause. "I need to talk to you. It's important. Very important." Pause. "It's not about Father Healey again, or any of that old . . . something else entirely." Pause. "Very important, Gene. I can't . . . it isn't . . . you won't . . ." Pause. Then his voice changed, became stronger. "I can't do this alone, Gene."

Bucky had never been able to do anything alone. Not when we were six, not when we were eleven, not when we were seventeen, not when he was twenty-three and it wasn't any longer me but Father Healey

who decided what he did. Not when he was twenty-seven and it was
me again deciding for him, more unhappy about that than I'd ever
been about anything in my life until Margie's accident.

Bucky recited his phone number, but he didn't hang up. I could hear
him breathing. Suddenly I could almost see him, somewhere out there,
sitting with the receiver pressed so close to his mouth it would look like
he was trying to swallow it. Hoping against hope that I might pick up
the phone after all. Worrying the depths of his skinny frantic soul for
what words he could say to make me do that.

"Gene . . . it's about . . . I shouldn't say this, but after all you're
a . . . were a . . . it's about those elderly deaths." Pause. "I work at
Kelvin Pharmaceutical now." And then the click.

What the hell could anybody make of any of that?

I limped to the elevator and caught a cab to St. Clare's Hospital.


Margie *was* worse, although the only way I could tell was that there
was one more tube hooked to her than there'd been last night. She lay
in bed in the same position she'd lain in for eighteen months and seven
days: curled head to knees, splinter-thin arms bent at the elbows. She
weighed ninety-nine pounds. Gastrostomy and catheter tubes ran into
her, and now an IV drip on a pole as well. Her beautiful brown hair,
worn away a bit at the back of her head from constant contact with the
pillow, was dull. Its sheen, like her life, had faded deep inside its brittle shafts, unrecoverable.

"Hello, Margie. I'm back."

I eased myself into the chair, leg straight out in front of me.

"Libby hasn't called yet. First week of classes, schedule to straighten
out, old friends to see—you know how it is." Margie always had. I
could see her and Libby shopping the week before Libby's freshman
year, laughing over the Gap bags, quarreling over the price of something I'd buy either of them now, no matter what it cost. Anything.

"It's pretty cool out for September, sweetheart. But the leaves haven't
changed yet. I walked across the Park just yesterday—all still green.
Composing myself for today. Which wasn't too bad. It's going to be a
good school year, I think."

*Have a great year!* Margie always said to me on the first day of
school, as if the whole year would be compressed in that first six hours
and twenty minutes. For three years she'd said it, the three years since
I'd been retired from the Force and limped into a career as a junior-high
teacher. I remembered her standing at the door, half-dressed for her sec-

retarial job at Time Warner, her silk blouse stretched across those generous breasts, the slip showing underneath. *Have a great day! Have a great five minutes!*

"Last period 7H looks like a zoo, Margie. But when doesn't last period look like a zoo? They're revved up like Ferraris by then. But both algebra classes look good, and there's a girl in 7A whose transcript is incredible. I mean, we're talking future Westinghouse Talent winner here."

*Talk to her,* the doctor had said. *We don't know what coma patients can and cannot hear.* That had been a year and a half ago. Nobody ever said it to me now. But I couldn't stop.

"There's a new sacrificial lamb in the room next to mine, eighth-grade English. She had a cat fight in there today. But I don't know, she might have more grit than she looks. And guess who called. Bucky Romano. After all this time. Thirteen years. He wants me to give him a call. I'm not sure yet."

Her teeth gapped and stuck out. The anti-seizure medication in her gastrostomy bag made the gum tissue grow too much. It displaced her teeth.

"I finally bought curtains for the kitchen. Like Libby nagged me to. Although they'll probably have to wait until she comes home at Thanksgiving to get hung. Yellow. You'd like them."

Margie had never seen this kitchen. I could see her in the dining room of the house I'd sold, up on a chair hanging drapes, rubbing at a dirty spot on the window. . . .

"Gene?"

"Hi, Susan." The shift nurse looked as tired as I'd ever seen her. "What's this new tube in Margie?"

"Antibiotics. She was having a little trouble breathing, and an X-ray showed a slight pneumonia. It'll clear right up on medication. Gene, you have a phone call."

Something clutched in my chest. *Libby.* Ever since that '93 Lincoln had torn through a light on Lexington while Margie crossed with a bag of groceries, any phone call in an unexpected place does that to me. I limped to the nurses' station.

"Gene? This is Vince. Romano. Bucky."

"Bucky."

"I'm sorry to bother you at . . . I was so sorry to hear about Margie, I left a message on your machine but maybe you haven't been home to . . . Listen, I need to see you, Gene. It's important. Please."

"It's late, Bucky. I have to teach tomorrow. I teach now, at—"

"*Please.* You'll know why when I see you. I have to see you."

I closed my eyes. "Look, I'm pretty tired. Maybe another time."

"*Please,* Gene. Just for a few minutes. I can be at your place in fifteen minutes!"

Bucky had never minded begging. I remembered that, now. Suddenly I didn't want him to see where I lived, how I lived, without Margie. What I really wanted was to tell him "no." But I couldn't. I never had, not our whole lives, and I couldn't now—why not? I didn't know.

"All right, Bucky. A few minutes. I'll meet you in the lobby here at St. Clare's."

"Fifteen minutes. God, thanks, Gene. Thanks so much, I really appreciate it, I need to—"

"*Okay.*"

"See you soon."

He didn't mind begging, and he made people help him. Even Father Healey had found out that. Coming in to Bucky's life, and going out.


The lobby of St. Clare's never changed. Same scuffed green floor, slashed gray vinyl couches mended with wide tape, information-desk attendant who looked like he could have been a bouncer at Madison Square Garden. Maybe he had. Tired people yelled and whispered in Spanish, Greek, Korean, Chinese. Statues of the Madonna and St. Clare and the crucified Christ beamed a serenity as alien here as money.

Bucky and I grew up in next-door apartments in a neighborhood like this one, a few blocks from Our Lady of Perpetual Sorrows. That's how we defined our location: "two doors down from the crying Broad." We made our First Communion together, and our Confirmation, and Bucky was best man when I married Marge. But by that time he'd entered the seminary, and any irreverence about Our Lady had disappeared, along with all other traces of humor, humility, or humanity. Or so I thought then. Maybe I wasn't wrong. Even though he always made straight As in class, Bucky-as-priest-in-training was the same as Bucky-as-shortstop or Bucky-as-third-clarinet or Bucky-as-altar-boy: intense, committed, shortsightedly wrong.

He'd catch a high pop and drop it. He'd know "Claire de Lune" perfectly, and be half a beat behind. Teeth sticking out, skinny face furrowed in concentration, he'd bend over the altar rail and become so enraptured by whatever he saw there that he'd forget to make the responses. We boys would nudge each other and grin, and later howl at him in the parking lot.

But his decision to leave the priesthood wasn't a howler. It wasn't even a real decision. He vacillated for months, growing thinner and more stuttery, and finally he'd taken a bottle of pills and a half pint of vodka. Father Healey and I found him, and had his stomach pumped, and Father Healey tried to talk him back into the seminary and the saving grace of God. From his hospital bed Bucky had called me, stuttering in his panic, to come get him and take him home. He was terrified. Not of the hospital—of Father Healey.

And I had, coming straight from duty, secure in my shield and gun and Margie's love and my beautiful young daughter and my contempt for the weakling who needed a lapsed-Catholic cop to help him face an old priest in a worn-out religion. God, I'd been smug.

"Gene?" Bucky said. "Gene Shaunessy?"

I looked up at the faded lobby of St. Clare's.

"Hello, Bucky."

"God, you look . . . I can't . . . you haven't changed a bit!"

Then he started to cry.


I got him to a Greek place around the corner on Ninth. The dinner trade was mostly over and we sat at a table in the shadows, next to a dirty side window with a view of a brick alley, Bucky with his back to the door. Not that he cared if anybody saw him crying. I cared. I ordered two beers.

"Okay, what is it?"

He blew his nose and nodded gratefully. "Same old Gene. You always just . . . never any . . ."

"Bucky. What the fuck is wrong?"

He said, unexpectedly, "You hate this."

Over his shoulder, I eyed the door. Starting eighteen months ago, I'd had enough tears and drama to last me the rest of my life, although I wasn't going to tell Bucky that. If he didn't get it over with . . .

"I work at Kelvin Pharmaceuticals," Bucky said, suddenly calmer. "After I left the seminary, after Father Healey . . . you remember . . ."

"Go on," I said, more harshly than I'd intended. Father Healey and I had screamed at each other outside Bucky's door at St. Vincent's, while Bucky's stomach was being pumped. I'd said things I didn't want to remember.

"I went back to school. Took a B.S. in chemistry. Then a Ph.D. You and I, about that time of . . . I wanted to call you after you were shot but . . . I could have tried harder to find you earlier, I know . . . anyway. I went to work for Kelvin, in the research department. Liked it. I met Tommy. We live together."

He'd never said. But, then, he'd never had to. And there hadn't been very much saying anyway, not back then, and certainly not at Our Lady of Perpetual Sorrows.

"I liked the work at Kelvin. Like it. Liked it." He took a deep breath. "I worked on Camineur. You take it, don't you, Gene?"

I almost jumped out of my skin. "How'd you know that?"

He grinned. "Not by any medical record hacking. Calm down, it isn't . . . people can't tell. I just guessed, from the profile."

He meant *my* profile. Camineur is something called a neurotransmitter uptake-regulator. Unlike Prozac and the other antidepressants that were its ancestors, it fiddles not just with serotonin levels but also with norepinephrine and dopamine and a half dozen other brain chemicals. It was prescribed for me after Margie's accident. Non-addictive, no bad side effects, no dulling of the mind. Without it, I couldn't sleep, couldn't eat, couldn't concentrate. Couldn't stop wanting to kill somebody every time I walked into St. Clare's.

I had found myself in a gun shop on Avenue D, trigger-testing a nine-millimeter, which felt so light in my hand it floated. When I looked at the thoughts in my head, I went to see Margie's doctor.

Bucky said, quietly for once, "Camineur was designed to prevent violent ideation in people with strong but normally controlled violent impulses, whose control has broken down under severe life stress. It's often prescribed for cops. Also military careerists and doctors. Types with compensated paranoia restrained by strong moral strictures. Nobody told you that the Camineur generation of mood inhibitors was that specific?"

If they did, I hadn't been listening. I hadn't been listening to much in those months. But I heard Bucky now. His hesitations disappeared when he talked about his work.

"It's a good drug, Gene. You don't have to feel . . . there isn't anything shameful about taking it. It just restores the brain chemistry to whatever it was before the trauma."

I scowled, and gestured for two more beers.

"All right. I didn't mean to . . . There's been several generations of neural pharmaceuticals since then. And that's why I'm talking to you."

I sipped my second beer, and watched Bucky drain his.

"Three years ago we . . . there was a breakthrough in neuropharm research, really startling stuff, I won't go into the . . . We started a whole new line of development. I was on the team. Am. On the team."

I waited. Sudden raindrops, large and sparse, struck the dirty window.

"Since Camineur, we've narrowed down the effects of neuropharms spectacularly. I don't know how much you know about this, but the big neurological discovery in the last five years is that repeated intense emotion doesn't just alter the synaptic pathways in the brain. It actually changes your brain structure from the cellular level up. With any intense experience, new structures start to be built, and if the experience is repeated, they get reinforced. The physical changes can make you, say, more open to risk-taking, or calmer in the face of stress. Or the physical structures that get built can make it hard or even impossible to function normally, even if you're trying with all your will. In other words, your life literally makes you crazy."

He smiled. I said nothing.

"What we've learned is how to affect only those pathways created by depression, only those created by fear, only those created by narcissistic rage . . . we don't touch your memories. They're there. You can see them, in your mind, like billboards. But now you drive past them, not through them. In an emotional sense."

Bucky peered at me. I said, not gently, "So what pills do *you* take to drive past your memories?"

He laughed. "I don't." I stayed impassive but he said hastily anyway, "Not that people who do are . . . it isn't a sign of weakness to take neuropharms, Gene. Or a sign of strength not to. I just . . . it isn't . . . I was waiting, was all. I was waiting."

"For what? Your prince to come?" I was still angry.

He said simply, "Yes."

Slowly I lowered my beer. But Bucky returned to his background intelligence.

"This drug my team is working on now . . . the next step was to go beyond just closing down negative pathways. Take, as just one example, serotonin. Some researcher said . . . there's one theory that serotonin, especially, is like cops. Having enough of it in your cerebral chemistry keep riots and looting and assault in the brain from getting out of control. But just holding down crime doesn't, all by itself, create prosperity or happiness. Or joy. For that, you need a new class of neuropharms that create positive pathways. Or at least strengthen those that are already there."

"Cocaine," I said. "Speed. Gin and tonic."

"No, no. Not a rush of power. Not a temporary high. Not temporary at all, and not isolating. The neural pathways that make people feel . . . the ones that let you . . ." He leaned toward me, elbows on the table. "Weren't there moments, Gene, when you felt so close to Margie it was like you crawled inside her skin for a minute? Like you *were* Margie?"

I looked at the window. Raindrops slid slowly down the dirty glass, streaking it dirtier. In the alley, a homeless prowled the garbage cans. "What's this got to do with the elderly suicides? If you have a point to make, make it."

"They weren't suicides. They were murders."

"Murders? Some psycho knocking off old people? What makes you think so?"

"Not some psycho. And I don't think so. I *know*."

"How?"

"All eight elderlies were taking J-24. That's the Kelvin code name for the neuropharm that ends situational isolation. It was a clinical trial."

I studied Bucky, whose eyes burned with Bucky light: intense, pleading, determined, inept. And something else, something that hadn't been there in the old days. "Bucky, that makes no sense. The NYPD isn't perfect, God knows, but they can tell the difference between suicide and murder. And anyway, the suicide rate rises naturally among old people, they get depressed—" I stopped. He had to already know this.

"That's just it!" Bucky cried, and an old Greek couple at a table halfway across the room turned to stare at him. He lowered his voice. "The elderly in the clinical trial *weren't* depressed. They were very carefully screened for it. No psychological, chemical, or social markers for depression. These were the . . . when you see old people in travel ads, doing things, full of life and health, playing tennis and dancing by candlelight . . . the team psychologists looked for our clinical subjects very carefully. *None* of them was depressed!"

"So maybe your pill made them depressed. Enough to kill themselves."

"No! No! J-24 couldn't . . . there wasn't any . . . it didn't make them depressed. I saw it." He hesitated. "And besides . . ."

"Besides what?"

He looked out at the alley. A waiter pushed a trolley of dirty dishes past our table. When Bucky spoke again, his voice sounded odd.

"I gave five intense years to J-24 and the research that led to it,

Gene. Days, evenings, weekends—eighty hours a week in the lab. Every minute until I met Tommy, and maybe too much time even after that. I know everything that the Kelvin team leaders know, everything that *can* be known about that drug's projected interaction with existing neurotransmitters. J-24 was my life."

As the Church had once been. Bucky couldn't do anything by halves. I wondered just what his position on "the team" had actually been.

He said, "We designed J-24 to combat the isolation that even normal, healthy people feel with age. You get old. Your friends die. Your mate dies. Your children live in another state, with lives of their own. All the connections you built up over decades are gone, and in healthy people, those connections created very thick, specific, strong neural structures. Any new friends you make in a nursing home or retirement community—there just aren't the years left to duplicate the strength of those neural pathways. Even when outgoing, undepressed, risk-taking elderlies try."

I didn't say anything.

"J-24 was specific to the neurochemistry of connection. You took it in the presence of someone else, and it opened the two of you up to each other, made it possible to genuinely—*genuinely*, at the permanent chemical level—imprint on each other."

"You created an *aphrodisiac for geezers?*"

"No," he said, irritated. "Sex had nothing to do with it. Those impulses originate in the limbic system. This was . . . emotional bonding. Of the most intense, long-term type. Don't tell me all you ever felt for Margie was sex!"

After a minute he said, "I'm sorry."

"Finish your story."

"It *is* finished. We gave the drug to four sets of volunteers, all people who had long-term terminal diseases but weren't depressed, people who were willing to take risks in order to enhance the quality of their own perceptions in the time left. I was there observing when they took it. They bonded like baby ducks imprinting on the first moving objects they see. No, not like that. More like . . . like . . ." He looked over my shoulder, at the wall, and his eyes filled with water. I glanced around to make sure nobody could see.

"Giacomo della Francesca and Lydia Smith took J-24 together almost a month ago. They were transformed by this incredible joy in each other. In knowing each other. Not each other's memories, but each other's . . . souls. They talked, and held hands, and you could just feel that they were completely open to each other, without all the psychological defenses we use to keep ourselves walled off. They knew each other. They almost *were* each other."

I was embarrassed by the look on his face. "But they didn't know each other like that, Bucky. It was just an illusion."

"No. It wasn't. Look, what happens when you connect with someone, share something intense with them?"

I didn't want to have this conversation. But Bucky didn't really need me to answer; he rolled on all by himself, unstoppable.

"What happens when you connect is that you exhibit greater risk taking, with fewer inhibitions. You exhibit greater empathy, greater attention, greater receptivity to what is being said, greater pleasure. And *all* of those responses are neurochemical, which in turn create, reinforce, or diminish physical structures in the brain. J-24 just reverses the process. Instead of the experience causing the neurochemical response, J-24 supplies the physical changes that create the experience. And that's not all. The drug boosts the *rate* of structural change, so that every touch, every word exchanged, every emotional response, reinforces neural pathways one or two hundred times as much as a normal life encounter."

I wasn't sure how much of this I believed. "And so you say you gave it to four old couples . . . does it only work on men and women?"

A strange look passed swiftly over his face: secretive, almost pained. I remembered Tommy. "That's all who have tried it so far. Can you . . . have you ever thought about what it would be like to be really merged, to know him, to be him—think of it, Gene! I could—"

"I don't want to hear about that," I said harshly. Libby would hate that answer. My liberal, tolerant daughter. But I'd been a cop. Lingering homophobia went with the territory, even if I wasn't exactly proud of it. Whatever Bucky's fantasies were about him and Tommy, I didn't want to know.

Bucky didn't look offended. "All right. But just imagine—an end to the terrible isolation that we live in our whole tiny lives. . . ." He looked at the raindrops sliding down the window.

"And you think somebody murdered those elderly for that? Who? Why?"

"I don't know."

"Bucky. Think. This doesn't make any sense. A drug company creates a . . . what did you call it? A neuropharm. They get it into clinical trials, under FDA supervision—"

"No," Bucky said.

I stared at him.

"It would have taken years. Maybe decades. It's too radical a departure. So Kelvin—"

"You knew there was no approval."

"Yes. But I thought . . . I never thought . . ." He looked at me, and suddenly I had another one of those unlogical flashes, and I saw that there was more wrong here even than Bucky was telling me. He believed that he'd participated, in whatever small way, in creating a drug that had led someone to murder eight old people. Never mind if it was true—Bucky believed it. He believed this same company was covering its collective ass by calling the deaths depressive suicides, when they could not have been suicides. And yet Bucky sat in front of me without chewing his nails to the knuckles, or pulling out his hair, or hating himself. Bucky, to whom guilt was the staff of life.

I'd seen him try to kill himself over leaving the Church. I'd watched him go through agonies of guilt over ignoring answering-machine messages from Father Healey. Hell, I'd watched him shake and cry because at ten years old we'd stolen three apples from a market on Columbus Avenue. Yet there he sat, disturbed but coherent. For Bucky, even serene. Believing he'd contributed to murder.

I said, "What neuropharms do you take, Bucky?"

"I told you. None."

"None at all."

"No." His brown eyes were completely honest. "Gene, I want you to find out how these clinical subjects really died. You have access to NYPD records—"

"Not any more."

"But you know people. And cases get buried there all the time, you used to tell me that yourself, with enough money you can buy yourself an investigation unless somebody high up in the city is really out to get you. Kelvin Pharmaceuticals doesn't have those kinds of enemies. They're not the Mob. They're just . . ."

"Committing murder to cover up an illegal drug trial? I don't buy it, Bucky."

"Then find out what *really* happened."

I shot back, "What do you think happened?"

"I don't know! But I do know this drug is a good thing! Don't you understand, it holds out the possibility of a perfect, totally open connection with the person you love most in the world. . . . Find out what happened, Gene. It wasn't suicide. J-24 doesn't cause depression. I *know* it. And for this drug to be denied people would be . . . it would be a sin."

He said it so simply, so naturally, that I was thrown all over again. This wasn't Bucky, as I had known him. Or maybe it was. He was still driven by sin and love.

I stood and put money on the table. "I don't want to get involved in this, Bucky. I really don't. But—one thing more—"

"Yeah?"

"Camineur. Can it . . . does it account for . . ." Jesus, I sounded like him. "I get these flashes of intuition about things I haven't been thinking about. Sometimes it's stuff I didn't know."

He nodded. "You knew the stuff before. You just didn't know you knew. Camineur strengthens intuitive right-brain pathways. As an effect of releasing the stranglehold of violent thoughts. You're more distanced from compulsive thoughts of destruction, but also more likely to make connections among various non-violent perceptions. You're just more intuitive, Gene, now that you're less driven."

*And I'm less Gene,* my unwelcome intuition said. I gazed down at Bucky, sitting there with his skinny fingers splayed on the table, an unBucky-like serenity weirdly mixed with his manic manner and his belief that he worked for a corporation that had murdered eight people. Who the hell was *he?*

"I don't want to get involved in this," I repeated.

"But you will," Bucky said, and in his words I heard utter, unshakable faith.


Jenny Kelly said, "I set up a conference with Jeff Connors and he never showed." It was Friday afternoon. She had deep circles around her eyes. Raccoon eyes, we called them. They were the badge of teachers who were new, dedicated, or crazy. Who sat up until 1:00 A.M. in a frenzy of lesson planning and paper correcting, and then arrived at school at 6:30 to supervise track or meet with students or correct more papers.

"Set up another conference," I suggested. "Sometimes by the third or fourth missed appointment, guilt drives them to show up."

She nodded. "Okay. Meanwhile, Jeff has my class all worked up over something called the Neighborhood Safety Information Network, where they're supposed to inform on their friends' brothers' drug activity, or something. It's somehow connected to getting their Social Services checks. It's got the kids all in an uproar. . . . I sent seventeen kids to the principal in three days."

"You might want to ease up on that, Jenny. It gives everybody—kids and administration—the idea that you can't control your own classroom."

"I can't," she said, so promptly and honestly that I had to smile. "But I *will*."

"Well, good luck."

"Listen, Gene, I'm picking the brains of everybody I can get to talk to me about this. Want to go have a cup of coffee someplace?"

"Sorry."

"Okay." She didn't look rebuffed, which was a relief. Today her earrings matched the color of her sweater. A soft blue, with lace at the neck. "Maybe another time."

"Maybe." It was easier than an outright no.

Crossing the parking lot to my car, I saw Jeff Connors. He slapped me a high-five. "Ms. Kelly's looking for you, Jeff."

"She is? Oh, yeah. Well, I can't today. Busy."

"So I hear. There isn't any such thing as the Neighborhood Safety Information Network, is there?"

He eyed me carefully. "Sure there is, Mr. S."

"Really? Well, I'm going to be at Midtown South station house this afternoon. I'll ask about it."

"It's, like, kinda new. They maybe don't know nothing about it yet."

"Ah. Well, I'll ask anyway. See you around, Jeff."

"Hang loose."

He watched my car all the way down the block, until I turned the corner.

The arrest room at Midtown South was full of cops filling out forms: fingerprint cards, On-line Booking System Arrest Worksheets, complaint reports, property invoices, requests for laboratory examinations of evidence, Arrest Documentation Checklists. The cops, most of whom had changed out of uniform, scribbled and muttered and sharpened pencils. In the holding pen alleged criminals cursed and slept and muttered and sang. It looked like fourth-period study hall in the junior high cafeteria.

I said, "Lieutenant Fermato?"

A scribbling cop in a Looney Tunes sweatshirt waved me toward an office without even looking up.

"Oh my God. Gene Shaunessy. Risen from the fuckin' dead."

"Hello, Johnny."

"Come *in*. God, you look like a politician. Teaching must be the soft life."

"Better to put on a few pounds than look like a starved rat."

We stood there clasping hands, looking at each other, not saying the things that didn't need saying anyway, even if we'd had the words, which we didn't. Johnny and I had been partners for seven years. We'd gone together through foot pursuits and high-speed chases and lost files and violent domestics and bungled traps by Internal Affairs and robberies-in-progress and the grueling boredom of the street. Johnny's divorce. My retirement. Johnny had gone into Narcotics a year before I took the hit that shattered my knee. If he'd been my partner, it might not have happened. He'd made lieutenant only a few months ago. I hadn't seen him in a year and a half.

Suddenly I knew—or the Camineur knew—why I'd come to Midtown South to help Bucky after all. I'd already lost too many pieces of my life. Not the life I had now—the life I'd had once. My real one.

"Gene—about Marge . . ."

I held up my hand. "Don't. I'm here about something else. Professional."

His voice changed. "You in trouble?"

"No. A friend is." Johnny didn't know Bucky; they'd been separate pieces of my old life. I couldn't picture them in the same room together for more than five minutes. "It's about the suicides at the Angels of Mercy Nursing Home. Giacomo della Francesca and Lydia Smith."

Johnny nodded. "What about it?"

"I'd like to see a copy of the initial crime-scene report."

Johnny looked at me steadily. But all he said was, "Not my jurisdiction, Gene."

I looked back. If Johnny didn't want to get me the report, he wouldn't. But either way, he *could*. Johnny'd been the best undercover cop in Manhattan, mostly because he was so good at putting together his net of criminal informers, inside favors, noncriminal spies, and unseen procedures. I didn't believe he'd dismantled any of it just because he'd come in off the street. Not Johnny.

"Is it important?"

I said, "It's important."

"All right," he said, and that was all that had to be said. I asked him instead about the Neighborhood Safety Information Network.

"We heard about that one," Johnny said. "Pure lies, but somebody's using it to stir up a lot of anti-cop crap as a set up for something or other. We're watching it."

"Watches run down," I said, because it was an old joke between us, and Johnny laughed. Then we talked about old times, and Libby, and his two boys, and when I left, the same cops were filling out the same forms and the same perps were still sleeping or cursing or singing, nobody looking at each other in the whole damn place.

By the next week, the elderly suicides had disappeared from the papers, which had moved on to another batch of mayhem and alleged brutality in the three-oh. Jenny Kelly had two more fights in her classroom. One I heard through the wall and broke up myself. The other Lateesha told me about in the parking lot. "That boy, Mr. Shaunessy, that Richie Tang, he call Ms. Kelly an ugly bitch! He say she be sorry for messing with *him!*"

"And then what?" I said, reluctantly.

Lateesha smiled. "Ms. Kelly, she yell back that Richie might act like a lost cause but he ain't lost to *her,* and she be damned if anybody gonna talk to her that way. But Richie just smile and walk out. Ms. Kelly, she be gone by Thanksgiving."

"Not necessarily," I said. "Sometimes people surprise you."

"Not me, they don't."

"Maybe even you, Lateesha."

Jenny Kelly's eyes wore permanent rings: sleeplessness, anger, smudged mascara. In the faculty room she sat hunched over her coffee, scribbling furiously with red pen on student compositions. I found myself choosing a different table.

"Hi, Gene," Bucky's voice said on my answering machine. "Please call if you . . . I wondered whether you found out any . . . give me a call. Please. I have a different phone number, I'll give it to you." Pause. "I've moved."

I didn't call him back. Something in the "I've moved" hinted at more pain, more complications, another chapter in Bucky's messy internal drama. I decided to call him only if I heard something from Johnny Fermato.

Who phoned me the following Tuesday, eight days after my visit to Midtown South. "Gene. John Fermato."

"Hey, Johnny."

"I'm calling to follow through on our conversation last week. I'm afraid the information you requested is unavailable."

I stood in my miniscule kitchen, listening to the traffic three stories below, listening to Johnny's cold formality. "Unavailable?"

"Yes. I'm sorry."

"You mean the file has disappeared? Been replaced by a later version? Somebody's sitting on it?"

"I'm sorry, the information you requested isn't available."

"Right," I said, without expression.

"Catch you soon."

"Bye, Lieutenant."

After he hung up I stood there holding the receiver, surprised at how much it hurt. It was a full five minutes before the anger came. And then it was distant, muffled. Filtered through the Camineur, so that it wouldn't get out of hand.

Safe.

Jeff Connors showed up at school after a three-day absence, wearing a beeper, and a necklace of thick gold links.

"Jeff, he big now," Lateesha told me, and turned away, lips pursed like the disapproving mother she would someday be.

I was patrolling the hall before the first bell when Jenny Kelly strode past me and stopped at the door to the boys' room, which wasn't really a door but a turning that hid the urinals and stalls from obvious view. The door itself had been removed after the fifth wastebasket fire in two days. Jeff came around the corner, saw Ms. Kelly, and stopped. I could see he was thinking about retreating again, but her voice didn't let him. "I want to see you, Jeff. In my free period." Her voice said he would be there.

"Okay," Jeff said, with no hustle, and slouched off, beeper riding on his hip.

I said to her, "He knows when your free period is."

She looked at me coolly. "Yes."

"So you've gotten him to talk to you."

"A little." Still cool. "His mother disappeared for three days. She uses. She's back now, but Jeff doesn't trust her to take care of his little brother. Did you even know he had a little brother, Gene?"

I shook my head.

"Why not?" She looked like Lateesha. Disapproving mother. The raccoon eyes were etched deeper. "This boy is in trouble, and he's one we don't have to lose. We can still save him. *You* could have, last year. He admires you. But you never gave him the time of day, beyond making sure he wasn't any trouble to *you*."

"I don't think you have the right to judge whether—"

"Don't I? Maybe not. I'm sorry. But don't you see, Jeff only wanted from you—"

"That's the bell. Good luck today, Ms. Kelly."

She stared at me, then gave a little laugh. "Right. And where were you when the glaciers melted? Never mind." She walked into her classroom, which diminished in noise only a fraction of a decibel.

Her earrings were little silver hoops, and her silky blouse was red.

After school I drove to the Angels of Mercy Nursing Home and pretended I was interested in finding a place for my aging mother. A woman named Karen Gennaro showed me a dining hall, bedrooms, activity rooms, a little garden deep in marigolds and asters, nursing facilities. Old people peacefully played cards, watched TV, sat by sunshiny windows. There was no sign that eighty-year-old Lydia Smith had thrown herself from the roof, or that her J-24-bonded boyfriend Giacomo della Francesco had stabbed himself to death.

"I'd like to walk around a little by myself now," I told Ms. Gennaro. "Just sort of get the feel of the place. My mother is . . . particular."

She hesitated. "We don't usually allow—"

"Mom didn't like Green Meadows because too many corridors were painted pale blue and she hates pale blue. She rejected Saint Anne's because the other women didn't care enough about their hairdos and so the atmosphere wasn't self-respecting. She wouldn't visit Havenview because there was no piano in the dining room. This is the tenth place I've reported on."

She laughed. "No wonder you sound so weary. All right, just check out with me before you leave."

I inspected the day room again, chatting idly with a man watching the weather channel. Then I wandered to the sixth floor, where Lydia Smith and Giacamo della Francesca had lived. I chatted with an elderly man in a wheelchair, and a sixteen-year-old Catholic Youth volunteer, and a Mrs. Locurzio, who had the room on the other side of Lydia Smith's. Nothing.

A janitor came by mopping floors, a heavy young man with watery blue eyes and a sweet, puzzled face like a bearded child.

"Excuse me—have you worked here long?"

"Four years." He leaned on his mop, friendly and shy.

"Then you must come to know the patients pretty well."

"Pretty well." He smiled. "They're nice to me."

I listened to his careful, spaced speech, a little thick on each initial consonant. "Are all of them nice to you?"

"Some are mean. Because they're sick and they hurt."

"Mrs. Smith was always nice to you."

"Oh, yes. A nice lady. She talked to me every day." His doughy face became more puzzled. "She died."

"Yes. She was unhappy with her life."

He frowned. "Mrs. Smith was unhappy? But she . . . no. She was happy." He looked at me in appeal. "She was *always* happy. Aren't you her friend?"

"Yes," I said. "I just made a mistake about her being unhappy."

"She was *always* happy. With Mr. Frank. They laughed and laughed and read books."

"Mr. della Francesca."

"He said I could call him Mr. Frank."

I said, "What's your name?"

"Pete," he said, as if I should know it.

"Oh, you're Pete! Yes, Mrs. Smith spoke to me about you. Just before she died. She said you were nice, too."

He beamed. "She was my friend."

"You were sad when she died, Pete."

"I was sad when she died."

I said, "What exactly happened?"

His face changed. He picked up the mop, thrust it into the rolling bucket. "Nothing."

"Nothing? But Mrs. Smith is dead."

"I gotta go now." He started to roll the bucket across the half-mopped floor, but I placed a firm hand on his arm. There's a cop intuition that has nothing to do with neuropharms.

I said, "Some bad people killed Mrs. Smith."

He looked at me, and something shifted behind his pale blue gaze.

"They didn't tell you that, I know. They said Mrs. Smith killed herself. But you know she was very happy and didn't do that, don't you. What did you see, Pete?"

He was scared now. Once, a long time ago, I hated myself for doing this to people like Pete. Then I got so I didn't think about it. It didn't bother me now, either.

"Mrs. Gennaro killed Mrs. Smith," I said.

Shock wiped out fear. "No, she didn't! She's a nice lady!"

"I say Mrs. Gennaro and the doctor killed Mrs. Smith."

"You're crazy! You're an asshole! Take it back!"

"Mrs. Gennaro and the doctor—"

"Mrs. Smith and Mr. Frank was all alone together when they went up to that roof!"

I said swiftly, "How do you know?"

But he was panicked now, genuinely terrified. Not of me—of what he'd said. He opened his mouth to scream. I said, "Don't worry, Pete. I'm a cop. I work with the cops you talked to before. They just sent me to double check your story. I work with the same cops you told before."

"With Officer Camp?"

"That's right," I said. "With Officer Camp."

"Oh." He still looked scared. "I told them already! I told them I unlocked the roof door for Mrs. Smith and Mr. Frank like they asked me to!"

"Pete—"

"I gotta go!"

"Go ahead, Pete. You did good."

He scurried off. I left the building before he could find Karen Gennaro.

A call to an old friend at Records turned up an Officer Joseph Camphausen at Midtown South, a Ralph Campogiani in the Queens Robbery Squad, a Bruce Campinella at the two-four, and a detective second grade Joyce Campolieto in Intelligence. I guessed Campinella, but it didn't matter which one Pete had talked to, or that I wouldn't get another chance inside Angels of Mercy. I headed for West End Avenue.

The sun was setting. Manhattan was filled with river light. I drove up the West Side Highway with the window down, and remembered how much Margie had liked to do that, even in the winter. *Real air, Gene. Chilled like good beer.*

Nobody at the Beth Israel Retirement Home would talk to me about the two old people who died there, Samuel Fetterolf and Rose Kaplan. Nor would they let me wander around loose. After my carefully guided tour, I went to the Chinese restaurant across the street and waited.

From every street-side window in Beth Israel I'd seen them head in here: well-dressed men and women visiting their parents and aunts and grandmothers after work. They'd stay an hour, and then they'd be too hungry to go home and cook, or maybe too demoralized to go home without a drink, a steady stream of overscheduled people dutifully keeping up connections with their old. I chose a table in the bar section, ordered, and ate slowly. It took a huge plate of moo goo gai pan and three club sodas before I heard it.

"How can you *say* that? She's not senile, Brad! She knows whether her friends are suicidal or not!"

"I didn't say she—"

"Yes, you did! You said we can't trust her perceptions! She's only old, not stupid!" Fierce thrust of chopsticks into her sweet and sour. She was about thirty, slim and tanned, her dark hair cut short. Preppy shirt and sweater. He wasn't holding up as well, the paunch and bald spot well underway, the beleaguered husband look not yet turned resentful.

"Joanne, I only said—"

"You said we should just discount what Grams said and leave her there, *even though* she's so scared. You always discount what she says!"

"I don't. I just—"

"Like about that thing at Passover. What Grams wanted was completely reasonable, and you just—"

"Excuse me," I said, before they drifted any more. The thing at Passover wouldn't do me any good. "I'm sorry, but I couldn't help overhear. I have a grandmother in Beth Israel, too, and I'm a little worried about her, otherwise I wouldn't interrupt, it's just that . . . my grandmother is scared to stay there, too."

They inspected me unsmilingly, saying nothing.

"I don't know what to do," I said desperately. "She's never been like this."

"I'm sorry," Brad said stiffly, "we can't help."

"Oh, I understand. Strangers. I just thought . . . you said something about your grandmother being frightened. . . . I'm sorry." I got up to leave, projecting embarrassment.

"Wait a minute," Joanne said. "What did you say your name was?"

"Aaron Sanderson."

"Joanne, I don't think—"

"Brad, if he has the same problem as—Mr. Sanderson, what is your grandmother afraid of? Is she usually nervous?"

"No, that's just it," I said, moving closer to their table. Brad frowned at me. "She's never nervous or jittery, and never depressed. She's fantastic, actually. But ever since those two residents died . . ."

"Well, that's just *it,*" Joanne said. Brad sighed and shifted his weight. "Grams was friendly with Mrs. Kaplan, and she told me Mrs. Kaplan would never in a million years commit suicide. She just *wouldn't.*"

"Same thing my grandmother said. But I'm sure there couldn't be actual danger in Beth Israel," I said. Dismiss what the witness said and wait for the contradiction.

"Why not?" Joanne said. "They could be testing some new medication . . . in fact, Grams said Mrs. Kaplan had volunteered for some clinical trial. She had cancer."

Brad said, "And so naturally she was depressed. Or maybe depression was a side effect of the drug. You read about that shit all the time. The drug company will be faced with a huge lawsuit, they'll settle, they'll stop giving the pills, and everybody's grandmother is safe. That simple."

"No, smartie." Joanne glared at him. "It's not that simple. Grams said she spent the afternoon with Mrs. Kaplan a week or so *after* she started the drug. Mrs. Kaplan was anything but depressed. She was really up, and she'd fallen in love with that Mr. Fetterolf who was also in the trial, and his daughter-in-law Dottie was telling me—"

"Joanne, let's go," Brad said. "I don't really feel like arguing here."

I said, "My grandmother knew Mr. Fetterolf slightly. And she's worried about his suicide—"

"So am *I*," Joanne said. "I keep telling and telling Brad—"

"Joanne, I'm going. You do what the hell you want."

"You can't just—all right, all right! Everything has to be your way!" She flounced up, threw me an apologetic look, and followed her husband out.

There were four Fetterolfs in the Manhattan phone directory. Two were single initials, which meant they were probably women living alone. I chose Herman Fetterolf on West Eighty-sixth.

The apartment building was nice, with a carpeted lobby and deep comfortable sofas. I said to the doorman, "Please tell Mrs. Dottie Fetterolf that there's a private investigator to talk to her about her father-in-law's death. My name is Joe Carter. Ask her if she'll come down to the lobby to talk to me."

He gave me a startled look and conveyed the message. When Mrs. Fetterolf came down, I could see she was ready to be furious at somebody, anybody. Long skirt swishing, long vest flapping, she steamed across the lobby. "You the private investigator? Who are you working for?"

"I'm not at liberty to say, Mrs. Fetterolf. But it's someone who, like you, has lost an elderly relative to suicide."

"Suicide! Ha! It wasn't any suicide! It was murder!"

"Murder?"

"They killed him! And no one will admit it!"

"What makes you think so?"

"Think? *Think?* I don't have to think, I *know!* One week he's fine, he's friends with this Mrs. Kaplan, they play Scrabble, they read books together, he's happy as a clam. Maybe even a little something gets going between them, who am I to say, more power to them. And then on the same night—the *same* night—he hangs himself and she walks in front of a bus! Coincidence? I don't think so . . . Besides, there would be a note."

"I beg your—"

"My father-in-law would have left a note. He was thoughtful that way. You know what I'm saying? He wrote everybody in the whole family all the time, nobody could even keep up with reading it all. He would have left a note for sure."

"Did he—"

"He was lonely after his wife died. Sarah. A saint. They met fifty-six years ago—"

In the end, she gave me her father-in-law's entire history. Also Rose Kaplan's. I wrote it all down.

When I called Johnny Fermato, I was told by a wary desk sergeant that Lieutenant Fermato would get back to me.

In my dreams.

"Somebody's being screwed over, Margie," I said. "And it's probably costing somebody else payoff money."

She lay there in the fetal position, her hands like claws. The IV was gone, but she was still connected by tubes to the humidified air supply, the catheter bag, the feeding pump. The pump made soft noises: *ronk, ronk.* I laid my briefcase on the bottom of her bed, which Susan would probably object to.

"It wasn't depression," I said to Margie. "Della Francesca and Mrs. Smith went up to the roof together. Alone together. Samuel Fetterolf and Rose Kaplan were in love." J-24 chemically-induced love.

The bag in Margie's feeding pump slowly emptied. The catheter bag slowly filled. Her ears were hidden under the dry, brittle, lifeless hair.

"Johnny Fermato knows something. Maybe only that the word's been passed down to keep the case closed. I did get the coroners' reports. They say 'self-inflicted fatal wounds.' All eight reports."

Somewhere in the hospital corridors, a woman screamed. Then stopped.

"Margie," I heard myself saying, "I don't want to come here any-more."

The next second, I was up and limping around the room. I put my forehead against the wall and ground it in. How could I say that to her? Margie, the only woman I'd ever loved, the person in the world I was closest to . . . On our wedding night, which was also her nineteenth birthday, she'd told me she felt like she could die from happiness. And I'd known what she meant.

And on that other night eight years later, when Bucky had done his pills-and-vodka routine, Marge had been with me when the phone rang. *Gene . . . Gene . . . I did it. . . .*

*Did what? Jesus, Bucky, it's after midnight. . .*

*But I don't . . . Father Healey . . .*

*Bucky, I gotta start my shift at eight tomorrow morning. Good-night.*

*Gene, who's calling at this hour?*

*. . . say . . . good-bye . . .*

*Of all the inconsiderate . . . the phone woke Libby!*

*Tell Father Healey I never would have made . . . good priests don't doubt like . . . I can't touch God anymore. . . .*

And then I'd known. I was out of the apartment in fifteen seconds. Shoes, pants, gun. In my pajama top I drove to the seminary, leaned on the bell. Bucky wasn't there, but Father Healey was. I searched the rooms, the chapel, the little meditation garden, all the while traf-fic noises drowning out the thumping in my chest. Father Healey shouting questions at me. I wouldn't let him in my car. Get away from me you bastard you killed him, you and your insistence on pushing God on a mind never tightly wrapped in the first place . . . Bucky wasn't at his mother's house. Now I had two people screaming at me.

I found him at Our Lady of Perpetual Sorrows. Where I should have looked first. He'd broken a stained glass window, just smashed it with a board, no subtlety. He was in front of the altar, breathing shallow, al-ready unconscious. EMS seemed to take forever to get there. The on-duty cops were faster; the stained-glass was alarm-wired.

But when it was over, Bucky's stomach pumped, sleeping it off at St. Vincent's, I had crawled back in bed next to Margie. Libby asleep in her little bedroom. I'd put my arms around my wife, and I'd vowed that after Bucky got out of the hospital, I'd never see him and his messy stu-pid dramas of faith again.

"I didn't mean that," I said to Margie, inert in her trach collar.

"Sweetheart, I didn't mean it. Of course I want to be here. I'll be here as long as you're breathing!"

She didn't move. IV bag emptying, catheter bag filling.

Susan came in, her nurse's uniform rumpled. "Hi, Gene."

"Hello, Susan."

"We're about the same tonight."

I could see that. And then the Camineur kicked in and I could see something else, in one of those unbidden flashes of knowledge that Bucky called heightened connective cognition. Bucky hadn't phoned me because he didn't really want to know what had happened to those old people. He already had enough belief to satisfy himself. He just wanted J-24 cleared publicly, and he wanted me to start the stink that would do it. He was handing the responsibility for Rose Kaplan and Samuel Fetterolf and Lydia Smith and Giacomo della Francesca to me. Just the way he'd handed to me the responsibility for his break with Father Healey the night of his attempted suicide. I'd been used.

"Fuck that!"

Susan turned, startled, from changing Marge's catheter bag. "I beg your pardon?"

Margie, of course, said nothing.

I limped out of the hospital room, ignoring the look on Susan's face. I was angrier than I had been in eighteen months. Anger pushed against the inside of my chest and shot like bullets through my veins.

Until the Camineur did its thing.


A dozen boys crowded the basketball hoop after school, even though it was drizzling. I limped toward my car. Just as I reached it, a red Mercedes pulled up beside me and Jeff Connors got out from the passenger side.

He wore a blue bandana on his head, and it bulged on the left side above the ear. Heavy bandaging underneath; somebody had worked on him. He also wore a necklace of heavy gold links, a beeper, and jacket of supple brown leather. He didn't even try to keep the leather out of the rain.

His eyes met mine, and something flickered behind them. The Mercedes drove off. Jeff started toward the kids at the hoops, who'd all stopped playing to watch the car. There was the usual high-fiving and competitive dissing, but I heard its guarded quality, and I saw something was about to go down.

Nothing to do with me. I unlocked my car door.

Jenny Kelly came hurrying across the court, through the drizzle. Her eyes flashed. "Jeff! Jeff!"

She didn't even know enough not to confront him in front of his customers. He stared at her, impassive, no sign of his usual likable hustle. To him, she might as well have been a cop.

"Jeff, could I see you for a minute?"

Not a facial twitch. But something moved behind his eyes.

"Please? It's about your little brother."

She was giving him an out: family emergency. He didn't take it.

"I'm busy."

Ms. Kelly nodded. "Okay. Tomorrow, then?"

"I'm busy."

"Then I'll catch you later." She'd learned not to argue. But I saw her face after she turned from the boys sniggering behind her. She wasn't giving up, either. Not on Jeff.

Me, she never glanced at.

I got into my car and drove off, knowing better than Jenny Kelly what was happening on the basketball court behind me, not even trying to interfere. If it didn't happen on school property, it would happen off it. What was the difference, really? You couldn't stop it. No matter what idealistic fools like Jenny Kelly thought.

Her earrings were little pearls, and her shirt, damp from the rain, clung to her body.


The whole next week, I left the phone off the hook. I dropped Libby a note saying to write me instead of calling because NYNEX was having trouble with the line into my building. I didn't go to the hospital. I taught my math classes, corrected papers in my own classroom, and left right after eighth period. I only glimpsed Jenny Kelly once, at a bus stop a few blocks from the school building. She was holding the hand of a small black kid, three or four, dressed in a Knicks sweatshirt. They were waiting for a bus. I drove on by.

But you can't really escape.

I spotted the guy when I came out of the metroteller late Friday afternoon. I'd noticed him earlier, when I dropped off a suit at the drycleaner's. This wasn't the kind of thing I dealt with any more—but it happens. Somebody you collared eight years ago gets out and decides to get even. Or somebody spots you by accident and suddenly remembers some old score on behalf of his cousin, or your partner, or some damn thing you yourself don't even recall. It happens.

I couldn't move fast, not with my knee. I strolled into Mulcahy's, which has a long aisle running between the bar and the tables, with another door to the alley that's usually left open if the weather's any good. The men's and ladies' rooms are off an alcove just before the alley, along with a pay phone and cigarette machine. I nodded at Brian Mulcahy behind the bar, limped through, and went into the ladies'. It was empty. I kept the door cracked. My tail checked the alley, then strode toward the men's room. When his back was to the ladies' and his hand on the heavy door, I grabbed him.

He wasn't as tall or heavy as I was—average build, brown hair, nondescript looks. He twisted in my grasp, and I felt the bulge of the gun under his jacket. "Stop it, Shaunessy! NYPD!"

I let him go. He fished out his shield, looking at me hard. Then he said, "Not here. This is an informant hangout—didn't you *know*? 284 West Seventieth, Apartment 8. Christ, why don't you fix your goddamn *phone?*" Then he was gone.

I had a beer at the bar while I thought it over. Then I went home. When the buzzer rang an hour and a half later, I didn't answer. Whoever stood downstairs buzzed for ten minutes straight before giving up.

That night I dreamed someone was trying to kill Margie, stalking her through the Times Square sleaze and firing tiny chemically poisoned darts. I couldn't be sure, dreams being what they are, but I think the stalker was me.


The Saturday mail came around three-thirty. It brought a flat manilla package, no return address, no note. It was a copy of the crime-scene report on the deaths of Lydia Smith and Giacomo della Francesca.

Seven years as partners doesn't just wash away. No matter what the official line has to be.

There were three eight-by-ten color crime scene photos: an empty rooftop; Mrs. Smith's body smashed on the pavement below; della Francesca's body lying on the floor beside a neatly made bed. His face was in partial shadow but his skinny spotted hands were clear, both clutching the hilt of the knife buried in his chest. There wasn't much blood. That doesn't happen until somebody pulls the knife out.

The written reports didn't say anything that wasn't in the photos.

I resealed the package and locked it in my file cabinet. Johnny had come through; Bucky had screwed me. The deaths were suicides, just like Kelvin Pharmaceuticals said, just like the Department said. Bucky's superconnective pill was the downer to end all downers, and he knew it, and he was hoping against hope it wasn't so.

Because he and Tommy had taken it together.

*I've moved,* Bucky had said in his one message since he told me about J-24. I'd assumed he meant that he'd changed apartments, or lovers, or lives, as he'd once changed from fanatic seminarian to fanatic chemist. But that's not what he meant. He meant he'd made his move with J-24, because he wanted the effect for himself and Tommy, and he refused to believe the risk applied to him. Just like all the dumb crack users I spent sixteen years arresting.

I dialed his number. After four rings, the answering machine picked up. I hung up, walked from the living room to the bedroom, pounded my fists on the wall a couple times, walked back and dialed again. When the machine picked up I said, "Bucky. This is Gene. Call me *now*. I mean it—I have to know you're all right."

I hesitated . . . he hadn't contacted me in weeks. What could I use as leverage?

"If you don't call me tonight, Saturday, by nine, I'll . . ." What? Not go look for him. Not again, not like thirteen years ago, rushing out in pants and pajama top, Margie calling after me, *Gene! Gene! For God's sake . . .*

I couldn't do it again.

"If you don't phone by nine o'clock, I'll call the feds with what I've found about J-24, without checking it out with you first. So *call me,* Bucky."

Usually on Saturday afternoon I went to the hospital to see Margie. Not today. I sat at my kitchen table with algebra tests from 7B spread over the tiny surface, and it took me an hour to get through three papers. I kept staring at the undecorated wall, seeing Bucky there. Seeing the photos of Lydia Smith and Giacomo della Francesca. Seeing that night thirteen years ago when Bucky had his stomach pumped. Then I'd wrench myself back to the test papers and correct another problem. *If train A leaves point X traveling at a steady fifty miles per hour at six* A.M. . . .

If a bullet leaves a gun traveling at one thousand five hundred feet per second, it can tear off a human head. Nobody realizes that but people who have seen it. Soldiers. Doctors. Cops.

After a while I'd realize I was staring at the wall again, and picked up another paper. *If 3X equals 2Y* . . . Some of the names on the papers I didn't even recognize. Who was James Dillard? Was he the tall quiet kid in the last row, or the short one in shoes held together with tape, who fell asleep most mornings? They were just names.

On the wall, I saw Jenny Kelly holding the hand of Jeff Connors' little brother.

At seven-thirty I shoved the papers into my briefcase and grabbed my jacket. Just before I left, I tried Bucky's number once more. No answer. I turned off the living room light and limped along the hall to the door. Just before I opened it, my foot struck something. Without even thinking about it, I flattened against the wall and reached behind me for the foyer light.

It was only another package. A padded mailer, nine by twelve, the cheap kind that leaks oily black stuffing all over you if you open it wrong. The stuffing was already coming out a little tear in one corner. There were no stamps, no address; it had been shoved under the door. Whoever had left it had gotten into the building—not hard to do on a Saturday, with people coming and going, just wait until someone else has unlocked the door and smile at them as you go in, any set of keys visible in your hand. In the upper left corner of the envelope was an NYPD evidence sticker.

I picked up the package just as the phone rang.

"Bucky! Where are—"

"Gene, this is Jenny Kelly. Listen, I need your help. Please! I just got a call from Jeff Connors, he didn't know who else to call. . . . The police have got him barricaded in a drug house someplace, they're yelling at him to come out and he's got Darryl with him, that's his little brother, and he's terrified—Jeff is—that they'll knock down the door and go in shooting. . . . God, Gene, please go! It's only four blocks from you, that's why I called, and you know how these things work . . . please!"

She had to pause for breath. I said tonelessly, "What's the address?"

She told me. I slammed the receiver down in the midst of her thank-yous. If she'd been in the room with me, I think I could have hit her.

I limped the four blocks north, forcing my damaged knee, and three blocks were gone before I realized I still had the padded envelope in my hand. I folded it in half and shoved it in my jacket pocket.

The address wasn't hard to find. Two cars blocked the street, lights whirling, and I could hear more sirens in the distance. The scene was all fucked up. A woman of twenty-one or twenty-two was screaming hysterically and jumping up and down: "He's got my baby! He's got a gun up there! He's going to kill my son!" while a uniform who looked about nineteen was trying ineptly to calm her down. Her clothes were torn and bloody. She smacked the rookie across the arm and his partner moved in to restrain her, while another cop with a bullhorn shouted up at the building. Neighbors poured out onto the street. The one uniform left was trying to do crowd control, funneling them away from the building, and nobody was going. He looked no older than the guy holding the woman, as if he'd had about six hours total time on the street.

I had my dummy shield. We'd all had our shields duplicated, one thirty-second of an inch smaller than the real shield, so we could leave the real one home and not risk a fine and all the paperwork if it got lost. When I retired, I turned in my shield but kept the dummy. I flashed it now at the rookie struggling with the hysterical girl. That might cost me a lot of trouble later, but I'd worry about that when the time came.

The street thinking comes back so fast.

"This doesn't look right," I shouted at the rookie over the shrieking woman. She was still flailing in his hold, screaming, "He's got my baby! He's got a gun! For Chrissake, get my baby before he kills him!" The guy with the bullhorn stopped shouting and came over to us.

"Who are you?"

"He's from Hostage and Barricade," the rookie gasped, although I hadn't said so. I didn't contradict him. He was trying so hard to be gentle with the screaming woman that she was twisting like a dervish while he struggled to cuff her.

"Look," I said, "she's not the mother of that child up there. He's the perp's little brother, and she sure the hell doesn't look old enough to be both their mother!"

"How do you—" the uniform began, but the girl let out a shriek that could have levelled buildings, jerked one hand free and clawed at my face.

I ducked fast enough that she missed my eyes, but her nails tore a long jagged line down my cheek. The rookie stopped being gentle and cuffed her so hard she staggered. The sleeve of her sweater rode up when he jerked her arms behind her back, and I saw the needle tracks.

Shit, shit, shit.

Two backup cars screamed up. An older cop in plain clothes got out, and I slipped my dummy shield back in my pocket.

"Listen, officer, I *know* that kid up there, the one with the baby. I'm his teacher. He's in the eighth grade. His name is Jeff Connors, the child with him is his little brother Darryl, and this woman is *not* their mother. Something's going down here, but it's not what she says."

He looked at me hard. "How'd you get that wound?"

"She clawed him," the rookie said. "He's from—"

"He phoned me," I said urgently, holding him with my eyes. "He's scared stiff. He'll come out with no problems if you let him, and leave Darryl there."

"You're his teacher? That why he called you? You got ID?"

I showed him my United Federation of Teachers card, driver's license, Benjamin Franklin Junior High pass. The uniforms had all been pressed into crowd control by a sergeant who looked like he knew what he was doing.

"Where'd he get the gun? He belong to a gang?"

I said, "I don't know. But he might."

"How do you know there's nobody else up there with him?"

"He didn't say so on the phone. But I don't know for sure."

"What's the phone number up there?"

"I don't know. He didn't give it to me."

"Is he on anything?"

"I don't know. I would guess no."

He stood there, weighing it a moment. Then he picked up the bullhorn, motioned to his men to get into position. His voice was suddenly calm, even gentle. "Connors! Look, we know you're with your little brother, and we don't want either of you to get hurt. Leave Darryl there and come down by yourself. Leave the gun and just come on down. You do that and everything'll be fine."

"He's going to kill my—" the woman shrieked, before someone shoved her into a car and slammed the door.

"Come on, Jeff, we can do this nice and easy, no problems for anybody."

I put my hand to my cheek. It came away bloody.

The negotiator's voice grew even calmer, even more reasonable.

"I know Darryl's probably scared, but he doesn't have to be, just come on down and we can get him home where he belongs. Then you and I can talk about what's best for your little brother. . . ."

Jeff came out. He slipped out of the building, hands on his head, going, "Don't shoot me, please don't shoot me, don't shoot me," and he wasn't the hustler of the eighth grade who knew all the moves, wasn't the dealer in big gold on the basketball court. He was a terrified thirteen-year-old in a dirty blue bandana, who'd been set up.

Cops in body armor rushed forward and grabbed him. More cops started in to the building. A taxi pulled up and Jenny Kelly jumped out, dressed in a low-cut black satin blouse and black velvet skirt.

"Jeff! Are you all right?"

Jeff looked at her, and I think if they'd been alone, he might have started to cry. "Darryl's up there alone. . . ."

"They'll bring Darryl down safe," I said.

"I'll take Darryl to your aunt's again," Jenny promised. A man climbed out of the taxi behind her and paid the driver. He was scowling. The rookie glanced down the front of Jenny's dress.

Jeff was cuffed and put into a car. Jenny turned to me. "Oh, your face, you're hurt! Where will they take Jeff, Gene? Will you go, too? Please?"

"I'll have to. I told them it was me that Jeff phoned."

She smiled. I'd never seen her smile like that before, at least not at me. I kept my eyes raised to her face, and my own face blank. "Who set him up, Jenny?"

"Set him up?"

"That woman was yelling she's Darryl's mother and Jeff was going to kill her baby. Somebody wanted the cops to go storming in there and start shooting. If Jeff got killed, the NYPD would be used as executioners. If he didn't, he'd still be so scared they'll own him. Who is it, Jenny? The same ones who circulated that inflammatory crap about a Neighborhood Safety Information Network?"

She frowned. "I don't know. But Jeff has been . . . there were some connections that . . ." She trailed off, frowned again. Her date came up to us, still scowling. "Gene, this is Paul Snyder. Paul, Gene Shaunessy. . . . Paul, I'm sorry, I have to go with Gene to wherever they're taking Jeff. I'm the one he really called. And I said I'd take Darryl to his aunt."

"Jenny, for Chrissake . . . we have tickets for the Met!"

She just looked at him, and I saw that Paul Snyder wasn't going to be seeing any more of Jenny Kelly's cleavage.

"I'll drive you to the precinct, Jenny," I said. "Only I have to be the first one interviewed, I have to be as quick as I can because there's something else urgent tonight. . . ." Bucky. Dear God.

Jenny said quickly, "Your wife? Is she worse?"

"She'll never be worse. Or better," I said before I knew I was going to say anything, and immediately regretted it.

"Gene . . ." Jenny began, but I didn't let her finish. She was standing too close to me. I could smell her perfume. A fold of her black velvet skirt blew against my leg.

I said harshly, "You won't last at school another six months if you take it all this hard. You'll burn out. You'll leave."

Her gaze didn't waver. "Oh, no, I won't. And don't talk to me in that tone of voice."

"Six months," I said, and turned away. A cop came out of the building carrying a wailing Darryl. And the lieutenant came over to me, wanting to know whatever it was I thought I knew about Jeff Connors' connections.


It was midnight before I got home. After the precinct house there'd been a clinic, with the claw marks on my face disinfected and a tetanus shot and a blood test and photographs for the assault charges. After that, I looked for Bucky.

He wasn't at his apartment, or at his mother's apartment. The weekend security guard at Kelvin Pharmaceuticals said he'd been on duty since four P.M. and Dr. Romano hadn't signed in to his lab. That was the entire list of places I knew to look. Bucky's current life was unknown to me. I didn't even know Tommy's last name.

I dragged myself through my apartment, pulling off my jacket. The light on the answering machine blinked.

My mind—or the Camineur—made some connections. Even before I pressed the MESSAGE button, I think I knew.

"Gene, this is Tom Fletcher. You don't know me . . . we've never met. . . ." A deeper voice than I'd expected but ragged, spiky. "I got your message on Vince Romano's machine. About the J-24. Vince . . ." The voice caught, went on. "Vince is in the hospital. I'm calling from there. St. Clare's, it's on Ninth at Fifty-first. Third floor. Just before he . . . said to tell you . . ."

I couldn't make out the words in the rest of the message.

I sat there in the dark for a few minutes. Then I pulled my jacket back on and caught a cab to St. Clare's. I didn't think I could drive.

The desk attendant waved me through. He thought I was just visiting Margie, even at this hour. It had happened before. But not lately.

Bucky lay on the bed, a sheet pulled up to his chin but not yet over his face. His eyes were open. Suddenly I didn't want to know what the sheet was covering—how he'd done it, what route he'd chosen, how long it had taken. All the dreary algebra of death. *If train A leaves the station at a steady fifty miles per hour* . . . There were no marks on Bucky's face. He was smiling.

And then I saw he was still breathing. Bucky, the ever inept, had failed a second time.

Tommy stood in a corner, as if he couldn't get it together enough to sit down. Tall and handsome, he had dark, well-cut hair and the kind of fresh complexion that comes with youth and exercise. He looked about fifteen years younger than Bucky. When had they taken the J-24 together? Lydia Smith and Giacomo della Francesca had killed themselves within hours of each other. So had Rose Kaplan and Samuel Fetterolf. How much did Tommy know?

He stood and held out his hand. His voice was husky. "You're Gene."

"I'm Gene."

"Tom Fletcher. Vince and I are—"

"I know," I said, and stared down at Bucky's smiling face, and wondered how I was going to tell this boy that he, too, was about to try to kill himself for chemically-induced love.

I flashed on Bucky and me sitting beside the rain-streaked alley window of the Greek diner. *What are you waiting for, Bucky, your prince to come?*

*Yes.* And, *Have you ever thought what it would be like to be really merged—to know him, to be him?*

"Tom," I said. "There's something we have to discuss."

"Discuss?" His voice had grown even huskier.

"About Bucky. Vince. You and Vince."

"What?"

I looked down at Bucky's smiling face.

"Not here. Come with me to the waiting room."

It was deserted at that hour, a forlorn alcove of scratched furniture, discarded magazines, too harsh fluorescent lights. We sat facing each other on red plastic chairs.

I said abruptly, "Do you know what J-24 is?"

His eyes grew wary. "Yes."

"What is it?" I couldn't find the right tone. I was grilling him as if he were under arrest and I were still a cop.

"It's a drug that Vince's company was working on. To make people bond to each other, merge together in perfect union." His voice was bitter.

"What else did he tell you?"

"Not much. What should he have told me?"

You never see enough, not even in the streets, to really prepare you. Each time you see genuine cruelty, it's like the first time. Damn you, Bucky. Damn you to hell for emotional greed.

I said, "He didn't tell you that the clinical subjects who took J-24 . . . the people who bonded . . . he didn't tell you they were all elderly?"

"No," Tom said.

"The same elderly who have been committing suicide all over in the city? The ones in the papers?"

"Oh, my God."

He got up and walked the length of the waiting room, maybe four good steps. Then back. His handsome face was gray as ash. "They killed themselves after taking J-24? Because of J-24?"

I nodded. Tom didn't move. A long minute passed, and then he said softly, "My poor Vince."

"Poor *Vince?* How the hell can you . . . don't you get it, Tommy boy? You're next! You took the bonding drug with poor suffering Vince, and your three weeks or whatever of joy are up and you're dead, kid! The chemicals will do their thing in your brain, super withdrawal, and you'll kill yourself just like Bucky! Only you'll probably be better at it and actually succeed!"

He stared at me. And then he said, "Vince didn't try to kill himself."

I couldn't speak.

"He didn't attempt suicide. Is that what you thought? No, he's in a catatonic state. And *I* never took J-24 with him."

"Then who . . . ?"

"God," Tom said, and the full force of bitterness was back. "He took it with God. At some church, Our Lady of Everlasting Something. Alone in front of the altar, fasting and praying. He told me when he moved out."

When he moved out. Because it wasn't Tommy that Bucky really wanted, it was God. It had always been God, for thirteen solid years. *Tell Father Healey I can't touch God any more. . . . Have you ever thought what it would be like to be really merged, to know him, to be him. . . . No. To know Him. To be Him. What are you waiting for, your Prince?*

*Yes.*

Tom said, "After he took the damned drug, he lost all interest in me. In everything. He didn't go to work, just sat in the corner smiling and laughing and crying. He was like . . . high on something, but not really. I don't know what he was. It wasn't like anything I ever saw before."

Nor anybody else. Merged with God. *They knew each other, they almost were each other. Think, Gene! To have an end to the terrible isolation in which we live our whole tiny lives. . . .*

"I got so *angry* with him," Tom said, "and it did no good at all. I just didn't count any more. So I told him to get out, and he did, and then I spent three days looking for him but I couldn't find him anywhere, and I was frantic. Finally he called me, this afternoon. He was crying. But again it was like I wasn't even really there, not me, Tom. He sure the hell wasn't crying over *me.*"

Tom walked to the one small window, which was barred. Back turned to me, he spoke over his shoulder. Carefully, trying to get it word-perfect.

"Vince said I should call you. He said, 'Tell Gene—it wears off. And then the grief and loss and anger . . . *especially* the anger that it's over. But I can beat it. It's different for me. They couldn't.' Then he hung up. Not a word to me."

I said, "I'm sorry."

He turned. "Yeah, well, that was Vince, wasn't it? *He* always came first with himself."

No, I could have said. God came first. And that's how Bucky beat the J-24 withdrawal. Human bonds, whether forged by living or chemicals, got scraped down as much as built up. But you didn't have to live in a three-room apartment with God, fight about money with God, listen to God snore and fart and say things so stupid you can't believe they're coming out of the mouth of your beloved, watch God be selfish or petty or cruel. God was bigger than all that, at least in Bucky's mind, was so big that He filled everything. And this time when God retreated from him, when the J-24 wore off and Bucky could feel the bond slipping away, Bucky slipped along after it. Deeper into his own mind, where all love exists anyway.

"The doctor said he might never come out of the catatonia," Tom said. He was starting to get angry now, the anger of self-preservation. "Or he might. Either way, I don't think I'll be waiting around for him. He's treated me too badly."

Not a long-term kind of guy, Tommy. I said, "But you never took J-24 yourself."

"No," Tom said. "I'm not stupid. I think I'll go home now. Thanks for coming, Gene. Good to meet you."

"You, too," I said, knowing neither of us meant it.

"Oh, and Vince said one more thing. He said to tell you it was, too, murder. Does that make sense?"

"Yes," I said. But not, I hoped, to him.


After Tom left, I sat in the waiting room and pulled from my jacket the second package. The NYPD evidence sticker had torn when I'd jammed the padded mailer in my pocket.

It was the original crime scene report for Lydia Smith and Giacomo della Francesca, the one Johnny Fermato must have known about when he sent me the phony one. This report was signed Bruce Campinella. I didn't know him, but I could probably pick him out of a line-up from the brief tussle in Mulcahy's: average height, brown hair, undistinguished looks, furious underneath. Your basic competent honest cop still outraged at what the system had for sale. And for sale at a probably not very high price. Not in New York.

There were only two photos this time. One I'd already seen: Mrs. Smith's smashed body on the pavement below the nursing home roof. The other was new. Della Francesca's body lying on the roof, not in his room, before the cover-up team moved him and took the second set of pictures. The old man lay face up, the knife still in his chest. It was a good photo; the facial expression was very clear. The pain was there, of course, but you could see the fury, too. The incredible rage. *And then the grief and loss and anger . . . especially the anger that it's over.*

Had della Francesca pushed Lydia Smith first, after that shattering quarrel that came from losing their special, unearthly union, and then killed himself? Or had she found the strength in her disappointment and outrage to drive the knife in, and then jumped? Ordinarily, the loss of love doesn't mean hate. Just how unbearable was it to have had a true, perfect, human end to human isolation—and then lose it? How much rage did that primordial loss release?

Or maybe Bucky was wrong, and it had been suicide after all. Not the anger uppermost, but the grief. Maybe the rage on della Francesca's dead face wasn't at his lost perfect love, but at his own emptiness once it was gone. He'd felt something so wonderful, so sublime, that everything else afterward fell unbearably short, and life itself wasn't worth the effort. No matter what he did, he'd never ever have its like again.

I thought of Samuel Fetterolf before he took J-24, writing everyone in his family all the time, trying to stay connected. Of Pete, straining every cell of his damaged brain to protect the memories of the old people who'd been kind to him. Of Jeff Connors, hanging onto Darryl even while he moved into the world of red Mercedes and big deals. Of Jenny Kelly, sacrificing her dates and her sleep and her private life in her frantic effort to connect to the students, who she undoubtedly thought of as "her kids." Of Bucky.

The elevator to the fifth floor was out of order. I took the stairs. The shift nurse barely nodded at me. It wasn't Susan. In Margie's room the lights had been dimmed and she lay in the gloom like a curved dry husk, covered with a light sheet. I pulled the chair closer to her bed and stared at her.

And for maybe the first time since her accident, I remembered.

*Roll the window down, Gene.*

*It's fifteen degrees out there, Margie!*

*It's real air. Chilled like good beer. It smells like a goddamn factory in this car.*

*Don't start again. I'm warning you.*

*Are you so afraid the job won't kill you that you want the cigarettes to do it?*

*Stop trying to control me.*

*Maybe you should do better at controlling yourself.*

The night I'd found Bucky at Our Lady of Perpetual Sorrows, I'd been in control. It was Bucky who hadn't. I'd crawled back in bed and put my arms around Marge and vowed never to see Bucky and his messy stupid dramas of faith ever again. Marge hadn't been asleep. She'd been crying. I'd had enough hysteria for one night; I didn't want to hear it. I wouldn't even let her speak. I stalked out of the bedroom and spent the night on the sofa. It was three days before I'd even talk to her so we could work it out and make it good between us again.

*Have a great year!* she'd said my first September at Benjamin Franklin. But it hadn't been a great year. I was trying to learn how to be a teacher, and trying to forget how to be a cop, and I didn't have much time left over for her. We'd fought about that, and then I'd stayed away from home more and more to get away from the fighting, and by the time I returned *she* was staying away from home a lot. Over time it got better again, but I don't know where she was going the night she crossed Lexington with a bag of groceries in front of that '93 Lincoln. I don't know who the groceries were for. She never bought porterhouse and champagne for me.

Maybe we would have worked that out, too. Somehow.

*Weren't there moments, Gene,* Bucky had said, *when you felt so close to Margie it was like you crawled inside her skin for a minute? Like you were Margie?* No. I was never Margie. We were close, but not that close. What we'd had was good, but not that good. Not a perfect merging of souls.

Which was the reason I could survive its loss.

I stood up slowly, favoring my knee. On the way out of the room I took the plastic bottle of Camineur out of my pocket and tossed it in the waste basket. Then I left, without looking back.

Outside, on Ninth Avenue, a patrol car suddenly switched on its lights and took off. Some kids who should have been at home swaggered past, heading downtown. I looked for a pay phone. By now Jenny Kelly would be done delivering Darryl to his aunt, and Jeff Connors was going to need better than the usual overworked public defender. I knew a guy at Legal Aid, a hotshot, who still owed me a long-overdue favor.

I found the phone and the connection went through.

# UNTO THE DAUGHTERS

*A story can begin anywhere: with a character, with a situation, with an image. This one began with a voice. The voice of the snake came to me, not by description ("extravagant," "rueful"), but in the voice, the exact words, of the first seven paragraphs. Obediently, I wrote them down.*

*Then I got stuck. The snake disappeared.*

*It was back a few days later, and I finished the story, although this time with more conscious participation. And then Eve does this. . . . No, I don't like that. How about the snake decides to go to . . . Eventually, about halfway through, the ending occurred to me, and then I figured out how to get there, checking periodically that I was still well inside the original voice.*

*That's how most of my stories get written. But I like it better when the voice just talks and I just write it down.*

THIS IS NOT THE WAY YOU HEARD THE STORY.

In the beginning, the tree was young. White blossoms scenting the air for a quarter mile. Shiny succulent fruit, bending the same boughs that held blossoms. Leaves of that delicate yellow-green that cannot, will not, last. Yet it did. *He* always did have gaudy taste. No restraint. Just look at the Himalayas. Or blowfish. I mean—really!

The woman was young, too. Pink curling toes, breasts as barely budded as the apple blossoms. And the man! My dear, those long, firm flanks alone could make you ache inside for hours. He could run five miles and not even be winded. He could make love to the woman five times a day. And did.

The flowers were young. The animals, tumbling and cavorting on the grass, were young. The fucking *beach sand* was young, clean evenly-shaped grains that only yesterday had been igneous rock. There was virgin rain.

Only I was old.

But it wasn't that. That was the first thing that came to your mind, wasn't it? Jealousy of glorious youth, revenge by the dried-up and jaded. Oh, you don't know, you sitting there so many centuries ahead. It wasn't that at all. I mean, I loved them both.

Looking at them, how could one not?

"Go away," Eve says. "I'm not going to eat one."

She sits cross-legged, braiding flowers into a crown. The flowers are about what you'd expect from Him, garish scarlet petals and a vulva-shaped pistil like a bad joke. Braiding them, her fingers are deft and competent. Some lion cubs tumble tiresomely on the grass.

"I want to give you a reason why you should eat one," I say, not gently.

"I've heard all your reasons."

"Not this one, Eve. This is a *new* reason."

She isn't interested. She knots the crown of flowers, puts it on her head, giggles, tosses it at the lions. It settles lopsided over one cub's left ear. The cub looks up with comic surprise, and Eve explodes into laughter.

Really, sometimes I wonder why I bother. She's so stupid, compared to the man.

I bother because she's so stupid compared to the man.

"Listen, Eve. *He* withholds knowledge from you two because He's selfish. What else would you call it to keep knowledge to yourself when you could just as well share it?"

"I don't need knowledge," Eve says airily. "What do I need knowledge for? And anyway, that's not a new reason. You've said that before."

"A tree, Eve. A fucking *tree*. To invest knowledge in. Doesn't that strike you as just a teeny bit warped? Mathematics in xylem, morality in fruit pulp? Astronomy rotting on the ground every time an apple falls. Don't you wonder what kind of a mind would do that?"

She only stares at me blankly. Oh, she's dumb. I mean!

I shout, in the temper of perfect despair, "Without knowledge, nothing will change!"

"Are *you* here again?" Adam says. I hadn't heard him climb over the rock behind us. He has a very quiet footstep for someone whose toenails have never ever been cut. Also a quiet, penetrating voice. Eve jumps up as if she's been shot.

"I thought I told you not to talk to this . . . thing ever again," Adam says. "Didn't I tell you that?"

Eve hangs her pretty head. "Yes, Adam. You did. I forgot."

He looks at her, and his face softens. That blooming skin, those sweet lips. Her hair falls forward, lustrous as night. I don't think my despair can go any deeper, but it does. She is so pretty. He will always for-

give her. And she will always forget everything he says two minutes
after he says it.

"Begone! You don't belong here!" Adam shouts, and throws a rock
at me. It hits just behind my head. It hurts like hell. One of the lion cubs
happily fetches it back, wagging a golden tail. The other one is still
wearing the lopsided crown of flowers.

As I slither away, half blind with pain, Eve calls after me. "I don't
*want* anything to change! I really don't!"

The hell with her.


"Just listen," I say. "Just put your entire tiny mind on one thing for
once and *listen* to me."

Eve sits sewing leaves into a blanket. Not cross-legged anymore:
She is six months pregnant. The leaves are wide and soft, with a sort
of furry nap on their underside. They appeared in the garden right
after she got pregnant, along with tough spiderwebs that make splendid thread. Why not a bush that grows little caps? Or tiny diapers with
plastic fastening tabs? Really, He has such a banal imagination.

Eve hums as she sews. Beside her is the cradle Adam made. It's
carved with moons and numbers and stars and other cabalistic signs:
a lovely piece of work. *Adam* has imagination.

"You have to *listen,* Eve. Not just hear—*listen.* Stop that humming.
I know the future—how could I know the future unless I am exactly
what I say I am? I know everything that's going to happen. I told you
when you'd conceive, didn't I? That alone should have convinced you.
And now I'm telling you that your baby will be a boy, and you'll call
him Cain, and he—"

"No, I'm going to call him Silas," Eve says. She knots the end of her
spider-thread and bites it off. "I *love* the name Silas."

"You're going to call him Cain, and he—"

"Do you think it would be prettier to embroider roses on this blanket, or daisies?"

"Eve, listen, if I can foretell the future then isn't it logical, isn't it reasonable for you to think—"

"I don't have to think," Eve says. "Adam does that for both of us,
plus all the forest-dressing and fruit-tending. He works so hard, poor
dear."

"*Eve*—"

"Roses, I think. In blue."

I can't stand it anymore. I go out into the constant, perpetual, monotonous sunshine, which smells like roses, like wisteria, like gardenia, like woodsmoke, like new-mown hay. Like heaven.


Eve has the baby at nine months, thirty-two seconds. She laughs as the small head slides out, which takes two painless minutes. The child is perfect.

"We'll call him Cain," Adam says.

"I thought we might call him Silas. I love the na—"

"Cain," Adam says firmly.

"All right, Adam."

He will never know she was disappointed.


"Eve," I say. "Listen."

She is bathing the two boys in the river, in the shallows just before the river splits into four parts and leaves the garden. Cain is diligently scrubbing his small penis, but Abel has caught at some seaweed and is examining how it hangs over his chubby fists. He turns it this way and that, bending his head close. He is much more intelligent than his brother.

"Eve, Adam will be back soon. If you'd just listen . . ."

"Daddy," Abel says, raising his head. He has a level gaze, friendly but evaluative, even at his age. He spends a lot of time with his father. "Daddy gone."

"Oh, yes, Daddy's gone to pick breadfruit in the west!" Eve cries, in a perfect ecstasy of maternal pride. "He'll be back tonight, my little poppets. He'll be home with his precious little boys!"

Cain looks up. He has succeeded in giving his penis the most innocent of erections. He smiles beatifically at Abel, at his mother, who does not see him because she is scrubbing Abel's back, careful not to drip soapstone onto his seaweed.

"Daddy pick breadfruit," Abel repeats. "Mommy not."

"Mommy doesn't want to go pick breadfruit," Eve says. "Mommy is happy right here with her little poppets."

"Mommy not," Abel repeats, thoughtfully.

"Eve," I say, "only with knowledge can you make choices. Only with truth can you be free. Four thousand years from now—"

"I am free," Eve says, momentarily startled. She looks at me. Her eyes are as fresh, as innocent, as when she was created. They open very wide. "How could anyone not think I'm perfectly *free?*"

"If you'd just listen—"

"Daddy gone," Abel says a third time. "Mommy not."

"Even thirty seconds of careful listening—"

"Mommy never gone."

"Tell that brat to shut up while I'm trying to talk to you!"

Wrong, wrong. Fury leaps into Eve's eyes. She scoops up both children as if I were trying to stone them, the silly bitch. She hugs them tight to her chest, breathing something from those perfect lips that might have been "Well!" or "Ugly!" or even "Help!" Then she staggers off with both boys in her arms, dripping water, Abel dripping seaweed.

"Put Abel down," Abel says dramatically. "Abel walk."

She does. The child looks at her. "Mommy do what Abel say!"

I go eat worms.

The third child is a girl, whom they name Sheitha.

Cain and Abel are almost grown. They help Adam with the garden dressing, the animal naming, whatever comes up. I don't know. I'm getting pretty sick of the whole lot of them. The tree still has both blossoms and fruit on the same branch. The river still flows into four exactly equal branches just beyond the garden: Pison, Gihon, Hiddekel, Euphrates. Exactly the same number of water molecules in each. I stop thinking He's theatrical and decide instead that He's compulsive. I mean—really. Fish lay the exact same number of eggs in each river.

Eve hasn't seen Him in decades. Adam, of course, walks with Him in the cool of every evening. Now the two boys go, too. Heaven knows what they talk about; I stay away. Often it's my one chance at Eve, who spends every day sewing and changing diapers and sweeping bowers and slicing breadfruit. Her toes are still pink curling delicacies.

"Eve, listen—"

Sheitha giggles at a bluebird perched on her dimpled knee.

"Adam makes all the decisions, decides all the rules, thinks up all the names, does all the thinking—"

"So?" Eve says. "Sheitha—you precious little angel!" She catches the baby in her arms and covers her with kisses. Sheitha crows in delight.

"Eve, listen—"

Miraculously, she does. She sets the baby on the grass and says seriously, "Adam says you aren't capable of telling the truth."

"Not *his* truth," I say. "Or His." But of course this subtlety of pronoun goes right over her head.

"Look, snake, I don't want to be rude. You've been very kind to me, keeping me company while I do my housework, and I appreciate—"

"I'm not being kind," I say desperately. Kind! Oh, my Eve . . . "I'm too old and tired for kindness. I'm just trying to show you, to get you to listen—"

"Adam's back," Eve says quickly. I hear him then, with the two boys. There is just time enough to slither under a bush. I lie there very still. Lately Adam has turned murderous toward me; I think he must have a special dispensation for it. *He* must have told Adam violence toward me doesn't count, because I have stepped out of my place. Which, of course, I have.

But this time Adam doesn't see me. The boys fall into some game with thread and polished stones. Sheitha toddles toward her daddy, grinning.

"We're just here to get something to eat," Adam says. "Ten minutes, is all—what, Eve, isn't there anything ready? What have you been doing all morning?"

Eve's face doesn't fall. But her eyes deepen in color a little, like skin that has been momentarily bruised. Of course, skin doesn't stay bruised here. Not here.

"I'm sorry, dear! I'll get something ready right away!"

"Please," Adam says. "Some of us have to work for a living."

She bustles quickly around. The slim pretty fingers are deft as ever. Adam throws himself prone into a bower. Sheitha climbs into his lap. She is as precocious as the boys were.

"Daddy go back?"

"Yes, my little sweetie. Daddy has to go cut more sugar cane. And name some new animals."

"Animals," Sheitha says happily. She loves animals. "Sheitha go."

Adam smiles. "No, precious, Sheitha can't go. Little girls can't go."

"Sheitha *go!*"

"No," Adam says. He is still smiling, but he stands up and she tumbles off his lap. The food is ready. Eve turns with a coconut shell of salad just as Sheitha is picking herself up. The baby stands looking up at her father. Her small face is crumpled in disappointment, in disbelief, in anguish. Eve stops her turning motion and looks, her full attention on Shetha's face.

I draw a deep breath.

The moment spins itself out, tough as spider-thread.

Eve breaks it. "Adam—can't you take her?"

He doesn't answer. Actually, he hasn't even heard her. He can't, in exactly the same way Eve cannot hear *Him* in the cool of the evening. You could argue that this exempts him from fault.

Eve picks up the baby and stands beside the bower. Fragrance rises from the newly-crushed flower petals where Adam was lying. When he and the boys have left again, I slither forward. Eve, the baby in her arms, has still not moved. Her head is bent. Sheitha is weeping, soft tears of vexation that will not, of course last very long. Not here. I don't have much time.

"Eve," I say. "Listen—"

I tell her how it will be for Sheitha after she marries Cain, who is not as sweet-tempered as his father. I tell her how it will be for Sheitha's daughter's daughter. I spare her nothing: not the expansion of the garden until the home bowers are insignificant. Not the debate over whether women have souls. Not foot-binding nor clitorectomy nor suttee nor the word "chattel." Sheitha, I say. Sheitha and Sheitha's daughter and Sheitha's daughter's daughter . . . I am hoarse before I'm done talking. Finally, I finish, saying for perhaps the fortieth or fiftieth time, "Knowledge is the only way to change it. Knowledge, and truth. Eve, listen—"

She goes with me to the tree. Her baby daughter in her arms, she goes with me. She chooses a bright red apple, and she chews her mouthful so completely that when she transfers it to Sheitha's lips there is no chance the baby could choke on it. Together, they eat the whole thing.

I am tired. I don't wait around for the rest: Adam's return, and his outrage that she has acted without him, his fear that now she knows things he does not. *His* arrival. I don't wait. I am too tired, and my gut twists as if I had swallowed something foul, or bitter. That happens sometimes, without my intending it. Sometimes I eat something with a vitamin I know I need, and it lies hard in my belly like pain.

This is not the way you heard the story.

But consider who eventually wrote that story down. Consider, too, who wiped up the ink or scrubbed the chisel or cleaned the printing office after the writing down was done. For centuries and centuries.

But not forever.

So this may not be the way you heard the story, but you, centuries and centuries hence, my sisters, know better. Finally. You know, yes, about Eve's screams on her childbed, and Sheitha's murder at the hands of her husband, and Sheitha's daughter's cursing of her rebellious mother as the girl climbed wilingly onto her husband's funeral pyre, and *her* daughter's harlotry, and *her* daughter's forced marriage at age nine to a man who gained control of all her camels and oases. You know all that, all the things I didn't tell poor Eve would happen anyway. But you know, too—as Eve would not have, had it not been for me—that knowledge can bring change. You sit cross-legged at your holodecks or in your pilot chairs or on your Councils, humming, and you finally know. Finally—it took you so fucking *long* to digest the fruit of knowledge and shit it out where it could fertilize anything. But you did. You are not stupid. More—you know that stupidity is only the soul asleep. The awakened sleeper may stumble a long time in the dark, but eventually the light comes. Even here.

I woke Eve up.

I, the mother.

So that may not be the way you heard the story, but it is the way it happened. And now—finally, finally—you know.

And can forgive me.

# EVOLUTION

*Science fiction is enamored of categorization. This story, for example, is "hard SF." Hard SF extrapolates realistically from known science, often (although not inevitably) in a near future setting. There's a built-in danger for such stories. In the next decade, "Evolution" will probably either become fact or become obsolete.*

*"Evolution" is built on world-wide concern, very real as I write this, over the idea of bacteria becoming resistant to antibiotics. Many diseases, including strains of tuberculosis and staphylococcus aureus, are already resistant to all antibiotics except vancomycin, the drug of last resort. Others, such as some enterococci, resist vancomycin as well. Few new antibiotics are in development because drug companies have found other lines of research to be more profitable.*

*This situation could go two ways. Bacteria might increase their resistance even more, which they are genetically well equipped to do. This could lead to recurrences of epidemics once thought subdued by modern medicine, including tuberculosis and staph. Hospitals would become fertile breeding grounds for these super-diseases: places you go to die, as they were in the nineteenth century. If you weren't infected when you went in, you would be when you came out.*

*Or, medical science might find a new way to defeat bacterial resistance to antibiotics. Already, promising work is being done at Yale on synthetic genes that make E. coli more sensitive to antibiotics. Such techniques would eliminate the crisis before it becomes one.*

*Either way, this story will no longer be a prediction of the future. Will it still be "hard science fiction"? I leave that to the categorizers.*

Somebody shot and killed Dr. Bennett behind the Food Mart on April Street!" Ceci Moore says breathlessly as I take the washing off the line.

I stand with a pair of Jack's boxer shorts in my hand and stare at her. I don't like Ceci. Her smirking pushiness, her need to shove her scrawny body into the middle of every situation, even ones she'd be better off leaving alone. She's been that way since high school. But we're neighbors; we're stuck with each other. Dr. Bennett delivered both Sean and Jackie. Slowly I fold the boxer shorts and lay them in my clothesbasket.

"Well, Betty, aren't you even going to *say* anything?"

"Have the police arrested anybody?"

"Janie Brunelli says there's no suspects." Tom Brunelli is one of Emerton's police officers, all five of them. He has trouble keeping his mouth shut. "Honestly, Betty, you look like there's a murder in this town every day!"

"Was it in the parking lot?" I'm in that parking lot behind the Food Mart every week. It's unpaved, just hard-packed rocky dirt sloping down to a low concrete wall by the river. I take Jackie's sheets off the line. Belle, Ariel, and Princess Jasmine all smile through fields of flowers.

"Yes, in the parking lot," Ceci says. "Near the Dumpsters. There must have been a silencer on the rifle, nobody heard anything. Tom found two .22 250 semiautomatic cartridges." Ceci knows about guns. Her house is full of them. "Betty, why don't you put all this wash in your dryer and save yourself the trouble of hanging it all out?"

"I like the way it smells line-dried. And I can hear Jackie through the window."

Instantly Ceci's face changes. "Jackie's home from school? Why?"

"She has a cold."

"Are you sure it's just a cold?"

"I'm sure." I take the clothespins off Sean's t-shirt. The front says SEE DICK DRINK. SEE DICK DRIVE. SEE DICK DIE. "Ceci, Jackie is not on any antibiotics."

"Good thing," Ceci says, and for a moment she studies her fingernails, very casual. "They say Dr. Bennett prescribed endozine again last week. For the youngest Nordstrum boy. *Without* sending him to the hospital."

I don't answer. The back of Sean's t-shirt says DON'T BE A DICK. Irritated by my silence, Ceci says, "I don't see how you can let your son wear that obscene clothing!"

"It's his choice. Besides, Ceci, it's a health message. About not drinking and driving. Aren't you the one that thinks strong health messages are a good thing?"

Our eyes lock. The silence lengthens. Finally Ceci says, "Well, haven't *we* gotten serious all of a sudden."

I say, "Murder is serious."

"Yes. I'm sure the cops will catch whoever did it. Probably one of those scum that hang around the Rainbow Bar."

"Dr. Bennett wasn't the type to hang around with scum."

"Oh, I don't mean he *knew* them. Some low-life probably killed him for his wallet." She looks straight into my eyes. "I can't think of any other motive. Can you?"

I look east, toward the river. On the other side, just visible over the tops of houses on its little hill, rise the three stories of Emerton Soldiers and Sailors Memorial Hospital. The bridge over the river was blown up three weeks ago. No injuries, no suspects. Now anybody who wants to go to the hospital has to drive ten miles up West River Road and cross at the Interstate. Jack told me that the Department of Transportation says two years to get a new bridge built.

I say, "Dr. Bennett was a good doctor. And a good man."

"Well, did anybody say he wasn't? Really, Betty, you should use your dryer and save yourself all that bending and stooping. Bad for the back. We're not getting any younger. Ta-ta." She waves her right hand, just a waggle of fingers, and walks off. Her nails, I notice, are painted the delicate fragile pinky-white of freshly unscabbed skin.

"You have no proof," Jack says. "Just some wild suspicions."

He has his stubborn face on. He sits with his Michelob at the kitchen table, dog-tired from his factory shift plus three hours overtime, and he doesn't want to hear this. I don't blame him. I don't want to be saying it. In the living room Jackie plays Nintendo frantically, trying to cram in as many electronic explosions as she can before her father claims the TV for Monday Night Football. Sean has already gone out with his friends, before his stepfather got home.

I sit down across from Jack, a fresh mug of coffee cradled between my palms. For warmth. "I know I don't have any proof, Jack. I'm not some detective."

"So let the cops handle it. It's their business, not ours. You stay out of it."

"I am out of it. You know that." Jack nods. We don't mix with cops, don't serve on any town committees, don't even listen to the news much. We don't get involved with what doesn't concern us. Jack never did. I add, "I'm just telling you what I think. I can do that, can't I?" and hear my voice stuck someplace between pleading and anger.

Jack hears it, too. He scowls, stands with his beer, puts his hand gently on my shoulder. "Sure, Bets. You can say whatever you want to me. But nobody else, you hear? I don't want no trouble, especially to you and the kids. This ain't our problem. Just be grateful *we're* all healthy, knock on wood."

He smiles and goes into the living room. Jackie switches off the Nintendo without being yelled at; she's good that way. I look out the kitchen window, but it's too dark to see anything but my own reflection, and anyway the window faces north, not east.

I haven't crossed the river since Jackie was born at Emerton Memorial, seven years ago. And then I was in the hospital less than twenty-four hours before I made Jack take me home. Not because of the infections, of course—that hadn't all started yet. But it has now, and what if next time instead of the youngest Nordstrum boy, it's Jackie who needs endozine? Or Sean?

Once you've been to Emerton Memorial, nobody but your family will go near you. And sometimes not even them. When Mrs. Weimer came home from surgery, her daughter-in-law put her in that back up-stairs room and left her food on disposable trays in the doorway and put in a chemical toilet. Didn't even help the old lady crawl out of bed to use it. For a whole month it went on like that—surgical masks, gloves, paper gowns—until Rosie Weimer was positive Mrs. Weimer hadn't picked up any mutated drug-resistant bacteria in Emerton Memorial. And Hal Weimer didn't say a word against his wife.

"People are scared, but they'll do the right thing," Jack said, the only other time I tried to talk to him about it. Jack isn't much for talking. And so I don't. I owe him that.

But in the city—in all the cities—they're not just scared. They're terrified. Even without listening to the news I hear about the riots and the special government police and half the population sick with the new germs that only endozine cures—sometimes. I don't see how they're going to have much energy for one murdered small-town doctor. And I don't share Jack's conviction that people in Emerton will automatically do the right thing. I remember all too well that sometimes they don't. How come Jack doesn't remember, too?

But he's right about one thing: I don't owe this town anything.

I stack the supper dishes in the sink and get Jackie started on her homework.


The next day, I drive down to the Food Mart parking lot.

There isn't much to see. It rained last night. Next to the Dumpster lie a wadded-up surgical glove and a piece of yellow tape like the police use around a crime scene. Also some of those little black cardboard boxes from the stuff that gets used up by the new holographic TV cameras. That's it.

"You heard what happened to Dr. Bennett," I say to Sean at dinner. Jack's working again. Jackie sits playing with the Barbie doll she doesn't know I know she has on her lap.

Sean looks at me sideways, under the heavy fringe of his dark bangs, and I can't read his expression. "He was killed for giving out too many antibiotics."

Jackie looks up. "Who killed the doctor?"

"The bastards that think they run this town," Sean says. He flicks the hair out of his eyes. His face is ashy gray. "Fucking vigilantes'll get us all."

"That's enough, Sean," I say.

Jackie's lip trembles. "Who'll get us all? Mommy . . ."

"Nobody's getting anybody," I say. "Sean, stop it. You're scaring her."

"Well, she should be scared," Sean says, but he shuts up and stares bleakly at his plate. Sixteen now, I've had him for sixteen years. Watching him, his thick dark hair and sulky mouth, I think that it's a sin to have a favorite child. And that I can't help it, and that I would, God forgive me, sacrifice both Jackie and Jack for this boy.

"I want you to clean the garage tonight, Sean. You promised Jack three days ago now."

"Tomorrow. Tonight I have to go out."

Jackie says, "Why should I be scared?"

"Tonight," I say.

Sean looks at me with teenage desperation. His eyes are very blue. "Not tonight. I have to go out."

Jackie says, "Why should I—"

I say, "You're staying home and cleaning the garage."

"No." He glares at me, and then breaks. He has his father's looks, but he's not really like his father. There are even tears in the corners of his eyes. "I'll do it tomorrow, Mom, I promise. Right after school. But tonight I have to go out."

"Where?"

"Just out."

Jackie says, "Why should I be scared? Scared of what? Mommy!"

Sean turns to her. "You shouldn't be scared, Jack-o-lantern. Everything's going to be all right. One way or another."

I listen to the tone of his voice and suddenly fear shoots through me, piercing as childbirth. I say, "Jackie, you can play Nintendo now. I'll clear the table."

Her face brightens. She skips into the living room and I look at my son. "What does that mean? 'One way or another'? Sean, what's going on?"

"Nothing," he says, and then despite his ashy color he looks me straight in the eyes, and smiles tenderly, and for the first time—the very first time—I see his resemblance to his father. He can lie to me with tenderness.

Two days later, just after I return from the Food Mart, they contact me.

The murder was on the news for two nights, and then disappeared. Over the parking lot is scattered more TV-camera litter. There's also a wine bottle buried halfway into the hard ground, with a bouquet of yellow roses in it. Nearby is an empty basket, the kind that comes filled with expensive dried flowers at Blossoms by Bonnie, weighted down with stones. Staring at it, I remember that Bonnie Widelstein went out of business a few months ago. A drug-resistant abscess, and after she got out of Emerton Memorial, nobody on this side of the river would buy flowers from her.

At home, Sylvia James is sitting in my driveway in her black Algol. As soon as I see her, I put it together.

"Sylvia," I say tonelessly.

She climbs out of the sportscar and smiles a social smile. "Elizabeth! How good to see you!" I don't answer. She hasn't seen me in seventeen years. She's carrying a cheese kuchen, like some sort of key into my house. She's still blonde, still slim, still well dressed. Her lipstick is bright red, which is what her face should be.

I let her in anyway, my heart making slow hard thuds in my chest. *Sean. Sean.*

Once inside, her hard smile fades and she has the grace to look embarrassed. "Elizabeth—"

"Betty," I say. "I go by Betty now."

"Betty. First off, I want to apologize for not being . . . for not standing by you in that mess. I know it was so long ago, but even so, I—I wasn't a very good friend." She hesitates. "I was frightened by it all."

I want to say, *You* were frightened? But I don't.

I never think of the whole dumb story any more. Not even when I look at Sean. Especially not when I look at Sean.

Seventeen years ago, when Sylvia and I were seniors in high school, we were best friends. Neither of us had a sister, so we made each other into that, even though her family wasn't crazy about their precious daughter hanging around with someone like me. The Goddards live on the other side of the river. Sylvia ignored them, and I ignored the drunken warnings of my aunt, the closest thing I had to a family. The differences didn't matter. We were Sylvia-and-Elizabeth, the two prettiest and boldest girls in the senior class who had an academic future.

And then, suddenly, I didn't. At Elizabeth's house I met Randolf Satler, young resident in her father's unit at the hospital. And I got pregnant, and Randy dumped me, and I refused a paternity test because if he didn't want me and the baby I had too much pride to force myself on any man. That's what I told everyone, including myself. I was eighteen years old. I didn't know what a common story mine was, or what a dreary one. I thought I was the only one in the whole wide world who had ever felt this bad.

So after Sean was born at Emerton Memorial and Randy got engaged the day I moved my baby "home" to my dying aunt's, I bought a Smith & Wesson revolver in the city and shot out the windows of Randy's supposedly empty house across the river. I hit the gardener, who was helping himself to the Satler liquor cabinet in the living room. The judge gave me seven-and-a-half to ten, and I served five, and that only because my lawyer pleaded post-partum depression. The gardener recovered and retired to Miami, and Dr. Satler went on to become Chief of Medicine at Emerton Memorial and a lot of other important things in the city, and Sylvia never visited me once in Bedford Hills Correctional Facility. Nobody did, except Jack. Who, when Sylvia-and-Elizabeth were strutting their stuff at Emerton High, had already dropped out and was bagging groceries at the Food Mart. After I got out of Bedford, the only reason the foster care people would give me Sean back was because Jack married me.

We live in Emerton, but not of it.

Sylvia puts her kuchen on the kitchen table and sits down without being asked. I can see she's done with apologizing. She's still smart enough to know there are things you can't apologize for.

"Eliz . . . Betty, I'm not here about the past. I'm here about Dr. Bennett's murder."

"That doesn't have anything to do with me."

"It has to do with all of us. Dan Moore lives next door to you."

I don't say anything.

"He and Ceci and Jim Dyer and Tom Brunelli are the ringleaders in a secret organization to close Emerton Memorial Hospital. They think the hospital is a breeding ground for the infections resistant to every antibiotic except endozine. Well, they're right about that—all hospitals are. But Dan and his group are determined to punish any doctor who prescribes endozine, so that no organisms develop a resistance to it, too, and it's kept effective in case one of *them* needs it."

"Sylvia—" the name tastes funny in my mouth, after all this time "—I'm telling you this doesn't have anything to do with me."

"And I'm telling you it does. We need you, Eliz . . . Betty. You live next door to Dan and Ceci. You can tell us when they leave the house, who comes to it, anything suspicious you see. We're not a vigilante group, Betty, like they are. We aren't doing anything illegal. We don't kill people, and we don't blow up bridges, and we don't threaten people like the Nordstrums who get endozine for their sick kids but are basically uneducated blue collar—"

She stops. Jack and I are basically uneducated blue collar. I say coldly, "I can't help you, Sylvia."

"I'm sorry, Betty. That wasn't what I meant. Look, this is more important than anything that happened a decade and a half ago! Don't you *understand?*" She leans toward me across the table. "The whole country's caught in this thing. It's already a public health crisis as big as the Spanish influenza epidemic of 1918, and it's only just started! Drug-resistant bacteria can produce a new generation every twenty minutes, they can swap resistant genes not only within a species but across *different* species. The bacteria are *winning*. And people like the Moores are taking advantage of that to contribute further to the break-down of even basic social decency."

In high school Sylvia had been on the debating team. But so, in that other life, had I. "If the Moores' group is trying to keep endozine from being used, then aren't they also fighting against the development of more drug-resistant bacteria? And if that's so, aren't they the ones, not you, who are ultimately aiding the country's public health?"

"Through dynamiting. And intimidation. And murder. Betty, I know you don't approve of those things. I wouldn't be here telling you about our countergroup if I thought you did. Before I came here, we looked very carefully at you. At the kind of person you are. Are now. You and your husband are law-abiding people, you vote, you make a contribu-tion to the Orphans of AIDS Fund, you—"

"How did you know about that? That's supposed to be a secret contribution!"

"—you signed the petition to protect the homeless from harass-ment. Your husband served on the jury that convicted Paul Keene of fraud, even though his real-estate scheme was so good for the economy of Emerton. You—"

"Stop it," I say. "You don't have any right to investigate me like I was some criminal!"

Only, of course, I was. Once. Not now. Sylvia's right about that—Jack and I believe in law and order, but for different reasons. Jack be-cause that's what his father believed in, and his grandfather. Me, because I learned in Bedford that enforced rules are the only thing that even half-way restrains the kind of predators Sylvia James never dreamed of. The kind I want kept away from my children.

Sylvia says, "We have a lot of people on our side, Betty. People who don't want to see this town slide into the same kind of violence there is in Albany and Syracuse and, worst case, New York."

A month ago, New York Hospital in Queens was blown up. The whole thing, with a series of coordinated timed bombs. Seventeen hun-dred people dead in less than a minute.

"It's a varied group," she continues. "Some town leaders, some housewives, some teachers, nearly all the medical personnel at the hospital. All people who care what happens to Emerton."

"Then you've got the wrong person here," I say, and it comes out harsher than I want to reveal. "I don't care about Emerton."

"You have reasons," Sylvia says evenly. "And I'm part of your reasons, I know. But I think you'll help us, Elizabeth. I know you must be concerned about your son—we've all observed what a good mother you are."

So she brought up Sean's name first. I say, "You're wrong again, Sylvia. I don't need you to protect Sean, and if you've let him get involved in helping you, you'll wish you'd never been born. I've worked damn hard to make sure that what happened seventeen years ago never touches him. He doesn't need to get mixed up in any way with your 'medical personnel at the hospital.' And Sean sure the hell doesn't owe this town anything, there wasn't even anybody who would take him in after my aunt died, he had to go to—"

The look on her face stops me. Pure surprise. And then something else.

"Oh my God," she says. "Is it possible you don't know? Hasn't Sean told you?"

"Told me what?" I stand up, and I'm seventeen years old again, and just that scared. Sylvia-and-Elizabeth.

"Your son isn't helping our side. He's working for Dan Moore and Mike Dyer. They use juveniles because if they're caught, they won't be tried as severely as adults. We think Sean was one of the kids they used to blow up the bridge over the river."

I look first at the high school. Sean isn't there; he hadn't even shown up for homeroom. No one's home at his friend Tom's house, or at Keith's. He isn't at the Billiard Ball or the Emerton Diner or the American Bowl. After that, I run out of places to search.

This doesn't happen in places like Emerton. We have fights at basketball games and grand theft auto and smashed store windows on Halloween and sometimes a drunken tragic car crash on prom night. But not secret terrorists, not counter-terrorist vigilante groups. Not in Emerton.

Not with my son.

I drive to the factory and make them page Jack.

He comes off the line, face creased with sweat and dirt. The air is filled with clanging machinery and grinding drills. I pull him outside the door, where there are benches and picnic tables for workers on break. "Betty! What is it?"

"Sean," I gasp. "He's in danger."

Something shifts behind Jack's eyes. "What kind of danger?"

"Sylvia Goddard came to see me today. Sylvia James. She says Sean is involved with the group that blew up the bridge, the ones who are trying to get Emerton Memorial closed, and . . . and killed Dr. Bennett."

Jack peels off his bench gloves, taking his time. Finally he looks up at me. "How come that bitch Sylvia Goddard comes to you with this? After all this time?"

"Jack! Is that all you can think of? Sean is in trouble!"

He says gently, "Well, Bets, it was bound to happen sooner or later, wasn't it? He's always been a tough kid to raise. Rebellious. Can't tell him anything."

I stare at Jack.

"Some people just have to learn the hard way."

"Jack . . . this is serious! Sean might be involved in terrorism! He could end up in jail!"

"Couldn't ever tell him anything," Jack says, and I hear the hidden satisfaction in his voice, that he doesn't even know is there. Not his son. Dr. Randy Satler's son. Turning out bad.

"Look," Jack says, "when the shift ends I'll go look for him, Bets. Bring him home. You go and wait there for us." His face is gentle, soothing. He really will find Sean, if it's possible. But only because he loves me.

My sudden surge of hatred is so strong I can't even speak.

"Go on home, Bets. It'll be all right. Sean just needs to have the nonsense kicked out of him."

I turn and walk away. At the turning in the parking lot, I see Jack walking jauntily back inside, pulling on his gloves.

I drive home, because I can't think what else to do. I sit on the couch and reach back in my mind, for that other place, the place I haven't gone to since I got out of Bedford. The gray granite place that turns you to granite, too, so you can sit and wait for hours, for weeks, for years, without feeling very much. I go into that place, and I become the Elizabeth I was then, when Sean was in foster care someplace and I didn't know who had him or what they might be doing to him or how I would get him back. I go into the gray granite place to become stone.

And it doesn't work.

It's been too long. I've had Sean too long. Jack has made me feel too safe. I can't find the stony place.

Jackie is spending the night at a friend's. I sit in the dark, no lights on, car in the garage. Sean doesn't come home, and neither does Jack. At two in the morning, a lot of people in dark clothing cross the back lawn and quietly enter Dan and Ceci's house next door, carrying bulky packages wrapped in black cloth.

Jack staggers in at six-thirty in the morning. Alone. His face droops with exhaustion.

"I couldn't find him, Betty. I looked everywhere."

"Thank you," I say, and he nods. Accepting my thanks. This was something he did for me, not for Sean. Not for himself, as Sean's stepfather. I push down my sudden anger and say, "You better get some sleep."

"Right." He goes down the narrow hallway into our bedroom. In three minutes he's snoring.

I let the car coast in neutral down the driveway. Our bedroom faces the street. The curtains don't stir.

The West River Road is deserted, except for a few eighteen-wheelers. I cross the river at the Interstate and start back along the east side. Three miles along, in the middle of farmland, the smell of burned flesh rolls in the window.

Cows, close to the pasture fence. I stop the car and get out. Fifteen or sixteen Holsteins. By straining over the fence, I can see the bullet holes in their heads. Somebody herded them together, shot them one by one, and started a half-hearted fire among the bodies with neatly cut firewood. The fire had gone out; it didn't look as if it was supposed to burn long. Just long enough to attract attention that hadn't come yet.

I'd never heard that cows could get human diseases. Why had they been shot?

I get back in my car and drove the rest of the way to Emerton Memorial.

This side of town is deathly quiet. Grass grows unmowed in yard after yard. One large, expensive house has old newspapers piled on the porch steps, ten or twelve of them. There are no kids waiting for school buses, no cars pulling out of driveways on the way to work. The hospital parking lot has huge empty stretches between cars. At the last minute I drive on through the lot, parking instead across the street in somebody's empty driveway, under a clump of trees.

Nobody sits at the information desk. The gift shop is locked. Nobody speaks to me as I study the directory on the lobby wall, even though two figures in gowns and masks hurry past. CHIEF OF MEDICINE, DR. RANDOLF SATLER. Third floor, east wing. The elevator is deserted.

It stops at the second floor. When the doors open a man stands there, a middle-aged farmer in overalls and work boots, his eyes red and swollen like he's been crying. There are tinted windows across from the elevators and I can see the back of him reflected in the glass. Coming and going. From somewhere I hear a voice calling, "Nurse, oh nurse, oh God . . ." A gurney sits in hallway, the body on it covered by a sheet up to the neck. The man in overalls looks at me and raises both hands to ward off the elevator, like it's some kind of demon. He steps backward. The doors close.

I grip the railing on the elevator wall.

The third floor looks empty. Bright arrows lead along the hallways: yellow for PATHOLOGY and LAB SERVICES, green for RESPIRATORY THERAPY, red for SUPPORT SERVICES. I follow the yellow arrow.

It dead-ends at an empty alcove with chairs, magazines thrown on the floor. And three locked doors off a short corridor that's little more than another alcove.

I pick the farthest door and pound on it. No words, just regular blows of my fist. After a minute, I start on the second one. A voice calls, "Who's there?"

I recognize the voice, even through the locked door. Even after seventeen years. I shout, "Police! Open the door!"

And he does. The second it cracks, I shove it hard and push my way into the lab.

*"Elizabeth?"*

He's older, heavier, but still the same. Dark hair, blue eyes . . . I look at that face every day at dinner. I've looked at it at soccer matches, in school plays, in his playpen. Dr. Satler looks more shaken to see me than I would have thought, his face white, sweat on his forehead.

"Hello, Randy."

"Elizabeth. You can't come in here. You have to leave—"

"Because of the staph? Do you think I care about that? After all, I'm in the hospital, right, Randy? This is where the endozine is. This place is safe. Unless it gets blown up while I'm standing here."

He stares at my left hand, still gripping the doorknob behind me. Then at the gun in my right hand. A seventeen-year-old Smith & Wesson, and for five of those years the gun wasn't cleaned or oiled, hidden under my aunt's garage. But it still fires.

"I'm not going to shoot you, Randy. I don't care if you're alive or dead. But you're going to help me. I can't find my son—" *your son* "—and Sylvia Goddard told me he's mixed up with that group that blew up the bridge. He's hiding with them someplace, probably scared out of his skull. You know everybody in town, everybody with power, you're going to get on that phone there and find out where Sean is."

"I would do that anyway," Randy says, and now he looks the way I remember him: impatient and arrogant. But not completely. There's still sweat on his pale face. "Put that stupid thing away, Elizabeth."

"No."

"Oh, for . . ." He turns his back on me and punches at the phone. "Cam? Randy Satler here. Could you . . . no, it's not about that . . . No. Not yet."

Cameron Witt. The mayor. His son is chief of Emerton's five cops.

"I need a favor. There's a kid missing. . . . I know that, Cam. You don't have to lecture *me* on how bad delay could . . . But you might know about this kid. Sean Baker."

"Pulaski. Sean Pulaski." He doesn't even know that.

"Sean Pulaski. Yeah, that one . . . okay. Get back to me . . . I told you. *Not yet.*" He hangs up. "Cam will hunt around and call back. Now will you put that stupid gun away, Elizabeth?"

"You still don't say thank you for anything." The words just come out. Fuck, fuck, fuck.

"To Cam, or to you for not shooting me?" He says it evenly, and the evenness is the only way I finally see how furious he is. People don't order around Dr. Randy Satler at gun point. A part of my mind wonders why he doesn't call security.

I said, "All right, I'm here. Give me a dose of endozine, just in case."

He goes on staring at me with that same level, furious gaze. "Too late, Elizabeth."

"What do you mean, too late? Haven't you got endozine?"

"Of course we do." Suddenly he staggers slightly, puts out one hand behind him, and holds onto a table covered with glassware and papers.

"Randy. You're sick."

"I am. And not with anything endozine is going to cure. Ah, Elizabeth, why didn't you just phone me? I'd have looked for Sean for you."

"Oh, right. Like you've been so interested and helpful in raising him."

"You never asked me."

I see that he means it. He really believes his total lack of contact with his son is my fault. I see that Randy gives only what he's asked to. He waits, lordly, for people to plead for his help, beg for it, and then he gives it. If it suits him.

I say, "I'll bet anything your kids with your wife are turning out really scary."

The blood rushes to his face, and I know I guessed right. His blue eyes darken and he looks like Jack looks just before Jack explodes. But Randy isn't Jack. An explosion would be too clean for him. He says instead, "You were stupid to come here. Haven't you been listening to the news?"

I haven't.

"The CDC publicly announced just last night what medical personnel have seen for weeks. A virulent strain of staphylococcus aureus has incorporated endozine-resistant plasmids from enterococcus." He pauses to catch his breath. "And pneumococcus may have done the same thing."

"What does that mean?"

"It means, you stupid woman, that now there are highly contagious infections that we have no drugs to cure. No antibiotics at all, not even endozine. This staph is resistant to them all. And it can live everywhere."

I lower the gun. The empty parking lot. No security to summon. The man who wouldn't get on the elevator. And Randy's face. "And you've got it."

"We've all got it. Everyone . . . in the hospital. And for forcing your way in here, you probably do, too."

"You're going to die," I say, and it's half a hope.

And he *smiles.*

He stands there in his white lab coat, sweating like a horse; barely able to stand up straight, almost shot by a woman he'd once abandoned pregnant, and he smiles. His blue eyes gleam. He looks like a picture I once saw in a book, back when I read a lot. It takes me a minute to remember that it was my high school World History book. A picture of some general.

"Everybody's going to die eventually," Randy says. "But not me right now. At least . . . I hope not." Casually he crosses the floor toward me, and I step backward. He smiles again.

"I'm not going to deliberately infect you, Elizabeth. I'm a *doctor.* I just want the gun."

"No."

"Have it your way. Look, how much do you know about the bubonic plague of the fourteenth century?"

"Nothing," I say, although I do. Why had I always acted stupider around Randy than I actually am?

"Then it won't mean anything to you to say that this mutated staph has at least that much potential—" again he paused and gulped air "—for rapid and fatal transmission. It flourishes everywhere. Even on doorknobs."

"So why the fuck are you *smiling?*" Alexander. That was the picture of the general. Alexander the Great.

"Because I . . . because the CDC distributed . . . I was on the national team to discover . . ." His face changes again. Goes even whiter. And he pitches over onto the floor.

I grab him, roll him face up, and feel his forehead. He's burning up. I bolt for the door. "Nurse! Doctor! There's a sick doctor here!"

Nobody comes.

I run down the corridors. Respiratory Therapy is empty. So is Support Services. I jab at the elevator button, but before it comes I run back to Randy.

And stand above him, lying there crumpled on the floor, laboring to breathe.

I'd dreamed about a moment like this for years. Dreamed it waking and asleep, in Emerton and in Bedford Hills and in Jack's arms. Dreamed it in a thousand ridiculous melodramatic versions. And here it is, Randy helpless and pleading, and me strong, standing over him, free to walk away and let him die. Free.

I wring out a towel in cold water and put it on his forehead. Then I find ice in the refrigerator in a corner of the lab and substitute that. He watches me, his breathing wheezy as old machinery.

"Elizabeth. Bring me . . . syringe in a box on . . . that table."

I do it. "Who should I get for you, Randy? Where?"

"Nobody. I'm not . . . as bad . . . as I sound. Yet. Just the initial . . . dyspnea." He picks up the syringe.

"Is there medicine for you in there? I thought you said endozine wouldn't work on this new infection." His color is a little better now.

"Not medicine. And not for me. For you."

He looks at me steadily. And I see that Randy would never plead, never admit to helplessness. Never ever think of himself as helpless.

He lowers the hand holding the syringe back to the floor. "Listen, Elizabeth. You have . . . almost certainly have . . ."

Somewhere, distantly, a siren starts to wail. Randy ignores it. All of a sudden his voice becomes much firmer, even though he's sweating again and his eyes burn bright with fever. Or something.

"This staph is resistant to everything we can throw it. We cultured it and tried. Cephalosporins and aminoglycosides and vancomycin, even endozine . . . I'll go into gram-positive septic shock. . . ." His eyes glaze, but after a moment he seems to find his thought again. "We exhausted all points of counterattack. Cell wall, bacterial ribosome, folic acid pathway. Microbes just evolve countermeasures. Like beta-lactamase."

I don't understand this language. Even talking to himself, he's making me feel stupid again. I ask something I do understand.

"Why are people killing cows? Are the cows sick, too?"

He focuses again. "Cows? No, they're not sick. Farmers use massive doses of antibiotics to increase meat and milk production. Agricultural use of endozine has increased the rate of resistance development by over a thousand percent since—Elizabeth, this is irrelevant! Can't you pay attention to what I'm saying for three minutes?"

I stand up and look down at him, lying shivering on the floor. He doesn't even seem to notice, just keeps on lecturing.

"But antibiotics weren't invented by humans. They were invented by the microbes themselves to use . . . against each other and . . . they had two billion years of evolution at it before we even showed up. . . . We should have—where are you going?"

"Home. Have a nice life, Randy."

He says quietly, "I probably will. But if . . . you leave now, you're probably dead. And your husband and kids, too."

"Why? Damn it, stop lecturing and tell me why!"

"Because you're infected, and there's no antibiotic for it, but there *is* another bacteria that will attack the drug-resistant staph."

I look at the syringe in his hand.

"It's a Trojan horse plasmid. That's a . . . never mind. It can get into the staph in your blood and deliver a lethal gene. One that will kill the staph. It's an incredible discovery. But the only way to deliver it so far is to deliver the whole bacteria."

My knees all of a sudden get shaky. Randy watches me from his position on the floor. He looks shakier himself. His breathing turns raspier again.

"No, you're not sick yet, Elizabeth. But you will be."

I snap, "From the staph germs or from the cure?"

"Both."

"You want to make me sicker. With two bacteria. And hope one will kill the other."

"Not hope. I *know*. I actually saw . . . it on the electromicrograph. . . ." His eyes roll, refocus. ". . . could package just the lethal plasmid on a transpon if we had time . . . no time. Has to be the whole bacteria." And then, stronger, "The CDC team is working on it. But *I* actually caught it on the electromicrograph!"

I say, before I know I'm going to, "Stop congratulating yourself and give me the syringe. Before you die."

I move across the floor toward him, put my arms around him to prop him in a sitting position against the table leg. His whole body feels on fire. But somehow he keeps his hands steady as he injects the syringe into the inside of my elbow. While it drains sickness into me I say, "You never actually wanted me, did you, Randy? Even before Sean?"

"No," he says. "Not really." He drops the syringe.

I bend my arm. "You're a rotten human being. All you care about is yourself and your work."

He smiles the same cold smile. "So? My work is what matters. In a larger sense than you could possibly imagine. You were always a weak sentimentalist, Elizabeth. Now, go home."

"Go *home*? But you said . . ."

"I said you'd infect everyone. And you will—with the bacteria that attacks staph. It should cause only a fairly mild illness. Jenner . . . smallpox . . ."

"But you said I have the mutated staph, too!"

"You almost certainly do. Yes . . . And so will everyone else, before long. Deaths . . . in New York State alone . . . passed one million this morning. Six and a half percent of the . . . the population. . . . Did you really think you could hide on your side of . . . the . . . river . . . ?"

"Randy!"

"Go . . . home."

I strip off his lab coat and wad it up for a pillow, bring more ice from the refrigerator, try to get him to drink some water.

"Go . . . home. Kiss everybody." He smiles to himself, and starts to shake with fever. His eyes close.

I stand up again. Should I go? Stay? If I could find someone in the hospital to take care of him—

The phone rings. I seize it. "Hello? Hello?"

"Randy? Excuse me, can I talk to Dr. Satler? This is Cameron Witt."

I try to sound professional. "Dr. Satler can't come to the phone right now. But if you're calling about Sean Pulaski, Dr. Satler asked me to take the message."

"I don't . . . oh, all right. Just tell Randy the Pulaski boy is with Richard and Sylvia James. He'll understand." The line clicks.

I replace the receiver and stare at Randy, fighting for breath on the floor, his face as gray as Sean's when Sean realized it was murder he'd gotten involved with. No, not as gray. Because Sean had been terrified, and Randy is only sick.

*My work is what matters.*

But how had Sean known to go to Sylvia? Even if he knew from Ceci who was on the other side, how did he know which people would hide him, would protect him when I could not, Jack could not? Sylvia-and-Elizabeth. How much did Sean actually know about the past I'd tried so hard to keep from touching him?

I reach the elevator, my finger almost touching the button, when the first explosion rocks the hospital.

It's in the west wing. Through the windows opposite the elevator banks I see windows in the far end of the building explode outward. Thick greasy black smoke billows out the holes. Alarms begin to screech.

*Don't touch the elevators.* Instructions remembered from high school, from grade-school fire drills. I race along the hall to the fire stairs. What if they put a bomb in the stairwell? What if *who* put a bomb in the stairwell? *A lot of people in dark clothing cross the back lawn and quietly enter Dan and Ceci's house next door, carrying bulky packages wrapped in black cloth.*

A last glimpse through a window by the door to the firestairs. People are running out of the building, not many, but the ones I see are pushing gurneys. A nurse staggers outside, three small children in her arms, on her hip, clinging to her back.

They aren't setting off any more bombs until people have a chance to get out.

I let the fire door close. Alarms scream. I run back to Pathology and shove open the heavy door.

Randy lies on the floor, sweating and shivering. His lips move but if he's muttering aloud, I can't hear it over the alarm. I tug on his arm. He doesn't resist and he doesn't help, just lies like a heavy dead cow.

There are no gurneys in Pathology. I slap him across the face, yelling "Randy! Randy! Get up!" Even now, even here, a small part of my mind thrills at hitting him.

His eyes open. For a second, I think he knows me. It goes away, then returns. He tries to get up. The effort is enough to let me hoist him over my shoulder in a fireman's carry. I could never have carried Jack, but Randy is much slighter, and I'm very strong.

But I can't carry him down three flights of stairs. I get him to the top, prop him up on his ass, and shove. He slides down one flight, bumping and flailing, and glares at me for a minute. "For . . . God's sake . . . Janet!"

His wife's name. I don't think about this tiny glimpse of his marriage. I give him another shove, but he grabs the railing and refuses to fall. He hauls himself—I'll never know how—back to a sitting position, and I sit next to him. Together, my arm around his waist, tugging and pulling, we both descend the stairs the way two-year-olds do, on our asses. Every second I'm waiting for the stairwell to blow up. Sean's gray face at dinner: *Fucking vigilantes'll get us all.*

The stairs don't blow up. The firedoor at the bottom gives out on a sidewalk on the side of the hospital away from both street and parking lot. As soon as we're outside, Randy blacks out.

This time I do what I should have done upstairs and grab him under the armpits. I drag him over the grass as far as I can. Sweat and hair fall in my eyes, and my vision keeps blurring. Dimly I'm aware of someone running toward us.

"It's Dr. Satler! Oh my God!"

A man. A large man. He grabs Randy and hoists him over his shoulder, a fireman's carry a lot smoother than mine, barely glancing at me. I stay behind them and, at the first buildings, run in a wide loop away from the hospital.

My car is still in the deserted driveway across the street. Fire trucks add their sirens to the noise. When they've torn past, I back my car out of the driveway and push my foot to the floor, just as a second bomb blows in the east wing of the hospital, and then another, and the air is full of flying debris as thick and sharp as the noise that goes on and on and on.

Three miles along the East River Road, it suddenly catches up with me. All of it. I pull the car off the road and I can't stop shaking. Only a few trucks pass me, and nobody stops. It's twenty minutes before I can start the engine again, and there has never been a twenty minutes like them in my life, not even in Bedford. At the end of them, I pray that there never will be again.

I turn on the radio as soon as I've started the engine.

"—in another hospital bombing in New York City, St. Clare's Hospital in the heart of Manhattan. Beleaguered police officials say that a shortage of available officers make impossible the kind of protection called for by Mayor Thomas Flanagan. No group has claimed credit for the bombing, which caused fires that spread to nearby businesses and at least one apartment house.

"Since the Centers for Disease Control's announcement last night of a widespread staphylococcus resistant to endozine, and its simultaneous release of an emergency counterbacteria in twenty-five metropolitan areas around the country, the violence has worsened in every city transmitting reliable reports to Atlanta. A spokesperson for the national team of pathologists and scientists responsible for the drastic countermeasure released an additional set of guidelines for its use. The spokesperson declined to be identified, or to identify any of the doctors on the team, citing fear of reprisals if—"

A burst of static. The voice disappears, replaced by a shrill hum.

I turn the dial carefully, looking for another station with news.


By the time I reach the west side of Emerton, the streets are deserted. Everyone has retreated inside. It looks like the neighborhoods around the hospital look. Had looked. My body still doesn't feel sick.

Instead of going straight home, I drive the deserted streets to the Food Mart.

The parking lot is as empty as everywhere else. But the basket is still there, weighted with stones. Now the stones hold down a pile of letters. The top one is addressed in blue Magic Marker: TO DR. BENNETT. The half-buried wine bottle holds a fresh bouquet, chrysanthemums from somebody's garden. Nearby a foot-high American flag sticks in the ground, beside a white candle on a styrofoam plate, a stone crucifix, and a Barbie doll dressed like an angel. Saran Wrap covers a leather-bound copy of The Prophet. There are also five anti-NRA stickers, a pile of seashells, and a battered peace sign on a gold chain like a necklace. The peace sign looks older than I am.

When I get home, Jack is still asleep.

I stand over him, as a few hours ago I stood over Randy Satler. I think about how Jack visited me in prison, week after week, making the long drive from Emerton even in the bad winter weather. About how he'd sit smiling at me through the thick glass in the visitors' room, his hands with their grease-stained fingers resting on his knees, smiling even when we couldn't think of anything to say to each other. About how he clutched my hand in the delivery room when Jackie was born, and the look on his face when he first held her. About the look on his face when I told him Sean was missing: the sly, secret, not-my-kid triumph. And I think about the two sets of germs in my body, readying for war.

I bend over and kiss Jack full on the lips.

He stirs a little, half wakes, reaches for me. I pull away and go into the bathroom, where I use his toothbrush. I don't rinse it. When I return, he's asleep again.

I drive to Jackie's school, to retrieve my daughter. Together, we will go to Sylvia Goddard's—Sylvia James's—and get Sean. I'll visit with Sylvia, and shake her hand, and kiss her on the cheek, and touch everything I can. When the kids are safe at home, I'll visit Ceci and tell her I've thought it over and I want to help fight the overuse of antibiotics that's killing us. I'll touch her, and anyone else there, and everyone that either Sylvia or Ceci introduces me to, until I get too sick to do that. If I get that sick. Randy said I wouldn't, not as sick as he is. Of course, Randy has lied to me before. But I have to believe him now, on this.

I don't really have any choice. Yet.

A month later, I am on my way to Albany to bring back another dose of the counterbacteria, which the news calls "a reengineered prokaryote." They're careful not to call it a germ.

I listen to the news every hour now, although Jack doesn't like it. Or anything else I'm doing. I read, and I study, and now I know what prokaryotes are, and beta-lactamase, and plasmids. I know how bacteria fight to survive, evolving whatever they need to wipe out the competition and go on producing the next generation. That's all that matters to bacteria. Survival by their own kind.

And that's what Randy Satler meant, too, when he said, "My work is what matters." Triumph by his own kind. It's what Ceci believes, too. And Jack.

We bring in the reengineered prokaryotes in convoys of cars and trucks, because in some other places there's been trouble. People who don't understand, people who won't understand. People whose family got a lot sicker than mine. The violence isn't over, even though the CDC says the epidemic itself is starting to come under control.

I'm early. The convoy hasn't formed yet. We leave from a different place in town each time. This time we're meeting behind the American Bowl. Sean is already there, with Sylvia. I take a short detour and drive, for the last time, to the Food Mart.

The basket is gone, with all its letters to the dead man. So are the American flag and the peace sign. The crucifix is still there, but it's broken in half. The latest flowers in the wine bottle are half wilted. Rain has muddied the Barbie doll's dress, and her long blonde hair is a mess. Someone ripped up the anti-NRA stickers. The white candle on a styrofoam plate and the pile of seashells are untouched.

We are not bacteria. More than survival matters to us, or should. The individual past, which we can't escape, no matter how hard we try. The individual present, with its unsafe choices. The individual future. And the collective one.

I search in my pockets. Nothing but keys, money clip, lipstick, tissues, a blue marble I must have stuck in my pocket when I cleaned behind the couch. Jackie likes marbles.

I put the marble beside the candle, check my gun, and drive to join the convoy for the city.

# ARS LONGA

*In 1993 Mike Resnick called me up to ask for a story for his anthology By Any Other Fame. He stipulated only that I tell him, in advance of writing the story, which celebrity I wanted to write about. He had contacted a lot of writers, and he didn't want duplication.*

*I pondered for a few weeks. When I called Mike and told him "Walt Disney," he said that Walt Disney was already taken. What, I complained, how can that be? It's only been two weeks! And I need Walt Disney! I must have Walt Disney! Allow me the head of Walt Disney!*

*Mike thought about it and agreed. His other claimant to Walt was David Gerrold, and Mike's reasoning was that David and I were such different writers that there was no remote chance we would use our joint celebrity in the same way.*

*Mike was right. David's Walt Disney became a dictator. Mine became . . . what selfless dedication made him.*

THE FIRST TIME I SAW WALT, I KNEW HE WOULD BE A GREAT MAN. OH, I know everybody and his brother says that about the famous, or those about to become famous. But in my case it's absolutely true. I saw that earnest little boy dressed in his hand-me-down knickers and torn shirt, and I just knew. I wouldn't say that if it wasn't true. The town of Marceline entrusted me with their precious children for fifty-two years, until my retirement. I'm a member in good standing of the First Congregational Church. You may ask anyone in Marceline about Annie Peeler's veracity.

I've never been interviewed for a newspaper before.

Would you like more tea, Mr. Snelling?

Yes, of course, about Walt. Of course I understand your time is limited and this will only be a small article, although I do think the papers might pay more attention to the fine arts instead of all these cheap movies and so-called pop songs with their suggestive lyrics and . . . Art is the thing that unites us, lifts us out of baser and more jaded selves. Art is what justifies our being.

Yes, I *did* tell Walt that. I told all my pupils that, right from the first day of school. It's a great mistake to think third-graders can't understand. Children hunger for greatness, and in a place like Marceline they see so little of it around them. That's why I've always hung fine art prints all around my classroom, even in the early years when they cost me most of my salary. I used to travel to Kansas City on the Atchison,

Topeka, and Santa Fe to buy them. Renoir and Rosetti and Monet and Whistler and of course Burne-Jones. Children will open like blossoms in the presence of great art, with proper guidance. I've always believed that. Why, when I graduated from Normal in 1894—

Yes. Walt.

As I say, I knew right away he was special. He sat at his desk in those patched hand-me-downs—his father, you know, was as mean with money as with everything else—drawing his little pictures in the margins of schoolbooks so old they had pages missing. I think they'd been his older brothers' books, and Walt's father just didn't give a hoot if all of Milton and most of long division had just been wantonly ripped out.

His mother? *What* mother?

Oh, don't write that down, I'm sorry I said it. It wasn't a very Christian thing to say, was it? I'm sure she did the best she could, poor thing, married to Elias Disney. Never any money, of course, and what was worse, no education or refinement, no chance to pass on a sense of the finer things in life. Just the same, to let him go around in those torn knickers, scrounging pencil stubs out of wastebaskets, sketching his little things in the margins of schoolbooks because no one recognized and nurtured his talent at home . . . If ever a boy needed mothering, it was young Walt.

I bought him his first sketchbook, you know, and a box of decent pencils. His little face just lit up. He was a grateful child, always, and quick to see an opportunity. Right away he started copying Edward Hicks's "The Peaceable Kingdom." He liked animal pictures, although of course later on I tried to steer him toward people. I always impressed on the children that the human form is the noblest expression of the painter's art.

Young Walt's first copy wasn't very good, of course—he completely missed the painting's spiritual dimension—but he kept at it all year, and gradually his drawing improved. I remembered he copied Burne-Jones's "The Mill" very credibly, and also Gaugin's "The Yellow Christ." Oh, yes, we had Gaugin, even though some of the parents didn't like it. Too strange and—I don't want you to get the wrong impression here, these are all lovely people in Marceline, good solid Christian people, but they do have provincial tastes. There's no getting around it. But I kept Gaugin up on my walls even when a delegation of parents went to the principal to object. I've always had a little rebellious streak of my own. And more important, of course, is that education must never bow to the trivial or the provincial. Education of the young must always embrace the highest of ideals and attainments.

Which is why I was glad when Walt's family moved to Kansas City at the end of the school year. Oh, of course I was torn up inside; some days I truly didn't think I could bear losing him. But I thought that in KC he could have proper art lessons, go to museums. . . . Ha! Just shows you how much I knew about Elias Disney!

He bought a newspaper route, you know, for the *Kansas City Star.* Little Walt and his big brother Roy had to get up at 3:30 in the morning to meet the delivery truck and deliver hundreds of papers before school, struggling through the snow and rain in the dark. It almost broke my heart when Walt told me that in the winter he'd lie down and doze in the corridors of apartment buildings, because they were warm, and in the summer he'd play with toys left overnight on the porches of children whose fathers weren't the skinflint, lucre-minded louts that Elias—

What? How did he tell me that? Oh, I went to KC every few months to visit him. By then I knew I was that poor, talented little boy's only hope. I met him during the noon recess of his school, a dreadful place full of coarse children and underbred teachers. It disgraced the name of education. I took Walt to a decent tearoom for lunch, and I brought him art supplies, and most of all I encouraged him. Never give up, I told him over and over. Look at Van Gogh. Look at Paul Cezanne, with his own dreadful father. There is more in life than daily drudgery to bring ephemeral journalism to uncaring philistines.

More tea?

Yes, Walt did continue to draw during those years. I remember a lovely still life, a fruit piece, a little bit in the style of Cezanne. Very promising. Of course, nearly all his time was taken up by the newspaper route, and finally I saw that something would have to be done. So when Walt was fourteen I went to see Elias Disney.

"You have to send that boy for Saturday lessons at the Art Institute," I said.

He squinted at me with his mean little eyes and didn't say anything. Walt had told me his father used to beat him. He'd stopped *that* by now, but he looked as if he wanted to beat me. But I stood my ground. And all the while his timid, ineffectual mother cowering in the background. I'm sorry, Mr. Snelling, but I really cannot respect a member of the fair sex who will not fight for her young. Had I ever been privileged to bear a child like Walt . . . but that's hardly germane to our interview, is it?

"I am prepared to pay for the lessons myself," I told Elias Disney. "All you must do is excuse Walt from work on Saturday. His obligation to his own talent is a higher one than to commerce."

Elias looked at me and spat his tobacco on the ground—a filthy habit, that, and one I was glad to see disappear. He said, "I always heard you was an interfering old maid."

Well, you can imagine the effect that had on me. I am directly descended from Ebenezer Zane, the frontier hero who saved the Ohio Valley from the savages. On my mother's side. I just drew myself up to my full height and said calmly, "Mr. Disney, I don't care how you insult me, that boy must have his chance. Art has called him, and your feelings and mine are irrelevant. If you will not allow me to give him the opportunity he deserves, then I will see that he wrenches it from you by moral force."

Well, Elias looked a little confused, and to tell the truth, so did Walt. He was still very young. But Elias's older three sons had already all run away from home, so maybe that's what made Elias back down. Or maybe Art can even touch a man like him, in his secret soul—would you be so rash as to deny the possibility, Mr. Snelling? I think not. At any rate, he spat again and said, "Ain't my lookout how you spend your money."

Immediately I pressed my advantage. "Then Walt may have Saturdays off? And carfare to the Art Institute?"

Elias nodded. I hid my triumph—it wouldn't have been Christian to gloat—and the very next week I took Walt to register at the Institute.

He didn't? Not anything about the Institute? Well, I'm afraid there's a reason for that. Let me just find the words to put this diplomatically.

There, I'm ready now. Are you writing this down?

The Art Institute is a good and worthy institution. But Kansas City, after all, is not New York. Had the young Walt Disney enrolled in an art school in New York, the greater sophistication and perspicacity of the teachers would have immediately led them to recognize his unusual talent. But in Kansas City, provincialism meant that his teachers were not as impressed with Walt as they should have been. That explains the mediocre response he received there. As I'm sure you know, the same negative reception initially greeted the Impressionists and the Pre-Raphaelites—why even Rosetti and Burne-Jones were initially scorned!

Not, of course, that I can approve of Rosetti's manner of living. But his art—

Please don't keep looking at your watch, Mr. Snelling. I assure you I'm telling this as fast as I can without leaving anything out.

Walt actually made good progress at the Art Institute. At the proper time, I bought him oils, brushes, and an easel. As much of my salary as was necessary went to support his art. That's what the profession of educator once meant to some of us. It was a calling, no less sacred than that of physician or minister, not merely a job to be unionized like any common workmen, as we see happening today. Put *that* in your paper.

The next thing that happened was that Elias Disney moved his family to Chicago. The newspaper route scheme had failed, of course, and now Elias was ready to try something else. A jelly factory, I believe. Walt went, too. I was devastated. Chicago was too far to visit regularly. But the Lord helps us to bear what we must, Mr. Snelling, and Art anoints her servants. Walt found a place on the McKinley High School paper, doing drawings and photography both.

Here I must trust you, Mr. Snelling. I want to tell the whole truth— you remember that I told you at the beginning of the interview that I revere truth—and yet not give you the wrong impression. Walt and I were as close as ever. We wrote each other every week. He was studying at the Chicago Academy of Fine Arts, and every month he sent me his work to critique. He relied utterly on my guidance, my greater education, my superior taste. But at this point in his life—he was seventeen, remember, young men are apt to be rebellious. That's only natural.

So sometimes—only sometimes—he sent me crude little line drawings, sketches of cute animals or smiling flowers. They were amusing, I suppose, but they represented a regression. He was so much better than that. His still lifes and rural landscapes were beginning to have real power. I remember especially a pastoral, somewhat in the style of Turner, that was remarkable for a boy his age. And then to spend his talent on debased line drawings!

Do you know the Biblical story of Onan, Mr. Snelling?

There, I've shocked you. Well, I did warn you that a life dedicated to Art can brook no evasions. And that was what young Walt, in his inexperience, was doing. Evading service to the highest ideals of Art and turning to the vulgar because it was easier.

I wrote him so, in the strongest possible terms. He replied by sending me drawings illustrating a children's fairy tale. It seems that he had gone to the motion pictures with a friend and seen Marguerite Clark in *Snow White and the Seven Dwarfs*. It had sparked something in his fertile mind, and he had translated that crude film into line drawings that, he thought, might illustrate a children's book.

How can I tell you what I felt? What would any mentor feel who sees real talent turning, in its youth and inexperience, to the lures of commerce that will corrupt it utterly?

I caught the next train to Chicago. I found him after school hours outside his father's factory, a pitiful concern already on the brink of failure. When Walt saw me, he turned as white as your shirt, Mr. Snelling.

"You are betraying yourself," I said quietly. I wanted him to be shocked by my lack of social preamble. I wanted him to realize how important this was.

We went to a tearoom and talked for hours. He had grown; he was good-looking, manly in figure but still unformed in soul. Oh, can you blame me that I fought so hard for that soul to belong to Art? If only more of our young people had someone to care about their futures!

And I reached him. At least, I think I did. He was sullen, which is certainly natural at sixteen, but he did promise me he would not stop painting what was best and true in the world. However, he *didn't* promise not to continue with his vulgar little line drawings.

And I didn't ask him to. I hadn't taught children for twenty-three years for nothing. One can only push so far, and then one must rely on righteous guilt.

I remember clearly one thing Walt said that day. I didn't hold the comment against him. I still don't. He was so young. He said, "There's no money in real art."

I said gently, "But there's soul in it."

And, of course, he had no answer to that.

The next month America entered the war. Walt wrote me that he'd joined the Navy. But all during his time at the Naval base in Connecticut, and all during his time in France driving supply trucks, he wrote me that he kept studying and learning, copying fine paintings. He wrote that he had a copy of Whistler's "The Little White Girl" in his kit bag, and wrinkled and stained though it became, he looked at it every night, drinking in the lines and composition.

It was only later that I learned about the cowboys he drew on the supply trucks, and the fake Croix de Guerre he painted on soldiers' leather jackets for ten francs each.

Well, I'm sure you can see where this is going, Mr. Snelling. I notice that you're not looking at your watch *now*. Isn't it amazing how all the epic human battles can be fought on such humble grounds? Altruism versus selfishness in every hospital. Civilization versus barbarism in every classroom. And the highest ideals of Art versus base commerce in letters carried by the humble Postal Service.

We had it out when Walt come home. He came to see me in Marceline, the first time he'd been back since he was nine. He used a portion of his Navy pay. That alone was proof to me that the values I had tried to give him had not been dulled by the roughness of war. He came to see me even before he visited his mother.

I waited for him in the parlor of my boarding house. I can still see that room, with its plush green sofa and red figured rug and Tiffany glass lamp above the round table. I remember it seemed incredible to me that the other boarders going in and out, good respectable souls that they were, had no idea of the importance of the meeting to come. And how Walt had changed! He was a man, still in uniform, with a man's power. But I knew that my power, that of Art, was at least equal to his. In fact, there is no power greater, save that of the Creator Himself.

"Hello, Miss Peeler," Walt said. He seemed nervous, and a little defiant. But so glad to see me!

"You've returned," I said, and then—I don't blush to admit this, Mr. Snelling—I cried a little. No one knew the fears I'd had for Walt's safety during the war. I made it my business that no one should know.

His defiance left him immediately. He sat beside me on the sofa and took my hands, and for nearly an hour he entertained me with stories of his gallant comrades in arms. People went past, watching us curiously, but I introduced him to no one. For that hour, doubly precious because of the battle to come, he was mine.

Let me say something here, Mr. Snelling. I count it as not the weakest proof of Walt's talent that he came to me in his hour of questioning. He was always attached to me, but this was more than mere attachment. Only the most idealistic and noblest of souls recognize that they can profit from the guidance of those that have trod the same way before. I am not, and never was, an artist. I was not entrusted with that gift myself. But I was a teacher, devoting my life to nurturing that which is highest in my students, and Walt at his crossroads recognized that.

He pulled a sketch pad from his traveling case.

"Now, I want you to look at this with an open mind. Promise me!" I had never seen his face so serious.

"I will," I said, and it was a solemn promise between us.

He opened the pad. Page after page of drawings of a mouse with a human face, dressed in red velvet pants with two huge pearl buttons, grinning merrily. "Mortimer," it said on some pages. Later in the sketchpad Mortimer Mouse was joined by a lady mouse. Both were shown boarding a plane powered by a dachshund wound up tight like a rubber band. The plane almost hits sketched-in mountains and trees.

At the end both mice parachute to safety, the girl with a great display of patched bloomers.

The drawing was unbelievably crude. "Mortimer's" head was no more than a circle, with an oblong circle for a snout. His so-called legs were mere lines. The whole was merry, mocking, vulgar, nauseatingly cute, without taste or real emotion or any meaning beyond the desire to provoke the most simple-minded laugh.

"It's preliminary sketches for an animated motion picture," Walt said. "Roy's already talked to some fellows at an outfit called Kansas City Film Ad Company. They do advertising, mostly, little one-minute animated shorts for local theaters. But they might be interested in trying for something bigger. This could be my opportunity!"

I remember that I closed my eyes. It was a prayer for eloquence.

"Walt," I finally said, "this is a turning point for the rest of your life. If you give your talent to . . . to *this,* it will be exactly like using a fine horsehair brush to paint a barn door. In a short time the brush is worn and damaged, unfit for anything else. But unlike a brush, dear Walt, your talent is not replaceable—once dulled, *you can never obtain another.* Your talent is given you only once, and to waste its freshness, its fine edge, on *cartoons . . .*"

For a moment I thought I couldn't go on. But then words found me. Art itself came to my rescue, giving my words wings. I spoke of Gaugin, turning his back on his comfortable stockbroker life to paint from his heart in the South Seas. I spoke of Delacroix, staying faithful to the patrician and the sublime despite the scorn heaped on him. I spoke of Art's sacred mission to capture the essence of man's soul, and of— oh!—the emptiness of the lives of those who accept tawdry, second-hand substitutes for that soul. I scarcely know what I said. I would have said anything to keep him faithful to the best that was in him, the highest of which he was capable.

He listened, but I wasn't reaching him. I could see that. He was only eighteen, and he was on fire with the vulgar hustle the war had brought to the cities. The post-war era—the first war, I mean—was a sad time for true culture, Mr. Snelling. Not that the present day is any better.

A cookie with your tea?

Oh, of course the story's not over! It's just that I never quite know how to tell people the next part. It always sounds . . . mystical. And in 1950, who has the spirituality to credit mystical intervention? Especially in what Art has become now? When I think of the soulless so-called Cubists, elevating technical exercises above the—

Yes. Of course. What actually happened on the green sofa.

I could see Walt was not persuaded. I had failed. The greatest talent it was ever my happiness to nurture was voluntarily turning himself over to Mammon. I was distraught. I begged, pleaded, argued. Finally, Walt left me, striding away with that sullen expression I knew so well from two and a half decades in the classroom. But you must remember—he was so young!

I followed him out to the street. He started to cross. I grabbed his sleeve. He shook himself free and ran into the street. And at that moment—the neighborhood where I boarded wasn't at all what it had once been, remember that please—at that moment a rat darted out from behind a trashcan in the adjacent alley. It ran straight toward me, and of course I screamed. Walt stopped in the middle of the street, and half-turned, and immediately was struck by one of Mr. Ford's mass-produced Model Ts.

Just give me a moment, please.

There.

Walt said that? I am glad of it. You see, he recognizes as well as I do that the accident was his true moment of decision. If it *was* an accident. Walt has always denied the mystical intervention of Art herself. Still, you men persist in thinking of yourselves as so much more rational than we women, do you not?

At any rate, Walt is certainly right when he says that dreadful time in hospital changed his life. I visited him every day, of course. We talked for hours. I took a formal leave from my classroom to be with him, and have never regretted it. Teaching goes on in many ways, Mr. Snelling, and education is never confined by four walls.

It was a year before Walt recovered from his injuries, which I'm sure he told you were extensive. There was damage to the lungs, ribs, and hips, followed by infection. Now, of course, we would have these wonderful new antibiotics to aid his recovery, but not then. All Walt had was the sustaining belief in the highest ideals of Art, which I strengthened and girded every day. He came out of the hospital a chastened man.

The rest I'm sure he's told you. He's worked thirty-two years now on the *Kansas City Star,* in the illustration department to be sure, but only to support himself. His real effort, his real soul, has gone into his painting. He has endured many hardships and disappointments—not unlike the masters before him. It's a disgrace to the world, of course, that he should only have his first show at forty-nine, but then the world has always been slow to acknowledge genuine merit. And of course Walt paints the true soul of his subjects, not like these cold travesties who think painting is about the paint, Mondrian and Rothko and this Pollock person. . . . When Walt's show opens next week, you'll see what I mean. His work bears comparison with the best of past masters. Why, there's one picture that might almost have been painted by Burne-Jones himself.

Dear me, I had no idea it was so late. Do you really have to go?

Well, let me leave you with just one summary quote for your paper. Let me see, I want to choose my words carefully. How about this: "Miss Annie Peeler has had faith in Mr. Walt Disney's talent from his childhood. His show at the Kansas City Public Library is long overdue, and this humble beginning will undoubtedly be the harbinger of acknowledgment by the art world. Miss Peeler will say of her own contribution to Mr. Disney's career only that she did no more than any proud member of our education system *should* do, striving always to keep our pupils' eyes fixed on the highest of which humanity is capable. If we do this, our children's success is inevitable."

There, how's that?

One last cup of tea?

# SEX EDUCATION

*Another genetic engineering story. This one was directly prompted by a news article. A British scientist succeeded in forcing a fertilized human zygote to divide into eight separate embryos. Each of the eight cloned embryos then began to grow normally into a human fetus. Only after this experiment was completed did the scientist check to see if the British equivalent of the AMA had any guidelines about this.*

*They didn't. Neither did the United States, then. In the years since, commissions have been formed, recommendations drawn up, laws passed. It is illegal in most of the developed world to fool around with human cloning, which of course doesn't mean that it won't happen anyway. The procedures are too easy (at least, compared with, say, building an atomic bomb). The temptations are too great. And—most important—the potential profits are too large. It will happen.*

*"Sex Education" is set in a world where certain kinds of human cloning are legal. But it explores ethical aspects of genetic engineering that apply in our universe as well.*

WHEN THE PEOPLE CAME, MOLLIE WAS PLAYING IN THE BACK YARD with Emily Gowan. They'd made an excellent fort out of the picnic table turned on its side and backed up to the wooden fence. From behind the table they could throw kooshballs, which were too soft and floppy to hurt, at Brandy. He wagged his tail and peered around in this funny way that sent Mollie and Emily into giggles. Mariah Carey played on Emily's boombox. Mollie threw another kooshball, orange and yellow. She didn't realize then that these weren't actually the first people; that there had been others.

"Mollie, dear, turn off the music and say hello to some friends of mine," Mommy said. She balanced on the grass in high heels, which sank into the dirt a half inch. It was weird that Mommy was dressed in her receptionist clothes in the middle of a Saturday morning. Usually she just wore jeans. Mollie came out from her fort.

"Hi."

"Hello, there," the man said heartily. He wasn't dressed up like Mommy, but he wore a big ring on his right hand. "I'm Mr. Berringer, and this is Mrs. Berringer."

"Call me Susie," the woman said to Mollie. She had long fluffy blonde hair and lines on her neck. Mollie wasn't supposed to call adults by their first names, which she thought was a stupid rule. She smiled at Mommy: *See?*

"Hi, Susie."

"My, you're a pretty little thing. Look at those eyes, Tom. And those gorgeous curls! Her hair is almost exactly the same color as mine!"

"Yeah," Mr. Berringer said. "Mollie, I'd like to ask you some questions, and I want you to answer truthfully, like a good girl. Mrs. Carter, I'd rather talk to Mollie alone, please."

Mollie looked at Mommy. Why should she have to answer this man's questions? But Mommy just nodded and went back into the house, her heels making a line of little holes in the grass. Brandy bounced up with a kooshball in his mouth.

"This is Brandy," Mollie said. "And my friend Emily Gowan."

The Berringers didn't say hi to Emily. Susie said, "Tom, don't let that dog drool on my dress!"

"Chill, Sue. Your damn dress is fine. Now, Mollie, are you ever sick?"

"Sick?" Mollie said. "You mean, like with a cold?"

"With anything."

"I had the chicken pox when I was little." She glanced at Emily. What business was it of his if she was ever sick? Emily looked down at her Reeboks. Brandy thrust the drippy kooshball into Mollie's hand.

"Did you miss any school last year because you got sick?" Mr. Berringer asked.

"No."

"The year before that?"

"No."

"Do you have a lot of friends?"

"Yes." Mollie scanned the house. Mommy stood in the kitchen window, watching.

"Who are your best friends?"

"Emily. Jennifer Sawicki. Sarah Romano."

"Do you ever get mad at your friends?"

Mollie glanced sideways at Emily. "Sometimes."

"Really, really mad? Enough to hit them?"

"No."

"Do you ever get really, really mad at your parents?"

"No."

"Not *ever*?"

"*No,*" Mollie said. She looked again to make sure Mommy was still in the window.

"Are you strong? Can you run fast?"

"I won the Third Grade Field Day race at school."

"Did you!" Mr. Berringer said. "Hear that, Suze?"

"I hear it." Susie smiled at Mollie, who didn't smile back.

Mr. Berringer said, "Do you like school?"

"Yes," Mollie said.

"Who was your teacher last year? Did you like her?"

"Mrs. Stallman. She was okay."

"What's your favorite subject?"

"Science." Mollie threw the kooshball for Brandy. He bounded after it.

"Tell me one thing you learned last year in science."

Mollie wanted to say "Why?" but she wasn't supposed to be rude to adults. Even when *they* were. She said, "We learned about the sun. We learned it stays hot because atoms smash together so hard they get joined up, and you get a new kind of atom and a lot of heat and light. It's called fusion." Brandy bought her back the kooshball, wetter than ever.

"Good!" Mr. Berringer said. "Fine! What was the lowest mark on your last report card, Mollie?"

"I got a B in Social Studies. All the rest were As."

The Berringers went on smiling at her. Mollie threw the ball again so she wouldn't have to look at them.

"Well, it's been good meeting you, Mollie," Mr. Berringer said. "Come on, Sue."

"Such incredibly blue eyes," Susie murmured.

When they'd gone, Emily said, "Who *were* those creepy people?"

"I don't know. Friends of my mother's, I guess. Let's go play Nintendo." She wanted to go inside and close the door of her room.

Emily said, "Did you see his diamond ring? They must be really rich."

Mollie didn't answer. Mommy wasn't in the kitchen; she'd walked the Berringers to their car. On the table lay all Mollie's report cards, along with a bunch of other papers. The third-grade report lay open on the top of the pile. Her B in social studies was printed clearly in Mrs. Stallman's purple ink.

Just after Christmas, when Mollie was halfway through the fourth grade, her mother knocked on Mollie's bedroom door. Mommy looked serious. Had she found out about the paint that Mollie and Emily had spilled in the garage? They'd cleaned it all up with some stuff from Emily's basement. Almost all up.

"Mollie, there are some people coming this afternoon to talk to you.

To ask you some questions," Mommy said. She had a piece of paper in her hand.

"People? What for?"

"It doesn't matter. Just answer all their questions politely. And wear your blue dress. But that's not what I want to talk to you about. I got a letter from your school."

So it wasn't the paint. Mollie tried to think what had happened at school before Christmas vacation. She couldn't remember anything bad. Mommy sat on the bed and patted the bedspread beside her. Mollie sat down.

"Mollie—" Mommy started, then stopped. She breathed deep and looked around the room, like she didn't know what to say next. Scared now, Mollie looked around, too. Her bedroom was pretty, with a new canopy bed and a white dresser with a big mirror and her own CD player. The whole house had been redecorated at the end of last summer, the same time Daddy bought the big new car.

"Mollie, this letter says your class will start sex education next semester. And before you do, I want to explain to you myself how babies get born. It's my responsibility to explain to you, not the school's."

Mollie clasped her hands in her lap and studied her fingers. She already knew about sex. Alexandra McCandless, who was in the fifth grade, told her and Emily and Jennifer Sawicki, in Jennifer's tree house. But not Sarah Romano. Alexandra made them all say "Fuck the holy ghost" before she'd tell them anything, and Sarah wouldn't say it, so she had to leave. But Mollie wasn't going to tell any of that to Mommy.

"When a man and a woman are married," Mommy said, "they lie in bed very close together and the man puts his penis in the woman's vagina. Little seeds go from him into her, and sometimes one of his seeds joins up with a little egg that's already in her body."

"Oh," Mollie said, because Mommy seemed to expect her to say something. "Like fusion."

"Like what?"

"Fusion. You know, in the sun. Two atoms smash together into each other, and they make a new kind of atom and a lot of energy."

Mommy smiled. "Well, I don't know as a sperm and egg 'smash together' exactly, but I guess it's sort of the same."

"Can I go now?"

"In a minute. The egg grows inside the woman until the baby's ready to be born."

Mollie blurted, "Does it hurt?"

"Does sex hurt?"

"No," Mollie said. She already knew that sex hurt, but only the first time. Alexandra McCandless said so. There was blood and crying and burning like you were on fire. After that it felt better than anything in the world and you would do anything to have it every night. "Does the baby getting born hurt?"

Mommy hesitated, which meant yes. "No, not really. There's some discomfort, but it's all worth it when you see your perfect little baby."

"Okay. Now can I go?"

"Mollie, don't be so impatient! I'm trying to explain something important here!"

"You explained it already."

"Well, there's more." Mommy pushed her hair back from her face and looked at her fingernails. "Sometimes a woman's egg and a man's sperm can't seem to join by themselves, for different reasons. So scientists help. They join a sperm from the father to an egg from the mother in a test tube, and when they're sure the two are really joined, they put the egg back in the mother."

"Oh," Mollie said. Alexandra hadn't said anything about this. How did they put the egg back in? Did they have to cut the woman open? Suddenly Mollie didn't want to know. "Is that all? Emily's waiting for me."

"If you'd just sit still and listen for even five minutes—"

So there was more. Mollie said, "I'm sorry, Mommy. But Emily's *waiting.*"

"Oh, Mollie, why do you make it so hard lately for me to talk to you?"

"I don't!"

"Yes, you do. And this is important. Your daddy and I have been saving money for your college education, you know we want you to be able to go—"

"Yes, yes," Mollie said, because she didn't want to hear yet again about how Mommy and Daddy couldn't go to college but Mollie must and so it was her responsibility to work hard at school. And make something of her life. And be the best Mollie she could be.

"It's so *complicated,*" Mommy said. "We do the best we can."

"I know you do," Mollie said. If *she'd* used that tone, Mommy would have called it whining.

"Mommy looked at her helplessly, and Mollie smiled, kissed her mother, and escaped.

She'd have to get Jennifer to ask Alexandra McCandless back to the treehouse. But Jennifer didn't like Alexandra since they had a fight over Luke Perry, so maybe Jennifer wouldn't do it.

Maybe Mollie wouldn't have to know any more just yet.

In February she turned ten. In March she got a new bike, a ten-speed, and an A on her project on the solar system. In April Alexandra's period started and she demonstrated to Mollie and Jennifer and Emily how to put in a Tampax; Mollie thought the whole thing was gross. In May, a truck pulled up beside Mollie when she and Emily were walking home from the library, and two people jumped out.

"There she is! Hey, Mollie, look this way!"

A camera flashed. A man in a suit shoved a microphone at her while a woman wearing jeans and carrying a camcorder walked backward in front of Mollie and Emily.

"Mollie, have you heard about the lawsuit the Berringers have filed about your embryonic clone?"

Mollie stared. What was an embryonic clone? She remembered the Berringers, from last summer. Susie said Mollie's hair was the same color as hers. Beside her, Emily clutched Mollie's hand.

The man said, "Clones were made of your embryo, Mollie. Before you were born. Twelve of them. Five have been sold and implanted so far—"

"Roger," the woman with the camcorder said, "maybe we shouldn't . . . You're scaring her."

"I'm not scared!" Mollie said, although she was. She squeezed Emily's hand.

"Good girl," the man said. "The babies born are just like you, Mollie, they're made of your genes. Didn't your parents tell you this? No? Except, the last baby was born with something wrong with it—Kelly, keep filming!"

"No," the woman said. "I didn't expect . . . Mollie, you go on home, honey."

"Damn it, Kelly, keep filming! We can edit it to her reaction!"

"*Look* at her! Mollie, go on home!"

Mollie bolted, dragging Emily with her. More people with microphones and cameras waited outside the house. "There she is!"

Mollie let go of Emily's hand. "Run, Emily!" Emily rushed to her own house. Then Mollie's father was there, lifting Mollie in his arms like she was still a little girl. He fought his way through the people, who shouted at him.

"Mr. Carter, what legal liability do you think you have for—"

"Is the rumor that something went wrong at Veritech going to affect your defense in—"

"Is Mollie aware of—"

Daddy carried Mollie through the front door and slammed it. "Irresponsible assholes! They should all be shot!"

Mollie wriggled free. "What's going on? Why are these people here!"

"Mollie, sweetheart—"

"Why, Mommy? What's an embryonic clone? Tell me!"

Her mother knelt on the floor beside Mollie. "I *tried* to tell you, Mollie. More than once. Remember, we had the first talk in your bedroom, and you didn't want—"

"This isn't your responsibility, Mollie," her father broke in. "And not ours, either. We just wanted to give you the best life we could. And the Berringers couldn't have a baby of their own, so we were helping them to have one just as perfect as you are. And for that good deed they're blaming *us!*"

"You're upsetting her, Paul."

"The *situation* is upsetting her! Those jackals outside, those assholes—"

"But what's an embryonic clone?" Mollie cried.

Her mother said, "It's when a sperm and an egg are joined in a scientist's laboratory, like I told you. Only instead of putting the embryo in the mommy right away, the scientists make it divide first, to get more just like it. Like . . . like making Xerox copies. Do you understand, Mollie?"

Mollie nodded. She felt calmer now, listening. This made sense.

Mommy stayed kneeling next to her. "Your extra embryos helped other people have babies just as wonderful as you. Only with the Berringers' baby, something went wrong while it was growing inside Mrs. Berringer. We never realized . . . never dreamed . . ."

Mollie said, "I see." Outside, more cars pulled up. "Only—"

"Only what, honey?" Mommy stood up, pushing her dark hair off her face.

"Only how will we get out with all those cars in the driveway?"

"Get out? Get out where?"

"Out of the garage!" Mollie said.

Daddy looked puzzled. "Why would we want to get out of the garage?"

"To go get the baby. The one the Berringers don't want."

Mommy and Daddy stared at her.

"The baby that's me," Mollie said.

They went on staring at her.

"Oh," Mollie said. "*Oh . . .*"

"Mollie. Honey . . ."

Mollie ran to her room and locked the door.

"You come back here!" Daddy called.

Her curtains were closed, but she could hear the reporters out on the sidewalk, talking and shouting questions. Mommy knocked but didn't try to force the door open.

Later, when Brandy scratched at her door, Mollie let him in. She sat on the bed hugging him hard, her ear pressed against his soft red fur.


Mommy and Daddy kept trying to talk to her about it. They kept explaining how they weren't responsible. Mollie had to listen, but she didn't have to say anything back, and she didn't.

After a few weeks, Mommy said they were taking Mollie to a therapist.

The reporters had gone away from the house. Mollie didn't go to school. She played with Brandy, and with Emily and Jennifer after school. Mollie could see they didn't want to talk about all this weird stuff, so she didn't. They just played Nintendo and Barbies and *Where in the World is Carmen Sandiego* on Emily's father's computer.

Mollie traded her Barbie, which had black hair and green eyes, for Jennifer's, which was blonde with blue eyes.

Mollie wasn't allowed to watch TV except when Mommy was in the living room. The newspaper stopped coming. When Mommy talked on the phone she always used the phone in her bedroom, and she locked the door. Mollie lifted the receiver in the kitchen very carefully, so Mommy wouldn't know she was there.

"—filed this morning," her father's voice said. "Both our counter-suits. The one against Veritech claims negligence as the cause of the birth defect. Bad refrigeration or deficient procedure, or something."

"Do you think that happened?" her mother asked.

"God, Libby, you can't express doubt now! You'll probably have to testify!"

"I know. Go on."

"Rizetti says Veritech will undoubtedly claim an implied risk in the procedure, even beyond what our contract specified, with neither fraud nor guarantees applicable. They'll ask for the case to be dismissed. Our countersuit against the Berringers includes asking for them to pay our court costs. After all, the baby is their problem, not ours, and they shouldn't saddle us with any negative consequences arising from it when we honored the contract completely. How's Mollie? Does she go to that therapist this afternoon?"

"At three. I'm so worried about her, Paul."

"Me, too."

"I tried to explain again to her that the cloned embryos are no different than delayed twinning, but she won't even listen to me. She stands there, but she's not really listening."

"Poor kid. It's those fucking irresponsible reporters!"

"I know."

"Call me after the appointment."

Mollie carefully set down the phone. By the time Mommy came to look for her, she was reading *Boxcar Children* in the living room.

The therapist was an old woman in a big, high-ceilinged room with rows of bookshelves. Her face was kind. She and Mollie sat facing each other in blue armchairs.

"A lot has happened to you in the last few weeks, Mollie."

"I guess," Mollie said.

"Some of it sounds a little bit scary."

Mollie didn't answer. She studied her hands, lying in her lap. She'd painted the tips of the fingernails gold with polish borrowed from Emily's big sister. The nails looked like small faces with short blonde hair.

"Are you feeling a little bit scared by everything that's happened?" the therapist said.

"I don't know."

"I think *I'd* be a little frightened."

"I guess."

"Do you miss going to school?"

"I don't know."

"You can return to school if you want to, Mollie. You have the right to make that decision for yourself."

Again Mollie didn't answer. She studied the tiny faces on her fingers. Ten of them.

"Mollie," the therapist said gently, "do you believe your parents love you?"

Mollie looked at the rows of books. Many of them had the same color backs, like they were part of a set. "Yes. They love me."

"And how does that—"

"They think I'm perfect."

"And how—"

"I want to go home now," Mollie said. She stood, leaving the therapist sitting by herself in the blue chair.

At home she closed her bedroom door and dragged her desk chair in front of it. Leaning toward her dresser mirror, she studied herself, in her sleeveless Esprit tee. Blue eyes, blonde curls, white even teeth. She knew she was pretty. And strong, and smart. And now there were five other baby Mollies someplace who were also pretty and strong and smart. Except for the one that wasn't.

And it wasn't anybody's fault, they all said. It wasn't Mommy and Daddy's fault because they were just helping the Berringers to have a baby like Mollie. It wasn't the scientists' fault because they were just helping, too. It wasn't the Berringers' fault because they didn't ask to have a baby that wasn't perfect. It wasn't the court's fault because somebody else had to pay the court money. No one was responsible.

But the clone baby, made out of Mollie's egg, wasn't pretty and strong and smart, and all the while Mollie knew whose responsibility that really was.

It was hers.

She waited until Daddy had left for work and Mommy was in the shower. She dressed in jeans and a sweater, pushed her hair up under a Buffalo Bills cap, and put on sunglasses. Although she didn't exactly look like a kid who had a good reason for not being in school, she didn't look like a dork either, which she would have in her blue dress. She put some things in her backpack, took thirty dollars from her mother's purse, and locked Brandy in the garage so he wouldn't follow her.

The address had been in the newspapers at Emily's house.

PROTOTYPE EMBRYOS ON TRIAL, one paper said. And HOW MUCH IS THAT BABY IN THE WINDOW? And, in a paper with very big lettering and lots of pictures, SHELLPORT SHIRLEY TEMPLE FLOPS IN RERUN.

Mollie had never taken the bus from Shellport to the city, but she'd seen it leave from in front of the park. She stood close to a woman in a flowered dress, and put the same amount of money in the slot that the woman had. No one noticed her.

The bus took forty minutes to get to the downtown terminal, which was just outside a mall. A lot more people pushed and shoved, but there were also more kids by themselves. Mollie went up to a woman in a pretty red suit carrying a briefcase.

"What bus do I take to get to Gerard Street?"

The woman smiled at her. "I'm not sure. You can ask inside." She pointed.

There was no line at the bus window. Heart hammering, Mollie asked her question.

"Bus 20. Leaves from Slot 6. You want to buy tokens?"

She hesitated. "Yes, please. Two."

Outside, she found slot 6. There was a long bench to wait on, but one end was occupied by three loud teenage boys. She stood by Slot 5.

The bus was full of kids carrying book bags that said SISTERS OF MERCY JUNIOR HIGH. Some of them weren't any bigger than Mollie. "So he laid this bitch at Christmas vacation and now she's knocked up," a boy said. "And my friend said—" Mollie turned away, watching street signs.

Gerard Street was long. It changed from stores to rows of small houses to regular houses like Mollie's to very big places with fancy flower beds. At the end, only a few women in maids' uniforms were left on the bus with Mollie.

There were no reporters at the Berringers' house. Mollie moved across the wide lawn from tree to tree, staying hidden. In the front was a big screened porch. She peered through the wire mesh; nobody there.

The back door wasn't locked.

Mollie wiped her hands on her jeans. They were sweaty, but cold. Her eyes burned. It was wrong to go into somebody's house. But not as wrong as everything else.

She left the back door open, and listened. No sounds. And then, somewhere to her left, a baby fussing.

The baby wasn't in a real nursery, like Jennifer's baby brother had. Instead there was a portacrib in the kitchen; maybe Susie had been cooking while she watched the baby. But the kitchen was empty. Through a window Mollie saw a woman in a side garden, picking daffodils. The woman wore a white uniform. She wasn't Susie.

Mollie walked slowly to the crib. She felt funny, light and cold at the same time. What if the baby had two heads, or no arms, or half a head? How much bad genes had Mollie given it?

She stumbled toward the crib.

The baby looked normal. It had blue eyes, and blonde fuzz, and was impossibly tiny. It was fussing a little, but not much.

The refrigerator turned on with a sudden clunk, and the baby jumped and screwed up its face.

Mollie picked her up, in her blankets. She knew to support the baby's head, because of Jennifer's baby brother. The baby stopped fussing. Mollie ran back through the house and out the door. The baby, held up against her shoulder, felt light. On the street, she started back toward the bus stop. This time, nobody else waited for the bus.

A man in a green track suit jogged toward her. Mollie gathered herself up to run, but the man smiled and said, "Out for a walk with your dolly?" and kept on going.

When the bus came, Mollie tried to hold the baby like a doll. The baby was getting heavier.

Halfway to the city, the baby began to wail. A few people glanced at her. Mollie kept her sunglasses on and jiggled the baby against her shoulder. It still cried. At the downtown stop, the busdriver started to say something to her, but Mollie hurried down the steps and ran into the mall.

In here nobody looked at her, even though the baby cried loudly. She went into a Rite Aid and bought some bottles with formula already in them, plus a package of Huggies. In the mall she sat on a bench and fed the bottle to the baby. A few women smiled at her, but nobody spoke until a black girl also carrying a baby sat down next to her.

"You be stuck with your brother, too?"

Mollie hesitated. "Sister."

The girl sighed. "Your mamma working?"

"Yes."

"Better than not working."

Mollie didn't answer. The other girl made her nervous. She was glad when after a few minutes the girl picked up her brother, who was old enough to hold a rattle, and drifted away.

Afterwards, Mollie wished she'd talked to her longer.

The baby finished the bottle and fell asleep. Mollie laid her on the bench and broke open the box of Huggies. She stuffed as many as would fit into her backpack and left the rest in the box. Maybe the black girl would come back and take them.

She found a number 18 bus and rode home.

On her block, she crept through the back yards with the sleeping baby, moving from bushes to garages to fences. Kids were still in school, even the high schoolers. Adults were at work. But her father's car was in the driveway, which meant her mother had called him to come home.

She crept to the cellar window, which she'd left unlatched. She laid the baby on the grass and slipped through the window onto Daddy's workbench. Then she pulled the baby through the window and carried her to the box behind the furnace, lined with a bedspread from the linen closet. Nobody went here since Mommy got the new washer and dryer in the new laundry room off the kitchen.

She changed the baby again and laid her in the box. Mollie still couldn't see anything wrong with the baby. She had all her toes and everything. While Mollie changed her, the baby woke up and regarded Mollie from big blue eyes the same shape as Mollie's own.

"Jessica," Mollie said. But that wasn't right. The baby didn't look like a Jessica. Ashley? Brittany? Nicole?

The baby regarded her solemnly. What was aortic stenosis?

"Don't cry," Mollie whispered. "Don't cry, Mollie."

She hid the diaper under an old sofa and snuck upstairs to her own room.


"One more time," her father said. He'd stopped shouting, but his face was still red. "Where were you for three hours?"

"In my room," Mollie said. Her throat hurt and her eyes burned.

"No, you weren't! Jesus Christ, Mollie, don't we have enough problems without you worrying everybody sick? It's your responsibility to tell your mother when you go out. Can't you act your age, for Chrissake?"

"Paul, calm down," Mollie's mother said. "Please."

"I was in my room," Mollie said. She wouldn't cry. She wouldn't.

"Mollie, you've never lied to us before," her mother said. *She* was crying. Mollie tried not to look at her. The door rang.

"Don't answer it, Paul," her mother said. "I don't want to see anybody just now."

Her father glanced at the window. "Christ, it's the cops."

Mollie looked at the dark window, but from this angle, all could she see was her own reflection. She looked instead at the floor. This part of the house wasn't over the furnace; only the fruit cellar was underneath her feet.

"Paul Carter? We'd like to ask you a few questions, please."

Mollie started to hum, so she wouldn't hear.

". . . disappeared this morning . . . whereabouts of both you and your wife . . . search the premises. . . ."

She beamed the humming through the floor, down to the baby.

"Not without a warrant," her father said. "What the hell is this, anyway? Why would *I* have her? We're fighting a lawsuit to avoid having to raise her!"

*—in the treetop, when the wind blows—*

"What are you really after?" her father shouted. "We have a lawsuit pending against these people! You're not coming in without a search warrant!"

*—the cradle will rock—*

"You just do that!" her father said. The door closed.

*—when the bough breaks—*

"Not possible," her mother whispered, and even through her humming, Mollie heard her. She looked up. Mommy and Daddy both stared at her. She hated them.

"Mollie," her mother whispered, "where were you this morning?"

"I was in my room," Mollie said.

She sprawled across her bed and pretended to sleep. Her mother opened the door. Light slanted across the pretty carpet, the expensive canopy bed. AVERAGE COST OF TEST TUBE BABY TOPS $80K, Emily's newspaper said. Mommy closed the door softly. A few minutes later Mollie went down to the basement.

The baby was crying. It was three hours since Mollie had fed her. Did babies always need to eat so soon? Mollie gave her another bottle and changed her diaper again. This time the diaper was poopy. Mollie got some on her hands. She breathed deep to keep from puking, and washed her hands in the old laundry tub.

But the baby was still crying. Mollie put her on her shoulder and walked, jouncing the baby with each step, the way she'd seen Jennifer's mother do. She hummed softly and patted the baby on the back. The baby stopped crying, but every time Mollie stopped walking, she started again.

"Please, sweet baby, please sweet baby . . ." Mollie crooned. Pretty soon it was a prayer, and then Mollie was crying, and the baby wouldn't stop crying, and Mollie's legs hurt but she had to keep going because nobody wanted this baby with the broken thing in her heart, nobody would accept the responsibility, and the baby was hers, was her, please sweet baby please sweet baby—

She was sobbing and walking and patting, and the baby was wailing, when feet clattered down the steps and her mother said, "Oh, my God." The policeman holding a piece of paper didn't say anything, and Mollie couldn't see him clearly anyway because her eyes were burning, but even through the burning she suddenly saw the revolving light beyond the cellar window, red and blue and red again, mirrored in the metal side of the cold furnace.

"I don't care!" Mollie screamed. "You want her to die!"

"Nobody wants the baby to die, Mollie," her father said. His face was all smoothed out and his eyes were wide open, like he was very surprised by something. Brandy crouched beside him, his furry face on the floor. "You don't understand."

"I understand nobody wants her! She's made out of me, and nobody wants her!"

"She's not made out of you. She's . . ."

"Nobody loves her because she's not perfect! I'm the only one who will take care of her!"

"Mollie, the baby will be placed in a foster—"

"I hate you!" Mollie screamed.

Her father reached for her. Her mother, on the phone with the therapist, fumbled with the receiver and dropped it. Outside, the trucks and cars and vans of the reporters clogged the street. Mollie shoved her father away and ran upstairs. Brandy raced after her.

"Mollie, you come back here!" her father shouted.

She didn't. She ran past her own room and into her parents' bedroom. Her eyes burned. There was the bed they did it on, with the gold trim and the green bedspread. They made babies here, her father putting his penis into her mother . . . *fucking*. And then the people had come, all the people she'd answered questions for and looked pretty for . . . been perfect for. . . . She grabbed her mother's nail scissors off the dresser and started hacking at her curls. Her father rushed into the room and started toward her.

She threw the nail scissors at him.

He stopped, gasping, even though the scissors had bounced off his arm.

"I hate you!" Mollie screamed. "You make babies out of me and don't love them when they're not . . . I'm not . . ."

Her father started toward her again. She grabbed a metal bookend and threw it at him. Then she grabbed the other one and threw it at the mirror, which shattered.

Her father gripped his arm. Her mother stood in the doorway with her fist in her mouth. Mollie flung everything around the room: clothes and drawers and books and pillows.

"I hate you!"

"Mollie! Stop it!" Her father, his arm bleeding, caught her and pinned her arms to her side. Another piece of the mirror fell out of the frame, into a silvery pile. Mollie could hear the baby cry even though the baby wasn't here anymore, the policeman had taken her away.

"Stop it! You hear me! Stop it!"

Crying and crying—

"Stop it! Mollie!"

She bit him hard.

He dropped her. Mollie backed away from him, suddenly calm. Downstairs, the baby cried.

Then the crying stopped.

In the abrupt silence, Mollie and her parents looked at each other. Her mother, dead white, said in a quavery voice, "Mollie, look at this room, you're . . . you're responsible for this mess. . . ."

"No," Mollie said. "I'm not." And then, "Nobody is."

Brandy tried to lick her hand, but Mollie pushed the dog away. She walked to her own room and shut the door.

# GRANT US THIS DAY

*Every writer balances continually between blatancy and obscurity. Make your point absolutely obvious through strongly patterned actions, conventional characters, and explicit exposition, and readers say, "That one was overwritten—really belabored it, didn't she?" Make your point cunningly subtle, naturalistically hinted at only through symbolism and suggestion, and readers say, "Huh?"*

*With "Grant Us This Day," I missed. No one who read the story in print seemed to realize what I was doing, which was a pretty good indicator that I hadn't succeeded in doing it. Virtually nobody I spoke to got the point. Consequently, this is the only story that has been altered for this collection. I have rewritten the last few paragraphs, in the springing-eternal hope that somebody will.*

WHEN I FINALLY FOUND GOD, HE WAS SLUMPED AT THE COUNTER IN a Detroit diner, stirring his coffee. The dissolving creamer made little spiral galaxies. He had a bad sunburn. I slid onto the next stool.

"God?"

He looked up. A little gray flecked his dark beard but on the whole he looked younger than I'd expected. Maybe thirty. Maybe twenty-eight. His jeans were grimy. "Who wants to know?"

"Daniel Smith." I held out my hand. He didn't take it. "Listen, God, I've been looking for you for a long time."

He said, "You got to read me my rights."

"What?"

"My Miranda rights. I know I screwed up, all right? But at least do it by the local rules. Let's get at least one part of this right."

"I'm not a cop," I said.

"Not a cop?"

"No."

"Just my luck." He slumped even lower on the stool, elbows resting on the counter, which bore some deep indescribable stain the shape of Africa. God traced it with one finger. Two teenage boys banged noisily through the front door; the waitress eyed them warily. "Then you're a divinity student, right? Colgate? Loyola?"

"No."

"You didn't find some ancient manuscript proving I exist in corporeal form?"

"No." The boys slid into a corner booth. Their jackets rode up, and I caught the flash of steel.

"You didn't consult a lama in a monastery on top of a Tibetan mountain—old, most old?"

"Not that either."

God sipped his coffee and made a face. "Then who the hell are you?"

"I'm from the Committee."

Even with his sunburn, he paled. "Oh, man."

"Well, that was one of the problems, certainly."

God slammed his spoon onto the counter and sat up straight. "Look, I know I screwed up. I know it has problems. I've already *admitted* that." He glanced around the diner. In the booth opposite the boys, a hooker sat with an enormously fat man eating a taco salad. He talked with his mouth full; she was asleep. The fat man hadn't noticed. The waitress limped past, carrying a platter of greasy burgers. She had one leg shorter than the other.

"Nonetheless," God said, surly now, "from the Committee's viewpoint I did everything right, so why bother me, man? I filled out the application in triplicate. I listed my previous work. I filed by the deadline. I submitted work that met your bureaucratic guidelines: neatness, originality, aptness of thought. What's more original than kangaroos? Or a hundred years' war? A hundred years for a single war! So why hassle me now?"

"Maybe," I said, looking at the fat man, who had noticed the hooker was asleep and was kicking her viciously, "you could have worked a little harder on 'neatness.'"

"Yeah, well, everybody's a critic." He slumped again, his brief surliness over. I couldn't read the expression on his face. "But that still doesn't explain what you're doing here. I know I didn't make the finals. I saw the list."

"Yes and no."

"What's that supposed to mean?" He rubbed his nose; it really was a wicked sunburn. It was going to peel something awful.

I said, "The list's changed. One finalist withdrew. You were the first name on the waiting list."

His eyes opened wide. "Really? Who withdrew?"

"I'm not at liberty to say. But now you're on the short list."

God bent his head to stare into his coffee. The flush on his neck wasn't all sunburn. This means so damn much to some of them. The waitress delivered the burgers to an old couple at a center table, both of them thin and quavery as parchment.

He said, "So what happens now?"

"The rules say you have a thousand years to revise, before the next round of voting. Off the record, let me say I think you should consider fairly substantial revision. The Committee liked certain aspects of your work, but the consensus was that the tone is uneven, and the whole lacks coherence."

"I'm not creating some cheap commercial piece here!"

"I know that. And nobody says you should. But still, any good work has a voice all its own, a coherence, a thematic pattern that clearly identifies the artist. Your work here—well, frankly, son, it's all over the map. The pieces don't adhere. The proportions are skewed. It lacks balance and unity."

God signaled for a piece of pie. The waitress limped over from the center table, where the old couple were holding hands. The fat man spoke low and fast to the hooker, leaning forward, his mouth twisted. The boys passed a plastic bag across the table, smirking at the room, daring anyone to notice.

God said, "I can't just—"

I held up my hand placatingly, "I know, I know—you can't just compromise your artistic integrity. And nobody's asking you to. Just be a little more consistent in tone and imagery."

God said, "No, you don't understand. It's not a question of artistic integrity. Not really." He leaned closer, suddenly earnest. I wondered if he had any ointment for that nose. "See—there's a spectrum you can work along. Call it 'intended meaningfulness.' At one end you have your absurdist pieces. Things happen in an unconnected manner. Nothing is predictable. Nothing is rational. Godot never shows." He smiled.

I didn't get the reference. Probably to his own work. Some of these guys think the grant Committee memorizes their every detail. The door opened on a gust of wind and a cop entered. The waitress brought God cherry pie on a thick beige plate.

"I don't think much of absurdist stuff," he continued. "I mean, where's the art? If literally anything can happen, why bother? But at the other end is all that tight moral order. Punish the bad, reward the good, solve the mysteries, give every act simple-minded motives and rational outcomes. B-o-r-i-n-g. And not all that just or compassionate, either, no

matter what those artists say. What's so compassionate about impos-
ing a single pattern on the lion and the ox? Or on the worm in the heart
of the rose, for that matter?"

"I wish you wouldn't be so self-referential. It's an annoying man-
nerism."

"But you get my point."

"Yes, I do. You go for texture. And density. And diversity. All com-
mendable. But not very commercial."

"I didn't think this was supposed to be a commercial competition!"

"It's not," I said. "But do you realize how many mediocre artists out
there justify their mediocrity by their lack of accessibility? Just because
they're not commercial doesn't mean they're grandly above all standards and judgements. Not every finger twitch is sacred just because it's
theirs."

"That's true." God slumped on his stool a third time. He certainly
was a volatile kid. But honest. Not many can see the line between self-
justification and true originality. I started to like him. The cop took a
seat at the end of the counter. The boys flipped the finger at his back.
The hooker wept softly. Her mascara smudged under her eyes.

"Look, son," I said, "don't take criticism so hard. Instead, *use* it.
You're still in the running, and you've got a thousand years. Rework
the more outre stuff to bring it in line with your major themes. Tone
down your use of color. Make the ending a little clearer. That's all I'm
suggesting. Give yourself a fighting chance."

He didn't say anything.

"After all, it's a pretty big grant."

Yes," he said tonelessly. He watched the hooker cry. Her fat pimp
showed her something in his hand; from this angle I couldn't see what.
The old couple rose to go, helping each other up. The waitress put an
order of fries in front of the cop and bent to rub her varicose veins.

"If you win, it could mean a major boost to your career. You have
a responsibility to your own talent."

"Yes."

"So think about revisions."

"The thing is," God said slowly, "I filled out the application forms
a long time ago. Before I began work. It looks pretty different to me
now. I do feel a responsibility to the work, but maybe not in the way
you mean."

Something in his voice turned me cold. I'd heard that tone before.
Recently. I pushed aside his pie, which he hadn't touched, and covered
his hand with mine. "Son—"

"Didn't you wonder why I thought at first that you were a cop?"

The real cop turned his head to glance at us. He ate the last of his fries, nodded at the waitress, and made for the door, brushing past the tottering old couple. The codger fumbled in his pocket for a tip.

I could hear the thickness in my voice. "Son—it doesn't work like that."

"Maybe it does for me." He looked directly into my eyes. His own were very dark, with layered depths, like fine ash. I wondered how I could have thought him only twenty-eight. The cop left, banging the door behind him. The fat pimp pulled the hooker to her feet. She was still crying. The old man laid a dollar bill, a quarter, and three pennies on the table.

I said, "So okay, you feel responsible. It's your work, the outlines are yours, even if it got away from you and took off in directions you never intended. That happens. It's still yours. *But that doesn't mean it's you.* It's your art, son, not your life. There's a difference, and it's crucial. The people who confuse the two aren't thinking straight."

He turned those dark eyes away from me, and shrugged. "I feel responsible, is all. For all of it. Even the part that got away from me."

Suddenly he smiled whimsically. "Accepting responsibility again would actually strengthen the imagery pattern, wouldn't it? A leitmotif. The Committee might actually like that."

They probably would. I said carefully, "A competition is no real reason to go native."

"It isn't my reason." Abruptly he flung out one hand. "Ah, don't you see? I love it. All of it. Even if it's flawed, even if I screwed up, even if I lose. I love it."

He did. I saw that now. He loved it. Loved *this*. The old couple tottered toward the door. The two teenage boys shot out of their booth. One of them grabbed the tip off the table; the other lunged for the old lady's purse, ripping it off her arm. She fell backwards, thin arms flailing, squeaking "oh oh oh oh . . ." Instantly the old man raised his cane and brought it down hard on the boy's head. He shrieked, and blood sprang onto his cheek. The boy, outraged, yelled "Fuck! What you go do that for, you old bastard!" Then both boys tore out the door.

The fat pimp helped the old woman up. He was very gentle. "You all right, ma'am?" The hooker, still crying, reached out one deft hand and stole the old man's wallet from his pocket. The old woman stood, shaky but unhurt. The pimp escorted them to the door, stopped, walked back to the hooker. Silently she handed him the wallet. His fat hands curled into fists. He returned the wallet to the old man, and all four of them left. The waitress leaned over in the silent diner and rubbed her varicose veins.

I have never wanted to be an artist myself.

There wasn't much else to say. Maybe God would actually go through with it again, maybe not. Sometimes these guys are more in love with the idea of artistic risk than with the actuality. But he *had* done it once. All of it, right up to the final artistic sacrifice. That set him apart. I couldn't tell him this—against Committee rules—but that part of his work was what had earned him the first position on the waiting list. It had been an impressive set-piece, especially amidst the uneven emotional tone of the rest of his work. And if he did it again, it would certainly strengthen the imagery pattern in his entry. He was right about that. His chances of winning would increase dramatically. If of course, he survived.

He had his place on the short list only because another candidate hadn't. "Withdrew" has a lot of meanings.

God grinned at me. Not a smile this time, an actual grin. "I'm sorry to be so stubborn. It's not like I don't appreciate your interest."

"Tell me something. Do you do all your own construction work?"

He rubbed his sunburned nose and laughed. "You know how it is. If you want something done right . . ."

"Yes. Well." I held out my hand and this time he took it, still grinning. He sat the counter stool almost jauntily. I'd been right to like him.

Outside, it was just getting dark. Clouds raced across the sky from the west, casting strange shadows. Litter blew in gusts at my feet: newspapers, styrofoam cups, a torn shirt. The shirt bore brown stains that might have been blood. The shadows lengthened, laying at right angles to each other.

Each work of art has its own internal pace; a thousand years is different here.

I thought I could hear them on the horizon, dragging the heavy wooden cross, howling about the thorned crown. Coming for him.

# FLOWERS OF AULIT PRISON

*Writers are possessed of two kinds of relatives: ones who complain you put them in your stories, and ones who complain you don't. My sister Kate is the latter. For years she has insisted that I should base a character on her, but unfortunately such a character hasn't yet coincided in my mind with a suitable story idea. In a way this is odd, since I write about sister-sister relationships quite frequently. One fueled my first award-nominated story, "Trinity," in 1983. One lies at the heart of "Margin of Error," included in this collection. And one is central to "Flowers of Aulit Prison." Although now that I think of it, perhaps Kate remains dissatisfied with these three stories not only because none of the six women is her, but also because each pair of sisters is locked in deadly rivalry.*

*This story isn't mainly about sisters, however. It's mainly about how we each shape reality, carry around a definite map of it in our heads, completely sure that the map is truth. Reality maps include memories ("The accident happened this way"), expectations, perceptions, evaluations, moral strictures. When people's maps diverge, you have disagreement and conflict. When most people's maps overlap to a very high degree, you have a homogenous society. When maps match almost exactly, you have World.*

*What creates a reality map? Experience partly. But since reality maps exist in the brain, and the brain runs on biochemical reactions, then the degree to which "my" reality is shaped by the compounds in my brain becomes an open question. This is an almost unexplored area of science, touching on the most fundamental of human questions: Who am I? Why do I think what I think?*

*There are, as yet, no answers. In the meantime, I created World as one way of looking at the questions.*

*Also in the meantime, I put a "Hurricane Kate" in one of my novels, but my sister didn't like that either. Some people are never satisfied.*

Mʏ sɪsᴛᴇʀ ʟɪᴇs sᴡᴇᴇᴛʟʏ ᴏɴ ᴛʜᴇ ʙᴇᴅ ᴀᴄʀᴏss ᴛʜᴇ ʀᴏᴏᴍ ꜰʀᴏᴍ ᴍɪɴᴇ.
She lies on her back, fingers lightly curled, her legs stretched straight as
elindel trees. Her pert little nose, much prettier than my own, pokes del-
icately into the air. Her skin glows like a fresh flower. But not with
health. She is, of course, dead.

I slip out of my bed and stand swaying a moment, with morning
dizziness. A Terran healer once told me my blood pressure was too low,
which is the sort of nonsensical thing Terrans will sometimes say—like
announcing the air is too moist. The air is what it is, and so am I.

What I am is a murderer.

I kneel in front of my sister's glass coffin. My mouth has that awful
morning taste, even though last night I drank nothing stronger than
water. Almost I yawn, but at the last moment I turn it into a narrow-
lipped ringing in my ears that somehow leaves my mouth tasting worse
than ever. But at least I haven't disrespected Ano. She was my only sib-
ling and closest friend, until I replaced her with illusion.

"Two more years, Ano," I say, "less forty-two days. Then you will
be free. And so will I."

Ano, of course, says nothing. There is no need. She knows as well
as I the time until her burial, when she can be released from the chemicals and glass that bind her dead body and can rejoin our ancestors.
Others I have known whose relatives were under atonement bondage

said the bodies complained and recriminated, especially in dreams, making the house a misery. Ano is more considerate. Her corpse never troubles me at all. I do that to myself.

I finish the morning prayers, leap up, and stagger dizzily to the piss closet. I may not have drunk pel last night, but my bladder is nonetheless bursting.

At noon a messenger rides into my yard on a Terran bicycle. The bicycle is an attractive design, sloping, with interesting curves. Adapted for our market, undoubtedly. The messenger is less attractive, a surly boy probably in his first year of government service. When I smile at him, he looks away. He would rather be someplace else. Well, if he doesn't perform his messenger duties with more courteous cheer, he will be.

"Letter for Uli Pek Bengarin."

"I am Uli Pek Bengarin."

Scowling, he hands me the letter and pedals away. I don't take the scowl personally. The boy does not, of course, know what I am, any more than my neighbors do. That would defeat the whole point. I am supposed to pass as fully real, until I can earn the right to resume being so.

The letter is shaped into a utilitarian circle, very businesslike, with a generic government seal. It could have come from the Tax Section, or Community Relief, or Processions and Rituals. But of course it hasn't; none of those sections would write to me until I am real again. The sealed letter is from Reality and Atonement. It's a summons; they have a job for me.

And about time. I have been home nearly six weeks since the last job, shaping my flowerbeds and polishing dishes and trying to paint a skyscape of last month's synchrony, when all six moons were visible at once. I paint badly. It is time for another job.

I pack my shoulder sack, kiss the glass of my sister's coffin, and lock the house. Then I wheel my bicycle—not, alas, as interestingly curved as the messenger's—out of its shed and pedal down the dusty road toward the city.

Frablit Pek Brimmidin is nervous. This interests me; Pek Brimmidin is usually a calm, controlled man, the sort who never replaces reality with illusion. He's given me my previous jobs with no fuss. But now he actually can't sit still; he fidgets back and forth across his small office, which is cluttered with papers, stone sculptures in an exaggerated style I don't like at all, and plates of half-eaten food. I don't comment on either the food or the pacing. I am fond of Pek Brimmidin, quite apart from my gratitude to him, which is profound. He was the official in R&A who voted to give me a chance to become real again. The other two judges voted for perpetual death, no chance of atonement. I'm not supposed to know this much detail about my own case, but I do. Pek Brimmidin is middle-aged, a stocky man whose neck fur has just begun to yellow. His eyes are gray, and kind.

"Pek Bengarin," he says, finally, and then stops.

"I stand ready to serve," I say softly, so as not to make him even more nervous. But something is growing heavy in my stomach. This does not look good.

"Pek Bengarin." Another pause. "You are an informer."

"I stand ready to serve our shared reality," I repeat, despite my astonishment. Of course I'm an informer. I've been an informer for two years and eighty-two days. I killed my sister, and I will be an informer until my atonement is over, I can be fully real again, and Ano can be released from death to join our ancestors. Pek Brimmidin knows this. He's assigned me every one of my previous informing jobs, from the first easy one in currency counterfeiting right through the last one, in baby stealing. I'm a very good informer, as Pek Brimmidin also knows. What's wrong with the man?

Suddenly Pek Brimmidin straightens. But he doesn't look me in the eye. "You are an informer, and the Section for Reality and Atonement has an informing job for you. In Aulit Prison."

So that's it. I go still. Aulit Prison holds criminals. Not just those who have tried to get away with stealing or cheating or child-snatching, which are, after all, normal. Aulit Prison holds those who are unreal, who have succumbed to the illusion that they are not part of shared common reality and so may do violence to the most concrete reality of others: their physical bodies. Maimers. Rapists. Murderers.

Like me.

I feel my left hand tremble, and I strive to control it and to not show how hurt I am. I thought Pek Brimmidin thought better of me. There is of course no such thing as partial atonement—one is either real or one is not—but a part of my mind nonetheless thought that Pek Brimmidin had recognized two years and eighty-two days of effort in regaining my reality. I have worked so hard.

He must see some of this on my face because he says quickly, "I am sorry to assign this job to you, Pek. I wish I had a better one. But you've been requested specifically by Rafkit Sarloe." Requested by the capital; my spirits lift slightly. "They've added a note to the request. I am authorized to tell you the informant job carries additional compensation. If you succeed, your debt will be considered immediately paid, and you can be restored at once to reality."

Restored at once to reality. I would again be a full member of World, without shame. Entitled to live in the real world of shared humanity, and to hold my head up with pride. And Ano could be buried, the artificial chemicals washed from her body, so that it could return to World and her sweet spirit could join our ancestors. Ano, too, would be restored to reality.

"I'll do it," I tell Pek Brimmidin. And then, formally, "I stand ready to serve our shared reality."

"One more thing, before you agree, Pek Bengarin." Pek Brimmidin is figeting again. "The suspect is a Terran."

I have never before informed on a Terran. Aulit Prison, of course, holds those aliens who have been judged unreal: Terrans, Fallers, the weird little Huhuhubs. The problem is that even after thirty years of ships coming to World, there is still considerable debate about whether *any* aliens are real at all. Clearly their bodies exist; after all, here they are. But their thinking is so disordered they might almost qualify as all being unable to recognize shared social reality, and so just as unreal as those poor empty children who never attain reason and must be destroyed.

Usually we on World just leave the aliens alone, except of course for trading with them. The Terrans in particular offer interesting objects, such as bicycles, and ask in return worthless items, mostly perfectly obvious information. But do any of the aliens have souls, capable of recognizing and honoring a shared reality with the souls of others? At the universities, the argument goes on. Also in market squares and pel shops, which is where I hear it. Personally, I think aliens may well be real. I try not to be a bigot.

I say to Pek Brimmidin, "I am willing to inform on a Terran."

He wiggles his hand in pleasure. "Good, good. You will enter Aulit Prison a Capmonth before the suspect is brought there. You will use your primary cover, please."

I nod, although Pek Brimmidin knows this is not easy for me. My primary cover is the truth: I killed my sister Ano Pek Bengarin two years and eighty-two days ago and was judged unreal enough for perpetual death, never able to join my ancestors. The only untrue part of the cover is that I escaped and have been hiding from the Section police ever since.

"You have just been captured," Pek Brimmidin continues, "and assigned to the first part of your death in Aulit. The Section records will show this."

Again I nod, not looking at him. The first part of my death in Aulit, the second, when the time came, in the kind of chemical bondage that holds Ano. And never ever to be freed—*ever*. What if it were true? I should go mad. Many do.

"The suspect is named 'Carryl Walters.' He is a Terran healer. He murdered a World child, in an experiment to discover how real people's brains function. His sentence is perpetual death. But the Section believes that Carryl Walters was working with a group of World people in these experiments. That somewhere on World there is a group that's so lost its hold on reality that it would murder children to investigate science."

For a moment the room wavers, including the exaggerated swooping curves of Pek Brimmidin's ugly sculptures. But then I get hold of myself. I am an informer, and a good one. I can do this. I am redeeming myself, and releasing Ano. I am an informer.

"I'll find out who this group is," I say. "And what they're doing, and where they are."

Pek Brimmidin smiles at me. "Good." His trust is a dose of shared reality: two people acknowledging their common perceptions together, without lies or violence. I need this dose. It is probably the last one I will have for a long time.

How do people manage in perpetual death, fed on only solitary illusion?

Aulit Prison must be full of the mad.

Traveling to Aulit takes two days of hard riding. Somewhere my bicycle loses a bolt, and I wheel it to the next village. The woman who runs the bicycle shop is competent but mean, the sort who gazes at shared reality mostly to pick out the ugly parts.

"At least it's not a *Terran* bicycle."

"At least," I say, but she is incapable of recognizing sarcasm.

"Sneaky soulless criminals, taking us over bit by bit. We should never have allowed them in. And the government is supposed to protect us from unreal slime, ha, what a joke. Your bolt is a nonstandard size."

"Is it?" I say.

"Yes. Costs you extra."

I nod. Behind the open rear door of the shop, two little girls play in a thick stand of moonweed.

"We should kill all the aliens," the repairer says. "No shame in destroying them before they corrupt us."

"Eurummmn," I say. Informers are not supposed to make themselves conspicuous with political debate. Above the two children's heads, the moonweed bends gracefully in the wind. One of the little girls has long brown neck fur, very pretty. The other does not.

"There, that bolt will hold fine. Where you from?"

"Rakfit Sarloe." Informers never name their villages.

She gives an exaggerated shudder. "I would never visit the capital. Too many aliens. They destroy *our* participation in shared reality without a moment's thought! Three and eight, please."

I want to say *No one but you can destroy your own participation in shared reality,* but I don't. Silently I pay her the money.

She glares at me, at the world. "You don't believe me about the Terrans. But I know what I know!"

I ride away, through the flowered countryside. In the sky, only Cap is visible, rising on the horizon opposite the sun. Cap glows with a clear white smoothness, like Ano's skin.

The Terrans, I am told, have only one moon. Shared reality on their world is, perhaps, skimpier than ours: less curved, less rich, less warm.

Are they ever jealous?


Aulit prison sits on a flat plain inland from the South Coast. I know that other islands on World have their own prisons, just as they have their own governments, but only Aulit is used for the alien unreal, as well as our own. A special agreement among the governments of World makes this possible. The alien governments protest, but of course it does them no good. The unreal is the unreal, and far too painful and dangerous to have running around loose. Besides, the alien governments are far away on other stars.

Aulit is huge and ugly, a straight-lined monolith of dull red stone, with no curves anywhere. An official from R&A meets me and turns me over to two prison guards. We enter through a barred gate, my bicycle chained to the guards', and I to my bicycle. I am led across a wide dusty yard toward a stone wall. The guards of course don't speak to me; I am unreal.

My cell is square, twice my length on a side. There is a bed, a piss pot, a table, and a single chair. The door is without a window, and all the other doors in the row of cells are closed.

"When will the prisoners be allowed to be all together?" I ask, but of course the guard doesn't answer me. I am not real.

I sit in my chair and wait. Without a clock, it's difficult to judge time, but I think a few hours pass totally without event. Then a gong sounds and my door slides up into the ceiling. Ropes and pulleys, controlled from above, inaccessible from inside the cell.

The corridor fills with illusionary people. Men and women, some with yellowed neck fur and sunken eyes, walking with the shuffle of old age. Some young, striding along with that dangerous mixture of anger and desperation. And the aliens.

I have seen aliens before, but not so many together. Fallers, about our size but very dark, as if burned crisp by their distant star. They wear their neck fur very long and dye it strange bright colors, although not in prison. Terrans, who don't even have neck fur but instead fur on their heads, which they sometimes cut into fanciful curves—rather pretty. Terrans are a little intimidating because of their size. They move slowly. Ano, who had one year at the university before I killed her, once told me that the Terran's world makes them feel lighter than ours does. I don't understand this, but Ano was very intelligent and so it's probably true. She also explained that Fallers, Terrans, and World people are somehow related far back in time, but this is harder to believe. Perhaps Ano was mistaken.

Nobody ever thinks Huhuhubs could be related to us. Tiny, scuttling, ugly, dangerous, they walk on all fours. They're covered with warts. They smell bad. I was glad to see only a few of them, sticking close together, in the corridor at Aulit.

We all move toward a large room filled with rough tables and chairs and, in the corner, a trough for the Huhuhubs. The food is already on the tables. Cereal, flatbread, elindel fruit—very basic, but nutritious. What surprises me most is the total absence of guards. Apparently prisoners are allowed to do whatever they wish to the food, the room, or each other, without interference. Well, why not? We aren't real.

I need protection, quickly.

I choose a group of two women and three men. They sit at a table with their backs to the wall, and others have left a respectful distance around them. From the way they group themselves, the oldest woman is the leader. I plant myself in front of her and look directly into her face. A long scar ridges her left cheek to disappear into grizzled neck fur.

"I am Uli Pek Bengarin," I say, my voice even but too low to be heard beyond this group. "In Aulit for the murder of my sister. I can be useful to you."

She doesn't speak, and her flat dark eyes don't waver, but I have her attention. Other prisoners watch furtively.

"I know an informer among the guards. He knows I know. He brings things into Aulit for me, in return for not sharing his name."

Still her eyes don't waver. But I see she believes me; the sheer outrage of my statement has convinced her. A guard who had already forfeited reality by informing—by violating shared reality—might easily turn it to less pernicious material advantage. Once reality is torn, the rents grow. For the same reason, she easily believes that I might violate my supposed agreement with the guard.

"What sort of things?" she says, carelessly. Her voice is raspy and thick, like some hairy root.

"Letters. Candy. Pel." Intoxicants are forbidden in prison; they promote shared conviviality, to which the unreal have no right.

"Weapons?"

"Perhaps," I say.

"And why shouldn't I beat this guard's name out of you and set up my own arrangement with him?"

"He will not. He is my cousin." This is the trickiest part of the cover provided to me by R&A Section: it requires that my would-be protector believe in a person who has kept enough sense of reality to honor family ties but will nonetheless violate a larger shared reality. I told Pek Brimmidin that I doubted that such a twisted state of mind would be very stable, and so a seasoned prisoner would not believe in it. But Pek Brimmidin was right and I was wrong. The woman nods.

"All right. Sit down."

She does not ask what I wish in return for the favors of my supposed cousin. She knows. I sit beside her, and from now on I am physically safe in Aulit Prison from all but her.

Next, I must somehow befriend a Terran.

This proves harder than I expect. The Terrans keep to themselves, and so do we. They are just as violent toward their own as all the mad doomed souls in Aulit; the place is every horror whispered by children trying to shock each other. Within a tenday I see two World men hold down and rape a woman. No one interferes. I see a Terran gang beat a Faller. I see a World woman knife another woman, who bleeds to death on the stone floor. This is the only time guards appear, heavily armored. A priest is with them. He wheels in a coffin of chemicals and immediately immerses the body so that it cannot decay to release the prisoner from her sentence of perpetual death.

At night, isolated in my cell, I dream that Frablit Pek Brimmidin appears and rescinds my provisional reality. The knifed, doomed corpse becomes Ano; her attacker becomes me. I wake from the dream moaning and weeping. The tears are not grief but terror. My life, and Ano's, hang from the splintery branch of a criminal alien I have not yet even met.

I know who he is, though. I skulk as close as I dare to the Terran groups, listening. I don't speak their language, of course, but Pek Brimmidin taught me to recognize the cadences of "Carryl Walters" in several of their dialects. Carryl Walters is an old Terran, with gray head fur cut in boring straight lines, wrinkled brownish skin, and sunken eyes. But his ten fingers—how do they keep the extra ones from tangling them up?—are long and quick.

It takes me only a day to realize that Carryl Walters's own people leave him alone, surrounding him with the same nonviolent respect that my protector gets. It takes me much longer to figure out why. Carryl Walters is not dangerous, neither a protector nor a punisher. I don't think he has any private shared realities with the guards. I don't understand until the World woman is knifed.

It happens in the courtyard, on a cool day in which I am gazing hungrily at the one patch of bright sky overhead. The knifed woman screams. The murderer pulls the knife from her belly and blood shoots out. In seconds the ground is drenched. The woman doubles over. Everyone looks the other way except me. And Carryl Walters runs over with his old-man stagger and kneels over the body, trying uselessly to save the life of a woman already dead anyway.

Of course. He is a healer. The Terrans don't bother him because they know that, next time, it might be they who have need of him.

I feel stupid for not realizing this right away. I am supposed to be *good* at informing. Now I'll make it up by immediate action. The problem, of course, is that no one will attack me while I'm under Afa Pek Fakar's protection, and provoking Pek Faker herself is far too dangerous.

I can see only one way to do this.

I wait a few days. Outside in the courtyard, I sit quietly against the prison wall and breathe shallowly. After a few minutes I leap up. The dizziness takes me; I worsen it by holding my breath. Then I ram as hard as I can into the rough stone wall and slide down it. Pain tears through my arm and forehead. One of Pek Fakar's men shouts something.

Pek Fakar is there in a minute. I hear her—hear all of them—through a curtain of dizziness and pain.

"—just *ran* into the wall, I saw it—"

"—told me she gets these dizzy attacks—"

"—head broken in—"

I gasp, through sudden real nausea, "The healer. The Terran—"

"The Terran?" Pek Fakar's voice, hard with sudden suspicion. But I gasp out more words, ". . . disease . . . a Terran told me . . . since childhood . . . without help I . . ." My vomit, unplanned but useful, spews over her boots.

"Get the Terran," Pek Fakar rasps to somebody. "And a towel!"

Then Carryl Walters bends over me. I clutch his arm, try to smile, and pass out.


When I come to, I am lying inside, on the floor of the eating hall, the Terran cross-legged beside me. A few World people hover near the far wall, scowling. Carryl Walters says, "How many fingers you see?"

"Four. Aren't you supposed to have five?"

He unbends the fifth from behind his palm and says, "You fine."

"No, I'm not," I say. He speaks childishly, and with an odd accent, but he's understandable. "I have a disease. Another Terran healer told me so."

"Who?"

"Her name was Anna Pek Rakov."

"What disease?"

"I don't remember. Something in the head. I get spells."

"What spells? You fall, flop on floor?"

"No. Yes. Sometimes. Sometimes it takes me differently." I look directly into his eyes. Strange eyes, smaller than mine, and that improbable blue. "Pek Rakov told me I could die during a spell, without help."

He does not react to the lie. Or maybe he does, and I don't know how to read it. I have never informed on a Terran before. Instead he says something grossly obscene, even for Aulit Prison: "Why you unreal? What you do?"

I move my gaze from his. "I murdered my sister." If he asks for details, I will cry. My head aches too hard.

He says, "I sorry."

Is he sorry that he asked, or that I killed Ano? Pek Rakov was not like this; she had some manners. I say, "The other Terran healer said I should be watched carefully by someone who knows what to do if I get a spell. Do you know what to do, Pek Walters?"

"Yes."

"Will you watch me?"

"Yes." He is, in fact, watching me closely now. I touch my head; there is a cloth tied around it where I bashed myself. The headache is worse. My hand comes away sticky with blood.

I say, "In return for what?"

"What you give Pek Fakar for protection?"

He is smarter than I thought. "Nothing I can also share with you." She would punish me hard.

"Then I watch you, you give me information about World."

I nod; this is what Terrans usually request. And where information is given, it can also be extracted. "I will explain your presence to Pek Fakar," I say, before the pain in my head swamps me without warning, and everything in the dining hall blurs and sears together.


Pek Fakar doesn't like it. But I have just given her a gun, smuggled in by my "cousin." I leave notes for the prison administration in my cell, under my bed. While the prisoners are in the courtyard—which we are every day, no matter what the weather—the notes are replaced by whatever I ask for. Pek Fakar had demanded a "weapon"; neither of us expected a Terran gun. She is the only person in the prison to have such a thing. It is to me a stark reminder that no one would care if all we un-real killed each other off completely. There is no one else to shoot; we never see anyone not already in perpetual death.

"Without Pek Walters, I might have another spell and die," I say to the scowling Pek Fakar. "He knows a special Terran method of flexing the brain to bring me out of a spell."

"He can teach this special method to me."

"So far, no World person has been able to learn it. Their brains are different from ours."

She glares at me. But no one, even those lost to reality, can deny that alien brains are weird. And my injuries are certainly real: bloody head cloth, left eye closed from swelling, skin scraped raw the length of my left cheek, bruised arm. She strokes the Terran gun, a boringly straight-lined cylinder of dull metal. "All right. You may keep the Terran near you—if he agrees. Why should he?"

I smile at her slowly. Pek Fakar never shows a response to flattery; to do so would be to show weakness. But she understands. Or thinks she does. I have threatened the Terran with her power, and the whole prison now knows that her power extends among the aliens as well as her own people. She goes on glaring, but she is not displeased. In her hand the gun gleams.

And so begin my conversations with a Terran.

Talking with Carryl Pek Walters is embarrassing and frustrating. He sits beside me in the eating hall or the courtyard and publicly scratches his head. When he is cheerful, he makes shrill horrible whistling noises between his teeth. He mentions topics that belong only among kin: the state of his skin (which has odd brown lumps on it) and his lungs (clogged with fluid, apparently). He does not know enough to begin conversations with ritual comments on flowers. It is like talking to a child, but a child who suddenly begins discussing bicycle engineering or university law.

"You think individual means very little, group means everything," he says.

We are sitting in the courtyard, against a stone wall, a little apart from the other prisoners. Some watch us furtively, some openly. I am angry. I am often angry with Pek Walters. This is not going as I'd planned.

"How can you say that? The individual is very important on World! We care for each other so that no individual is left out of our common reality, except by his own acts!"

"Exactly." Pek Walters says. He has just learned this word from me. "You care for others so no one left alone. Alone is bad. Act alone is bad. Only together is real."

"Of course," I say. Could he be stupid after all? "Reality is always shared. Is a star really there if only one eye can perceive its light?"

He smiles and says something in his own language, which makes no sense to me. He repeats it in real words. "When tree falls in forest, is sound if no person hears?"

"But—do you mean to say that on your star, people believe they . . ." What? I can't find the words.

He says, "People believe they always real, alone or together. Real even when other people say they dead. Real even when they do something very bad. Even when they murder."

"But they're not real! How could they be? They've violated shared reality! If I don't acknowledge you, the reality of your soul, if I send you to your ancestors without your consent, that is proof that I don't understand reality and so am not seeing it! Only the unreal could do that!"

"Baby not see shared reality. Is baby unreal?"

"Of course. Until the age when children attain reason, they are unreal."

"Then when I kill baby, is all right, because I not kill real person?"

"Of course it's not all right! When one kills a baby, one kills its chance to become real, before it could even join its ancestors! And also all the chances of the babies to which it might become ancestor. No one would kill a baby on World, not even these dead souls in Aulit! Are you saying that on Terra, people would kill babies?"

He looks at something I cannot see. "Yes."

My chance has arrived, although not in a form I relish. Still, I have a job to do. I say, "I have heard that Terrans will kill people for science. Even babies. To find out the kinds of things that Anna Pek Rakov knew about my brain. Is that true?"

"Yes and no."

"How can it be yes *and* no? Are children ever used for science experiments?"

"Yes."

"What kinds of experiments?"

"You should ask, what kind children? Dying children. Children not born yet. Children born . . . wrong. With no brain, or broken brain."

I struggle with all this. Dying children . . . he must mean not children who are really dead, but those in the transition to join their ancestors. Well, that would not be so bad, provided the bodies were then allowed to decay properly and release the souls. Children without brains or with broken brains . . . not bad, either. Such poor unreal things would be destroyed anyway. But children not born yet . . . in or out of the mother's womb? I push this away, to discuss another time. I am on a different path.

"And you never use living, real children for science?"

He gives me a look I cannot read. So much of Terran expression is still strange "Yes. We use. In some experiments. Experiments who not hurt children."

"Like what?" I say. We are staring directly at each other now. Suddenly I wonder if this old Terran suspects that I am an informer seeking information, and that is why he accepted my skimpy story about having spells. That would not necessarily be bad. There are ways to bargain with the unreal once everyone admits that bargaining is what is taking place. But I'm not sure whether Pek Walters knows that.

He says, "Experiments who study how brain work. Such as, how memory work. Including shared memory."

"Memory? Memory doesn't 'work.' It just is."

"No. Memory work. By memory-building pro-teenz." He uses a Terran word, then adds, "Tiny little pieces of food," which makes no sense. What does food have to do with memory? You don't eat memories, or obtain them from food. But I am further down the path, and I use his words to go further still.

"Does memory in World people work with the same . . . 'pro-teenz' as Terran memory?"

"Yes and no. Some same or almost same. Some different." He is watching me very closely.

"How do you know that memory works the same or different in World people? Have Terrans done brain experiments on World?"

"Yes."

"With World children?"

"Yes."

I watch a group of Huhuhubs across the courtyard. The smelly little aliens are clustered together in some kind of ritual or game. "And have you, personally, participated in these science experiments on children, Pek Walters?"

He doesn't answer me. Instead he smiles, and if I didn't know better, I'd swear the smile was sad. He says, "Pek Bengarin, why you kill your sister?"

The unexpectedness of it—now, so close to almost learning something useful—outrages me. Not even Pek Fakar has asked me that. I stare at him angrily. He says, "I know, I not should ask. Wrong for ask. But I tell you much, and answer is important—"

"But the question is obscene. You should not ask. World people are not so cruel to each other."

"Even people damned in Aulit Prison?" he says, and even though I don't know one of the words he uses, I see that yes, he recognizes that I am an informer. And that I have been seeking information. All right, so much the better. But I need time to set my questions on a different path.

To gain time, I repeat my previous point. "World people are not so cruel."

"Then you—"

The air suddenly sizzles, smelling of burning. People shout. I look up. Aka Pek Fakar stands in the middle of the courtyard with the Terran gun, firing it at the Huhuhubs. One by one they drop as the beam of light hits them and makes a sizzling hole. The aliens pass into the second stage of their perpetual death.

I stand and tug on Pek Walters's arm. "Come on. We must clear the area immediately or the guards will release poison gas."

"Why?"

"So they can get the bodies into bondage chemicals, of course!" Does this alien think the prison officials would let the unreal get even a little bit decayed? I thought that after our several conversations, Pek Walters understood more than that.

He rises slowly, haltingly, to his feet. Pek Fakar, laughing, strolls toward the door, the gun still in her hand.

Pek Walters says, "World people not cruel?"

Behind us, the bodies of the Huhuhubs lie sprawled across each other, smoking.

The next time we are herded from our cells into the dining hall and then the courtyard, the Huhuhub corpses are of course gone. Pek Walters has developed a cough. He walks more slowly, and once, on the way to our usual spot against the far wall, he puts a hand on my arm to steady himself.

"Are you sick, Pek?"

"Exactly," he says.

"But you are a healer. Make the cough disappear."

He smiles, and sinks gratefully against the wall. "Healer, heal own self."

"What?"

"Nothing. So you are informer, Pek Bengarin, and you hope I tell you something about science experiments on children on World."

I take a deep breath. Pek Fakar passes us, carrying her gun. Two of her own people now stay close beside her at all times, in case another prisoner tries to take the gun away from her. I cannot believe anyone would try, but maybe I'm wrong. There's no telling what the unreal will do. Pek Walters watches her pass, and his smile is gone. Yesterday Pek Fakar shot another person, this time not even an alien. There is a note under my bed requesting more guns.

I say, "*You* say I am an informer. I do not say it."

"Exactly," Pek Walters says. He has another coughing spell, then closes his eyes wearily. "I have not an-tee-by-otics."

Another Terran word. Carefully I repeat it. " 'An-tee-by-otics'?"

"Pro-teenz for heal."

Again that word for very small bits of food. I make use of it. "Tell me about the pro-teenz in the science experiments."

"I tell you everything about experiments. But only if you answer questions first."

He will ask about my sister. For no reason other than rudeness and cruelty. I feel my face turn to stone.

He says, "Tell me why steal baby not so bad for make person unreal always."

I blink. Isn't this obvious? "To steal a baby doesn't damage the baby's reality. It just grows up somewhere else, with some other people. But all real people of World share the same reality, and anyway after the transition, the child will rejoin its blood ancestors. Baby stealing is wrong, of course, but it isn't a really serious crime."

"And make false coins?"

"The same. False, true—coins are still shared."

He coughs again, this time much harder. I wait. Finally he says, "So when I steal your bicycle, I not violate shared reality too much, because bicycle still somewhere with people of World."

"Of course."

"But when I steal bicycle, I violate shared reality a little?"

"Yes." After a minute I add, "Because the bicycle is, after all, *mine*. You . . . made my reality shift a little without sharing the decision with me." I peer at him; how can all this not be obvious to such an intelligent man?

He says, "You are too trusting for be informer, Pek Bengarin."

I feel my throat swell with indignation. I am a *very good* informer. Haven't I just bound this Terran to me with a private shared reality in order to create an exchange of information? I am about to demand his share of the bargain when he says abruptly, "So why you kill your sister?"

Two of Pek Fakar's people swagger past. They carry the new guns. Across the courtyard a Faller turns slowly to look at them, and even I can read fear on that alien face.

I say, as evenly as I can manage, "I fell prey to an illusion. I thought that Ano was copulating with my lover. She was younger, more intelligent, prettier. I am not very pretty, as you can see. I didn't share the reality with her, or him, and my illusion grew. Finally it exploded in my head, and I . . . did it." I am breathing hard, and Pek Fakar's people look blurry.

"You remember clear Ano's murder?"

I turn to him in astonishment. "How could I forget it?"

"You cannot. You cannot because memory-building pro-teenz. Memory is strong in your brain. Memory-building pro-teenz are strong in your brain. Scientific research on World children for discover what is structure of pro-teenz, where is pro-teenz, how pro-teenz work. But we discover different thing instead."

"What different thing?" I say, but Pek Walters only shakes his head and begins coughing again. I wonder if the coughing spell is an excuse to violate our bargain. He is, after all, unreal.

Pek Fakar's people have gone inside the prison. The Faller slumps against the far wall. They have not shot him. For this moment, at least, he is not entering the second stage of his perpetual death.

But beside me, Pek Walters coughs blood.


He is dying. I am sure of it, although of course no World healer comes to him. He is dead anyway. Also, his fellow Terrans keep away, looking fearful, which makes me wonder if his disease is catching. This leaves only me. I walk him to his cell, and then wonder why I can't just stay when the door closes. No one will check. Or, if they do, will care. And this may be my last chance to gain the needed information, before either Pek Walters is coffined or Pek Fakar orders me away from him because he is too weak to watch over my supposed blood sickness.

His body has become very hot. During the long night he tosses on his bunk, muttering in his own language, and sometimes those strange alien eyes roll in their sockets. But other times he is clearer, and he looks at me as if he recognizes who I am. Those times, I question him. But the lucid times and unlucid ones blur together. His mind is no longer his own.

"Pek Walters. Where are the memory experiments being conducted? In what place?"

"Memory . . . memories . . ." More in his own language. It has the cadences of poetry.

"Pek Walters. In what place are the memory experiments being done?"

"At Rafkit Sarloe," he says, which makes no sense. Rafkit Sarloe is the government center, where no one lives. It is not large. People flow in every day, running the Sections, and out to their villages again at night. There is no square measure of Rafkit Sarloe that is not constantly shared physical reality.

He coughs, more bloody spume, and his eyes roll in his head. I make him sip some water. "Pek Walters. In what place are the memory experiments being done?"

"At Rafkit Sarloe. In the Cloud. At Aulit Prison."

It goes on and on like that. And in the early morning, Pek Walters dies.

There is one moment of greater clarity, somewhere near the end. He looks at me, out of his old, ravaged face gone gaunt with his transition. The disturbing look is back in his eyes, sad and kind, not a look for the unreal to wear. It is too much sharing. He says, so low I must bend over him to hear, "Sick brain talks to itself. You not kill your sister."

"Hush, don't try to talk. . . ."

"Find . . . Brifjis. Maldon Pek Brifjis, in Rafkit Haddon. Find . . ." He relapses again into fever.

A few moments after he dies, the armored guards enter the cell, wheeling the coffin full of bondage chemicals. With them is the priest. I want to say, *Wait, he is a good man, he doesn't deserve perpetual death*—but of course I do not. I am astonished at myself for even thinking it. A guard edges me into the corridor and the door closes.

That same day, I am sent away from Aulit Prison.

"Tell me again. Everything," Pek Brimmidin says.

Pek Brimmidin is just the same: stocky, yellowing, slightly stooped. His cluttered office is just the same. Food dishes, papers, overelaborated sculptures. I stare hungrily at the ugly things. I hadn't realized how much I'd longed, in prison, for the natural sight of curves. I keep my eyes on the sculptures, partly to hold back my question until the proper time to ask it.

"Pek Walters said he would tell me everything about the experiments that are, yes, going on with World children. In the name of science. But all he had time to tell me was that the experiments involve 'memory-building pro-teenz,' which are tiny pieces of food from which the brain constructs memory. He also said the experiments were going on in Rafkit Sarloe and Aulit Prison."

"And that is all, Pek Bengarin?"

"That is all."

Pek Brimmidin nods curtly. He is trying to appear dangerous, to scare out of me any piece of information I might have forgotten. But Frablit Pek Brimmidin can't appear dangerous to me. I have seen the real thing.

Pek Brimmidin has not changed. But I have.

I ask my question. "I have brought to you all the information I could obtain before the Terran died. Is it sufficient to release me and Ano?"

He runs a hand through his neck fur. "I'm sorry I can't answer that, Pek. I will need to consult my superiors. But I promise to send you word as soon as I can."

"Thank you," I say, and lower my eyes. *You are too trusting for be informer, Pek Bengarin.*

Why didn't I tell Frablit Pek Brimmidin the rest of it, about 'Maldon Pek Brifjis' and 'Rafkit Haddon' and not really killing my sister? Because it is most likely nonsense, the ravings of a fevered brain. Because this 'Maldon Pek Brifjis' might be an innocent World man, who does not deserve trouble brought to him by an unreal alien. Because Pek Walters's words were personal, addressed to me alone, on his deathbed. Because I do not want to discuss Ano with Pek Brimmidin's superiors one more useless painful time.

Because, despite myself, I trust Carryl Pek Walters.

"You may go," Pek Brimmidin says, and I ride my bicycle along the dusty road home.

I make a bargain with Ano's corpse, still lying in curled-finger grace on the bed across from mine. Her beautiful brown hair floats in the chemicals of the coffin. I used to covet that hair desperately, when we were very young. Once I even cut it all off while she slept. But other times I would weave it for her, or braid it with flowers. She was so pretty. At one point, when she was still a child, she wore eight bid rings, one on each finger. Two of the bids were in negotiation between the boys' fathers and ours. Although older, I have never had a single bid.

Did I murder her?

My bargain with her corpse is this: If the Reality & Atonement Section releases me and Ano because of my work in Aulit Prison, I will seek no further. Ano will be free to join our ancestors; I will be fully real. It will no longer matter whether or not I killed my sister, because both of us will again be sharing in the same reality as if I had not. But if Reality & Atonement holds me unreal still longer, after all I have given them, I will try to find this "Maldon Pek Brifjis."

I say none of this aloud. The guards at Aulit Prison knew immediately when Pek Walters died, inside a closed and windowless room. They could be watching me here, now. World has no devices to do this, but how did Pek Walters know so much about a World man working with a Terran science experiment? Somewhere there are World people and Terrans in partnership. Terrans, as everyone knows, have all sorts of listening devices we do not.

I kiss Ano's coffin. I don't say it aloud, but I hope desperately that Reality & Atonement releases us. I want to return to shared reality, to the daily warmth and sweetness of belonging, now and forever, to the living and dead of World. I do not want to be an informer any more.

Not for anyone, even myself.


The message comes three days later. The afternoon is warm and I sit outside on my stone bench, watching my neighbor's milkbeasts eye her sturdily fenced flowerbeds. She has new flowers that I don't recognize, with blooms that are entrancing but somehow foreign—could they be Terran? It doesn't seem likely. During my time in Aulit Prison, more people seem to have made up their minds that the Terrans are unreal. I have heard more mutterings, more anger against those who buy from alien traders.

Frablit Pek Brimmidin himself brings the letter from Reality and Atonement, laboring up the road on his ancient bicycle. He has removed his uniform, so as not to embarrass me in front of my neighbors. I watch him ride up, his neck fur damp with unaccustomed exertion, his gray eyes abashed, and I know already what the sealed message must say. Pek Brimmidin is too kind for his job. That is why he is only a low-level messenger boy all the time, not just today.

These are things I never saw before.

*"You are too trusting for be informer, Pek Bengarin."*

"Thank you, Pek Brimmidin," I say. "Would you like a glass of water? Or pel?"

"No, thank you, Pek," he says. He does not meet my eyes. He waves to my other neighbor, fetching water from the village well, and fumbles meaninglessly with the handle of his bicycle. "I can't stay."

"Then ride safely," I say, and go back in my house. I stand beside Ano and break the seal on the government letter. After I read it, I gaze at her a long time. So beautiful, so sweet-natured. So loved.

Then I start to clean. I scrub every inch of my house, for hours and hours, climbing on a ladder to wash the ceiling, sloshing thick soapsuds in the cracks, scrubbing every surface of every object and carrying the more intricately shaped outside into the sun to dry. Despite my most intense scrutiny, I find nothing that I can imagine being a listening device. Nothing that looks alien, nothing unreal.

But I no longer know what is real.

Only Bata is up; the other moons have not risen. The sky is clear and starry, the air cool. I wheel my bicycle inside and try to remember everything I need.

Whatever kind of glass Ano's coffin is made of, it is very tough. I have to swing my garden shovel three times, each time with all my strength, before I can break it. On the third blow the glass cracks, then falls leisurely apart into large pieces that bounce slightly when they hit the floor. Chemicals cascade off the bed, a waterfall of clear liquid that smells only slightly acrid.

In my high boots I wade close to the bed and throw containers of water over Ano to wash off chemical residue. The containers are waiting in a neat row by the wall, everything from my largest wash basin to the kitchen bowls. Ano smiles sweetly.

I reach onto the soggy bed and lift her clear.

In the kitchen, I lay her body—limp, soft-limbed—on the floor and strip off her chemical-soaked clothing. I dry her, move her to the waiting blanket, take a last look, and wrap her tightly. The bundle of her and the shovel balances across the handles of my bicycle. I pull off my boots and open the door.

The night smells of my neighbor's foreign flowers. Ano seems weightless. I feel as if I can ride for hours. And I do.

I bury her, weighted with stones, in marshy ground well off a deserted road. The wet dirt will speed the decay, and it is easy to cover the grave with reeds and toglif branches. When I've finished, I bury my clothes and dress in clean ones in my pack. Another few hours of riding and I can find an inn to sleep in. Or a field, if need be.

The morning dawns pearly, with three moons in the sky. Everywhere I ride are flowers, first wild and then cultivated. Although exhausted, I sing softly to the curving blooms, to the sky, to the pale moonlit road. Ano is real, and free.

Go sweetly, sweet sister, to our waiting ancestors.

Two days later I reach Rafkit Haddon.

It is an old city, sloping down the side of a mountain to the sea. The homes of the rich either stand on the shore or perch on the mountain,

looking in both cases like rounded great white birds. In between lie a
jumble of houses, market squares, government buildings, inns, pel
shops, slums and parks, the latter with magnificent old trees and
shabby old shrines. The manufacturing shops and warehouses lie to the
north, with the docks.

I have experience in finding people. I start with Rituals & Processions. The clerk behind the counter, a pre-initiate of the priesthood, is
young and eager to help. "Yes?"

"I am Ajma Pek Goranalit, attached to the household of Menanlin.
I have been sent to inquire about the ritual activity of a citizen, Maldon Pek Brifjis. Can you help me?"

"Of course," she beams. An inquiry about ritual activity is never
written; discretion is necessary when a great house is considering honoring a citizen by allowing him to honor their ancestors. A person so
chosen gains great prestige—and considerable material wealth. I picked
the name "Menanlin" after an hour's judicious listening in a crowded
pel shop. The family is old, numerous, and discreet.

"Let me see," she says, browsing among her public records. "Brifjis
. . . Brifjis . . . it's a common name, of course . . . which citizen, Pek?"

"Maldon."

"Oh, yes . . . here. He paid for two musical tributes to his ancestors
last year, made a donation to the Rafkit Haddon Priest House. . . . Oh!
And he was chosen to honor the ancestors of the house of Choulalait!"

She sounds awe-struck. I nod. "We know about that, of course. But
is there anything else?"

"No, I don't think so . . . wait. He paid for a charity tribute for the
ancestors of his clu merchant, Lam Pek Flanoe, a poor man. Quite a
lavish tribute, too. Music, and three priests."

"Kind," I said.

"Very! Three priests!" Her young eyes shine. "Isn't it wonderful
how many truly kind people share reality?"

"Yes," I say. "It is."

I find the clue merchant by the simple method of asking for him in
several market squares. Sales of all fuels are of course slow in the summer; the young relatives left in charge of the clu stalls are happy to chat
with strangers. Lam Pek Flanoe lives in a run-down neighborhood just
behind the great houses by the sea. The neighborhood is home to servants and merchants who provide for the rich. Four more glasses of pel
in three more pel shops, and I know that Maldon Pek Brifjis is currently
a guest in the home of a rich widow. I know the widow's address. I
know that that Pek Brifjis is a healer.

A healer.

*Sick brain talks to itself. You not kill your sister.*

I am dizzy from four glasses of pel. Enough. I find an inn, the kind where no one asks questions, and sleep without the shared reality of dreams.

It takes me a day, disguised as a street cleaner, to decide which of the men coming and going from the rich widow's house is Pek Brifjis. Then I spend three days following him, in various guises. He goes a lot of places and talks to a lot of people, but none of them seem unusual for a rich healer with a personal pleasure in collecting antique water carafes. On the fourth day I look for a good opportunity to approach him, but this turns out to be unnecessary.

"Pek," a man says to me as I loiter, dressed as a vendor of sweet flatbreads, outside the baths on Elindel Street. I have stolen the sweets before dawn from the open kitchen of a bake shop. I know at once that the man approaching me is a bodyguard, and that he is very good. It's in the way he walks, looks at me, places his hand on my arm. He is also very handsome, but that thought barely registers. Handsome men are never for such as me. They are for Ano.

Were for Ano.

"Come with me, please," the bodyguard says, and I don't argue. He leads me to the back of the baths, through a private entrance, to a small room apparently used for private grooming of some sort. The only furniture is two small stone tables. He checks me, expertly but gently, for weapons, looking even in my mouth. Satisfied, he indicates where I am to stand, and opens a second door.

Maldon Pek Brifjis enters, wrapped in a bathing robe of rich imported cloth. He is younger than Carryl Walters, a vigorous man in a vigorous prime. His eyes are striking, a deep purple with long gold lines radiating from their centers. He says immediately, "Why have you been following me for three days?"

"Someone told me to," I say. I have nothing to lose by an honest shared reality, although I still don't fully believe I have anything to gain.

"Who? You may say anything in front of my guard."

"Carryl Pek Walters."

The purple eyes deepen even more. "Pek Walters is dead."

"Yes," I say. "Perpetually. I was with him when he entered the second stage of death."

"And where was that?" He is testing me.

"In Aulit Prison. His last words instructed me to find you. To . . . ask you something."

"What do you wish to ask me?"

"Not what I thought I would ask," I say, and realize that I have made the decision to tell him everything. Until I saw him up close, I wasn't completely sure what I would do. I can no longer share reality with World, not even if I went to Frablit Pek Brimmidin with exactly the knowledge he wants about the scientific experiments on children. That would not atone for releasing Ano before the Section agreed. And Pek Brimmidin is only a messenger, anyway. No, less than a messenger: a tool, like a garden shovel, or a bicycle. He does not share the reality of his users. He only thinks he does.

As I had thought I did.

I say, "I want to know if I killed my sister. Pek Walters said I did not. He said 'sick brain talks to itself,' and that I had not killed Ano. And to ask *you*. Did I kill my sister?"

Pek Brifjis sits down on one of the stone tables. "I don't know," he says, and I see his neck fur quiver. "Perhaps you did. Perhaps you did not."

"How can I discover which?"

"You cannot."

"Ever?"

"Ever." And then, "I am sorry."

Dizziness takes me. The "low blood pressure." The next thing I know, I lie on the floor of the small room, with Pek Brifjis's fingers on my elbow pulse. I struggle to sit up.

"No, wait," he says. "Wait a moment. Have you eaten today?"

"Yes."

"Well, wait a moment anyway. I need to think."

He does, the purple eyes turning inward, his fingers absently pressing the inside of my elbow. Finally he says, "You are an informer. That's why you were released from Aulit Prison after Pek Walters died. You inform for the government."

I don't answer. It no longer matters.

"But you have left informing. Because of what Pek Walters told you. Because he told you that the skits-oh-free-nia experiments might have . . . No. It can't be."

He too has used a word I don't know. It sounds Terran. Again I struggle to sit up, to leave. There is no hope for me here. This healer can tell me nothing.

He pushes me back down on the floor and says swiftly. "When did your sister die?" His eyes have changed once again; the long golden flecks are brighter, radiating from the center like glowing spokes. "Please, Pek, this is immensely important. To both of us."

"Two years ago, and 152 days."

"Where? In what city?"

"Village. Our village. Gofkit Ilo."

"Yes," he says. "*Yes*. Tell me everything you remember of her death. Everything."

This time I push him aside and sit up. Blood rushes from my head, but anger overcomes the dizziness. "I will tell you nothing. Who do you people think you are, ancestors? To tell me I killed Ano, then tell me I didn't, then say you don't know—to destroy the hope of atonement I had as an informer, then to tell me there is no other hope—no, there might be hope—no, there's not—how can you live with yourself? How can you twist people's brains away from shared reality and offer *nothing to replace it!*" I am screaming. The bodyguard glances at the door. I don't care: I go on screaming.

"You are doing experiments on children, wrecking their reality as you have wrecked mine! You are a murderer—" But I don't get to scream all that. Maybe I don't get to scream any of it. For a needle slides into my elbow, at the inner pulse where Maldon Brjfis has been holding it, and the room slides away as easily as Ano into her grave.

A bed, soft and silky, beneath me. Rich wall hangings. The room is very warm. A scented breeze whispers across my bare stomach. Bare? I sit up and discover I am dressed in the gauzy skirt, skimpy bandeau, and flirting veil of a prostitute.

At my first movement, Pek Brifjis crosses from the fireplace to my bed. "Pek. This room does not allow sound to escape. Do not resume screaming. Do you understand?"

I nod. His bodyguard stands across the room. I pull the flirting veil from my face.

"I am sorry about that," Pek Brifjis says. "It was necessary to dress you in a way that accounts for a bodyguard carrying a drugged woman into a private home without raising questions."

A private home. I guess that this is the rich widow's house by the sea. A room that does not allow sound to escape. A needle unlike ours: sharp and sure. Brain experiments. "Skits-oh-fren-ia."

I say, "You work with the Terrans."

"No," he says. "I do not."

"But Pek Walters . . ." It doesn't matter. "What are you going to do with me?"

He says, "I am going to offer you a trade."

"What sort of trade?"

"Information in return for your freedom."

And he says he does not work with Terrans. I say, "What use is freedom to me?" although of course I don't expect him to understand that. I can never be free.

"Not that kind of freedom," he says. "I won't just let you go from this room. I will let you rejoin your ancestors, and Ano."

I gape at him.

"Yes, Pek. I will kill you and bury you myself, where your body can decay."

"You would violate shared reality like that? For *me?*"

His purple eyes deepen again. For a moment, something in those eyes looks almost like Pek Walters's blue ones. "Please understand. I think there is a strong chance you did not kill Ano. Your village was one where . . . subjects were used for experimentation. I think that is the true shared reality here."

I say nothing. A little of his assurance disappears. "Or so I believe. Will you agree to the trade?"

"Perhaps," I say. Will he actually do what he promises? I can't be sure. But there is no other way for me. I cannot hide from the government all the years until I die. I am too young. And when they find me, they will send me back to Aulit, and when I die there they will put me in a coffin of preservative chemicals . . .

I would never see Ano again.

The healer watches me closely. Again I see the Pek Walters look in his eyes: sadness and pity.

"Perhaps I will agree to the trade," I say, and wait for him to speak again about the night Ano died. But instead he says, "I want to show you something."

He nods at the bodyguard who leaves the room, returning a few moments later. By the hand he leads a child, a little girl, clean and well-dressed. One look makes my neck fur bristle. The girl's eyes are flat and unseeing. She mutters to herself. I offer a quick appeal for protection to my ancestors. The girl is unreal, without the capacity to perceive shared reality, even though she is well over the age of reason. She is not human. She should have been destroyed.

"This is Ori," Pek Brifjis says. The girl suddenly laughs, a wild demented laugh, and peers at something only she can see.

"Why is it here?" I listen to the harshness in my own voice.

"Ori was born real. She was made this way by the scientific brain experiments of the government."

"Of the government! That is a lie!"

"Is it? Do you still, Pek, have such trust in your government?"

"No, but . . ." To make me continue to earn Ano's freedom, even after I had met their terms . . . to lie to Pek Brimmidin . . . those offenses against shared reality are one thing. The destruction of a real person's physical body, as I had done with Ano's (had I?) is another, far far worse. To destroy a *mind*, the instrument of perceiving shared reality . . . Pek Brifjis lies.

He says, "Pek, tell me about the night Ano died."

"Tell me about this . . . thing!"

"All right." He sits down in a chair beside my luxurious bed. The thing wanders around the room, muttering. It seems unable to stay still.

"She was born Ori Malfisit, in a small village in the far north—"

"What village?" I need desperately to see if he falters on details.

He does not. "Gofkit Ramloe. Of real parents, simple people, an old and established family. At six years old, Ori was playing in the forest with some other children when she disappeared. The other children said they heard something thrashing toward the marshes. The family decided she had been carried off by a wild kilfreit—there are still some left, you know, that far north—and held a procession in honor of Ori's joining their ancestors.

"But that's not what happened to Ori. She was stolen by two men, unreal prisoners promised atonement and restoration to full reality, just as you were. Ori was carried off to Rafkit Sarloe, with eight other children from all over World. There they were given to the Terrans, who were told that they were orphans who could be used for experiment. The experiments were ones that would not hurt or damage the children in any way."

I look at Ori, now tearing a table scarf into shreds and muttering. Her empty eyes turn to mine, and I have to look away.

"This part is difficult," Pek Brifjis says. "Listen hard, Pek. The Terrans truly did not hurt the children. They put ee-lek-trodes on their heads . . . you don't know what that means. They found ways to see which parts of their brains worked the same as Terran brains and which did not. They used a number of tests and machines and drugs. None of it hurt the children, who lived at the Terran scientific compound and were cared for by World childwatchers. At first the children missed their parents, but they were young, and after a while they were happy."

I glance again at Ori. The unreal, not sharing in common reality, are isolated and therefore dangerous. A person with no world in common with others will violate those others as easily as cutting flowers. Under such conditions, pleasure is possible, but not happiness.

Pek Brifjis runs his hand through his neck fur. "The Terrans worked with World healers, of course, teaching them. It was the usual trade, only this time we received the information and they the physical reality: children and watchers. There was no other way World could permit Terrans to handle our children. Our healers were there every moment."

He looks at me. I say, "Yes," just because something must be said.

"Do you know, Pek, what it is like to realize you have lived your whole life according to beliefs that are not true?"

"No!" I say, so loudly that Ori looks up with her mad, unreal gaze. She smiles. I don't know why I spoke so loud. What Pek Brifjis said has nothing to do with me. Nothing at all.

"Well, Pek Walters knew. He realized that the experiments he participated in, harmless to the subjects and in aid of biological understanding of species differences, were being used for something else. The roots of skits-oh-free-nia, misfiring brain sir-kits—" He is off on a long explanation that means nothing to me. Too many Terran words, too much strangeness. Pek Brifjis is no longer talking to me. He is talking to himself, in some sort of pain I don't understand.

Suddenly the purple eyes snap back to mine. "What all that means, Pek, is that a few of the healers—our own healers, from World—found out how to manipulate the Terran science. They took it and used it to put into minds memories that did not happen."

"Not possible!"

"It is possible. The brain is made very excited, with Terran devices, while the false memory is recited over and over. Then different parts of the brain are made to . . . to recirculate memories and emotions over and over. Like water recirculated through mill races. The water gets all scrambled together. . . . No. Think of it this way: different parts of the brain send signals to each other. The signals are forced to loop together, and every loop makes the unreal memories stronger. It is apparently in common use on Terra, although tightly controlled."

*Sick brain talks to itself.*

"But—"

"There are no objections possible, Pek. It is real. It happened. It happened to Ori. The World scientists made her brain remember things that had not happened. Small things, at first. That worked. When they tried larger memories, something went wrong. It left her like this. They were still learning; that was five years ago. They got better, much better. Good enough to experiment on adult subjects who could then be returned to shared reality."

"One can't plant memories like flowers, or uproot them like weeds!"

"These people could. And did."

"But—*why?*"

"Because the World healers who did this—and they were only a few—saw a different reality."

"I don't—"

"They saw the Terrans able to do everything. Make better machines than we can, from windmills to bicycles. Fly to the stars. Cure disease. Control nature. Many World people are afraid of Terrans, Pek. And of Fallers and Huhuhubs. Because their reality is superior to ours."

"There is only one common reality," I said. "The Terrans just know more about it than we do!"

"Perhaps. But Terran knowledge makes people uneasy. And afraid. And jealous."

*Jealous. Ano saying to me in the kitchen, with Bata and Cap bright at the window, "I will too go out tonight to see him! You can't stop me! You're just jealous, a jealous ugly shriveled thing that not even your lover wants, so you don't wish me to have any—" And the red flood swamping my brain, the kitchen knife, the blood—*

"Pek?" the healer says. "Pek?"

"I'm . . . all right. The jealous healers, they hurt their own people, World people, for revenge on the Terrans—that makes no sense!"

"The healers acted with great sorrow. They knew what they were doing to people. But they needed to perfect the technique of inducing controlled skits-oh-free-nia . . . they *needed* to do it. To make people angry at Terrans. Angry enough to forget the attractive trade goods and rise up against the aliens. To cause war. The healers are mistaken, Pek. We have not had a war on World in a thousand years; our people cannot understand how hard the Terrans would strike back. But you must understand: the outlaw scientists thought they were doing the right thing. They thought they were creating anger in order to save World.

"And another thing—with the help of the government, they were careful not to make any World man or woman permanently unreal. The adults manipulated into murder were all offered atonement as informers. The children are all cared for. The mistakes, like Ori, will be allowed to decay someday, to return to her ancestors. I will see to that myself."

Ori tears the last of the scarf into pieces, smiling horribly, her flat eyes empty. What unreal memories fill her head?

I say bitterly, "Doing the right thing . . . letting me believe I killed my sister!"

"When you rejoin your ancestors, you will find it isn't so. And the means of rejoining them was made available to you: the completion of your informing atonement."

But now that atonement never will be completed. I stole Ano and buried her without Section consent. Maldon Brifjis, of course, does not know this.

Through my pain and anger I blurt, "And what of *you*, Pek Brifjis? You work with these criminal healers, aiding them in emptying children like Ori of reality—"

"I don't work with them. I thought you smarter, Pek. I work against them. And so did Carryl Walters, which is why he died in Aulit Prison."

"Against them?"

"Many of us do. Carryl Walters among them. He was an informer. And my friend."

Neither of us says anything. Pek Brifjis stares into the fire. I stare at Ori, who has begun to grimace horribly. She squats on an intricately woven curved rug which looks very old. A reek suddenly fills the room. Ori does not share with the rest of us the reality of piss closets. She throws back her head and laughs, a horrible sound like splintering metal.

"Take her away," Pek Brifjis says wearily to the guard, who looks unhappy. "I'll clean up here." To me he adds, "We can't allow any servants in here with you."

The guard leads away the grimacing child. Pek Brifjis kneels and scrubs at the rug with chimney rags dipped in water from my carafe. I remember that he collects antique water carafes. What a long way that must seem from scrubbing shit, from Ori, from Carryl Walters coughing out his lungs in Aulit Prison, among aliens.

"Pek Brifjis—did I kill my sister?"

He looks up. There is shit on his hands. "There is no way to be absolutely sure. It is possible you were one of the experiment subjects from your village. You would have been drugged in your house, to awake with your sister murdered and your mind altered."

I say, more quietly than I have said anything else in this room, "You will really kill me, let me decay, and enable me to rejoin my ancestors?"

Pek Brifjis stands and wipes the shit from his hands. "I will."

"But what will you do if I refuse? If instead I ask to return home?"

"If you do that, the government will arrest you and once more promise you atonement—if you inform on those of us working to oppose them."

"Not if I go first to whatever part of the government is truly working to end the experiments. Surely you aren't saying the *entire* government is doing this . . . thing."

"Of course not. But do you know for certain which Sections, and which officials in those Sections, wish for war with the Terrans, and which do not? *We* can't be sure. How can you?"

Frablit Pek Brimmidin is innocent, I think. But the thought is useless. Pek Brimmidin is innocent, but powerless.

It tears my soul to think that the two might be the same thing.

Pek Brifjis rubs at the damp carpet with the toe of his boot. He puts the rags in a lidded jar and washes his hands at the washstand. A faint stench still hangs in the air. He comes to stand beside my bed.

"Is that what you want, Uli Pek Bengarin? That I let you leave this house, not knowing what you will do, whom you will inform on? That I endanger everything we have done in order to convince you of its truth?"

"Or you can kill me and let me rejoin my ancestors. Which is what you think I will choose, isn't it? That choice would let you keep faith with the reality you have decided is true, and still keep yourself secret from the criminals. Killing me would be easiest for you. But only if I consent to my murder. Otherwise, you will violate even the reality you have decided to perceive."

He stares down at me, a muscular man with beautiful purple eyes. A healer who would kill. A patriot defying his government to prevent a violent war. A sinner who does all he can to minimize his sin and keep it from denying him the chance to rejoin his own ancestors. A believer in shared reality who is trying to bend the reality without breaking the belief.

I keep quiet. The silence stretches on. Finally it is Pek Brifjis that breaks it. "I wish Carryl Walters had never sent you to me."

"But he did. And I choose to return to my village. Will you let me go, or keep me prisoner here, or murder me without my consent?"

"Damn you," he says, and I recognize the word as one Carryl Walters used, about the unreal souls in Aulit Prison.

"Exactly," I say. "What will you do, Pek? Which of your supposed multiple realities will you choose now?"


It is a hot night, and I cannot sleep.

I lie in my tent on the wide empty plain and listen to the night noises. Rude laughter from the pel tent, where a group of miners drinks far too late at night for men who must bore into hard rock at dawn. Snoring from the tent to my right. Muffled lovemaking from a tent farther down the row, I'm not sure whose. The woman giggles, high and sweet.

I have been a miner for half a year now. After I left the northern village of Gofkit Ramloe, Ori's village, I just kept heading north. Here on the equator, where World harvests its tin and diamonds and pel berries and salt, life is both simpler and less organized. Papers are not necessary. Many of the miners are young, evading their government service for one reason or another. Reasons that must seem valid to them. Here government sections rule weakly, compared to the rule of the mining and farming companies. There are no messengers on Terran bicycles. There is no Terran science. There are no Terrans.

There are shrines, of course, and rituals and processions, and tributes to one's ancestors. But these things actually receive less attention than in the cities, because they are more taken for granted. Do you pay attention to air?

The woman giggles again, and this time I recognize the sound. Awi Pek Crafmal, the young runaway from another island. She is a pretty thing, and a hard worker. Sometimes she reminds me of Ano.

I asked a great many questions in Gofkit Ramloe. *Ori Malfisit*, Pek Brifjis said her name was. *An old and established family*. But I asked and asked, and no such family had ever lived in Gofkit Ramloe. Wherever Ori came from, and however she had been made into that unreal and empty vessel shitting on a rich carpet, she had not started her poor little life in Gofkit Ramloe.

Did Maldon Brifjis know I would discover that, when he released me from the rich widow's house overlooking the sea? He must have. Or maybe, despite knowing I was an informer, he didn't understand that I would actually go to Gofkit Ramloe and check. You can't understand everything.

Sometimes, in the darkest part of the night, I wish I had taken Pek Brifjis's offer to return me to my ancestors.

I work on the rock piles of the mine during the day, among miners who lift sledges and shatter solid stone. They talk, and curse, and revile the Terrans, although few miners have as much as seen one. After work the miners sit in camp and drink pel, lifting huge mugs with dirty hands, and laugh at obscene jokes. They all share the same reality, and it binds them together, in simple and happy strength.

I have strength, too. I have the strength to swing my sledge with the other women, many of whom have the same rough plain looks as I, and who are happy to accept me as one of them. I had the strength to shatter Ano's coffin, and to bury her even when I thought the price to me was perpetual death. I had the strength to follow Carryl Walters's words about the brain experiments and seek Maldon Brifjis. I had the strength to twist Pek Brifjis's divided mind to make him let me go.

But do I have the strength to go where all of that leads me? Do I have the strength to look at Frablit Brimmidin's reality, and Carryl Walters's reality, and Ano's, and Maldon Brifjis's, and Ori's—and try to find the places that match and the places that don't? Do I have the strength to live on, never knowing if I killed my sister, or if I did not? Do I have the strength to doubt everything, and live with doubt, and sort through the millions of separate realities on World, searching for the true pieces of each—assuming that I can even recognize them?

Should anyone have to live like that? In uncertainty, in doubt, in loneliness. Alone in one's mind, in an isolated and unshared reality.

I would like to return to the days when Ano was alive. Or even to the days when I was an informer. To the days when I shared in World's reality, and knew it to be solid beneath me, like the ground itself. To the days when I knew what to think, and so did not have to.

To the days before I became—unwillingly—as terrifyingly real as I am now.

# SUMMER WIND

*My generation is getting older.*

*So is every other generation extant, of course, but we Baby Boomers seem to take it more personally. We had such very high expectations, and such a great amount of hubris. We were going to revolutionize the culture, end war, find true love, colonize Mars, and never ever give up the dream that there are no limits to the human soul.*

*Well, there are, of course. Human strength, like human frailty, seldom leads us in whatever direction we thought we wanted to go. I was dwelling on this shocking verity when Ellen Datlow asked me for a story for* Ruby Slippers, Golden Tears, *the third volume of her series of retold fairy tales. Instantly I chose "Sleeping Beauty." That tale has been retold before, perhaps more times than any other except "Cinderella." However, Ellen let me re-shape it again, here as a struggle not against timeless sleep, but against the burdens of being fully awake while time inexorably keeps passing.*

Sometimes she talked to them. Which of course was stupid, since they could neither hear nor answer. She talked anyway. It made the illusion of company.

Her favorite to talk to was the stableboy, frozen in the stableyard beside the king's big roan, the grooming brush still in his upraised hand. The roan was frozen too, of course, brown eyes closed, white forelock blowing gently in the summer wind. She used to be a little frightened of the roan, so big it was, but not of the stableboy, who had had merry red lips and wide shoulders and dark curling hair.

He had them still.

Every so often she washed off a few of them: the stableboy, or the cook beside his pots, or the lady-in-waiting sewing in the solarium, or even the man and woman in the north bedchamber, locked in naked embrace on the wide bed. None of them ever sweated or stank, but still, there was the dust—dust didn't sleep—and after years and years the people became coated in fine, gray powder. At first she tried to whisk them clean with a serving maid's feather duster, but it was very hard to dust eyelashes and earlobes. In the end she just threw a pot of water over them. They didn't stir, and their clothes dried eventually, the velvets and silks a little stiff and water-marked, the coarse-woven breeches and skirts of the servants none the worse off. Better, maybe. And it wasn't as if any of them would catch cold.

"There you are," she said to the stableboy. "Now, doesn't that feel better? To be clean?"

Water glistened in his black curls.

"I'm sure it must feel better."

A droplet fell onto his forehead, slid over his smooth brown cheeks, came to rest in the corner of his mouth.

"It was not supposed to happen this way, Corwin."

He didn't answer, of course. She reached out one finger and patted the droplet from his sleeping lips. She put the finger in her own mouth and sucked it.

"How many years was *I* asleep? How many?"

His chest rose and fell gently, regularly.

She wished she could remember the color of his eyes.

A few years later, the first prince came. Or maybe it wasn't even the first. Briar Rose was climbing the steps from the cool, dark chambers under the castle, her spread skirt full of wheat and apples and cheese as fresh as the day they were stored. She passed the open windows of the Long Gallery and heard a tremendous commotion.

Finally! At last!

She dropped her skirts; wheat and apples rolled everywhere. Rose rushed through the Gallery and up the steps to her bedchamber in the highest tower. From her stone window she could just glimpse him beyond the castle wall, the moat, the circle of grass between moat and Hedge. He sat astride a white stallion on the far side of the Hedge, hacking with a long silver sword. Sunlight glinted on his blond hair.

She put her hand to her mouth. The slim white fingers trembled.

The prince was shouting, but wind carried his words away from her. Did that mean the wind would carry hers toward him? She waved her arms and shouted.

"Here! Oh, brave prince, here I am! Briar Rose, princess of all the realm! Fight on, oh good prince!"

He didn't look up. With a tremendous blow, he hacked a limb from the black Hedge, so thick and interwoven it looked like metal, not plant. The branch shuddered and fell. On the backswing, the sword struck smaller branches to the prince's right. They whipped aside and then snapped back, and a thorn-studded twig slapped the prince across the eyes and blinded him. He screamed and dropped his sword. The sharp blade caught the stallion in the right leg. It shied in pain. The blinded prince fell off, directly into the Hedge, and was impaled on thorns as long as a man's hand and hard as iron.

Rose screamed. She rushed down the tower steps, not seeing them, not seeing anything. Over the drawbridge, across the grass. At the Hedge she was forced to stop by the terrible thorns, as thick and sharp on this side as on the other. She couldn't see the prince, but she could hear him. He went on screaming for what seemed an eternity, although of course it wasn't.

Then he stopped.

She sank onto the green grass, sweet with unchanging summer, and buried her face in her apple-smelling skirts. Somewhere, faintly on the wind, she heard a sound like old women weeping.

After that, she avoided all the east-facing windows. It was years before she convinced herself that the prince's body was, must be, gone from the far side of the Hedge. Even though the carrion birds did not stay for nearly that long.

Somewhere around the thirteenth year of unchanging summer, the second prince came. Rose almost didn't hear him. For months, she had rarely left her tower chamber. Blankets draped the two stone windows, darkening the room almost to blackness. She descended the stone steps only to visit the storage rooms. The rest of the long hours, she lay on her bed and drank the wine stored deep in the cool cellars under the castle. Days and nights came and went, and she lifted the gold goblet to her lips and let the red forgetfulness slide down her throat and tried not to remember. Anything.

After the first unmemorized months of this, she caught sight of herself in her mirror. She found another blanket to drape over the treacherous glass.

But still the chamberpot must be emptied occasionally, although not very often. Rose shoved aside the blanket over the south window and leaned far out to dump the reeking pot into the moat far below. Her bleary eyes caught the flash of a sword.

He was red-headed this time, hair the color of warm flame. His horse was black, his sword set with green stones. Emeralds, perhaps. Or jade. Rose watched him, and not a muscle of her face moved.

The prince slashed at the Hedge, rising in his stirrups, swinging his mighty sword with both hands. The air rang with his blows. His bright hair swirled and leaped around his strong shoulders. Then his left leg

caught on a thorn and the Hedge dragged him forward. The screaming started.

Rose let the edge of the blanket drop and stood behind it, the un-
emptied chamber pot splashing over her trembling hands. She thought
she heard sobs, the dry juiceless sobs of the very old, but of course the
chamber was empty.

She lost a year. Or maybe more than a year; she couldn't be sure. There
was only the accumulation of dust to go by, thick on the Gallery floor,
thick on the sleeping bodies. A year's worth of drifting dust.

When she came again to herself, she lay outside, on the endlessly
green summer grass. Her naked body was covered with scars. She
walked, dazed, through the castle. Clothes on the sleepers had been
slashed to ribbons. Mutilated doublets, breeches, sleeves, redingotes,
kirtles. Blood had oozed from exposed shoulders and thighs where the
knife had cut too deep, blood now dried on the sleeping flesh. In the
north bedchamber, the long tumbled hair of the woman had been
hacked off, her exposed scalp clotted with blood, her lips still smiling
as she slept in her lover's arms.

Rose stumbled, hand to her mouth, to the stableyard. Corwin sat beside the big roan, black curls unshorn, tunic unslashed. Beside him,
ripped and bloody, lay Rose's own dress, the blue dress with pink
forget-me-nots she had worn for the ball on her sixteenth birthday.

She buried it, along with all the other ruined clothing and the bloody
rags from washing the clotted wounds, in a deep hole beside the Hedge.

On the wind, old women keened.

Although the spinning wheel was heavy, she dragged it down the
tower stairs to the Long Gallery. For a moment she looked curiously at
the sharp needle, but for only a moment. The storage rooms held wool
and flax, bales of it, quintals of it. There were needles and thread and
colored ribbon. There were wooden buttons, and jeweled buttons, and
carved buttons of a translucent white said to be the teeth of faraway animals large enough to lay siege to a magic Hedge. Briar Rose knew better, but she took the white buttons and smoothed them between her
fingers.

She weaved and sewed and embroidered new clothes for every
sleeper in the castle, hundreds of people. Pages and scullery maids and
mummers and knights and ladies and the chapel priest and the king's
fool, for whom she made a particolored doublet embroidered with

small sharp thorns. She weaved clothes for the chancellor and the pastry chef and ~~the seneschal and~~ the falconer and the captain of the guards and the king and queen, asleep on their thrones. For herself Rose weaved a simple black dress and wore it every day. Sometimes, tugging a chemise or kirtle or leggings over an unresisting sleeping body, she almost heard voices on the summer breeze. Voices, but no words.

She spun and weaved and embroidered sixteen hours a day, for years. She frowned as she worked, and a line stitched itself across her forehead, perpendicular to the lines in her neck. Her golden hair fell forward and interferred with the spinning and so she bound it into a plait, and saw the gray among the gold, and shoved the plait behind her back.

She had finished an embroidered doublet for a sous-cook and was about to carry it to the kitchen when she heard a great noise without the walls.

Slowly, with great care, Rose laid the sous-cook's doublet neatly on the polished Gallery floor. Slowly, leaning against the stone wall to ease her arthritic left knee, she climbed the circular stairwell to her bedchamber in the tower.

He attacked the Hedge from the northwest, and he had brought a great retinue. At least two dozen young men hacked and slashed, while squires and pages waited behind. Flags snapped in the wind; horses pawed the ground; a trumpet blared. Rose had no trouble distinguishing the prince. He wore a gold circlet in his glossy dark hair, and the bridle of his golden horse was set with black diamonds. His sword hacked and slashed faster than the others', and even from the high tower, Rose could see that he smiled.

She unfurled the banner she had embroidered, fierce yellow on black, with the two curt words: BE GONE! None of the young men looked up. Rose flapped the banner, and a picture flashed through her mind, quick as the prince's sword: her old nurse, shaking a rug above the moat, freeing it of dust.

The prince and his men continued to hack at the Hedge. Rose called out—after all, she could hear them, should they not be able to hear her? Her voice sounded thin, pale. She hadn't spoken in years. The ghostly words disappeared in the other voices, the wordless ones on the summer wind. No one noticed her.

The prince fell into the Hedge, and the screaming began, and Rose bowed her head and prayed for them, the lost souls, the ones for whom she would never spin doublets or breeches or whispered smiles like the one on the woman with hacked-off hair asleep in her shared bed in the north chamber.

Her other dead.


After years, decades, everyone in the castle was clothed, and dusted, and pillowed on embroidered cushions rich with intricate designs in jewelled-colored thread. The pewter in the kitchen gleamed. The wooden floor of the Long Gallery shone. Tapestries hung bright and clean on the walls.

Rose no longer sat at the spinning wheel. Her fingers were knotted and twisted, the flesh between them thin and tough as snakeskin. Her hair, too, had thinned but not toughened, its lustrous silver fine as spun flax. When she brushed it at night, it fell around her sagging breasts like a shower of light.

Something was happening to the voices on the wind. They spun their wordless threads more strongly, more distinctly, especially outside the castle. Rose slept little now, and often she sat in the stableyard through the long unchanging summer afternoon, listening. Corwin slept beside her, his long lashes throwing shadows on his downy cheeks. She watched him, and listened to the spinning wind, and sometimes her lined face turned slowly in a day-long arc, as if following a different sun than the one that never moved.

"Corwin," she said in her quavery voice, "did you hear that?"

The wind hummed over the cobblestones, stirred the forelock of the sleeping roan.

"There are almost words, Corwin. No, better than words."

His chest rose and fell.

"I am old, Corwin. Too old. Princes are much younger men."

Sunlight tangled in his fresh black curls.

"They aren't really supposed to be words. Are they."

Rose creaked to her feet. She walked to the stableyard well. The oak bucket swung suspended from its windlass, empty. Rose put a hand on the winch, which had become very hard for her twisted hands to turn, and closed her eyes. The wind spun past her, then through her. Her ears roared. The bucket descended of itself, filled with water. Cranked back up. Rose opened her eyes.

"Ah," she said quietly. And then, "So."

The wind blew.

She hobbled through the stableyard gate to the Hedge. One hand she laid on it, and closed her eyes. The wind hummed in her head, barely rustling the summer grass.

When she opened her eyes, nothing about the Hedge had changed.

"So," Rose said, and went back into the bailey, to dust the royal guard.

But each day she sat in the wordless wind, or the wind whose words were not what mattered, or in her own mind. And listened.

No prince had arrived for decades. A generation, Rose decided; a generation who knew the members of the retinue led by the young royal on the black horse. But that generation must grow older, and marry, and give birth to children, and one day a trumpet sounded and men shouted and banners snapped in the wind.

It took Rose a long time to climb the tower staircase. Often she paused to rest, leaning against the cool stone, hand pressed to her heart. At the top she paused again, to look curiously around her old room, the one place she never cleaned. The bedclothes lay dirty and sodden on the stained floor. Rose picked them up, folded them across the bed, and hobbled to a stone window.

The prince had just begun to hack at the Hedge. He was the handsomest one yet: hair and beard of deep burnished bronze, dark blue doublet strained across strong shoulders, silver fittings on epaulets and sash. Rose's vision had actually improved with age; she could see his eyes. They were the green of stained-glass windows in bright sun.

She knew better, now, than to call to him. She stared at his hacking and slashing, at the deadly Hedge, and then closed her eyes. She let the wind roar in her ears, and through her head, and into the places that had not existed when she was young. Not even when she heard him scream did she open her eyes.

But finally, when the screams stopped as quickly as they had come, she leaned through the tower window and scanned the ground far below. The prince lay on the trampled grass, circled by kneeling, shouting men. Rose watched him wave them away, rise unsteadily, and remount his horse. She saw the horrified gaze he bent upon the Hedge.

Later, after they had all ridden away, she made her way back down the steps, over the drawbridge, across the grass to the Hedge. It loomed as dark, as thick, as impenetrable as ever. The black thorns pointed in all directions, in and out, and nothing she could do with the wind could change them at all.

———————

But then, one day, the Hedge melted.

Rose was very old. Her silver plait had become a bother and she'd cut it, trimming her hair into a neat white cap. There were ten hairs on her chin, which sometimes she remembered to pull out and sometimes she didn't. Her body had gone skinny as a bird's, with thin bird bones, except for a soft rounded belly that fluttered when she snored. The arthritis in her hands had eased and they, too, were skinny, long darting hands, worn and capable as a spinning shuttle. Her sunken blue eyes spun power.

She was sitting on the unchanging grass when she heard the tumult behind the Hedge. Creakily she rose to start for the tower. But there was no need. Before her eyes the black thorns melted, running into the ground like so much dirty water from washing the kitchen floor. And then the rest of the Hedge melted. Beside her a sleeping groom stirred, and beside the drawbridge, another.

The prince rode through the dissolving Hedge as if it had never been. He had brown hair, gold sash, a chestnut horse. As he dismounted, the solid mass of muscle in his thighs shifted above his high polished boots.

"The bedchamber of the princess—where is it?"

Rose pointed at the highest tower.

He strode past her, trailed by his retinue. When the last squire had crossed the drawbridge, Rose followed.

All was commotion. Guards sprang forward, found themselves dressed in embroidered velvet, and spun around, bewildered, drawn swords in their hand. Ladies bellowed for pages. The falconer dashed from the mews, wearing a doublet of white satin slashed over crimson, the peregrine on his wrist fitted with gold-trimmed jesses with ivory bells.

Rose hobbled to the stableyard. The king's roan pawed and snorted. Men ran to and fro. A serving wench lowered the bucket into the well, on her head a coif sewn with gold lace.

Only Corwin noticed Rose. He stood a whole head taller than she— surely it had only been a half head difference, once? He glanced at her, away, and then back again, puzzlement on his fresh, handsome face. His eyes, she saw, were gray.

"Do I know you, good dame?"

"No," Rose said.

"Did you come, then, with the visitors?"

"No, lad."

He studied her neat black dress, cropped hair, wrinkled face. Her eyes. "I thought I knew everyone who lived in the castle."

She didn't answer. A slow flush started in his smooth brown cheeks. "Where do you live, mistress?"

She said, "I live nowhere you have ever been, lad. Nor could go." His puzzlement only deepened, but she turned and hobbled away. There was no way she could explain.

There was shouting now, in the high tower, drifted down on the warm summer air. Through the open windows of the Long Gallery, Rose saw the queen rush past, her long velvet skirts swept over her arm. A nearly bald woman in a lace nightdress rushed from the north bed-chamber, screaming. Soon they would start to search, to ask questions, to close the drawbridge.

She hobbled over it, through the place where the Hedge had been, now a bare circle like a second, drier moat. And they were waiting for her just beyond, half concealed in a grove of trees, seven of them. Old women like her, power in their glances, voices like the spinning wind.

Rose said, "Is this all there is, then, for the life I have lost? This magic?"

"Yes," one of them said.

"It is no little thing," another said quietly. "You have brought a prince back to life. You have clothed a fiefdom. You have seen, as few do, what and who you are."

Rose thought about that. The woman who had spoken, her spine curved like a bow, gazed steadily back.

The first old woman repeated sharply, "It is no little thing you have gained, sister."

Rose said, "I would rather have had my lost life."

And to that there was no answer. The women shrugged, and linked arms with Rose, and the eight set out into the world that hardly, as yet, recognized how badly it needed them. And perhaps never would.

# ALWAYS TRUE TO THEE, IN MY FASHION

*Don't you hate it when a joke falls flat?*

*This story, yet another centering on designer drugs to affect the mind, was intended as a light parody of fashion. Not just fashion in clothing, which is all too easy to parody, but fashion in lifestyle. One year magazines celebrate "The New Seriousness": supposedly Americans are giving up their frivolous hedonism and turning to the search for spiritual answers. The next year heralds the arrival of "A Return to Individual Style." Then conservatism, in politics and sofas alike. We're into national pride. No, we're into mindless fun. We're into cocooning. We're into family values, but only until the kids are in bed, when "The Nineties Romantic: Sensuousness Grows Up" dictates our actions, nightdress, and lighting (halogen torchieres that glow pink). How can you get funnier than this desire to carve up ageless human activities and feeling, label each piece, and market each as a "new fashion"?*

*A few critics, however, thought that "Always True to Thee, In My Fashion" was another of my stories looking seriously at the consequences of genetic tinkering. They then identified, quite correctly, all of the story's scientific implausibilities and problems.*

*Ah, well. I still think it's funny.*

RELATIONSHIPS FOR THE AUTUMN SEASON WERE CASUAL AND UNCON-structed, following a summer where fashion had been unusually colorful and intense. Suzanne liked wearing the new feelings. They were light and cool, allowing her a lot of freedom of movement. The offhand affection made her feel unencumbered, graceful.

Cade wasn't so sure.

"It sounds bloody boring," he said to Suzanne, holding the pills in his hand. "Love isn't supposed to be so boring. At least the summer fashions offered a few surprises."

Boxes from the couture houses spilled around their bedroom. Suzanne, of course, had done the ordering. Karl Lagerfeld, Galliano, Enkia for Christian LaCroix, and of course Suzanne's own special designer and friend, Sendil. Cade stood in the middle of an explosion of slouchy tweeds and off-white linen, wearing his underwear and his stubborn look.

"But the summer feelings were so heavy," Suzanne said. She dropped a casual kiss on the top of Cade's head. "Come on, Cadie, at least give it a try. You have the body for casual emotions, you know. They look so good on you."

This was true. Cade was lean and loose-jointed, with a small head on long neck: a body made for easy carelessness. Backlit by their wide bedroom windows, he already looked coolly nonchalant: an Edwardian aristocrat, perhaps, or one of those marvelously blase American river-boat gamblers who couldn't be bothered to sweat. The environment helped, of course. Suzanne always did their V-R, and for autumn she'd programmed unlined curtains, cool terra cotta tiles, oyster-white walls. All very informal and composed, nothing trying very hard. But she'd left the windows natural. That, too, was perfect: too nonchalant about the view of London to bother reprogramming its ugliness. Only Suzanne would have thought of this touch. Their friends would be so jealous.

"Come on, Cade, try the feelings on." But he only went on looking troubled, holding the pills in his long-fingered hand.

Suzanne began to feel impatient. Cade was wonderful, of course, but he could be so conservative. He really hadn't liked the summer fashions—and they had been so much fun! Suzanne knew she looked good in those kinds of dramatic, highly colored feelings. They went well with her voluptuous body and small, sharp teeth. People had noticed. She'd had two passionate adulteries, one knife fight with Kittery, one duel fought over her, two midnight reconciliations, and one weepy parting from Cade at sunset on the edge of a sea, which had been V-Red into wine-dark roils for the occasion. Very satisfying.

But the summer was over. Really, Cade should be more willing to vary his emotional wardrobe. Sometimes she even wondered if she might be better off with another lover . . . Mikhail, maybe, or even Jastinder . . . but no, of course not. She loved Cade. They belonged to each other forever. Cade was the bedrock of her life. If only he weren't so stubborn!

"Have you ever thought," he said, not looking at her, "that we might skip a fashion season? Just let it go by and wear something old, off alone together? Or even go naked?"

"What an idea," she said lightly.

"We could try it, Suzanne."

"We could also move out of the towers and live down there along the Thames among the starving and dirty-mattressed thugs. Equally appealing."

*Wrong, wrong.* Cade turned away from her. In another minute he would put the pills back in their little bottle. Suzanne decided to try playfulness. She twined her arms around his neck, and flashed her eyes at him. "You are vast, Cade. You contain multitudes. Do you really think it's fair, mmmm, that you deny me all your multitudes, when I'm so ready to love them all?"

Reluctantly, he smiled. " 'Multitudes,' is it?"

"And I *want* them all. All the Cades. I'm greedy, you know." She rubbed against him.

"Well . . ."

"Come on, Cade. For me." Another rub, and after it she danced away, laughing.

He could never resist her. He swallowed the pills, then reached out his arms. Suzanne eluded them.

"Not yet. After they take effect."

"Suzanne . . ."

"Tomorrow." Casually, she blew him an affectionate kiss and sauntered toward the door, leaving him gazing after her. Cade wanting her, and she offhand and insouciant.

It was going to be a wonderful autumn.


The next day was unbelievably exciting, more arousing even than when she'd walked in on Cade and Kittery in the summer bedroom, and they'd had the shouting and pleading and knife fight. This was arousing in a different way. Suzanne had strolled in to the apartment in midmorning, half an hour late. "There you are, then," she'd said casually to Cade.

He looked up from his reader, his long-limbed body sprawled across the chair. "Oh, hallo."

"How are you?"

He shrugged, then made a negligent gesture with one graceful slim-fingered hand.

Suzanne draped herself across his lap, gazing abstractedly out the window. Today London looked even uglier than usual: cold, gray, dirty.

"Do you mind awfully?" Cade said. "I'm in the middle of this article."

"And so absorbed that you don't notice me, mmmmm?" Suzanne moved against him.

Cade smiled, pecked her cheek, and gave her a careless nudge. "Off you go, then." He returned to his reader. Suzanne stood and stretched.

The rush of blood to her nipples and thighs startled her. He really was indifferent to her! She would have to actually work at getting him interested, winning him from his casual reading. . . . God, it was exciting!

She would succeed, of course. She always did. But why hadn't she ever realized before how much more interesting the victory was when she'd have to struggle for it? She hadn't been this aroused in years.

"Cade . . ." She leaned over him and nibbled on his ear. "Sweet Cade . . ."

He tilted his head to look up at her, eyebrows raised. The drugs had done something to his eyes, or to her perception of them; they looked lighter, more opaque. Suzanne laughed softly. "Come on, it will be so good. . . ."

"Ok, all right. If you insist."

He rose from his chair, turned to pick up the dropped reader. He nudged an antique vase a quarter-inch to the right on one of Sendil's occasional tables. He rubbed his left elbow, gazing out the window. Suzanne took his hand, and they ambled toward the bedroom.

And it was wonderful. The most interesting show in years. Really, the fashion designers were geniuses.

"Cade, Flavia and Mikhail have invited us to a water fete on Saturday. Do you want to go?"

He looked up from his screen, where he was checking his portfolio on the New York Stock Exchange. He didn't even look annoyed that she'd interrupted. "Do you want to go?"

"I asked *you*."

"I don't care."

Suzanne bit her lip. "Well, what shall I tell Flavia?"

"Whatever you like, love."

"Well, then . . . I thought I might fly to Paris this weekend." She paused. "To see Guillaume."

He didn't even twitch. "Whatever you like, love."

"Cade—do you care if I visit Guillaume? For an entire weekend?" In the summer, a threat to visit Guillaume, a former lover who still adored Suzanne, had produced drama that went on for sixteen straight hours.

"Oh, Suzanne, don't be tiresome. Of course you can visit Guillaume if you want." Cade blew her a casual kiss.

She charged across the room, seized his hand, and dragged him away from the terminal. His eyebrows rose slightly.

But afterward, as Cade lay deeply asleep, Suzanne wondered. Maybe he'd actually been right, after all, about the current fashions. Not that it hadn't been exciting to work at arousing him, but . . . she wasn't supposed to be working. She was supposed to feel just as detached and casual as Cade. That was the bloody trouble with fashion—no matter what the designers said, one size never did fit all. The individual drug responses were too different. Well, no matter. Tomorrow she'd just increase her dosage. Until she, and not Cade, was the more casual. The sought after, rather than the seeker.

The way it was supposed to be.

"Cade . . . Cade?"

"Oh, Suzanne. Do come in."

He sat up in bed, unselfconscious, unruffled. Beside him, Flavia emerged languidly from the off-white sheets. She said, "Suzanne, darling. I *am* sorry. We didn't expect you so soon. Shall I leave?"

Suzanne crossed the room to the dresser. This was more like it. A little movement, for a change—a little *action*. Really, casual was all very well, but how many evenings could one spend in off-hand conversation? Almost she was grateful to Flavia. Not that she would show it, of course. But Flavia was giving her the perfect excuse to put on an entirely different demeanor. She had rather missed changing for dinner.

From the dresser top she picked up a string of pearls and toyed with them, a careful appearance of anger suppressed under a facade of sophisticated control. "Cade . . . how could you?"

Flavia said, "Perhaps I *had* better leave, hadn't I? See you later, darlings." She activated a V-R dress from her necklace—easy unconstricting lines in a subtle taupe, Suzanne noted—and left.

Cade said, "Suzanne—"

"I trusted you, Cade!"

"Oh, rot," he said. "You're making a fuss over nothing."

"Nothing! You call—"

"Really, Suzanne. Flavia hardly matters."

" 'Hardly'? And just what does that mean?"

"Oh, Suzanne, you know what it means. Really, don't make yourself ridiculous over trifles." And Cade yawned, stretched, and went to sleep.

*To sleep.*

Suzanne thought of waking him. She thought of pounding on him with her small fists, of dumping him on the floor, of packing her bags and leaving a note. But, really, all those things *would* look rather ridiculous. People would hear about it, snicker . . . and even if they didn't, even if Cade kept her bad taste to himself, there was still the fact that the two of them would know it had happened. Suzanne had lost her cool poise. She had been as embarrassing as Kittery, the season Kittery showed up at a geisha party dressed in the crude emotions of a political revolutionary. Even if Cade were to keep this incident private, Suzanne winced at the idea of his thinking her as gauche as Kittery, as capable of such a major fashion faux pas. No, no. Better to let it pass.

Cade snored softly. Suzanne lay beside him, fists clenched, waiting for winter.

Finally, the new fashions were out! Suzanne went to Paris for the pre-season shows, sitting in the first row at each important couture house, exultant. She saw, and was seen, and was happy.

The designers had outdone themselves, especially Suwela for Karl Lagerfield. The feeling was tremulous, ingenue, all the tentative sharp sweetness of virgin love. Pink, pale blue, white—lots of white—with indrawn gasps and wide-eyed sexual exploration. Ruffles and flowers and heart flutterings at a lingering look. Gianfranco Ferre showed a marvelous silk, flowing biocloth abloom with living forget-me-nots, accessorized with innocence barely daring to touch the male model's hand. At Galliano, the jackets were matched with flounced bonnets and a blushing fear that a too-passionate kiss would lead . . . where? The models' knees trembled with nervous anticipation. And the ever-faithful Sendil showed an empire-waist ballgown in muslin—muslin!—that, he whispered to Suzanne, had been inspired solely by her.

Suzanne wanted everything. She spent more money than ever before at a preview. She could hardly wait for the official opening of the season. Cade and she, once more thirteen years old, with love new and sparkling and fraught with sweet tension. . . . While she waited for opening day, she had her hair grown long, her hips slimmed, and her eyes widened and colored to huge blue orbs.

Maybe they could give a party. Everyone tremulous with anticipation and virgin hopes . . . wasn't there something called "spin the bottle"? She could ask the computer.

It was going to be a wonderful winter.

"No," Cade said.

"No?"

"Oh, don't look so crushed, love. Well, maybe, then. I mean, what does it matter, really?"

"What does it *matter*?" Suzanne cried. "Cade, it's the start of the season!"

He eyed her with amusement. But under the amusement was something else, the now-familiar feeling that he found her faintly ridiculous, casually distasteful. God, she couldn't wait to get him out of this wretched understated nonchalance.

Suzanne made an effort to speak lightly. "Well, if it doesn't matter, then there's no reason not to go for a bit of a change, is there?"

He flicked at a speck of dust on his sleeve. "I suppose not. But, then, love, no reason to go for change either, is there? This suits us well enough, don't you think?"

Suzanne tried not to bite her lip clear through. It was too close to opening day for tissue repair. "Well, perhaps, but one wants some variety, all the same. . . ."

He shrugged. "I don't, actually."

She cried, "But, Cade—!"

"Oh, Suzanne, don't get so worked up, it's quite tiresome. Can't we discuss it later?"

"But—"

"I have lunch with Jastinder. Or Kittery. Or somebody. Care to come? No? Well, suit yourself, love."

He waved to her and sauntered out.


She couldn't budge him. He didn't resist her; he just wasn't interested. Careless. Indifferent.

Opening day came. Suzanne stood in the bedroom, biting her bottom lip. What to do? Everything was ready. She'd programmed the room for pale pink walls with white wood molding, filmy curtains fluttering in the breeze, a view of gardens filled with lavender and June roses and wisteria and anything else the computer said was old-fashioned. The scent simulator was running overtime. Around Suzanne were the half-unpacked boxes of flouncy silks and sweet girlish slip-dresses and little kid slippers. Plus, of course, the white jackets and copper-toed boots for Cade. Who had glanced at the entire thing with amused negligence, and then gone out somewhere for a stroll.

"But you can't!" Suzanne had cried. "It's opening day! And you're still dressed in . . . *that*."

"Oh, love, what does it matter?" Cade had said. "I'm comfortable. And isn't all this stuff just a bit . . . twee? Isn't it, now?"

"But Cade—"

"I rather like what I'm used to."

"You're not used to it!" Suzanne had cried in anguish. "You can't be! You've only had it for a season!"

"Really? I guess so. Seems longer," Cade said. "See you later, love. Or not."

Now Suzanne scowled at the pills in her hand. There was a real problem here. If she took them, she would be garbed in the gentle sweet tremulousness of youth. Gentle, sweet, tremulous—and ineffective. That was the whole point. Ingenues were acted upon, not actors. But without the whole force of her will, could she persuade Cade to stop being such an ass?

On the other hand, if she didn't take the pills, she would be dressed wrong for the occasion. She pictured showing up at the Donnison lunch in the Alliani Towers, at the afternoon reception in the Artificial Islands, at Kittery's party tonight, dressed badly, shabbily, in last season's worn-out feelings . . . no, *no*. She couldn't. She had a reputation to maintain. And everyone would think that she couldn't afford new feelings, that she had lost all her money in data-atoll speculation or some other ghastly nouveau thing. . . . Damn Cade!

He came back from his stroll a few hours later, whistling carelessly. The vid was already crammed with "Where are you?" messages from their friends at the Donnison lunch. Breathless, ingenue messages, from people having a wonderful youthful time. And there was Cade, cool and off-hand in those detestable boring tweeds, daring to *whistle*. . . .

"Where have you *been?*" Suzanne said. "Don't you know how late we are? Come on, get dressed!"

"Don't whine, Suzanne, it's terribly unattractive."

"I never whine!" she cried, stung.

"Well, then, don't do whatever you're doing. Come lie down beside me instead."

It was the most assertive thing he'd said in months. Encouraged, Suzanne lay with him on the bed, trying to control her panic. Maybe if she were sweet enough to him . . .

"You haven't dressed yet, either, have you, love?" Cade said. He was smiling. "That isn't the tentative embrace of an ingenue."

"Would you like that?" Suzanne said hopefully. "I can just change . . ."

"Actually, no. I've been thinking, Suzanne. I don't want to get all tricked out as some sort of ersatz boy-child, and you don't want to go on wearing these casual emotions. So what about what I suggested at the end of last summer? Let's just go naked for a while. See what it's like."

"No!" Suzanne shrieked.

She hadn't known she was going to do it. She never shrieked like that—not she, Suzanne! Except, of course, when fashion decreed it, and that didn't really count. . . . What was she thinking? Of course it counted, it was the only thing that kept them all safe. To go *naked* in front of each other, Good God what was Cade thinking? Civilized people didn't parade around naked, everything personal on display for any passing observer to pick over and chortle at, nude and helplessly exposed in their deepest feelings!

Or lack of them.

She struggled to sound casual. And she succeeded—or last season's pills did. "Cade . . . I don't want to go naked. Really, I don't think you're being very fair. We had it your way for a season. Now it should be my turn."

A long silence. For a moment Suzanne thought he'd actually fallen asleep. If he had *dared* . . .

"Suzanne," he said finally, "it's my detached impression that you always have it your way."

It hurt so much that Suzanne's legs trembled as she climbed off the bed. How could he say that? She always thought in terms of the two of them! Always! She went into the bathroom and closed the door. Shaky, she leaned against the wall, and caught sight of herself in the mirror. She looked lovely. Blue eyes wide with surprised hurt, pale lip trembling, like a young girl suddenly cut to her vulnerable heart. . . .

And she hadn't even yet taken the season's pills!

Cade would have to come around. He would simply *have* to.


He didn't. Suzanne argued. She stormed. She begged. Finally, after missing three days of wonderful parties—irreplaceable parties, a season only opened once, after all—she dressed herself in the pills and a white cotton frock, and pleaded with him tremulously, weeping delicate, sweet tears. Cade only laughed affectionately, and hugged her casually, and went off to do something else off-hand and detestable.

She dissolved the pills in his burgundy.

It bothered her, a little. They had always been honest with each other. And besides, it was such a scary thing for a young girl to do, her fingers shook the whole time as she broke open the capsules and a single shining crystalline tear dropped into the glass (how much salt would one tear add? Cade had a keen palate.) But she did it. And, wide-eyed, she handed him the glass, her girlish bosom heaving with silent emotion. Then she excused herself and went to take a scented bath in pink bubbles and to do her hair in long drooping ringlets.

By the time she came out, Cade was waiting for her. He held a single pink rose, and his eyes met hers shyly, for just a moment, as he handed it to her. They went for a walk before dinner along a beach, and the stars came out one by one, and when he took her hand, Suzanne thought her heart would burst. At the thought that he might kiss her, the V-R waves blurred a little, and her breath came faster.

It was going to be a wonderful winter.

"Suzanne," Cade said, very low. "Sweet Suzanne . . ."

"Yes, Cade?"

"I have something to tell you."

"Yes?" Emotion thrilled through her.

"I don't like burgundy."

"What . . . but you . . ."

"At least not that burgundy. I didn't drink it. But I did run it through the molecular analyzer."

She pulled away from his hand. Suddenly, she was very afraid.

"I'm so disappointed in you, Suzanne. I rather hoped that whatever fashion said, we at least trusted each other."

"What . . ." She had trouble getting the words out, damn this tremulous high-pitched voice. "What are you going to do?"

"Do?" He laughed carelessly. "Why do anything? It's not really worth making a fuss over, is it?"

Relief washed over her. It was last season's fashion. He was still wearing it, and it was keeping him casual about her betrayal. Nonchalant, off-hand. Oh, thank heavens. . . .

"But I think maybe we should live apart for a bit. Till things sort themselves out. Don't you think that would be best?"

"Oh no! No!" Girlish protest, in a high sweet girlish voice. When what she wanted was to grab him and force her body against his and convince him to change his mind by sheer brute sexuality . . . but she couldn't. Not dressed like this. It would be ludicrous.

"Cade . . ."

"Oh, don't take it so hard, love. I mean, it's not the end of the world, is it? You're still you, and I'm still me. Be good, now." And he loped off down the beach and out the apartment door.

Suzanne turned off the V-R. She sat in the bare-walled apartment and cried. She loved Cade, she really did. Maybe if she agreed to go naked for a season . . . but, no. That wasn't how she loved Cade, or how he loved her, either. They loved each other for their multiplicity of selves, their basic and true complexity, expressed outwardly and so well through the art of change. That was what kept love fresh and romantic, wasn't it? Change. Growth. Variety.

Suzanne cried until she had no tears left, until she was completely drained. (It felt rather good, actually. Ingenues were allowed so much wild sorrow.) Then she called Sendil, at home, on a shielded frequency.

"Sendil? Suzanne."

"Suzanne? What is it? I can't see you, my dear."

"The vid's malfunctioning, I have audio only. Sendil, I've got some rather awful news."

"What? Oh, are you all right?"

"I'm . . . oh, please understand! I'm so alone! I need you!" Her voice trembled. She had his complete attention.

"Anything, love. Anything at all!"

"I'm . . ." Her girlish voice dropped to a whisper drenched in shame. "I'm . . . *enceinte*. And Cade . . . Cade won't marry me!"

"Suzanne!" Sendil cried. "Oh my God! What a master stroke! Are you going to keep it going all season?"

"I'm . . . I'm going away. I can't . . . face anyone."

"No, of course not. Oh my God, darling, this will just *make* your reputation!"

Suzanne said acidly, "I was under the impression it was already made," realized her mistake, and dropped back into ingenue. It wasn't hard, really; all she had to do was take a deep breath and give herself up to the drugs. She said gaspingly, "But I can't . . . I can't face it completely by myself. I'm just not strong enough. So you're the only person I'm telling. Will you come see me in my shame?"

"Oh, Suzanne, of course I'll stand by you," Sendil said, boyish emotion making his voice husky. Sendil always took a dose and a half of fashion.

"I leave tomorrow," Suzanne gasped. "I'll write you, dear faithful Sendil, to tell you where to visit me. . . ." She'd get a holo of her body looking pregnant, custom-made. "Oh, he just threw me away! I feel so wretched!"

"Of course you do," Sendil breathed. "Poor innocent! Seduced and abandoned! What can I do to cheer you up?"

"Nothing. Oh, wait . . . maybe if I know my shame won't go on forever . . . but, oh, Sendil, I couldn't ask you what follows this season! I know you'd never let out a peep in advance!"

"Well, not ordinarily, of course, but in this case, for you . . ."

"You're the *only* one I'm going to let visit me, to hear about everything that happens. Everyone else will simply have to play along with you."

"Ahh." Sendil's voice thickened with emotion. "I'd do anything to cheer you up, darling. And believe me, you'll love the next season. After a whole season away, everyone will be panting to see how you look, every eye will be trained on you . . . and the look is going to be a return to military! You're just made for it, darling, and it for you!"

"Military," Suzanne breathed. Sendil was right. It was perfect. Uniforms and swords and guns and stern, disciplined command breaking into bawdy barracks-room physicality at night . . . officers pulling rank in the bedroom. . . . *That's an order, soldier—Yes, sir!* . . . The sexual and social possibilities were tremendous. And Cade would never skip two seasons of fashion. She would come back from the winter's exile with everyone buzzing about her, and then Cade in the uniform of, say, the old Royal Guards . . . and herself outranking him (she'd find out somehow what rank he'd chosen, bribery or something), able to command his allegiance, keeping a military bearing and so having to give away nothing of herself. . . .

It was going to be a wonderful spring.

# DANCING ON AIR

*There is not, I have discovered, a large intersection between fans of science fiction and fans of ballet. Those who celebrate Judith Merril are unlikely to celebrate Merrill Ashley, and vice-versa. So when asked what this story is "about," I usually answer, "Genetic engineering, the exploitation of other species, and the various traps of motherhood." Respectable SF answers, the first two. A respectable literary answer, that last one. Answers that are, of course, true . . . but only to the reader. To the writer, this story is a chance to linger over words like* grand jeté *and* fouette of adage.

*I always wanted to be a dancer. Since this is an unlikely as alchemy, instead I write stories like this, for the pleasure of those of us dwelling in the intersection.*

# ONE

> *"When a man has been guilty of a mistake, either in order-
> ing his own affairs, or in directing those of State, or in com-
> manding an army, do we not always say, So-and-so has
> made a false step in this affair? And can making a false step
> derive from anything but lack of skill in dancing?"*
>
> —Moliere

SOMETIMES I UNDERSTAND THE WORDS. SOMETIMES I DO NOT UNDER-
stand the words.

Eric brings me to the exercise yard. A man and a woman stand
there. The man is tall. The woman is short. She has long black fur on
her head. She smells angry.

Eric says, "This is Angel. Angel, this is John Cole and Caroline
Olson."

"Hello," I say.

"I'm supposed to understand that growl?" the woman says. "Might
as well be Russian!"

"Caroline," the man says, "you promised . . ."

"I know what I promised." She walks away. She smells very angry.
I don't understand. My word was *hello*. *Hello* is one of the easy words.

The man says, "Hello, Angel." He smiles. I sniff his shoes and bark.
He smells friendly. I smell two cats and a hot dog and street tar and a
car. I feel happy. I like cars.

The woman comes back. "If we have to do this, then let's just do it,
for Chrissake. Let's sign the papers and get out of this hole."

John Cole says, "The lawyers are all waiting in Eric's office."

Eric's office smells of many people. I go to my place beside the door.
I lie down. Maybe later somebody takes me in the car.

A woman looks at many papers and talks. "A contract between Bio-
mod Canine Protection Agency, herein referred to as the party of the

first part, and the New York City Ballet, herein referred to as the party of the second part, in fulfillment of the requirements of Columbia Insurance Company, herein referred to as the party of the third part, as those requirements are set forth in Policy 438-69, Section 17, respecting prima ballerina Caroline Olson. The party of the first part shall furnish genetically-modified canine protection to Caroline Olson under, and not limited to, the following conditions. . . ."

The words are hard.

I think words I can understand.

My name is Angel. I am a dog. I protect. Eric tells me to protect. No people can touch the one I protect except safe people. I love people I protect. I sleep now.

"Angel," Eric says from his chair. "Wake up now. You must protect."

I wake up. Eric walks to me. He sits next to me. He puts his voice in my ear.

"This is Caroline. You must protect Caroline. No one must hurt Caroline. No one must touch Caroline except safe people. Angel— *protect Caroline.*"

I smell Caroline. I am very happy. I protect Caroline.

"Jesus H. Christ," Caroline says. She walks away.

I love Caroline.


We go in the car. We go very far. Many people. Many smells. John drives the car. John is safe. He may touch Caroline. John stops the car. We get out. There are many tall buildings and many cars.

"You sure you're going to be okay?" John Cole says.

"You've protected your investment, haven't you?" Caroline snarls. John drives away.

A man stands by the door. The man says, "Evening, Miss Olson."

"Evening, Sam. This is my new guard dog. The company insists I have one, after . . . what's been happening. They say the insurance company is paranoid. Yeah, sure. I need a dog like I need a knee injury."

"Yes, ma'am. Doberman, isn't he? He looks like a goooood ol' dog. Hey, big fella, what's your name?"

"Angel," I say.

The man jumps and makes a noise. Caroline laughs.

"Bioenhanced. Great for my privacy, right? Rover, Sam is safe. Do you hear me? Sam is *safe.*"

I say, "My name is Angel."

Caroline says, "Sam, you can relax. Really. He only attacks on command, or if I scream, or if he hasn't been told a person is safe and that person touches me."

"Yes, Ma'am." Sam smells afraid. He looks at me hard. I bark and my tail moves.

Caroline says, "Come on, Fido. Your spy career is about to begin."

I say, "My name is Angel."

"Right," Caroline says.

We go in the building. We go in the elevator. I say, "Sam has a cat. I smell Sam's cat."

"Who the fuck cares," Caroline says.

I am a dog.

I must love Caroline.

# TWO

Two days after the second ballerina was murdered, Michael Chow, senior editor of *New York Now* and my boss, called me into his office. I already knew what he wanted, and I already knew I didn't want to do it. He knew that, too. We both knew it wouldn't make any difference.

"You're the logical reporter, Susan," Michael said. He sat behind his desk, always a bad sign. When he thought I'd want an assignment, he leaned casually against the front of the desk. Its top was cluttered with printouts; with disposable research cartridges, some with their screens alight; with pictures of Michael's six children. *Six.* They all looked like Michael: straight black hair and a smooth face like a peeled egg. At the apex of the mess sat a hardcopy of the *Times* 3:00 P.M. on-line lead: AUTOPSY DISCOVERS BIOENHANCERS IN CITY BALLET DANCER. "You have an in. Even Anton Privitera will talk to you."

"Not about this. He already gave his press conference. Such as it was."

"So? You can get to him as a parent and leverage from there."

My daughter Deborah was a student in the School of American Ballet, the juvenile province of Anton Privitera's kingdom. For thirty years he had ruled the New York City Ballet like an annointed tyrant. Sometimes it seemed he could even levy taxes and raise armies, so exalted was his reputation in the dance world, and so good was his business manager John Cole at raising funds and enlisting corporate patrons.

Dancers had flocked to the City Ballet from Europe, from Asia, from South America, from the serious ballet schools in the patrolled zones of America's dying cities. Until biohancers, the New York City Ballet had been the undisputed grail of the international dance world.

Now, of course, that was changing.

Privitera was dynamic with the press as long as we were content with what he wished us to know. He wasn't going to want to discuss the murder of two dancers, one of them his own.

A month ago Nicole Heyer, a principal dancer with the American Ballet Theater, had been found strangled in Central Park. Three days ago the body of Jennifer Lang had been found in her modest apartment. Heyer had been a bioenhanced dancer who had come to the ABT from the Stuttgart Ballet. Lang, a minor soloist with the City Ballet, had of course been natural. Or so everybody thought until the autopsy. The entire company had been bioscanned only three weeks ago, Artistic Director Privitera had told the press, but apparently these particular viro-enhancers were so new and so different that they hadn't even shown up on the scan.

I wondered how to make Michael understand the depth of my dislike for all this.

"Don't cover the usual police stuff," Michael said, "nor the scientific stuff on bioenhancement. Concentrate on the human angle you do so well. What's the effect of these murders on the other dancers? Has it affected their dancing? Does Privitera seemed more confirmed in his company policy now, or has this shaken him enough to consider a change? What's he doing to protect his dancers? How do the parents feel about the youngsters in the ballet school? Are they withdrawing them until the killer is caught?"

I said, "You don't have any sensitivity at all, do you, Michael?"

He said quietly, "Your girl's seventeen, Susan. If you couldn't get her to leave dancing before, you're not going to get her to leave now. Will you do the story?"

I looked again at the scattered pictures of Michael's children. His oldest was at Harvard Law. His second son was a happily married househusband, raising three kids. His third child, a daughter, was doing six-to-ten in Rock Mountain Maximum Security State Prison for armed robbery. There was no figuring it out. I said, "I'll do the story."

"Good," he said, not looking at me. "Just hold down the metaphors, Susan. You're still too given to metaphors."

"*New York Now* could use a few metaphors. A feature magazine isn't supposed to be a TV holo bite."

"A feature magazine isn't art, either," Michael retorted. "Let's all keep that in mind."

"You're in luck," I said. "As it happens, I'm not a great lover of art."

I couldn't decide whether to tell Deborah I had agreed to write about ballet. She would hate my writing about her world under threat.

Which was a reason both for and against.


September heat and long, cool shadows fought it out over the wide plaza of Lincoln Center. The fountain splashed, surrounded by tourists and students and strollers and derelicts. I thought Lincoln Center was ugly, shoebox architecture stuck around a charmless expanse of stone unredeemed by a little splashing water. Michael said I only felt that way because I hated New York. If Lincoln Center had been built in Kentucky, he said, I would have admired it.

I had remembered to get the electronic password from Deborah. Since the first murder, the New York State Theater changed it weekly. Late afternoon was heavy rehearsal time; the company was using the stage as well as the studios. I heard the Spanish bolero from the second act of *Coppelia*. Deborah had been trying to learn it for weeks. The role of Swanilda, the girl who pretends to be a doll, had first made the brilliant Caroline Olson a superstar.

Privitera's office was a jumble of dance programs, costume swatches, and computers. He made me wait for him twenty minutes. I sat and thought about what I knew about bioenhanced dancers, besides the fact that there weren't supposed to have been any at City Ballet.

There were several kinds of bioenhancement. All of them were experimental, all of them were illegal in The United States, all of them were constantly in flux as new discoveries were made and rushed onto the European, South American, and Japanese markets. It was a new science, chaotic and contradictory, like physics at the start of the last century, or cancer cures at the start of this one. No bioenhancements had been developed specifically for ballet dancers, who were an insignificant portion of the population. But European dancers submitted to experimental versions, as did American dancers who could travel to Berlin or Copenhagen or Rio for the very expensive privilege of injecting their bodies with tiny, unproven biological "machines."

Some nanomachines carried programming that searched out deviations in the body and repaired them to match surrounding tissue. This speeded the healing of some injuries some of the time, or only erratically, or not at all, depending on whom you believed. Jennifer Lang had been receiving these treatments, trying desperately to lessen the injury rate that went hand in hand with ballet. The nanomachines were highly experimental, and nobody was sure what long-term effect they might have, reproducing themselves in the human body, interacting with human DNA.

Bone builders were both simpler and more dangerous. They were altered viruses, reprogrammed to change the shape or density of bones. Most of the experimental work had been done on old women with advanced osteoporosis. Some grew denser bones after treatment. The rest didn't. In ballet, the legs are required to rotate 180 degrees in the hip sockets—the famous "turn out" that had destroyed so many dancers' hips and knees. If bones could be altered to swivel 180 degrees *naturally* in their sockets, turn out would cause far less strain and disintegration. Extension could also be higher, making easier the spectacular *arabesques* and *grand battement* kicks.

If the bones of the foot were reshaped, foot injuries could be lessened in the unnatural act of dancing on toe.

Bioenhanced leg muscles could be stronger, for higher jumps, greater speed, more stamina.

Anything that helped metabolic efficiency or lung capacity could help a dancer sustain movements. They could also help her keep down her weight without anorexia, the secret vice of the ballet world.

Dancers in Europe began to experiment with bioenhancement. First cautiously, clandestinely. Then scandalously. Now openly, as a mark of pride. A dancer with the Royal Ballet or the Bolshoi or the Nederlands Dans Theater who didn't have his or her body enhanced was considered undevoted to movement. A dancer at the New York City Ballet who did have his or her body enhanced was considered undevoted to art.

Privitera swept into his office without apology for being late. "Ah, there you are. What can I do for you?" His accent was very light, but still the musical tones of his native Tuscany were there. It gave his words a deceptive intimacy.

"I've come about my daughter, Deborah Anders. She's in the D level at SAB. She's the one who—"

"Yes, yes, yes, I know who she is. I know all my dancers, even the very young ones. Of course. But shouldn't you be talking with Madame Alois? She is the director of our school."

"But you make all the important decisions," I say, trying to smile winningly.

Privitera sat on a wing chair. He must have been in his seventies, yet he moved like a young man: straight strong back, light movements. The famous bright blue eyes met mine shrewdly. His vitality and physical presence on stage had made him a legendary dancer; now he was simply a legend. Whatever he decided the New York City Ballet should be, it became. I didn't like him. That absolute power bothered me—even though it was merely power over an art form seen by only a fraction of the people who watched soccer or football.

"I have three questions about Deborah, Mr. Privitera. First—and I'm sure you hear this all the time—can you give me some idea of her chances as a professional dancer? She'll have to apply to college this fall, if she's going to go, and although what she really wants is to dance professionally, if that's not going to happen then we need to think about other—"

"Yes, yes," Privitera said, swatting away this question like the irrelevancy he considered it to be. "But dance is never a second choice, Ms. Anders."

"Matthews," I said. "Susan Matthews. Anders is Deborah's name."

"If Deborah has it in her to be a dancer, that's what she will be. If not—" He shrugged. People who were not dancers ceased to exist for Anton Privitera.

"That's what I want to know. Does she have it in her to be a professional dancer? Her teachers say she has good musicality and rhythm, but . . ."

My hands gripped together so tightly the skin was gray.

"Perhaps. Perhaps. You must leave it to me to judge when the time comes."

"But that's what I'm saying," I said, as agreeably as I could. "The time *has* come. College—"

"You cannot hurry art. If Deborah is meant to be a dancer, she will become one. Leave it to me, dear."

*Dear.* It was what he called all his dancers. I saw that it had just slipped out. *Leave it to me, dear. I know best.* How often did he say that in class, in rehearsal, during a choreography session, before a performance?

The muted strains of *Coppelia* drifted through the walls. I said, "Then let me ask my second question. As a parent, I'm naturally concerned about Deborah's safety since these awful murders. What steps has City Ballet taken to ensure the safety of the students and dancers?"

The intense eyes contracted to blue shards. But I could see the moment he decided the question was within a parent's right to ask. "The police do not think there is danger to the students. This . . . madman, this *bestia,* apparently attacks only full-fledged dancers, soloists and principals who have tried to reach art through medicine and not through dancing. No dancer in my company or my school is bioenhanced. My dancers believe as I do: You can achieve art only through talent and work, through opening yourself to the dance, not through mechanical aids. What they do at the ABT—that is *not art!* Besides," he added, with an abrupt descent to the practical, "students cannot afford bioenhancing operations."

Idealism enforced by realism—I saw the combination that kept the City Ballet a success, despite the technically superior performances of bioenhanced dancers. I could almost hear dancers and patrons alike: *"The only real ballet." "Dance that preserves the necessary illusion that the performers' bodies and the audience's are fundamentally the same." "My dear, he's simply the most wonderful man, saving the precious traditions that made dance great in the first place. We've pledged twenty thousand dollars—"*

I decided to push. "But Jennifer Lang apparently found a way to afford illegal bioenhancements that—"

"That has nothing to do with your Deborah," Privitera said, standing in one fluid movement. His blue eyes were arctic. "Now if you will excuse me, many things call me."

"But you haven't said what you *are* doing for the students' safety," I said, not rising from my chair, trying to sound as if my only interest were parental. "Please, I need to know. Deborah . . ."

He barely repressed a sigh. "We have increased security, Ms. Anders. Electronic surveillance both at SAB and Lincoln Center has been added to, with specifics that I cannot discuss. We have hired additional escorts for those students performing small professional roles who must leave Lincoln Center after ten at night. We have created new emphasis on teaching our young dancers the importance, the complete *necessity,* of training their bodies for dance, not relying on drugs and operations that can only offer tawdry imitations of the genuine experience of art."

I doubted City Ballet had actually done all that: it had only been three days since Jennifer Lang's murder. But Privitera's rhetoric helped me ask my last questions.

"Have any other parents withdrawn their sons and daughters from SAB? For that matter, have any of your dancers altered their performance schedules? How has the company as a whole been affected?"

Privitera looked at me with utter scorn. "If a dancer—even a student dancer—leaves me because some *bestia* is killing performers who do what I have insisted my dancers *not* do—such a so-called dancer should leave. There is no place for such a dancer in my school or my company. Don't you understand, Ms. Anders—this is the *New York City Ballet.*"

He left. Through the open door the music was clear: still the Spanish dance from *Coppelia*. The girl who turned herself into a beautiful doll.

Michael was right. I was definitely too given to metaphors.

As I walked down the hall, it occurred to me that Privitera hadn't mentioned increased bioscanning. Surely that would make the most sense—discover which dancers were attaining their high jumps and strong *developpés* through bioenhancement, and then eliminate those dancers from the purity of the company? Before some *bestia* did it first.

Deborah, I knew, was taking an extra class in Studio 3. I shouldn't go. If I went, we would only fight again. I pushed open the door to Studio 3.

I sat on a hard small chair with the ballet mothers waiting for the class to end. I knew better than to talk to any of them. They all wanted their daughters to succeed in ballet.

Barre warmups were over. The warm air smelled of rosin on wood. Dancers worked in the center of the floor, sweat dripping off their twirling and leaping bodies. *Bourées, pirouettes, entrechats.* "*Non, non!*" the teacher called, a retired French dancer whom I had never seen smile. "When you jump, your arms must help. They must pull you through from left to right. Like this."

Deborah did the step wrong. "*Non, non!*" the teacher called. "Like this!"

Deborah still did it wrong. She grimaced. I felt my stomach tighten.

Deborah tried again. It was still wrong. The teacher gestured toward the back of the room. Deborah walked to the barre and practiced the step alone while the rest of the class went on leaping. *Plié, relevé,* then . . . I didn't know the names of the rest of these steps. Whatever they were, she was still doing them wrong. Deborah tried over and over again, her face clenched. I couldn't watch.

When Deborah was fourteen, she ran away from home in St. Louis to her father's hovel in New York, the same father she had not seen since she was three. She wanted to dance for Anton Privitera, she said. I demanded that Pers, whom I had divorced for desertion, send her back. He refused. Deborah moved into his rat-trap on West 110th, way outside Manhattan's patrolled zone. The lack of police protection didn't deter her, the filthy toilet down the hall didn't deter her, the nine-year-old who was shot dealing sunshine on the stoop next door didn't deter her. When I flew to New York, she cried but refused to go home. She wanted to dance for Anton Privitera.

You can't physically wrestle a fourteen-year-old onto a plane. You can argue, and scream, and threaten, and plead, and cry, but you cannot physically move her. Not without a court order. I filed for breach of custody.

Pers did the most effective thing you can do in the New York judicial system: nothing. Since Pers was an indigent periodically on public assistance, the court appointed a public defender for him. The public defender had 154 cases. He asked for three continuances in a row. The judge had a docket full six months ahead. In less than a year and a half Deborah would be sixteen, legally entitled to leave home. She auditioned for Privitera, and the School of American Ballet accepted her.

Another kid was shot, this one on the subway just before Pers's stop. She was twelve. A boy was knifed, a young mother was raped, houses were torched. Pers's lawyer resigned. Another was appointed, who immediately filed for a continuance.

I quit my job with *St. Louis Online* and moved to New York. I left behind a new promotion, a house I loved, and a man I had just started to care about. I found work on Michael's magazine, for half the prestige and two-thirds the salary, in a city twice as expensive and three times as dangerous. I took a two-room apartment on West Seventy-fifth, shabby but decent, just inside the patrolled zone. From my living room window I could see the shimmer of the electronic fence marking the zone. The shimmer bent to exclude all of Central Park south of Seventieth. I bought a gun.

After a few tense weeks, Deborah moved in with me. We lived with piles of toe shoes and surgical tape, with leotards and tights drying on a line strung across the living room, with *Dance* magazine in tattered third-hand copies that would go on to be somebody else's fourth-hand copies, with bunions and inflamed tendons and pulled ligaments. We lived with Deborah's guilt and my anger. At night I lay awake on the pull-out sofa, staring at the ceiling, remembering the day Deborah had started kindergarten and I had opened a college fund for her. She refused now to consider college. She wanted to dance for Anton Privitera.

Privitera had not yet invited her to join the company. She had just turned seventeen. This was her last year with the School. If she weren't invited into the corps de ballet this year, she could forget about dancing for the New York City Ballet.

I sat with the ballet mothers and watched. Deborah's extension was not as high as some of the other girls', her strength not always enough to sustain a slow, difficult move.

So glamorous! the ballet mothers screeched. So beautiful! So wonderful for a girl to know so young what she wants to do with her life! The ballet mothers apparently never saw the constant injuries, the fatigue, the competition that made every friend a deadly rival, the narrowing down of a young world until there is only one definition of success: Do I get to dance for Privitera? Everything else is failure. Life and death, determined at seventeen. "I don't know what I'll do if Jeannie isn't asked to join the company," Jeannie's mother told me. "It would be like we both died. Maybe we would."

"You're so unfair, Mom!" Deborah shouted at me periodically in the tiny, jammed apartment. "You never see the good side of dancing! You're so against me!"

Is it so unfair to hope that your child will be forced out of a life that can only break her body and her heart? A life whose future will belong only to those willing to become human test tubes for inhuman biological experiments?

Nicole Heyer, the dead ABT dancer, had apparently come to the United States from Germany because she could not compete with the dazzlingly bioenhanced dancers in her own country. Jennifer Lang, an ordinary girl from an ordinary Houston family, had lacked the money for major experimentation. To finance her bioenhancements in European labs, she had rented herself out as a glamorous and expensive call girl. Fuck a ballerina: That was how her killer had gotten into her apartment.

In her corner of Studio 3, Deborah finally got the sequence of steps straight, although I could see she was wobbly. She rejoined the class. The room had become as steamy as a Turkish bath. Students ran and leapt the whole length of the hall, corner to corner, in groups of six. "*Grand jeté* in third *arabesque*," Madame called. "*Non, non,* more extension, Lisa. Victoria, more quick—*vite! vite!* One, two . . . next group."

Deborah ran, jumped, and crashed to the ground.

I stood. Jeannie's mother put a hand on my arm. "You can't go to her," she said matter-of-factly. "You'll interfere with her discipline."

Madame ran gnarled hands over Deborah's ankle. "Lisa, help her to the side. Ninette, go tell the office to send the doctor. *Alors,* next group, *grand jeté* in third *arabesque* . . ."

I shook off Jeannie's mother's hand and walked slowly to where Deborah sat, her face twisted in pain.

"It's nothing, Mom."

"Don't move it until the doctor gets here."

"I said it's nothing!"

It was a sprain. The doctor taped it and said Deborah shouldn't dance for a week.

At home she limped to her room. An hour later I found her at the barre.

"Deborah! You heard what the doctor said!"

Her eyes were luminous with tears: Odette as the dying swan, Giselle in the mad scene. "I have to, Mom! You don't understand! They're casting *Nutcracker* in two weeks! I have to be there, dancing!"

"Deborah—"

"I can dance through the injury! Leave me alone!"

Deborah had never yet been cast in Privitera's *Nutcracker*. I watched her transfer her weight gingerly to the injured ankle, wince, and *plié*. She wouldn't meet my eyes in the mirror.

Slowly I closed the door.

That night we had tickets to see *Coppelia*. Caroline Olson skimmed across the stage, barely seeming to touch ground. Her *grands jetés* brought gasps from the sophisticated New York ballet audience. In the final act, when Swanilda danced a tender *pas de deux* with her lover Franz, I could see heads motionless all over the theater, lips slightly parted, barely breathing. Franz turned her slowly in a liquid *arabesque,* her leg impossibly high, followed by *pirouettes*. Swanilda melted from one pose to another, her long silken legs forming a perfect line with her body, flesh made light and strong and elegant as the music itself.

Beside me, I felt Deborah's despair.

# THREE

CAROLINE JUMPS. SHE JUMPS WITH HER HIND LEGS OUT STRAIGHT, ONE IN front and one in back. She runs in circles and jumps again. Dmitri catches her.

"No, no," Mr. Privitera says. "Not like that. *Promenade en couronne, attitude, arabesque effacé.* Now the lift. Dimitri, you are handling her like a sack of grain. Like this."

Mr. Privitera picks up Caroline. My ears raise. But Mr. Privitera is safe. Mr. Privitera can touch Caroline. Dmitri can touch Caroline. Carlos can touch Caroline.

Dmitri says, "It's the damn *dog*. How am I supposed to learn the part with him staring at me, ready to tear me from limb to limb? How the hell am I supposed to concentrate?"

John Cole sits next to me. John says, "Dmitri, there's no chance Angel will attack you. His biochip is state-of-the-art programming. I told you. If you're in his 'safe' directory, you'd have to actually attack Caroline yourself before Angel would act, unless Caroline told you otherwise. There's no real danger to break your concentration."

Dmitri says, "And what if I drop her accidentally? How do I know that won't look like an attack to that dog?"

Caroline sits down. She looks at John. She looks at Dmitri. She does not look at me. She smiles.

John says, "A drop is not an attack. Unless Caroline screams—and we all know she never does, no matter what the injury—there's no danger. Believe me."

"I don't," Dmitri says.

Everybody stands quiet.

Mr. Privitera says, "Caroline, dear, let me drop you. Stand up. Ready—lift."

Caroline smells surprised. She stands. Mr. Privitera picks up Caroline. She jumps a little. He picks her up over his head. She falls down hard. My ears raise. Caroline does not scream. She is not hurt. Mr. Privitera is safe. Caroline said Mr. Privitera is safe.

"See?" Mr. Privitera says. He breathes hard. "No danger. Positions, please. *Promenade en couronne, attitude, arabesque effacé,* lift."

Dmitri picks up Caroline. The music gets loud. John says in my ear, "Angel—did Caroline go away from her house last night?"

"Yes," I say.

"Where did Caroline go?"

"Left four blocks, right one block. Caroline gave money."

"The bakery," John says. "Did she go away to any more places, or did she go home?"

"Caroline goes home last night."

"Did anyone come to Caroline's house last night?"

"No people come to Caroline's house last night."

"Thank you," John says. He pats me. I feel happy.

Caroline looks at us. A woman ties a long cloth on Caroline's waist. The woman gives Caroline a piece of wood. Yesterday I ask John what the wood is. Yesterday John says it is a fan. The music starts, faster. Caroline does not jump. Yesterday Caroline jumps with the fan.

"Caroline?" Mr. Privitera says. "Start here, dear."

Caroline jumps. She still looks at John. He looks at me.

Some woman here smells of yogurt and a bitch collie in heat.


Caroline opens the bedroom door. She comes out. She wears jeans on her hind legs. She wears a hat on her head. It covers all her fur. She walks to the door. She says to me, "Stay, you old fleabag. You hear me? Stay!"

I walk to the door.

"Christ." Caroline opens the door a little way. She pushes her body through the door. She closes the door. I push through the door hard with her.

"I said stay!" Caroline opens the door again. She pushes me. I do not go inside. Caroline goes inside. I follow Caroline.

"Take two," Caroline says. She opens the door. She walks away. She goes back. She closes the door. She opens the door. She closes the door. She turns around. She goes through the door and closes it hard. She is very fast. I am inside alone.

"Gotcha, Fido!" Caroline says through the door.

I howl. I throw me against the door. I bark and howl. The light goes on in my head. I howl and howl.

Soon Caroline comes through the door. A man holds her arm. He smells of iron. He talks to a box.

"Subject elected to return to her apartment, sir, rather than have me accompany her to her destination. We're in her apartment now."

Caroline grabs the box. "John, you shit, how *dare* you! You had the dog biowired! That's an invasion of privacy, I'll sue your ass off, I'll quit the company, I'll—"

"Caroline," John's voice said. I look. There is no John smell. John is not here. Only John's voice is here. "You have no legal grounds. This man is allowed to accompany you, according to the protection contract you signed. *You* signed it, my dear. As for quitting the City Ballet . . . That's up to you. But while you dance for us, Angel goes where you do. If he gets too excited over not seeing you, the biosignal triggers. Just where were you going that you didn't want Angel with you?"

"To turn tricks on street corners!" Caroline yells. "And I bet he has a homing device embedded in him, too, doesn't he?"

She smells very angry. She is angry at me. I lie on the floor. I put my paws on my head. It is not happy here.

The man says, "Departing the apartment now, sir." He leaves. He takes the small box.

Caroline sits on the floor. Her back is against the door. She looks at me. My paws are on my head. Caroline smells angry.

Nothing happens.

A little later Caroline says, "I guess it's you and me, then. They set it up that way. I'm stuck with you."

I do not move move my paws. She still smells angry.

"All right, let's try another approach. Disarm the enemy from within. Psychological sabotage. You don't have any idea what I'm talking about, do you? What did they give you, a five-year-old's IQ? Angel . . ."

I look at Caroline. She says my right name.

". . . tell me about Sam's cat."

"What?"

"Sam's cat. You said that first day you came home with me that you smelled a cat on Sam, the day doorman. Do you still smell it? Can you tell what kind of cat it is?"

I am confused. Caroline says nice words. Caroline smells angry. Her back is too straight. Her fur is wrong.

"Is it a male cat or a female cat? Can you tell that?"

"A female cat," I say. I remember the cat smell. My muscles itch.

"Did you want to chase it?"

"I must never chase cats. I must protect Caroline."

Caroline's smell changes. She leans close to my ear.

"But did you *want* to chase it, Angel? Did you want to get to behave like a dog?"

"I want to protect Caroline."

"Hoo boy. They did a job on you, didn't they, boy?"

The words are too hard. Caroline still smells a little angry. I do not understand.

"It's nothing compared to what they're doing in South America and Europe," she says. Her body shakes.

"Are you hurt?" I say.

Caroline puts a hand on my back. The hand is very soft. She says no words.

I am happy. Caroline talks to me. She tells me about dancing. Caroline is a dancer. She jumps and runs in circles. She stands high on her hind legs. People come in cars to watch her. The people are happy when Caroline dances.

We walk outside. I protect Caroline. We go many places. Caroline gives me cake and hot dogs. There are many smells. Sometimes Caroline and I follow the smells. We see many dogs and many cats. The man with the small box comes with us sometimes. John says the man is safe.

"What if I tell Angel you're not 'safe'?" Caroline says to the man. He follows us on a long walk. "What if I order him to tear you limb to limb?" She smells angry again.

"You don't have programming override capacity. The biochip augmenting his bioenhancement is very specific, Ms. Olson. I'm hard-wired in."

"I'll bet," Caroline says. "Did anybody ask Angel if he wants this life?"

The man smiles.

We go to Lincoln Center every day. Caroline dances there. She dances in the day. She dances at night. More people watch at night.

John asks me where Caroline and I go. Every day I tell him.

Nobody tries to touch Caroline. I protect her.

"I can't do it," Caroline tells a man on the street corner. The man stands very close to Caroline. I growl soft. "For God's sake, Stan, don't touch me. The dog. And I'm probably being watched."

"Do they care *that* much?"

"I could blow the whistle on the whole unofficial charade," Caroline says. She smells tired. "No matter what Privitera's delusions are. But then we'd lose our chance, wouldn't we?"

"Thanks for the time," the man says, loud. He smiles. He walks away.

Later John says, "Who did Caroline talk to?"

"A man," I say. "He wants the time."

Later Caroline says, "Angel, we're going tonight to see my mother."

# FOUR

DEMONSTRATORS DYED THE FOUNTAIN AT LINCOLN CENTER BLOOD RED. They marched around the gruesome jets of water, shouting and resisting arrest. I sprinted across the plaza, trying to get there to see which side they were on before the police carted all of them away. Even from this distance I could tell they weren't dancers, not with those thick bodies. The electronic placards dissolved from HOW MANY MUST DIE FROM DENYING EVOLUTION! to FREE MEDICAL RESEARCH FROM GOVERNMENT STRAITJACKETS! to MY BODY BELONGS TO ME! Pro-human bioenhancement, then. A holograph projector, which a cop was shutting down, spewed out a ten-foot-high holo of Jane and June Welsh, Siamese twins who had been successfully separated only after German scientists had bioenhanced their bodies to force alterations in major organs. The holo loop showed the attached twins dragging each other around, followed by the successfully separated twins waving gaily. The cop did something and Jane and June disappeared.

"They died," I said to a demonstrator, a slim boy wearing a FREE MY BODY! button. "Ultimately, neither of their hearts could stand the stress of bioenhancement."

He glared at me. "That was their risk to take, wasn't it?"

"Their combined IQ didn't equal your weight. How could they evaluate risk?"

"This is a *revolution*, lady. In any revolution you have casualties that—" A cop grabbed his arm. The boy took a wild swing at him and the cop pressed his nerve gun to the boy's neck. He dropped peacefully, smiling.

Abruptly more people gathered, some of them wilier than the boy. Demonstrators stood with their hands on their heads, singing slogans. Media robocams zoomed in from the sky; the live crews would be here in minutes. A group of counterdemonstrators formed across the plaza, in front of the Met. I backed away slowly, hands on my head, not singing—and stopped abruptly halfway across the chaotic plaza.

An old woman in a powerchair was watching the demonstration with the most intense expression I had ever seen. It was as if she were watching a horrifying execution, judging it judiciously as art. Bodyguards flanked the chair. She wore an expensive, pale blue suit and large, perfectly matched pearls. Her wrinkled, cold face was completely familiar. This was how Caroline Olson would look in forty years, if she refused all cosmetic treatment.

She caught me watching her. Her expression didn't change. It passed over me as if I didn't exist.

I took the chance. "Ms. Olson?"

She didn't deny the name. "Yes?"

"I'm a reporter with *New York Now,* doing an article on the New York City Ballet. I'd like to ask you a few questions about your daughter Caroline, if that's all right."

"I never give interviews."

"Yes, ma'am. Just a few informal questions—you must be so proud of Caroline. But are you worried about her safety in light of the recent so-called ballerina murders?"

She shocked me. She smiled. "No, not at all."

"You're *not?*"

She gazed at the break-up of the demonstration. "Do you know the work on dancers' bodies they're doing in Berlin?"

"No, I—"

"Then you have no business interviewing anyone on the subject." She watched the last of the demonstrators being dragged away by the cops. "The New York City ballet is finished. The future of the art lies with bioenhancement."

I must have looked like a fish, staring at her with my mouth working. "But Caroline is the prima ballerina, she's only twenty-six—"

"Caroline had a good run. For a dancer." She made a signal, an imperious movement of her hand, and one of the bodyguards turned her chair and wheeled it away.

I trotted after it. "But, Ms. Olson, are you saying you think your daughter and her whole company *should* be replaced by bioenhanced dancers because they can achieve higher lifts, fewer injuries, more spectacular turn out—"

"I never give interviews," she said, and the other bodyguard moved between us.

I gazed after her. She had spoken about Caroline as if her daughter were an obsolete Buick. It took me a moment to remember to pull out a notebook and tell it what she had said.

Someone dumped something into the fountain. Immediately the red disappeared and the water spouted clear once more. A bioenhanced dog trotted over and lapped at the water, the dog's owner patiently holding the leash while his pink-furred, huge-eyed poodle drank its fill.


After an hour at a library terminal at *New York Now*, I knew that Anna Olson was a major contributor to the American Ballet Theater but not to the New York City Ballet, where her daughter had chosen to dance. Caroline's father was dead. He had left his widow an East Side mansion, three Renoirs, and a fortune invested in Peruvian sugar, Japanese weather-control equipment, and German pharmaceuticals. According to *Ballet News*, mother and daughter were estranged. To find out more than that, I'd need professional help.

Michael didn't want to do it. "There's no money for that kind of research, Susan. Not to even mention the ethics involved."

"Oh, come on, Michael. It's no worse than using criminal informers for any other story."

"This isn't your old newspaper job, Susie. We're a feature magazine, remember? We don't use informants, and we don't do investigative reporting." He leaned against his desk, his peeled-egg face troubled.

"The magazine doesn't have to do any investigating at all. Just give me the number. I know you know it. If I'd been doing the job I should have for the last two years instead of sulking because I hate New York, I'd know it, too. Just the number, Michael. That's all. Neither you nor the magazine will even be mentioned."

He ran his hand through his hair. For the first time, I noticed that it was thinning. "All right. But Susan—don't get obsessed. For your own sake." He looked at the picture of his daughter doing time in Rock Mountain.

I called the Robin Hood and arranged to see him. He was young—they all are—maybe as young as twenty, operating out of a dingy apartment in Tribeca. I couldn't judge his equipment: beyond basic literacy, computers are as alien to me as dancers. Like dancers, they concentrate on one aspect of the world, dismissing the rest.

The Robin Hood furnished the usual proofs that he could tap into private databanks, that he could access government records, and that his translation programs could handle international airline d-bases. He promised a two-day turnaround. The price was astronomical by my standards, although probably negligible by his. I transferred the credits from my savings account, emptying it.

I said, "You do know that the original Robin Hood transferred goods for free?"

He said, not missing a beat, "The original Robin Hood didn't have to pay for a Seidman-Nuwer encryptor."

I really hadn't expected him to know who the original Robin Hood was.

When I got home, Deborah had fallen asleep across her bed, still dressed in practice clothes. The toes of her tights were bloody. A new pair of toe shoes were shoved between the bedroom door and the door jamb; she softened the stiff boxes by slamming the door on them. There were three email messages for her from SAB, but I erased them all. I covered her, closed her door, and let her sleep.


I met with the Robin Hood two days later. He handed me a sheaf of hardcopy. "The City Ballet injury records show two injuries for Caroline Olson in the last four years, which is as far back as the files are kept. One shin splint, one pulled ligament. Of course, if she had other injuries and saw a private doctor, that wouldn't show up on their records, but if she did see one it wasn't anybody on the City Ballet Recommended Physician List. I checked that."

"Two injuries? In four *years?*"

"That's what the record shows. These here are four-year records of City Ballet bioscans. All negative. Nobody shows any bioenhancement, not even Jennifer Lang. These are the City Ballet attendance figures over ten years, broken down by subscription and single-event tickets."

I was startled; the drop in attendance over the last two years was more dramatic than the press had ever indicated.

"This one is Mrs. Anna Olson's tax return for last year. All that income—all of it—is from investments and interests, and none of it is tied up in trusts or entails. She controls it all, and she can waste the whole thing if she wants to. You asked about unusual liquidation of stock in the last ten years: There wasn't any. There's no trust fund for Caroline Olson. This is Caroline's tax return—only her salary with City Ballet, plus guest appearance fees. Hefty, but nothing like what the old lady controls.

"This last is the air flight stuff you wanted: No flights on major commercial airlines out of the country for Caroline in the last six years, except when the City Ballet did its three international tours, and then Caroline flew pretty much with everybody else in the group. Of course if she did go to Rio or Copenhagen or Berlin, she could have gone by chartered plane or private jet. My guess is private jet. Those aren't required to file passenger lists."

It wasn't what I'd hoped to find. Or rather, it was half of what I'd hoped. No dancer is injured that seldom. It just doesn't happen. I pictured Caroline Olson's amazing extension, her breathtaking leaps; she reached almost the height expected of male superstars. And her crippled horror of a mother had huge amounts of money. *"Caroline had a good run."*

I would bet my few remaining dollars that Caroline Olson was bioenhanced, no matter what her bioscans said. Jennifer Lang's had been negative, too. Apparently the DNA hackers were staying one step ahead of the DNA security checkers. Although it was odd that the records didn't show a single dancer trying to get away with bioenhancement, not even once, even in the face of Privitera's fervency. There are always some people who value their own career advancement over the received faith.

But I had assumed that Caroline would have needed to leave the country. Bioenhancement labs are large, full of sensitive and costly and nonportable equipment, and dozens of technicians. Not easy to hide. Police investigators had traced both Jennifer Lang and Nicole Heyer to Danish labs. I didn't think one could exist illegally in New York.

Maybe I was wrong.

The Robin Hood watched me keenly. In the morning light from the window he looked no older than Deborah. He had thick brown hair, nice shoulders. I wondered if he had a life outside his lab. So many of them didn't.

"Thanks," I said.

"Susan—"

"What?"

He hesitated. "I don't know what you're after with this data. But I've worked with friends of Michael's before. If you're thinking about trying to leverage anything to do with human bioenhancement . . ."

"Yeah?"

"Don't." He looked intently at his console. "That's out of both our leagues. Magazine reporters are very small against the kind of high-stakes shit those guys are into."

"Thanks for the advice," I said. And then, on impulse, "Would you by any chance like a home-cooked meal? I have a daughter about your age, seventeen, she's a dancer. . . ."

He stared at me in disbelief. He shook his head. "You're a *client,* Susan. And anyway, I'm twenty-six. And I'm married." He shook his head again. "And if you don't know enough not to ask a Robin Hood to dinner, you really don't know enough to mess around with bioenhancement. That stuff's life or death."

Life or death. Enough for a bioenhancement corporation to murder two dancers?

But I rejected that idea. It was always too easy to label the corporations the automatic bad guys. That was the stuff of cheap holovids. Most corporate types I knew just tried to keep ahead of the IRS.

I said, "Most life-and-death stuff originates at home."

I could feel him shaking his head as I left, but I didn't turn around.

# FIVE

CAROLINE AND I RIDE IN A TAXI. IT IS LATE AT NIGHT. WE RIDE ACROSS the park. Then we ride more. Caroline says words to a gate. A man opens the door to a very big house. He smells surprised. He wears pajamas. "Miss Caroline!"

"Hello, Seacomb. Is my mother in?"

"She's asleep, of course. If there's an emergency—"

"No emergency. But my apartment pipes sprung a leak and I'll be spending the night here. This is my dog, Angel. Angel, Seacomb is safe."

"Of course, Miss," Seacomb says. He smells very unhappy. "It's just—"

"Just that you have orders not to let me use this house?"

"No, Miss," the man says. "My orders are to let me use the house as you choose. Only—"

"Of course they are," Caroline says. "My mother wants me to grovel back here. She's been panting for that. Well, here I am. Only she's taken a sleeping pill and is out cold until morning, right?"

"Yes, Miss," the man says. He smells very unhappy. There are no cats or dogs in this place, but there are mice. The mice droppings smell interesting.

"I'll sleep in the downstairs study. And, oh, Seacomb, I'm expecting guests. Please disable the electric gate. They'll use the back entrance, and I'll let them in myself. You needn't take any trouble about it."

"It's no trouble to—"

"I said I'll let them in myself."

"Yes, Miss," Seacomb says. He smells very very unhappy.

He leaves. Caroline and I go down stairs. Caroline drinks. She gives me water. I smell a mouse in a cupboard. My ears raise. There are interesting things here.

"Well, Angel, here we are at my mother's house. Do you remember your mother, boy?"

"No," I say. I am confused. The words are a little hard.

"There are some people coming for a party. Some dancers. Kristine Meyers is coming. You remember Kristine Meyers?"

"Yes," I say. Kristine Meyers dances with Caroline. They run in circles and jump high. Caroline jumps higher.

"We're going to talk about dancing, Angel. This is a prettier house than mine to talk about dancing. This is a good house for a party, which is what we're going to have. My mother lets me use her house for parties. Remember that, boy."

Later Caroline opens the door. Some people stand there. We go into the basement. Kristine Meyers is there. She smells frightened. Some men are with her. They carry papers. They talk a long time.

"Here, Angel, have a pretzel," a man says. "It's a party."

Some people dance to a radio. Kristine smells angry and confused. Her fur stands up. Caroline says words to her. The words are hard. The words are long. I have a pretzel. Nobody touches Caroline.

We are there all night. Kristine cries.

"Her boyfriend is gone," Caroline says to me.

In early morning we go home. We go in a taxi. Somebody is sick in the taxi yesterday. It smells bad. Caroline sleeps. I sleep. Caroline does not go to class.

In the afternoon we go to Lincoln Center. Kristine is there. She sleeps on a couch in the lounge. Caroline dances with Dmitri.

John Cole bends close to my ear. "You went out with Caroline all last night."

"Yes," I say.

"Where did you go?"

"We go to Caroline's mother's house. We go to a party. Caroline's mother lets Caroline use her house for parties."

"Who was at this party?"

"Dancers. Kristine is at the party. Kristine is safe."

John looks at Kristine. She still sleeps on the couch.

"Who else was at the party? What did they do?"

I remember hard. "Dancers are at the party. We eat pretzels. We talk about dancing. People dance to the radio. Nobody touches Caroline. There is music."

John's body relaxes. "Good," he says. "Okay."

"I like pretzels," I say. But John does not give me a pretzel today.


Caroline and I walk in the park. There are many good smells. Caroline sits under a tree. The long fur on her head falls down. She pats my head. She gives me a cookie.

"It's easy for you, isn't it, Angel?" Caroline says.

I say, "The words are hard."

"You like being a dog? A bioenhanced servant dog?"

"The words are hard."

"Are you happy, Angel?"

"I am happy. I love Caroline."

She pats my head again. The sun is warm. The smells are good. I close my eyes.

"I love to dance," Caroline says. "And I hate that I love it."

I open my eyes. Caroline smells unhappy.

"Goddamn it, I love it anyway. I do. Even though it wasn't my choice. You didn't choose what you are, either, did you, Angel? They goddamn made you what they needed you to be. Yet you love it. And for you there's no account due."

The words are too hard. I put my nose into Caroline's front legs. She puts her front legs around me. She holds me tight.

"It's not *fair*," Caroline whispers into my fur.

Caroline does not hold me yesterday. She holds me today. I am happy. But Caroline smells unhappy.

Where is my happy if Caroline smells unhappy?

I do not understand.

# SIX

DEBORAH DIDN'T GET CAST IN *NUTCRACKER*. AN SAB TEACHER TOLD her she might want to consider auditioning for one of the regional companies rather than City Ballet—a death sentence, from her point of view. She told me this quietly, without histrionics, sitting cross-legged on the floor sewing ribbons onto a pair of toe shoes. Not wanting to say the wrong thing, I said nothing, contenting myself with touching her hair, coiled at the nape of her neck into the ballerina bun. Two days later she told me she was dropping out of high school.

"I need the time to dance," she said. "You just don't understand, Mom."

The worst thing I could do was let her make me into the enemy. "I do understand, honey. But there will be lots of time to dance after you finish school. And if you don't—"

"Finishing is a year away! I can't afford the time. I have to take more classes, work harder, get asked into the company. *This year*. I'm sorry, Mom, but I just can't waste my time on all that useless junk in school."

I locked my hands firmly on my lap. "Well, let's look at this reasonably. Suppose after all you do get asked to join the company—"

"I *will* be asked! I'll work so hard they'll have to ask me!"

"All right. Then you dance with them until, say, you're thirty-five. At thirty-five you have over half your life left. You saw what happened to Carla Cameri and Maura Jones." Carla's hip had disintegrated;

Maura's Achilles tendon had forced her into retirement at thirty-two. Both of them worked in a clothing store, for pitifully small salaries. Dancers didn't get pensions unless they'd been with the same company for ten years, a rarity in the volatile world of artistic directors with absolute power, who often fired dancers because they were remaking a company into a different "look."

I pressed my point. "What will you do at thirty or thirty-five with your body debilitated and without even a high school education?"

"I'll teach. I'll coach. I'll go back to school. Oh, Mom, how do I know? That's decades away! I have to think about what I need to do for my career now!"

No mother love is luminous enough to make a sixteen-year-old see herself at thirty-five.

I said, "No, Deborah. You can't quit school. I'd have to sign for you, and I won't."

"Daddy already did."

We looked at each other. It was too late; she'd already made me into the enemy. Because she needed one.

She said, in a sudden burst of passion, "You don't understand! You never felt about your job the way I feel about ballet! You never loved anything enough to give up everything else for it!" She rushed to her room and slammed the door. I put my head in my hands.

After a while, I started to laugh. I couldn't help it. *Never loved anything enough to give up everything else for it.*

Right.

Pers wasn't available to yell at. I phoned six times. I left messages on email, even though I had no idea whether he had a terminal. I made the trip out of the protected zone to his apartment. The area was worse than I remembered: glass, broken machinery, shit, drug paraphernalia. The cab driver was clearly eager to leave, but I made him wait while I questioned a kid who came out of Pers's building. The boy, about eight, had a long pus-encrusted cut down one cheek.

"Do you know when Pers Anders usually comes home? He lives in 2C."

The kid stared at me, expressionless. The cab driver leaned out and said, "One more minute and I'm leaving, lady."

I pulled out a twenty-dollar bill and held it close to me. "When does Pers Anders usually come home?"

"He moved."

"Moved?"

"Left his stuff. He say he go someplace better than this shithole. I hear him say it. Don't you try to prong me, lady. You give me that money."

"Do you know the address?"

He greeted this with the scorn it deserved. I gave him the money.

Deborah left school and started spending all day and much of the night at Lincoln Center. Finally I walked over to SAB and caught her just before a partnering class. She had twisted a bright scarf around her waist, over her leotard, and her sweaty hair curled in tendrils where it had escaped her bun.

"Deborah, why didn't you tell me your father had moved?"

She looked wary, wiping her face with a towel to gain time. "I didn't think you'd care. You hate him."

"As long as you still visit him, I need to know where he is."

She considered this. Finally she gave me the address. It was a good one, in the new luxury condos where the old main library had been.

"How can Pers afford *that?*"

"He didn't say. Maybe he's got a job. Mom, I have class."

"Pers is allergic to jobs."

"Mom, Mr. Privitera is teaching this class *himself!*"

I didn't stay to watch class. On the way out, I passed Privitera, humming to himself on his way to elate or cast down his temple virgins.


The police had released no new information on the ballerina murders.

I turned in the article on the New York City Ballet. It seemed to me neither good nor bad; everything important about the subject didn't fit the magazine's focus. There weren't too many metaphors. Michael read it without comment. I worked on an article about computerized gambling, and another about holographic TV. I voted in the Presidential election. I bought Christmas presents.

But every free minute, all autumn and early winter, I spent at the magazine library terminals, reading about human bioenhancement, trying to guess what Caroline Olson was having done to herself. What might someday lie in Deborah's future, if she were as big a fool then as she was being now.

"Don't get obsessed," Michael had said.

The literature was hard to interpret. I wasn't trained in biology, and as far as I could see, the cutting-edge research was chaotic, with various discoveries being reported one month, contradicted the next. All the experiments were carried out in other countries, which meant they were reported in other languages, and I didn't know how far to trust the biases of the translators. Most of them seemed to be other scientists in the same field. This whole field seemed to me like a canoe rushing toward the falls: nobody in charge, both oars gone, control impossible.

I read about splendid, "revolutionary" advances in biological nanotechnology that always seemed under development, or not quite practical yet, or hotly disputed by people practicing other kinds of revolutionary advances. I read about genesplicing retroviruses and setting them loose in human organs to accomplish potentially wonderful things. Elimination of disease. Perfect metabolic functioning. Immortality. The studies were always concerned with one small, esoteric facet of scientific work, but the "Conclusions" sections were often grandiose, speculating wildly.

I even picked up hints of experimental work on altering genetic makeup *in vitro,* instead of trying to reshape adult bodies. Some scientists seemed to think this might actually be easier to accomplish. But nowhere in the world was it legal to experiment on an embryo not destined for abortion, an embryo that would go on to become a human being stuck with the results of arbitrary and untested messing around with his basic cellular blueprints. Babies were not tinker toys—or dogs. The Copenhagen Accord, signed twenty-seven years by most technologically civilized countries, had seen to that. The articles on genetic modification *in vitro* were carefully speculative.

But then so was nearly everything else I read. The proof was walking around in inaccessible foreign hospitals, or living anonymously in inaccessible foreign cities—the anonymity of the experimental subjects seemed to be a given, which also made me wonder how many of them were experimental casualties. And if so, of what kind.

Michael wasn't going to want any article built on this tentative speculation. Lawsuits would loom. But I was beyond caring what Michael wanted.

I learned that the Fifth International Conference on Human Bioenhancement was going to be held in Paris in late April. After paying the Robin Hood, I had no money left for a trip to Paris. Michael would have to pay for it. I would have to give him a reason.

One night in January I did a stupid thing. I went alone to Lincoln Center and waited by the stage door of the New York State Theater. Caroline Olson came out at 11:30, dressed in jeans and parka, accompanied only by a huge black Doberman on the most nominal of leashes.

They walked south on Broadway, to an all-night restaurant. I sat myself at the next table.

For the last few months, her reviews had not been good. "A puzzling and disappointing degeneration," said the *New Yorker.* "Technical sloppiness not associated with either Olson or Privitera," said *Dance Magazine.* "This girl is in trouble, and Anton Privitera had better find out what kind of trouble and move to correct it," said the *Times Online.*

Caroline ate abstractly, feeding bits to the dog, oblivious to the frowns of a fastidious waiter who was undoubtedly an out-of-work actor. Up close, the illusion of power and beauty I remembered from *Coppelia* evaporated. She looked like just another mildly pretty, self-absorbed, overly thin young woman. Except for the dog, the waiter/actor didn't give her a second glance.

"We go now?" the dog said.

I choked on my sandwich. Caroline glanced at me absently. "Soon, Angel."

She went on eating. I left, waited for her, and followed her home. She and the dog lived on Central Park South, a luxury building where the late-night electronic surveillance system greeted them both by name.

I took a cab home. Deborah had never mentioned that the City Ballet prima ballerina was protected by a bioenhanced Doberman. She knew I'd written the story about the ballerina murders. Anton Privitera hadn't mentioned it, either, in his press conference about dancer safety. I wondered why not. While I was parceling out wonder, I devoted some to the question of City Ballet's infrequent, superficial, and always-negative bioscans. Shouldn't a company devoted to the religion of "natural art" be more zealous about ferreting out heretics?

Unless, of course, somebody didn't really want to know.

Privitera? But that was hard to reconcile with his blazing, intolerant sincerity.

It occurred to me that I had never seen an admittedly bioenhanced dancer perform. Until tonight, I'd gone to finished performances rarely and only with Deborah, who of course scorned such perverts and believed that they had nothing to teach her.

She was out when I got back to our apartment. Each week, it seemed, she was gone more. I fell asleep, waiting for her to come home.

# SEVEN

Snow falls. It is cold. Caroline and I walk to Lincoln Center. A man takes Caroline's purse. He runs. Caroline says "Shit!" Then she says, "Angel? Go stop him!" She drops my leash.

I run and jump on the man. He screams. I do not hurt him. Caroline says *stop him*. She does not say *attack him*. So I stand on the man's chest and growl and nip at his foreleg. He brings out a knife. Then I bite him. He drops the knife and screams again. The police come.

"Holy shit," Caroline says to me. "You really do that. You really do."

"I protect Caroline," I say.

Caroline talks to police. Caroline talks to reporters. I get a steak to eat.

I am happy.

The snow goes away. The snow is there many many days, but it goes away. We visit Caroline's mother's house for two more parties in the basement. It gets warm in the park. Ducks live in the water again. Flowers grow. Caroline says not to dig up flowers.

I lie backstage. Caroline dances on stage. John and Mr. Privitera stand beside me. They smell unhappy. John's shoes smell of tar and food and leaves and cats and other good things. I sniff John's shoes.

"She looks exhausted," John says. "She's giving it everything she's got, but it's just not there, Anton."

Mr. Privitera says no words. He watches Caroline dance.

"William Scholes attacked again in the *Times*. He said that watching her had become painful—'like watching a reed grown stiff and brittle.' "

"I will talk to her again," Mr. Privitera says.

"Scholes called the performance 'a travesty,' " John says.

Caroline comes backstage. She limps. She wipes her face with a towel. She smells afraid.

"Dear, I'd like to see you," Mr. Privitera says.

We go to Caroline's dressing room. Caroline sits down. She trembles. Her body smells sick. I growl. Caroline puts a hand on my head.

Mr. Privitera says, "First of all, dear, I have good news for all of us. The police have caught that unspeakable murderer who killed Jennifer Lang and the ABT dancer."

Caroline sits up a little straighter. Her smell changes. "They did! How?"

"They caught him breaking into the Plaza Hotel room where Marie D'Arbois is staying while she guests with ABT."

"Is Marie—"

"She's fine. She wasn't alone, she had a lover or something with her. The madman just got careless. The police are holding back the details. Marie, of course, is another of those bioenhanced dancers. I don't know if you ever saw her dance."

"I did," Caroline says. "I thought she was wonderful."

Caroline and Mr. Privitera look hard at each other. They smell ready to attack. But they do not attack. I am confused. Mr. Privitera is safe. He may touch Caroline.

Mr. Privitera says, "We must all be grateful to the police. Now there's something else I need to discuss with you, dear."

Caroline closes her hand on my fur. She says, "Yes?"

"I want you to take a good long rest, dear. You know your dancing has deteriorated. You tell me you're not doing drugs or working sketchily, and I believe you. Sometimes it helps a dancer to take a rest from performing. Take class, eat right, get strong. In the fall we'll see."

"You're telling me you're cutting me from the summer season at Saratoga."

"Yes, dear."

Caroline is quiet. Then she says, "There's nothing wrong with me. My timing has just been a little off, that's all."

"Then take the summer to work on your timing. And everything else."

Mr. Privitera and Caroline look hard at each other again. Caroline's hand still pulls my fur. It hurts a little. I do not move.

Mr. Privitera leans close to Caroline. "Listen, dear. *Jewels* was one of your best roles. But tonight . . . and not just *Jewels*. You wobbled and wavered through *Starscape*. Your Nikiya in the 'Shades' section of *La Bayadère* was . . . embarrassing. There is no other word. You danced as if you had never learned the steps. And you couldn't even complete the *Don Quixote pas de deux* at the gala."

"I fell! Dancers get injured all the time! My injury rate compared to—"

"You've missed rehearsals and even performances," Mr. Privitera said. He stands up. "I'm sorry, dear. Take the summer. Rest. Work. In the fall, we'll see."

Caroline says, "What about the last two weeks of the season?"

Mr. Privitera says, "I'm sorry, dear."

He walks to the door. He puts his hand on the door. He says, "Oh, at least you won't have to be burdened with that dog anymore. Now that the madman's been caught, I'll have John notify the protection agency to come pick it up."

Caroline raises her head. Her fur all stands up. She smells angry. Soon she runs out the door. Mr. Privitera is gone. She runs to the offices. "John! John, you bastard!"

The office hall is dark. The doors do not open. John is not here.

Caroline runs up steps to the offices. She falls. She falls down some of the steps and hits the wall. She lies on the floor. She holds her hind foot and smells hurt.

"Angel," she says. "Go get somebody to help me."

I go to the lounge. One dancer is there. She says, "Oh! I'm sorry, I didn't know that anybody—Angel?"

"Caroline is hurt," I say. "Come. Come fast."

She comes. Caroline says, "Who are you? No, wait—Deborah, right? From the corps?"

"No, I'm not . . . I haven't been invited to join the corps yet. I'm a student at SAB. I'm just here a lot. . . . Are you hurt? Can you stand?"

"Help me up," Caroline says. "Angel, Deborah is safe."

Deborah tries to pick up Caroline. Caroline makes a little noise. She cannot stand. Deborah gets John. He picks up Caroline.

"It's nothing," she says. "No doctor. Just get me a cab. . . . Dammit, John, don't fuss, it's nothing!" She looks at John hard. "You want to take Angel away from me."

John smells surprised. He says, "Who told you that?"

"His Majesty himself. But now you've decided whatever you thought I was doing so privately doesn't matter any more, is that right?"

"It's a mistake. Of course you can keep the dog. Anton doesn't understand," John says. He smells angry.

"No, I'll just bet he doesn't," Caroline says. "You might have picked a kinder way to tell me I'm through at City Ballet."

"You're not through, Caroline," John says. Now he smells bad. His words are not right. He smells like the man who takes Caroline's purse.

"Right," Caroline says. She sits in the cab.

Deborah steps back. She smells surprised.

"I'm keeping the dog," Caroline says. "So we're in agreement, aren't we, John? Come on, Angel. Let's go home."

We go to class. Caroline cannot dance. She tries and then stops. She sits in a corner. Mr. Privitera sits in another corner. Caroline watches Deborah. The dancers raise one hind leg. They spin and jump.

Madame holds up her hand. The music stops. "Deborah, let us see that again, *s'il vous plait*. Alone."

The other dancers move away. They look at each other. They smell surprised. The music starts again and Deborah raises one hind leg very high. She spins and jumps.

Mr. Privitera says, "Let me see the bolero from *Coppelia*. Madame says you know it."

"Y-yes," Deborah says. She dances alone.

"Very nice, dear," Mr. Privitera says. "You are much improved."

The other dancers look at each other again.

Everybody dances.

Caroline watches Deborah hard.

# EIGHT

DEBORAH'S FACE LOOKED LIKE EVERY CHRISTMAS MORNING IN THE EN-
tire world. She grabbed both my hands. "They invited me to join the
company!"

My suitcase lay open on the bed, surrounded by discarded clothes I
wasn't taking to the bioenhancement conference in Paris. My daughter picked up a pile of spidersilk blouses and hurled them into the air.
In the soft April air from the open window the filmy, artificial material drifted and danced. "I can't believe it! They asked me to join the
company! I'm in!"

She whirled around the tiny room, rising on toe in her street shoes,
laughing and exclaiming. My silence went unnoticed. Deborah did an
*arabesque* to the bedpost, then plopped herself down on my best dress.
"Don't you want to know what happened, Mom?"

"What happened, Deborah?"

"Well, Mr. Privitera came to watch class, and Madame asked me to
repeat the variation alone. God, I thought I'd die. Then *Mr. Privitera*—not Madame—asked me to do the bolero from *Coppelia*. For an
awful minute I couldn't remember a single step. Then I did, and he said
it was very nice! He said I was much improved!"

Accolades from the king. But even in my numbness I could see there
was something she wasn't telling me.

"I thought you told me the company doesn't choose any new
dancers this close to the end of the season?"

She sobered immediately. "Not usually. But Caroline Olson was fired. She missed rehearsals and performances, and she wasn't even taking the trouble to prepare her roles. Her reviews have been awful."

"I saw them," I said.

Deborah looked at me sharply. "Ego, I guess. Caroline's always been sort of a bitch. So apparently they're not letting her go to Saratoga, because Tina Patrochov and a guest artist are dividing her roles, and Mr. Privitera told Jill Kerrigan to learn Tina's solo from *Sleeping Beauty.* So that left a place in the corps de ballet, and they chose me!"

I had had enough time to bring myself to say it.

"Congratulations, sweetheart."

"When does your plane for Paris leave?"

This non sequitur—if it was that—turned me back to my packing. "Seven tonight."

"And you'll be gone ten days. You'll have a great time in Paris. Maybe the next time the company goes on tour, I'll go with them!"

She whirled out of the room.

I sat at the end of the bed, holding onto the bedpost. When Deborah was three, she'd wanted a ride on a camel. Somehow it had become an obsession. She talked about camels in daycare, at dinnertime, at bedtime. She drew pictures of camels, misshapen things with one huge hump. Camels were in short supply in St. Louis. Ignore it, everyone said, kids forget these things, she'll get over it. Deborah never forgot. She didn't get over it. Pers had just left us, and I was consumed with the anxiety of a single parent. Finally I paid a friend to tie a large wad of hay under a blanket on his very old, very swaybacked horse. A Peruvian camel, I told my three-year-old. A very special kind. You can have a ride.

"That's not a camel," Deborah had said, with nostril-lifted disdain. "That's a heffalunt!"

I read last week in *World* that the animal-biotech scientists have built a camel with the flexible trunk of an elephant. The trunk can lift up to forty-five pounds. It was expected to be a useful beast of burden in the Sahara.

I finished packing for Paris.


Paris in April was an unending gray drizzle. The book and software stalls along the Seine kept up their electronic weather shields, giving them the hazy, streaming-gutter look of abandoned outhouses. The gargoyles on Notre Dame looked insubstantial in the rain, irrelevant in the face of camels with trunks. The French, as usual, conspired to make

Americans—especially Americans who speak only rudimentary French—feel crass and barbaric. My clothes were wrong. My desire for a large breakfast was wrong. The Fifth International Conference on Human Bioenhancement had lost my press credentials.

The conference was held in one of the huge new hotels in Neuilly, near the Eurodisney Gene Zoo. I couldn't decide if this was an attempt to provide entertainment or irony. Three hundred scientists and doctors, a hundred press, and at least that many industrial representatives, plus groupies, thronged the hotel. The scientists presented papers; the industrial reps, mostly from biotech or pharmaceutical firms, presented "infoforums." The moment I walked in, carrying provisional credentials, I felt the tension, a peculiar kind of tension instantly recognizable to reporters. Something big was going on. Big and unpleasant.

From the press talk in the bar I learned that the presentation to not miss was Thursday night by Dr. Gerard Taillebois of the Pasteur Institute, in conjunction with Dr. Greta Erbland of Steckel and Osterhoff. This pairing of a major research facility with a commercial biotech firm was common in Europe. Sometimes the addition of a hospital made it a triumvirate. A hand-written addendum on the program showed that the presentation had been moved from the Napoleon Room to the Grand Ballroom. I checked out the room; it was approximately the size of an airplane hangar. Hotel employees were setting up acres of chairs.

I asked a *garçon* to point out Dr. Taillebois to me. He was a tall, bald man in his sixties or seventies who looked like he hadn't slept or eaten in days.

Wednesday night I went to the Paris Opera Ballet. The wet pavement in front of the Opera House gleamed like black patent leather. Patrons dripped jewels and fur. This gala was why Michael had funded my trip; my first ballet article for *New York Now* had proved popular, despite its vapidity. Or maybe because of it. Tonight the famous French company was dancing an eclectic program, with guest artists from the Royal Ballet and the Kirov. Michael wanted five thousand words on the oldest ballet company in the world.

I watched bioenhanced British dancers perform the wedding *pas de deux* from *Sleeping Beauty,* with its famous fishdives; Danish soloists in twentieth-century dances by Georges Balanchine; French ballerinas in contemporary works by their brilliant choreographer Louis Dufort. All of them were breathtaking. In the new ballets, especially choreographed for these bioenhanced bodies, the dancers executed sustained movements no natural body would have been capable of making at all, at a speed that never looked machinelike. Instead the dancers were flashes of light: lasers, optic signals, nerve impulses surging across the stage and triggering pleasure centers in the brains of the delighted audience.

I gaped at one *pas de trois* in which the male dancer lifted two women at once, holding them aloft in swallow lifts over his head, one on each palm, then turning them slowly for a full ninety seconds. It wasn't a bench-pressing stunt. It was the culmination of a yearning, lyrical dance, as tender as any in the great nineteenth-century ballets. The female dancers were lowered slowly to the floor, and they both flowed through a *fouette of adage* as if they hadn't any bones.

Not one dancer had been replaced in the evening's program due to injury. I tried to remember the last time I'd seen a performance of the New York City Ballet without a last-minute substitution.

During intermission, profoundly depressed, I bought a glass of wine in the lobby. The eddying crowd receded for a moment, and I was face to face with Anna Olson, seated regally in her powerchair and flanked by her bodyguards. Holding tight to her hand was a little girl of five or six, dressed in a pink party dress and pink tights, with wide blue eyes, black hair, and a long slim neck. She might have been Caroline Olson fifteen years ago.

"Ms. Olson," I said.

She looked at me coldly, without recognition.

"I'm Susan Matthews. We met at the private reception for Anton Privitera at Georgette Allen's," I lied.

"Yes?" she said, but her eyes raked me. My dress wasn't the sort that turned up at the private fundraisers of New York billionaires. I didn't give her a chance to cut me.

"This must be your—" granddaughter? Caroline, an only child, had never interrupted her dancing career for pregnancy. niece? grandniece? "—your ward."

"*Je m'appelle Marguerite,*" the child said eagerly. "*Nous regardons le ballet.*"

"Do you study ballet, Marguerite?"

"*Mais oui!*" she said scornfully, but Anna Olson made a sign and the bodyguards deftly cut me off from both of them. By maneuvering around the edge of the hall, I caught a last, distant glimpse of Marguerite. She waited patiently in line to go back to her seat. Her small feet in pink ballet slippers turned out in a perfect fifth position.

Thursday afternoon I drove into Paris to rent an electronic translator for the presentation by Taillebois and Erbland. The translators furnished by the conference were long since claimed. People who had rented them for the opening talks simply hung onto them, afraid to miss anything. The Taillebois/Erbland presentation would include written handouts in French, English, German, Spanish, Russian, and Japanese, but not until the session was over. I was afraid to miss anything, either.

I couldn't find a electronic translator with a brand name I trusted. I settled for a human named Jean-Paul, from a highly recommended commercial agency. He was about four feet ten, with sad brown eyes and a face wrinkled into fantastic crevasses. He told me he had translated for Charles de Gaulle during the crisis in Algeria. I believed him. He looked older than God.

We drove back to Neuilly in the rain. I said, "Jean-Paul, do you like ballet?"

"*Non*," he said immediately. "It is too slippery an art for me."

"Slippery?"

"Nothing is real. Girls are spirits of the dead, or joyous peasants, or other silly things. Have you ever seen any real peasants, Mademoiselle? They are not joyous. And girls lighter than air land on stage with a thump!" He illustrated by smacking the dashboard with his palm. "Men die of love for those women. Nobody dies for love. They die for money, or hate, but not love. *Non.*"

"But isn't all art no more than illusion?"

He shrugged. "Not all illusion is worth creating. Not silly illusions. Dancers wobbling on tippy toes . . . *non, non.*"

I said carefully, "French dancers can be openly bioenhanced. Not like in the United States. To some of us, that gives the art a whole new excitement. Technical, if not artistic."

Jean-Paul shrugged again. "Anybody can be bioenhanced, if they have the money. Bioenhancement, by itself it does not impress me. My grandson is bioenhanced."

"What does he do?"

Jean-Paul twisted his body toward me in the seat of the car. "He is a soccer player! One of the best in the world! If you followed the sport, you would know his name. Claude Despreaux. Soccer—now *there* is illusion worth creating!"

His tone was exactly Anton Privitera's, talking about ballet.


Thursday evening, just before the presentation, I finally caught Deborah at home. Her face on the phonevid was drawn and strained. "What's wrong?"

"Nothing, Mom. How's Paris?"

"Wet. Deborah, you're not telling me the truth."

"Everything's fine! I just . . . just had a complicated rehearsal today."

The corps de ballet does not usually demand complicated rehearsals. The function of the corps is to move gracefully behind the soloists and principal dancers; it's seldom allowed to do anything that will distract from their virtuosity. I said carefully, "Are you injured?"

"No, of course not. Look, I have to go."

"Deborah . . ."

"They're waiting for me!" The screen went blank.

Who was waiting for her? It was 1:00 A.M. in New York.

When I called back, there was no answer.

I went to the Grand Ballroom. Jean-Paul had been holding both our seats, lousy ones, since noon. An hour later, the presentation still had not started.

The audience fidgeted, tense and muttering. Finally a woman dressed in a severe suit entered. She spoke German. Jean-Paul translated into my ear.

"Good evening. I am Katya Waggenschauser. I have an announcement before we begin. I regret to inform you that Dr. Taillebois will not appear. Dr. Taillebois . . . he . . ." Abruptly she ran off the stage.

The muttering rose to an astonished roar.

A man walked on stage. The crowd quieted immediately. Jean-Paul translated from the French, "I am Dr. Valois of the Pasteur Institute. Shortly Dr. Erbland will begin the presentation. But I regret to inform you that Dr. Taillebois will not appear. There has been an unfortunate accident. Dr. Taillebois is dead."

The murmuring rose, fell again. I heard reporters whispering into camphones in six languages.

"In a few moments Dr. Erbland will make her and Dr. Taillebois's presentation. Please be patient just a few moments longer."

Eventually someone introduced Dr. Erbland, a long and fulsome introduction, and she walked onto the stage. A thin, tall woman in her sixties, she looked shaken and pale. She opened by speaking about how various kinds of bioenhancement differed from each other in intent, procedure, and biological mechanism. Most bioenhancements were introduced into an adult body that had already finished growing. A few, usually aimed at correcting hereditary problems, were carried out on infants. Those procedures were somewhat closer to the kinds of genetic re-engineering—it was not referred to merely as "bioenhancement"—that produced new strains of animals. And as with animals, science had long known that it was possible to manipulate pre-embryonic human genes in the same way, *in vitro*.

The audience grew completely quiet.

*In vitro* work, Dr. Erbland said, offered by its nature fewer guides and guarantees. There were much coded redundancies in genetic information, and that made it difficult to determine long-term happenings. The human genome map, the basis of all embryonic re-engineering, had been complete for forty years, but "complete" was not the same as "understood." The body had many genetic behaviors that researchers were only just beginning to understand. No one could have expected that when embryonic re-engineering first began, as a highly experimental undertaking, that genetic identity would be so stubborn.

Stubborn? I didn't know what she meant. Apparently, neither did anybody else in the audience. People scarcely breathed.

This experimental nature of embryonic manipulation in humans did not, of course, stop experimentation, Dr. Erbland continued. Before such experimentation was declared illegal by the Copenhagen Accord, many laboratories around the world had advanced science with the cooperation of voluntary subjects. Completely voluntary, she said. She said it three times.

I wondered how an embryo volunteered.

These voluntary subjects had been re-engineered using variants of the same techniques that produced *in vitro* bioenhancements in other mammals. Her company, in conjunction with the Pasteur Research Institute, had been pioneers in the new techniques. For over thirty years.

Thirty years. My search of the literature had found nothing going back that far. At least not those available on the standard scientific nets. If such "re-engineered" embryos had been allowed to fully gestate, and had survived, they were just barely within the cut-off date for legal existence. Were we talking about embryos or people here?

Dr. Erbland made a curious gesture: raising both arms from the elbow, then letting them fall. It looked almost like a plea. Was she making a public confession of breaking international law? Why would she do that?

Over such a long time, Dr. Erbland continued, the human genetic identity, encoded in "jumping genes" in many unsuspected redundant ways, reasserted itself. This was the subject of her and Dr. Taillebois's work. Unfortunately, the effect on the organism—completely unanticipated by anyone—could be biologically devestating. This first graphic showed basal DNA changes in a re-engineered embryo created twenty-five years ago. The subject, a male, was—

A holograph projected a complicated, three-dimensional genemap.

The scientists in the audience leaned forward intently. The non-scientists looked at each other.

As the presentation progressed, anchored in graphs and formulas and genemap holos, it became clear even to me what Dr. Erbland was actually saying.

European geneticists had been experimenting on embryos as long as thirty years ago, and never stopped. They had allowed some of those embryos to become people. Against international law, and without knowing the long-term effects. And now the long-term effects, like old bills, were coming due, and those people's bodies were destroying themselves at the genetic level.

We had engineered a bioenhanced cancer to replace the natural one we had conquered.

It was a few moments before I noticed that Jean-Paul had stopped translating. He sat like stone, his wrinkled face lengthened in sorrow.

The audience forgot this was a scientific conference. "How many people have been re-engineered at an embryonic level?" someone shouted in English. "Total number worldwide!"

Someone else shouted, *"A todos van à morir?"*

*"Les lois internationales—"*

*"Der sagt—"*

Dr. Erbland broke into a long, passionate speech, clearly not part of the prepared presentation. I caught the word *"sagt"* several times: *law.* I remembered that Dr. Erbland worked for a commercial biotech firm wholly owned by a pharmaceutical company.

The same company in which Anna Olson owned a fortune in stock.

Jean-Paul said quietly, "My grandson. Claude. He was one of those embryos. They told us it was safe. . . ."

I looked at the old man, slumped forward, and I couldn't find any sympathy for him. That appalled me. A cherished grandson . . . But they had agreed, Claude's parents, to roulette with a child's life. In order to produce a superior soccer player. *"Soccer—now there is an illusion worth creating."*

I remembered Anna Olson at the demonstration by the Lincoln Center fountain: *"Caroline had a good run. For a dancer."* Caroline Olson, Deborah said, had been fired because she missed rehearsals and performances. The *Times* had called her last performance "a travesty." Because her body was eating itself at a genetic level, undetectable by the City Ballet bioscans that assumed you could compare new DNA patterns to the body's original, which no procedure completely erased. But for Caroline, the original itself had carried the hidden blueprint for destruction. For twenty-six years.

The ultimate ballet mother had made Caroline into what Anna Olson needed her to be. For as long as Caroline might last.

And then I remembered little Marguerite, standing with her perfect turn out in fifth position.

I stood and pushed my way to the exit. I had to get out of that room. Nobody else left. Dr. Erbland, rattled and afraid, tried to answer questions shouted in six languages. I shoved past a woman who was punching her neighbor. *Gendarmes* appeared as if conjured from the floorboards. Maybe that would be next.

The hardcopies of Dr. Taillebois's original presentation were stacked neatly on tables in the lobby. I took one in English. As I went out the door, I heard a *gendarme* say clearly to somebody, *"Oui, il s'a suicide, Dr. Taillebois."*

I didn't want to stay an hour longer in Paris. I packed at the hotel and changed my ticket at Orly. On the plane home I made myself read the Taillebois/Erbland paper. Most of it was incomprehensible to me; what I understood was obscene. I kept seeing Marguerite in her pink ballet slippers, Caroline staggering on stage. If my lack of sympathy for Taillebois and Erbland was a lack in me, then so be it.

For the first time since Deborah had entered the School of American Ballet, and despite the dazzling performances at the Paris Opera, I found myself respecting Anton Privitera.


When I landed at Kennedy, at almost midnight, there was a message from the electronic gate keeper, "Call this number immediately. Urgent and crucial." I didn't recognize the number.

Deborah. An accident. I raced to the nearest public phone. But it wasn't a hospital; it was an attorney's office.

"Ms. Susan Matthews? Hold, please."

A man's face came on the screen. "This is James Beecher, Ms. Matthews. I'm attorney for Pers Anders. He's being held without bail, pending trial. He left a message for you, most urgent. The message is—"

"Trial? On what charges?" But I think I already knew. The well-cut suit on the lawyer. The move to an expensive neighborhood. Pers was working for somebody, and there weren't very many things he knew how to do.

"The charges are dealing in narcotics. First-degree felony. The message is—"

"Sunshine, right? No, that wouldn't have been expensive enough for Pers," I said bitterly. "Designer viruses? Pleasure center beanos?"

"The message is, 'Don't look in the caverns of the moon.' That's all." The screen went blank.

I stared at it anyway. When Deborah was tiny, in the brief period a million years ago when Pers and I were still together and raising her, she had a game she loved. She'd hide a favorite toy somewhere and call out, "Don't look in the closet! Don't look under the bed! Don't look in the sock drawer!" The toy was always wherever she said not to look. The caverns of the moon was what she called her bedroom, but that was much later, long after Pers had deserted us both but before she tracked him down in New York. I didn't know that he even knew about it.

*Don't look in the caverns of the moon.*

I took a helo right to the Central Park landing stage, charging it to the magazine. The last five blocks I ran, past the automated stores that never sleep and the night people who had just gotten up. Deborah wasn't home; she didn't expect me back from Paris until tomorrow. I tore apart her bedroom, and in an old dance bag I found it, flattened between the mattress and box spring. No practiced criminal, my Deborah.

The powder was pinkish, with no particular odor. There was a lot of it. I had no idea what it was; probably it had a unique name to go with a unique formula matched to some brain function. What kind of father would use his own daughter as a courier for this designer-gene abyss? Would the cops have already have been here if I'd come home a day later? An hour later?

I flushed it all down the toilet, including the dance bag, which I first cut into tiny pieces. Then I searched the rest of the apartment, and then I searched it again. There were no more drugs. There was no money.

She wasn't running stuff for Pers for free. Not Deborah. She had spent the money somewhere.

*"They asked me to join the company! He said it was very nice! He said I was much improved!"*

I made myself sit and think. It was one o'clock in the morning. Lincoln Center would be locked and dark. She might be at a restaurant with other dancers; she might be staying the night with a friend. I called other SAB students. Each answered sleepily. Deborah wasn't there. Ninette told me that after the evening performance Deborah had said she was going home.

"Well, yes, Ms. Matthews, she did seem a little tense," Ninette said, stifling a yawn, her long hair tousled on the shoulders of her nightgown. "But it was only her second night in actual performance, so I thought . . ." The young voice trailed off. I wasn't going to be told whatever this girl thought. Clearly I was an interfering mother.

You bet I was.

I waited another hour. Deborah didn't come home. I called a cab and went to Caroline Olson's apartment on Central Park South.

It had to be Caroline. She must have known she herself was bioenhanced, and I had seen her dance before her downfall: the complete abandon to ballet, the joy. Maybe she thought that helping other dancers to illegal bioenhancement was a favor to them, a benefit. She might be making a distinction—the same one Dr. Erbland had made—between the ultimately destructive re-engineering done to her *in vitro* and the bioenhancements done to European dancers. Or maybe she didn't connect her own sudden deterioration with how her mother had genetically consecrated her to ballet.

Or maybe she did. Maybe she knew that her meteoric success was what was now killing her. Maybe she was so sick and so enraged that she *wanted* to destroy other dancers along with her. If she couldn't dance out her full career, then neither would they.

Or maybe she thought it was worth it. A short life but a brilliant one. Anything for art. Most dancers ended up crippling their bodies anyway, although more slowly. The great Suzanne Farrell had ended up with a plastic hip, her pelvis destroyed by constant turnout. Mikhail Baryshnikov ruined his knees. Miranda Mains was unable to walk by the time she was twenty-eight. Maybe Caroline Olson thought no sacrifice was too great for ballet, even a life.

But not my Deborah's.

I buzzed the security system of Caroline's apartment for five solid minutes. There was no answer. Finally the system said politely, "Your party does not answer. Further buzzing may constitute legal harrassment. You should leave now."

I got back in the cab, chewing on my thumb. I felt that kind of desperation you think you can't live through; it consumes your belly, chokes your breath. The driver waited indifferently. *Where?* God, in New York they could be anywhere.

Anywhere nobody would think to look for illegal genetic operations. Anywhere safe, and protected, and easily accessible by dancers, without suspicion.

I gave the driver Anna Olson's address, remembered from the tax return pirated by the Robin Hood. Then I transferred the gun from my purse to my pocket.

I think I wasn't quite sane.

# NINE

CAROLINE AND I RIDE IN A TAXI. I LIKE TAXIS. I PUT MY HEAD OUT THE window. The taxi has many smells. We stop at Deborah's house. Caroline and I go get Deborah.

"I've changed my mind," Deborah says. Her door is open only a little. She stands behind her door. "I'm not going."

"Yes, you are," Caroline says.

Deborah says, "You're not my mother!"

Caroline changes her smell. She has a cane to walk. She leans on her cane. Her voice gets soft. "No, I'm not your mother. And I'm not going to push you like a mother. Believe me, Deborah, I know what that's like. But as a senior dancer, I'm going to ask you to come with me. I'm willing to beg you to come. It's that important. Not just to you, but to me."

Deborah looks at the floor.

"Don't be embarrassed. Just understand that I mean it. I'll beg, I'll grovel. But first I'm asking, as a senior member of the company."

Deborah looks up. She smells angry. "Why do you care? It's my life!"

"Yes. Yours and Privitera's." Caroline closes her eyes. "You owe him something, too. No, don't consider that. Just come because I'm asking you."

Deborah still smells angry. But she comes.

We ride in the taxi to Caroline's mother's house. I say, "Is there a party tonight?"

Deborah laughs. It sounds funny. Caroline says, "Yes, Angel. Another party. With music and dancers and talking. And you can have some pretzels."

"I like pretzels," I say. "Does Deborah like pretzels?"

"No," Deborah says, and now she smells scared.

We go in the back way. Caroline has a key. People come to the basement. Someone starts music. "Not so loud!" a man says.

"No, it's all right," Caroline says. "My mother's still in Europe, and the staff is on vacation while she's gone. We have the place to ourselves."

A woman brings me a pretzel. People talk. Caroline and Deborah and two men talk in the corner. I don't hear the words. The words at parties are very hard. I watch Caroline, and eat pretzels, and watch two people dance to the radio.

"Christ," the man dancer says, "is this fake revelry really necessary?"

"Yes," the woman says. She looks at me. "Caroline says yes."

In the corner, two men show Deborah some papers. Caroline sits with them. Deborah starts to cry.

I watch Caroline. Deborah may touch Caroline. The two men may touch Caroline. But Caroline says parties are happy. No people smell happy. I do not understand.

The buzzer rings.

Nobody moves. People look at each other. Caroline says, "Is the gate still open? Let it go. It's probably kids. There's nobody home but us."

The buzzer rings and rings. Then it stops. Caroline talks to Deborah. The door opens at the top of the stairs.

A man with Caroline takes a bottle from his pocket very fast. He puts the papers on the floor and pours the bottle on it. The papers disappear. "All right, everybody, this is a party," he says.

Steps run down the stairs. A voice calls, "Wait! You can't go down there! Young woman! You can't go down there!" The voice is angry. It is Caroline's mother.

I walk to Caroline. She smells surprised.

A woman comes into the basement. She holds a gun. My ears raise. I stand next to Caroline.

"Nobody move," the woman says. Deborah says, "Mom!"

Caroline looks at the woman, then at Deborah, then at the woman. She walks with her cane to the woman.

"Stay right there," the woman says. She smells angry and scared. I move with Caroline.

"Christ, you sound like a bad holovid," Caroline says. "You're Deborah's mother? What the hell do you think you're doing here?"

From the top of the stairs Caroline's mother calls, "Caroline! What is the meaning of this?"

The woman says very fast, "Deborah, you're making a terrible mistake. Bioenhancement may help your dancing for a while, but it could also kill you. The conference on genetics in Paris—they presented scientific proof that one kind of bioenhancement kills, and if they're just finding that out know about enhancements done twenty-five years ago—then who knows what kind of insane risk you're running with these other kinds? Don't take my word for it, it's online this morning. Pers was arrested, damn him, and I found your drug stash just before the police did. That's how you're paying for this, isn't it? Debbie—how could you be such a damn *fool?*"

"Wait a minute," Caroline says. She leans on her cane. "You thought we brought Deborah here *to bioenhance her?*" Caroline starts to laugh. She puts her hand on her face. "Oh my God!"

Caroline's mother calls from the top of the stairs, "I'm phoning the police."

Caroline says, very fast, "Go bring her down here, James. You'll have to lift her out of her chair and carry her. Keith, get her chair." The two men run up the stairs.

Caroline is shaking. I stand beside her. I growl. The woman still has the gun. She points the gun at Caroline. I wait for Caroline to tell me *Attack.*

The woman says, "Don't try to deny it. You'd do anything for ballet, wouldn't you? All of you. You're sick—but you're not murdering my daughter!"

Caroline's face changes. Her smell changes. I feel her hand on my head. Her hand shakes. Her body shakes. I smell anger bigger than other angers. I wait for *Attack.*

Deborah says, "You're all wrong, Mom! Just like you always are! Does this look like a bioenhancement lab? *Does it?* These people aren't enhancing me—they're trying to talk me out of it! These two guys are doctors and they're trying to 'deprogram' me—just like you tried to program me all my life! You never wanted me to dance, you always tried to make me into this cute little college-bound student that *you* needed me to be. Never what *I* needed!"

The men carry Caroline's mother and Caroline's mother's chair down the steps. They put Caroline's mother in the chair. Caroline's mother also smells angry. But Caroline smells more angry than everybody.

Caroline says, "Sound familiar, Mother dear? What Deborah's saying? What did *you* learn at the genetic conference? What I've been telling you for months, right? Your gift to dance is dying. Because you wanted a prima ballerina at any price. Even if I'm the one to pay it."

Caroline's mother says, "You love dance. You wanted it as much as I did. You were a star."

"I never got to find out if I would have been one anyway! That isn't so inconceivable, is it? And then I might have still been dancing! But instead I was . . . *made*. Molded, sewed, carpentered. Into what you needed me to be."

Deborah's mother lowers her gun. Her eyes are big. Caroline's mother says, "You were a star. You had a good run. Without me, you might have been nothing. Worthless."

A man says, very soft, "Jesus H. Christ."

Caroline is shaking hard. I am afraid she will fall again. Her hand is on her cane. The cane shakes. Her other hand is on me.

Caroline says, "You cold, self-centered bitch—"

A little girl runs down the stairs.

The little girl says, *"Tante Anna! Tante Anna! Ou êtes-vous?"* She stops at the bottom of the steps. She smells afraid. *"Qui sont tout ces gens?"*

Caroline looks at the little girl. The little girl has no shoes. She has long black fur on her head. Her hind feet go out like Caroline's feet when Caroline dances. The toes look strange. I don't understand the little girl's feet.

Caroline says again, "You cold, self-centered bitch." Her voice is soft now. She stops shaking. "When did you have her made? Five years ago? Six? A new model with improved features? Who will decay all the sooner?"

Caroline's mother says, "You are a hysterical fool."

Caroline says, "Angel—attack. Now."

I attack Caroline's mother. I knock over the chair. I bite her foreleg. Someone screams, "Caroline! For God's sake! Caroline!" I bite Caroline's mother's head. I must protect Caroline. This person hurts Caroline. I must protect Caroline.

A gun fires and I hurt and hurt and hurt—

I love Caroline.

# TEN

THE TOWN OF SARATOGA, WHERE THE AMERICAN BALLET THEATER IS dancing its summer season, is itself a brightly colored stage. Visitors throng the racetrack, the brand-new Electronics Museum, the historical battle sites. In 1777, right here, Benedict Arnold and his half-trained revolutionaries stopped British forces under General John Burgoyne. It was the first great victory of freedom over the old order.

Until this year, the New York City Ballet danced here every summer. But the Performing Arts Center chose not to renew the City Ballet contract. In New York, too, City Ballet attendance is half of what it was only a few years ago.

The Saratoga pavillion is open to the countryside. Ballet lovers fill the seats, spread blankets up the sloping lawn, watch dancers accompanied not only by Tchaikovsky or Chopin but also by crickets and robins. In Saratoga, the ballet smells of freshly mown grass. The classic "white ballets"—*Swan Lake, Les Sylphides*—are remembered green. Small girls whose first taste of dance is at Saratoga will dream, for the rest of their life, of toe shoes skimming over wildflowers.

I take my seat, in the back of the regular seating, as the small orchestra finishes tuning up. The conductor enters to the usual thunderous applause, even though nobody here knows his name and very few care. They have come to see the dancers.

Debussy floats out over the countryside. *Afternoon of a Faun:* slow, melting. On the nearly bare stage, furnished only with barre and mirrors, a male dancer in practice clothes wakes up, stretches, warms up his muscles in a series of low, languorous moves.

A girl appears in the mirror, which isn't really a mirror but an empty place in the backdrop. A void. She, too, stretches, poses, pliés. Both dancers watch the mirrors. They are so absorbed in their own reflections that they only gradually become aware of each other's presence. Even then, they exist for each other only as foils, presences to dance to. In the end the girl will step back through the mirror. There is the feeling that for the boy, she may not really have existed at all, except as a dream.

It is Deborah's first lead in a one-act ballet. Her extension is high, her turnout perfect, her movements sure and strong and sustained, filled with the joy of dancing. I can barely stand to look at her. This is her reward, her grail, for continuing her bioenhancement. She isn't dancing for Anton Privitera, but she is dancing. A year and a half of bioenhancement, bought legally now in Copenhagen and paid for by selling her story to an eager press, has given her the physical possibilities to match her musicality, and her rhythm, and her drive.

The faun finally touches the girl, turning her slowly *en attitude*. Deborah smiles. This is her afternoon. She's willing to pay whatever price the night demands, even though science has no idea yet what, for her kind of treatments, it might be.

Privitera must have known that some of his dancers were bioenhanced. The completely inadequate bioscans at City Ballet, the phenomenally low injury rate of his prima ballerina—Privitera must have known. Or maybe his staff let him remain in official ignorance, keeping from him any knowledge of heresy in the ranks. There was a rumor that Privitera's business manager John Coles even tried to keep Caroline from "deprogramming" dancers who wanted bioenhancement. The rumor about Coles was never substantiated. But in the last year, City Ballet has been struggling to survive. Too many patrons have withdrawn their favor. The mystique of natural art, like other mystiques, didn't last forever. It had a good run.

"If you could have chosen, and that was the *only* way you could have had the career, would you have chosen the embryonic engineering anyway?" was the sole thing Deborah asked Caroline in jail, through bullet-proof plastic glass and electronic speaking systems, under the hard eyes of matrons. Caroline, awaiting trial for second-degree murder, didn't seem to mind Deborah's brusqueness, her self-absorption. Caroline was silent a long time, her gaunt face lengthened from the girlish roundness I remembered. Then she said to Deborah, "No."

"I would," Deborah said.

Caroline only looked at her.

They're here, Caroline and her dog. Somewhere up on the grass, Caroline in a powerchair, Angel hobbling on the three legs my bullet left him. Caroline was acquitted by reason of temporary insanity. They didn't let Angel stay with her during the trial. Nor did they let him testify, which would have been abnormal but not impossible. Five-year-olds can testify under some circumstances, and Angel has the biochip-and-reengineered intelligence of a five-year-old. Maybe it wouldn't have been so abnormal. Or maybe all of us, not just Anton Privitera, will have to change our definition of abnormal.

Five-year-olds know a lot. It was Marguerite who cried out, *"Vous avez assassiné ma tante Anna!"* She knew whom I was aiming at, even if the police did not. But Marguerite couldn't know how much I loathed the old woman who had made her daughter into what the mother needed her to be—just as I, out of love, had tried to do to mine.

On stage Deborah *pirouettes*. Maybe her types of bioenhancement will be all right, despite the growing body of doubts collected by Caroline's doctor allies. When the first cures for cancer were developed from reengineered retroviruses, dying and desperate patients demanded they be administered without long, drawn-out FDA testing. Some of the patients died even sooner, possibly from the cures. Some lived until ninety. The edge of anything is a lottery, and protection doesn't help— not against change, or madmen, or errors of judgement. *I protect Caroline*, Angel kept saying after I shot him, yelping in pain between sentences. *I protect Caroline*.

Deborah flows into a *retiré*, one leg bent at the knee, and rises on toe. Her face glows. Her partner lifts her above his head and turns her slowly, her feet perfectly arched in their toe shoes, dancing on air.